THE
LIGHT

The Light
ISBN: 978-1-9163945-0-6

First published in Great Britain
in 2020 through Ingram Spark
Self-Publishing

Copyright © Dean Jones
www.thelightdeanjones.com

Dean Jones has asserted his right under
the Copyright, Design and Patents Act
1988 to be identified as the author of this
work.

disclaimer

This book is sold subject to the condition
that it shall not, by way of trade or
otherwise, be lent, resold, hired out, or
otherwise circulated without the author's
prior consent in any form of binding or
cover and without a similar condition,
including this condition, being imposed on
the subsequent publisher.

Typeset in the UK at The Joy of Pages
www.thejoyofpages.co.uk

This book started off as something to pass the time. It was never intended to become a novel, or even intended for publication. There are too many people to name, but thanks to the great support and encouragement around me, what started off as a pass-time has escalated into what it is today. I would like to thank everyone who believed in me and for the influence they gave me. I would like to thank my mother Julia Jones for her consistent support and assistance, Samuel Charles and Georgie Clarke for the military input, Rachel Cullen for her huge contribution towards the writing and grammar, Mandy Ward for her essential knowledge and advice, Lesley Jones for her editing and invaluable insights into writing, Natasha Mackenzie for the fantastic book cover and last but not least David Hambling for the formatting and professional advice and support that will be continuous throughout my writing career.

THE
LIGHT

☥ ℔ ▽

DEAN JONES

PROLOGUE

WAR IS COMING! A war the like of which Earth has never seen. Satan's power is growing stronger and stronger, and his evil is seeping into the world. Soon not even the Lord's strongest angels will hold back the force that intends to destroy His creation... and the Lord himself!

'Can you feel that?' Asked Darius, an angelic soldier sworn to protect the humans and Earth.

'Satan!' A voice said from the group of angels.

Darius agreed, looking surprised and shocked. 'Three times in twenty days he has shown his presence. He has never done this before.'

The angels stood silent and expressionless, not knowing what to do or say. Another angel flew down from above and landed next to Darius; his magnificent twenty-foot glossy silver wings folded and disappeared into his back. He was tall and athletic with dark hair that shone and bright blue eyes.

'Michael.' Darius welcomed him, bowing his head; the others followed suit.

'Again,' said Michael. It was more a statement than a question.

There was silence. Michael was deep in thought, trying to understand the situation. 'I don't like this. Darius, take Jade and Kleo and kill the possessed human. It's too late to save their life, but we can still save their soul. I don't want there to be any exchange of words.'

'It only takes one to kill a possessed,' said Darius.

'This is what troubles me. Satan knows we will just push him back to hell again – why keep coming back?' Said Michael. 'I'm taking no chances. Three of you go – save the human's soul, then get straight back here!'

'Yes, Michael,' said Darius. 'Jade, Kleo, let's go.'

All three marched towards the portal that would take them to Earth and simultaneously touched bright white orbs on their golden belts. Each made a whirring noise before releasing flexible metal armour which wrapped around their entire bodies. Magnificent swords appeared on their thighs and beautiful white wings burst from their backs, expanding to fifteen feet.

All three stopped by the circular portal in heaven's floor, gave each other a nod and jumped through one by one.

CHAPTER 1

Darius and Jade were ahead of Kleo as the three angels flew towards Earth like meteors. They landed outside a derelict house, miles from any town or village, that looked like it had been abandoned many years ago. Kleo could sense Satan's presence inside.

'The possessed human is upstairs,' said Darius. 'Stay close to me.'

Darius led the way gracefully to the front door and tried the handle; it was unlocked. The door creaked as he pushed it open, but no doubt their presence was noticed anyway, Kleo thought.

It was pitch-black inside and the air was dry and cold with a smell of old decay and death. Darius walked through a cobweb as he entered; he wiped his face and headed for the stairs in front of him. He led the way up the stairs and took each step light as a feather.

Once all three were at the top of the staircase, they continued to the last room at the back of the house. The possessed human was in this room;

not only could Kleo sense him, but there was a black mist coming out from under the door. This mist was known to the angels as the darkness that oozed out of humans possessed by Satan.

Darius took hold of the door handle and drew his sword. 'You two stay right behind me. I'll do this quickly!'

Darius opened the door and, in a flash, stood behind the possessed middle-aged man, his sword to the man's throat. The man was kneeling in the centre of the empty room. Normally Darius would have severed his head instantly, but something was wrong. The weight of Satan's presence grew stronger, and the black mist already oozing out of the man's mouth, nose and ears increased. It spread across the floor, crept up the walls and touched the ceiling.

Kleo felt a pressure in his abdomen; it intensified, threw him off his feet and pinned him to the wall. Next to him, he saw the same had happened to Jade.

Darius was not moving; he was observing Jade and Kleo pinned to the wall by an invisible force and looked distressed.

It confused Kleo; he knew Satan should not have such strength on Earth. His powers here should be weak, which was why it never took over one angel to send his presence back to hell.

'You come into my house, uninvited, and try to behead me?' Said Satan through the possessed man, in a deep, cracked voice. Then he chuckled. 'No, we will not be having that this time, Darius!'

The black mist around Darius's feet made its way up his legs. He was clearly trying to cut off the man's head, but he seemed incapacitated. And he was oddly quiet, which troubled

Kleo immensely. The black mist now completely covered his body. It crept up his neck, and into his mouth, nose and ears. Kleo felt a jolt of shock and disbelief as he sensed Darius's essence slipping away. Darius looked at Jade and Kleo as if to say he was sorry, and Kleo felt helpless. Darius's eyes rolled to the back of his head, and there was an explosion of light.

Darius was gone; only a floating ball of light remained where he once stood. The possessed man tilted his head back, opened his mouth and consumed the ball of light.

'Darius belongs to me now,' said Satan, and a smile crept across the man's face, 'but do not despair, he will be well looked after. I have a message for all my angelic brothers and sisters. War is coming. I have more power than you could ever imagine, and now even Father cannot stop me. I will first destroy his Earth and his hideous creation of humanity. Then I will come for heaven and Father himself. Any angels that bow down and serve me will be spared. The rest will experience untold torture and torment for all eternity!'

The possessed man started to convulse. His arms and legs twisted and snapped as his body bent into impossible positions. With one final twist, his spine snapped. The man's broken body dropped to the floor, as did Jade and Kleo.

The black mist seeped away into the floor and in just a few seconds was completely gone, along with Satan's presence.

Kleo and Jade got up and looked at each other in horror, then ran to escape the house. Michael was outside with eight other angels.

'We felt Satan's power – what happened? Where is Darius?' Asked Michael.

'He's gone,' replied Kleo.

'What do you mean, gone?'

'Satan somehow overpowered us all. There was nothing we could do. Darius is gone, Satan took his soul.'

The angels looked at each other in confusion; Michael stood, speechless.

'But that's impossible. Father saw to it that Satan could not have such power on Earth,' said one angel.

'Well, he does, and that's not all. He said war is coming, and any angel that wants to be spared must bow down and serve him,' said Jade.

'Never!' Shouted another angel, and spat on the floor.

'I must see Father. Follow me,' said Michael. He raised his sword and sliced the air, creating a portal back to heaven. Once all the angels entered, the portal disappeared.

CHAPTER 2

Oliver was surrounded by bright light and struggled to see. He tried to figure out where he was, but all he could see was white.

Where am I? He thought, looking around in all directions.

Though confused, he felt at peace and somehow knew he had nothing to fear. A faint voice said something, but he could not make it out.

'Who's there, where am I?' He asked.

'Protect him,' a voice said.

Oliver did not understand, but before he could say anything else, he realised he was in his church. He looked down and there was a baby boy in his arms.

'Protect him,' the voice repeated.

Oliver experienced a sudden feeling of dread; he felt trapped, surrounded by some concealed horror.

'Protect him,' the voice said again. Oliver looked up and saw a dark, shadowy figure standing by the church entrance.

The entity was made up of a black mist and reached towards him and the baby. Oliver became consumed by fear. He started to panic and wanted to escape, but he could not move.

'PROTECT HIM!' The voice screamed one last time and Oliver jumped up out of bed, short of breath and sweating profusely.

It was a dream, the same dream he had been having for weeks.

'Fuck's sake,' he said, and reached for the glass of water on his bedside table.

The alarm clock read 05.35 a.m. and showed the date: 18 April 2014. He finished his water and got up to go to the bathroom. His house, as always, was a mess. On his way to the bathroom, he had to step over dirty washing and tripped on a shoe. He switched on the bathroom light, looked at himself in the mirror and considered whether he was going insane.

After he washed his face with cold water, he looked in the mirror again, grasped his crucifix and closed his eyes. *Protect him... protect who, and from what?*

He shook his head and brushed his teeth. Fortunately, Oliver had planned to be up for six anyway; he had a funeral service to conduct at ten. So, after brushing his teeth he went back into the bedroom and got dressed for the day. He grabbed himself a cereal bar from the kitchen and left, eating it on the go. Outside, a couple were just getting out of a taxi. Oliver gave them a friendly smile and walked around the corner to his church. He glanced at the sign at the entrance: 'St Michael's', and, although he knew it was a sin, he felt proud.

He thought about what he would say at the service for Mr O'Connor. The O'Connor family were very nice people and Oliver felt especially bad for the twin eight-year-old girls now without a father. Mr O'Connor had been the victim of a pulmonary embolism. The paramedics had done everything they could, but he died before he reached the hospital. Oliver's words would have to give courage and strength to Mrs O'Connor and the children, and also show what a great man Mr O'Connor was.

Eager to prepare the church, Oliver ran to the entrance, unlocked the doors and entered.

* * *

The day went so fast. People were leaving after the service, which had gone well. He had managed not to upset Mrs O'Connor too much and at one point even made her smile.

'Goodbye, Mrs O'Connor, and remember, you know where I am if you need me, any time, and no matter how trivial,' said Oliver as he ushered the remaining congregation out of church.

Oliver stood waving goodbye to everyone at the entrance as they got back in their cars to travel to the wake. He noticed a woman sitting on the wall outside the church. He waited for all the cars to leave before he approached her.

'Hello there, can I help you?' He asked.

'I'm sorry, I didn't mean to bother you, it's silly really,' said the woman, and got up to walk away.

'I could do with a little silly, to be honest. Take my mind off that poor family. Please come inside,' said Oliver, and walked back into the church.

The woman hesitated at first but followed Oliver into the body of the church.

'Wow,' she said.

Oliver turned and saw she was eyeing the beautiful images in the stained-glass windows. 'They are quite something, are they not?'

For a second, he was taken aback; the woman was remarkably pretty. She had long red hair full of volume, a pale face with freckles around her nose and a smooth, clear complexion. She was wearing a red hand-knitted jumper with slim blue jeans and flat black shoes. Oliver guessed she was in her early twenties and it was obvious she was pregnant.

'I love them,' she said, still staring at the windows.

'Why thank you, erm... and your name is?'

'Oh, sorry, I'm Jessica. Nice to meet you.'

'I'm Father Hall, but if it makes you more comfortable, please call me Oliver.' He reached out and they shook hands. 'So, you have something silly to tell me?'

Jessica took a deep breath and exhaled loudly. Once she got her composure, she was ready to talk. 'Well... my mother keeps calling me silly, but I know it's the truth. I don't know what to think about it, I'm just so confused. It would be nice to have an answer if you know what I mean?'

'Well, I may have one if you tell me what it is,' said Oliver with a little chuckle.

'Please don't think I'm crazy.'

'I will not think you're crazy,' said Oliver reassuringly.

Jessica took another deep breath, then explained. 'I'm five months pregnant with a baby boy...' She paused. 'But... I... I haven't slept with anyone in over ten months. How can I be pregnant?' She paused again and watched Oliver, waiting for his response.

Oliver froze; for a second, he could have sworn he heard the voice in the back of his mind saying, 'Protect him.' Then he realised she was standing in the exact spot where he had been standing in all his dreams. 'A boy?' He managed to ask.

Jessica looked at him, confused. 'My mother would have burst out laughing at this point, but you look like you've seen a ghost. Are you okay?' She asked.

Just like in his dreams, the voice at the back of his mind said, 'Protect him.'

It triggered the fear that always accompanied the dreams; he got a sudden hot flush and his heart raced. 'Yes, I'm fine,' said Oliver, as he lost consciousness and passed out.

* * *

'Father Hall... Oliver, wake up, are you okay?' Asked a female voice.

Oliver opened his eyes, but everything was blurry. After giving them a rub, he saw Jessica was fanning him with her hand.

Oliver looked around. He was on the floor in the church. 'What happened?'

'You passed out when I told you about my baby. You've been out for a few minutes – are you okay?'

'I feel fine. Your baby?' Said Oliver, confused; then it came back to him and he jumped up to his feet. He looked at Jessica and started backing away.

'Do you think I'm crazy?' Asked Jessica with a sad look.

'No, no, of course not. It's just... it's...' He paused. 'I have a bit of a headache,' was all he could think of to say.

'A headache?' Asked Jessica speculatively.

'Yes, a headache,' said Oliver. 'Would it be possible to talk about this another time, over lunch maybe?'

Jessica thought about it for a few seconds. 'Lunch sounds great. How's tomorrow?'

'Tomorrow's fine. If you meet me here at two o'clock, there's a really nice cafe just around the corner.'

'See you at two then,' said Jessica with a smile. 'Are you sure you're feeling well enough to be alone?'

'Yes, thank you, I just need some water. I'll be fine.'

'Okay,' said Jessica, and turned to leave. 'See you tomorrow. Hope your headache gets better.'

'Thanks, see you tomorrow.'

As the doors closed behind her, Oliver took a seat on one of the pews and put his face in his hands. 'I'm going insane!'

CHAPTER 3

THE THREE ARCHANGELS, Michael, Gabriel and Raphael, sat on their thrones, conversing. Each throne was unique, both in design and colour. Michael's was red and blue with engravings of angels in battle. Gabriel's was white with a pinch of blue and engravings of angels playing trumpets. Raphael's was entirely green with engravings of fish, plants and trees.

The entrance to their Father's throne room was behind them, a one thousand-foot high golden gate with sculptures of angels and humans sculpted into it. Below them were millions of angels and human souls, all gathered together to hear the Lord's message from Gabriel.

Ready to enunciate the news to his audience, Gabriel stood and approached the edge of the ledge they were upon. He put his trumpet to his lips and blew, sending a booming, harmonious melody across heaven.

'Brothers... sisters...' Silence gradually fell. 'We have dark times ahead... Father has spoken, and he has foretold of a great darkness entering the world of humanity. Lucifer's strength and legions have grown beyond comprehension.' Gabriel started walking from side to side with his hands behind his back. 'With every soul he claims, his power grows and grows, and it has grown so much that soon, even without the key to open the bottomless pit, he will be able to break the barrier between hell and Earth. He will open portals around the world and send his demons to possess, spread terror and kill the people of the Earth, thus gathering more souls and power. Once strong enough, he will walk the Earth to consume the souls of the faithful. When he gains enough souls for the power he needs, his gaze will turn towards heaven. He will open portals between Earth and heaven and bring the war to us.' Gabriel paused, and the listeners started talking amongst themselves, horrified at the information. 'Satan has sent a message and confirmed he will continue on this path. He warned that any angel standing in his way will be tossed into eternal torment unless they surrender to his will.' The objections became louder, the crowd disgusted at the notion.

'Brothers, sisters, please calm down,' said Michael. He stood next to Gabriel and placed his hand on his shoulder.

Gabriel continued. 'Father has advised that all of you remain here and do not attempt to help as this comes to pass. Losing anyone of you to Satan's torment, as happened to Darius, would be devastating. This will test not only humanity's faith in Our Lord but also all of ours. There will be those who lose their faith and may even aid Satan, but know this: Father has already sent a saviour to Earth, an unborn child, and he is our only chance of stopping Satan.'

There was a long pause as the news settled in. Gabriel turned and took his seat on his throne.

'We must watch over this saviour and do what we do best. We will advise and guide the humans to a righteous path, through thoughts and signs alone. Go to Earth at your own peril. That is all,' said Michael.

* * *

Oliver woke up and glanced over at the time. It was 10.20 a.m. He heard rain clattering against his window and guessed it would be a wet, miserable Saturday morning. He rubbed his eyes, stretched and sat up. As he sat on the edge of his bed, he realised he had a dreamless night's sleep.

'Finally, a decent night's sleep,' he said to himself, and smiled as he got up to get dressed. He had chosen what he would wear the night before and it was already ironed and hanging on his wardrobe door. A plain black shirt and dark blue jeans, the most stylish and expensive clothes he owned. He put them on, then made his way into the kitchen. He sat at his dining table, grabbed the remote for his battered old TV, and turned up the volume to watch the news.

Missing thirty-five-year-old Derek Johnson, husband and father of two, has been found murdered. The discovery was made an hour ago in an abandoned house, three miles away from his home in Devon. A coroner is yet to confirm the cause of death, but the police believe, due to his multiple broken bones, he was beaten to death. Derek was last seen two days ago walking his dog through a field by a fellow dog walker. The dog has also been found dead, with a broken neck, a mile away from the abandoned house. The police have no suspects at present but have told our reporters they will use every resource at their disposal to find who committed this brutal offence. They urge anyone with any information to come forward,' said the female reporter.

Oliver sighed and turned off the TV. It really was a miserable Saturday morning, he thought. He quickly brushed his teeth and left for St Michael's.

* * *

Jessica arrived at two o'clock sharp. Oliver had just locked up when he turned and saw her standing behind him.

She smiled and waved at him. 'Hi, Father, are you feeling better?'

'Hi, Jessica, I'm fine, thank you. How are you?'

Jessica was wearing a dark red raincoat, which really brought out the colour of her hair, slim-fit light blue jeans and black leather boots. 'Much better now the rain has stopped. My umbrella's broken so I would have got soaked if I hadn't got a taxi.'

'Ha, lucky you. I got a little caught in that rain – I'm still damp. Forgot to grab a jacket on my way out.'

'Well, you look very handsome.'

'Thank you,' said Oliver, slightly embarrassed, but smiling, 'shall we head for lunch?'

'Show me the way,' said Jessica and walked alongside him.

They arrived at the cafe and sat at a table by the window. A waitress approached them and asked if she could take their order.

'I'll have a cheeseburger and chips please, and a cappuccino,' said Oliver.

The waitress looked at Jessica, and after a moment she gave her order. 'Can I have the omelette and a caramel latte, please?'

'Yes, that's fine. I'll bring your drinks over in just a second, and food will be about ten minutes. If you need anything else, my name is Vanessa. Just give me a shout.' She smiled and walked back to the kitchen.

'She was nice,' said Jessica.

'Yeah, the staff are superb here, so is the food. Alice does a good job running this place. I cannot wait for this burger, I'm starving,' said Oliver.

'I'm hungry too. I haven't eaten at all today,' said Jessica, and her stomach rumbled so loud that Oliver heard it from across the table.

'Sounds like it too. Well, it shouldn't be too long. So, let's get to know each other a little better. Where are you from?' Asked Oliver.

'I live in Chelsea at the moment, but I grew up in Wembley. My parents and my younger brother Aaron are still there. Aaron is ten and a little terror.'

'How old are you, if you don't mind me asking?'

'How old do you think I am?'

'I'm really not good with ages,' said Oliver, and wished he'd never asked.

'One cappuccino and one caramel latte,' said Vanessa, placing the drinks on the table. 'Your food won't be long now.'

'So, how old do you think?' Asked Jessica again, smiling.

'Twenty-two?' He guessed, though he thought maybe twenty-three or four.

'Close, I'm twenty-four. Twenty-five next year,

twenty-third of February. What about you? I guess twenty-seven.'

'Ha, bang on, I'm twenty-seven.'

'Seriously?'

'Seriously, I'm twenty-seven, eighth of August 1986. Good guess. I've lived in London for five years, but I was born and raised in Birmingham. I moved here after some family issues and wanted to have a fresh start.'

Oliver regretted bringing up the past he would rather forget, so he changed the subject. 'So, about your baby. You really have had no intercourse to get pregnant?'

'None whatsoever. I've gone over it in my head, over and over, and there's not one occasion when it could have happened. It's so scary, I'm so confused.'

'Well, hopefully together we can find out exactly what's going on and why. If it makes you feel any better, I believe you. As you can imagine, the church hears many claims of conception by divine intervention, or miraculous conception without intercourse – none are ever true. You would be amazed by the number of women who believe they are carrying the son of God, and it will be the second coming. However, with you... you will think I'm crazy now, but I've been having these dreams for weeks and–' Before Oliver could finish there was a loud smash from the kitchen, followed by a scream. 'What the–' said Oliver; Jessica shrugged her shoulders.

Oliver got up and headed towards the kitchen, as did another man who Oliver had not noticed until now, but he welcomed the assistance. The man looked to be in his late twenties; he had a fresh look about him, clean-shaven, with tidy, short black hair.

They entered the kitchen, completely ignoring the 'staff only' sign. Vanessa was on the floor having a seizure.

Alice, the manager, was standing in the corner by the back door holding Oliver's food. 'She just tried to bite me. I pushed her away and she started fitting.'

There was some sort of black liquid running out of Vanessa's eyes and mouth.

Oliver knelt beside her, grabbed her shoulders and gave her a little shake. 'Vanessa, are you okay, can you hear me?'

'We should put her in the recovery position,' suggested the other man.

Oliver agreed, but before he had a chance to think Vanessa grabbed him and threw him across the room. He slammed into a wall and fell to the floor.

Alice let out another scream and Vanessa jumped up; her eyes had become jet black and she looked at the other man, then at Alice.

Alice threw Oliver's burger into Vanessa's face and screamed, trying to open the back door. Vanessa grabbed a kitchen knife, ran at Alice and stabbed her through her neck. The look on Alice's face was one of pure horror. Blood poured out of her mouth and the wound; she fell to her knees and toppled over, bleeding out onto the kitchen floor.

Vanessa's attention switched to the other man; she pounced on him, taking them both to the floor. She tried desperately to bite his face and neck, snapping and snarling. It seemed to take all his strength just to hold her back, just inches from his face. The black liquid that oozed from her dripped and splattered all over him.

'Help!' He shouted.

Oliver got himself up and grabbed a frying pan off the wall beside him; he smashed Vanessa over the back of the head. She rolled over twice and hit a storage cabinet.

'What's going on?' Asked Jessica as she opened the kitchen door.

Seeing the opportunity to flee, Vanessa, on all fours like an animal, barged past Jessica into the dining area. She jumped onto a table, then through the cafe window, out onto the street.

'Jessica, phone an ambulance. She's been hurt,' instructed Oliver as he pointed at Alice.

'Are you okay?' Oliver asked the other man as he pulled him up from the floor.

'I'm fine, thanks,' he said, wiping his face. 'I'm DC Cole. Quick let's get her before she hurts someone.'

Once outside, they saw a group of people surrounding a car. Vanessa was lying across the windscreen and appeared to be dead. In front of them was an articulated lorry. Its hazards were flashing and there was blood splattered over the front of it. Oliver put two and two together and guessed the lorry must have smashed into her and sent her into the parked car's windscreen. The driver of the lorry was sitting on the kerb with his face in his hands. Cole ran to Vanessa, and Oliver went to the lorry driver.

'Are you okay? What happened?' Asked Oliver.

'She just came out of nowhere – there was nothing I could do,' said the lorry driver, on the verge of tears.

'It's okay. There was nothing you could have done. There's something wrong with her. She just attacked us, she's completely out of control,' said

Oliver, looking back at the cafe and Jessica, who was crying with a hand covering her mouth.

Cole came over to Oliver. 'She's dead. What the hell just happened?'

'I have no idea... one second she's serving us drinks, the next she's trying to kill us. I've never seen anything like it,' said Oliver. 'Then she got hit by this lorry.'

'It's so strange... just before I hit her, there was a flash of light to my left. It drew my attention to her, but it wasn't enough, I couldn't stop the lorry in time,' said the driver and put his face back into his hands. 'I'm so sorry.'

Jessica joined the group. 'The emergency services are on the way. Alice is dead, she's been stabbed in the neck,' said Jessica, tears streaming down her face. Oliver took her into his arms to comfort her and looked around, at a loss.

* * *

After giving statements to the police and being checked over by paramedics, Oliver, Jessica and Cole were given the all-clear to leave.

'Have they said anything to you about what happened to Vanessa?' Asked Oliver.

'It's too early to tell. They'll know more once they've performed an autopsy and checked her blood results,' said Cole.

'So, you're a detective constable?' Said Oliver.

'Yes, I've been one for a few years now. I've never actually been a witness in an investigation before though. They will expect me to do a thorough statement on this tomorrow.'

'I don't envy you. I'm Father Hall, by the way, I'm the parish priest at St Michael's church on Chester Square,' said Oliver, and reached out his hand.

'It's a pleasure to meet you.' They shook hands.

'Jessica West, nice to meet you,' said Jessica, and shook Cole's hand.

'Nice to meet you too,' said Cole. 'Well, I'd love to stay and chat, but I have a dinner reservation at seven and it's six now. I'll be in touch if I need any more information from you both.'

'That's fine,' said Oliver, 'do you need my address?'

'I got your details from the officers, so that's okay. Here's my number if you need me for anything. Have a good night,' said Cole, and passed them both a business card.

'Thank you,' said Jessica.

'Enjoy your evening,' said Oliver, and Cole walked away. 'Well, what a day.'

'Yeah, it's been horrible. I've never seen a dead body before. Now I've seen two,' said Jessica, looking sorrowful. 'I don't think I'll be able to sleep tonight.'

'Well, I'm always here if you need someone to talk to,' said Oliver.

'Thank you, that means a lot. Would you mind if I just stayed with you for a bit, make my way home once I've calmed down?'

'No, I don't mind at all. My place is just a short walk from here, and you're welcome to come back until you're feeling better. I was just going to watch a movie and order some Chinese, so some company would be great,' said Oliver with a smile.

Jessica looked relieved. 'That sounds perfect, thank you.'

'My pleasure. You must excuse the mess though, I'm afraid. I'm always so busy. I rarely have time to clean up.'

'Don't worry, I'm just grateful to you for having me,' said Jessica.

Oliver smiled, and they started their walk.

When they neared his house, Oliver felt nervous. He very rarely had guests, and he regretted leaving the place in such a state.

A man wearing a black hoodie walked towards them from the direction of Oliver's house. The man looked at Oliver; he was very pale and had a nasty scar under his right eye. Oliver didn't recognise him and had not seen him in the area before.

They reached the house, and Oliver opened the door for Jessica.

'Thank you,' she said, and made her way inside.

Oliver turned to see the stranger was looking back at him. Oliver looked away and followed Jessica.

* * *

When he got back into his car, he took down his hood and cursed himself for letting the priest see him. He was a professional and that was way too sloppy. 'Damn it!' He said and hit the steering wheel.

He took out his mobile phone and dialled a number. After a few rings, someone answered.

'He saw me as I was walking away from his house. He was with a woman. I thought it was a couple, never considered it to be him... I know... Yes. Yes, I understand. There was nothing suspicious in his house... I will.' He ended the call, started his car and drove away.

* * *

Oliver offered Jessica a drink. 'Tea or coffee?'

'Tea, please,' replied Jessica, 'one sugar.'

'The TV remote is on the table, feel free to watch whatever,' said Oliver.

Jessica turned on the TV in the living room and browsed through the channels.

'Shall I order us some food or just put a pizza in? I have ham and pineapple or Texas BBQ chicken?' Said Oliver.

'Pizza's fine. Texas BBQ, please.'

Oliver put the pizza in the oven, made the drinks, then sat next to Jessica. 'So where were we in the cafe before all the madness happened?'

'You were saying something about a dream you'd been having, I think?' Said Jessica.

'Oh, yes, that was it, the dream. Well, what I was saying was that I do believe you. Usually I'd be very sceptical because people will sometimes do or say anything for attention. Yet I don't think this is the case with you, and I don't think you coming to me was by chance. I believe there is a genuine mystery surrounding the conception of your unborn child, and I want to help you figure out what it is.'

'Thank you, Oliver, you have no idea how much that means to me,' said Jessica. 'And what about this dream?'

'It's been a recurring dream. I'm holding a baby boy in my church, in the exact spot where you stood when you first told me. Then there's a voice saying, "protect him".'

'Really?'

'Yeah, it's been disturbing my sleep for weeks. I was actually starting to get worried. I thought the dreams may have been a sign of a serious medical condition. I'm not sure if it's coincidence, but after seeing you it seems the dreams may have stopped. Last night was the best night's sleep I've had in so long. One other thing – I could have sworn I heard the voice again yesterday when you spoke to me in the church.'

'The one saying, "protect him"?'

'Yes, that same voice and the same words,' confirmed Oliver. 'I know it's strange, but I know what I heard. There's one other thing you should know, too.'

'What's that?'

'At the end of all the dreams there's a man, or something in the shape of a man, made up of black smoke or fog. It's hard to describe, but he is reaching for the baby in my arms, and all my instincts are screaming at me to run. To be honest, I've never felt fear like it.'

'Are you saying someone will try to hurt my baby?' Asked Jessica, looking horrified.

Oliver took her hand. 'What I'm saying is, if you truly have become pregnant without having intercourse, and somehow my dreams are connected to this baby, then I suggest we keep all of this to ourselves. I'd advise that you make up a story about how you got pregnant and not divulge to anyone else that you're not sure how you conceived.'

After a brief pause Jessica replied, 'I suppose you're right – it can't hurt to have a story. It's not like anyone will believe this anyway. If anyone asks I can always say I had a one-night stand and I don't know who the father is. I'll just say he bailed on me the following morning because neither of us wanted it to go any further.'

'Are you comfortable with that?' Asked Oliver.

'I'll have to be – it's better than being laughed at or being called mental. It's decided, that's the story. I was really drunk, slept with a stranger and got pregnant. Very classy.'

'Are you sure that's what you want?'

'I can't think of anything better, so yeah, it will have to do.'

'Okay,' said Oliver. A movie continued after a commercial break on the television. 'I haven't seen this in ages, I love this film,' he said, and turned up the volume.

They made themselves comfortable. Oliver was happy to let the movie take his mind off the day's events.

CHAPTER 4

Oliver woke up on his sofa to his mobile phone ringing on the coffee table. There was a slice of pizza left over and the TV was still on. Jessica was asleep in his bedroom; he had suggested she stay after she had nearly fallen asleep during the movie they had been watching. He reached over for his mobile; it was a number he did not recognise.

'Hello?' Oliver rubbed the sleep from his eyes.

'Hi, Father Hall, it's DC Cole. Sorry if I woke you.'

'It's fine, how can I help?' Said Oliver, and made his way into the kitchen.

'I just had to make sure you were okay. I need to get hold of Jessica too.'

'Jessica is here. She's fine, other than being quite upset over what happened yesterday. Is everything okay?'

'There's something you two need to know.'

'What is it?'

'I had a phone call this morning from a friend at Scotland Yard. He told me there were a lot of attacks last night, just like the one we encountered with Vanessa. Normal people just switching out of nowhere and attacking anyone in sight, the same black liquid coming out their faces. It's believed to be some sort of disease or virus, but no one really knows. Many people have been killed and injured. The majority were asleep when the attacks took place, so they couldn't even defend themselves. The emergency services have struggled to keep on top of the situation.'

'Are you serious?' Asked Oliver as he turned on his battered TV.

The news was on and scrolling across the bottom of the screen was: 'BREAKING NEWS: Deadly unknown virus leaves thirty-eight dead, twenty of whom were infected, and over forty injured in an hour of mayhem in London.'

'Yes, totally serious,' said Cole. 'It all started around 3 a.m. and ended an hour later. The alleged infected all had some type of seizure and died around the same time. It's so strange, no one has any answers. You and Jessica should stay indoors if you can until some sense is made of all of this.'

'Understood. I'll let Jessica know as soon as she wakes up. Thank you for the phone call, DC Cole.'

'No problem, Father Hall. Stay safe.'

'I will, bye.'

Oliver put his mobile in his pocket and shook his head in disbelief. Thirty-eight dead, he thought, and there will probably be more if they don't figure out what's going on. He switched on the kettle and made two teas. He looked at the TV and the news was showing some horrendous injuries people had received during the attacks. He turned the TV off; what little appetite he'd had was now gone. He walked back into the living room with the tea. Jessica had woken up and was sitting on the sofa.

'Oh good, you're awake, I've made us drinks. I've put one sugar in like you had last night,' said Oliver, passing her the drink.

'Thank you,' said Jessica. 'What time is it?'

'It's just gone eight.'

'I have to get to my mum's for ten. I promised I'd go shopping with her today.'

Oliver sat down. 'You might want to hear what's happened before you leave. I've just got off the phone with DC Cole. Last night there were more attacks like our encounter with Vanessa. Check this out,' he said, grabbed the TV remote and turned up the volume.

Jessica's eyes were glued to the TV whilst Oliver drank his tea.

Oliver's phone vibrated in his pocket. Grateful for the distraction from the disturbing images on the TV, he opened the text message. It was from a number he did not recognise, and it read: *'You need to ditch your phone and hide. They are looking for you. A friend.'*

Oliver tried to send a message back saying: *'Think you have the wrong number,'* but the message would not go through.

'How weird.'

'I know, how mad is all this?' Said Jessica, gazing at the TV.

'I meant... never mind,' said Oliver, and put his phone back in his pocket.

'I need to phone my parents and make sure they're okay,' said Jessica, and left the room.

Oliver turned off the TV and continued to drink his tea. His phone vibrated again. Another message, this time from a different number:

'Seriously, ditch the phone and leave. There are some bad people coming for you and they can track your phone.'

Oliver was annoyed and tried to call the number, but it was not recognised. It baffled him. He had just received a message from the number, so how could it not be recognised?

Jessica came back into the room. 'Everyone is fine, thank God. The news said that public transport hasn't been affected, so for peace of mind I'm heading to my parents.'

'Are you sure you're okay to travel alone?' Asked Oliver. 'I would come with you, but it's Sunday... with everything that's happened people will be looking for support from the church.'

'I'll be fine. I'll get there as fast as I can and I'll let you know when I get there.'

'Well, please be careful – if you see anyone acting crazy with black eyes, run. Please don't forget to call when you arrive.'

'Don't worry, I'll be okay, and I won't forget. Thanks for having me, Oliver.'

'No problem. Bye, Jess,' said Oliver, and got up to hug her goodbye.

'Bye, I'll speak to you soon.'

Jessica left the house and Oliver got ready for church.

* * *

In a busy shopping centre three miles away from Oliver's house, Steven disconnected from the public Wi-Fi and packed away his laptop.

'Do you think he will act on the texts?' Asked Nicole.

'Not a chance,' replied Steven as he took her hand and headed into a crowd of people, 'but we had to try. Keep your hood up and head down. We don't want any cameras to see our faces.'

The pair made their way down into the London underground and got onto the Tube. Luckily it was not very busy; besides a few people at the other end, their carriage was practically empty.

'So, if you knew he wouldn't act on the messages, why even bother?'

'Because I didn't just send him messages. I also put a rather destructive virus into the phone's global positioning system. Now if anyone tries to hack the phone and track its position, it will rapidly destroy the hard drive of the computer trying to access it,' said Steven.

'Very clever,' said Nicole, smiling.

'I'm not just a pretty face,' joked Steven. 'Right, let's get changed, we only have a few more stops.'

Nicole took off her black backpack and pulled out two pairs of trainers and two tracksuits, one grey and one blue.

Steven was currently wearing a black shirt, a pair of black skinny jeans and black boots. Nicole was wearing a black wig, a black T-shirt, a black skirt and black boots.

The tracksuits were large, and it was easy for the pair to pull them over their clothes and change into them. They took off their boots and put on the trainers. Nicole took off her wig and stuffed the lot into the backpack.

'My stop's coming up. Remember - leave the backpack on here. We want to disappear, and that will give us away if we're being watched,' said Steven.

'I will, don't worry. So, you'll meet me at my mum's in an hour?' Said Nicole.

'Yeah, no longer than an hour, I promise,' said

Steven, preparing to get off.

'I don't want us to split up,' said Nicole with a frown.

'It's only an hour, babe.'

'An hour's too long,' said Nicole, and put on a sad face.

'You're making it extremely difficult for me to see my other bitches,' said Steven with a cheeky wink.

'Shut up,' said Nicole, and punched him playfully in the arm.

'Love you,' said Steven and reached in for a kiss.

'I love you too,' said Nicole and met his lips with hers.

The doors opened and Steven got off. Nicole watched him walk away as the doors closed and the train left the station.

* * *

In the window of the second-floor apartment opposite St Michael's church, he looked at his reflection. As he ran his finger over his facial scar, memories he would rather forget flooded back.

'Alexander!' A voice shouted from behind him.

'What?' Alexander shouted back.

'Did you not hear me? I've been talking to you. He has called, he wants to know if you've made any progress with the priest.'

Alexander gave the bulky, bearded man a most sinister look. The man trembled and looked away.

'Speak of the devil,' said Alexander, who was looking out of the window at Oliver approaching the church. 'Tell him progress will be made soon. I know the priest's every move... when the time comes we'll be ready.'

The bearded man nodded his head and left the room.

* * *

As Oliver approached the church, he noticed two blacked-out four-by-fours parked outside, and two suited men standing at the church doors.

'Morning, can I help you two?' Asked Oliver.

'Father Hall?' Said one of the men.

'That's me, and you are?'

'He is waiting for you inside,' said the man, ignoring Oliver's question, and he opened the church doors.

'Who's inside?' Asked Oliver and made his way towards the entrance.

Whilst stepping aside, the man gestured for Oliver to go inside. Once he was inside, the doors were closed behind him. There was an eerie silence inside. As he walked further in he could see that, by the altar, under the crucifix, someone was praying. Oliver made his way towards them, and as he got closer, he realised who this may be.

'Excuse me, sorry to bother you, but may I ask who you are?'

The man stood and turned to face him. He was about fifty years old, wore red robes and clasped a gold cross.

Oliver dropped to the floor and knelt before him. 'Your Lordship.'

'Please, Father Hall, stand,' said the man, and took Oliver's hand to help him rise.

'I do not understand, why would you be here?' Asked Oliver.

The man opened his arms, embraced Oliver and kissed both his cheeks. 'So, you know who I am?'

'Of course, you're the Right Reverend Christopher Smith, Auxiliary Bishop of Westminster, My Lord. Why would you be here?'

'I've been sent here by His Eminence Alberto Cardinal Luvini, under instruction from the Holy Father, to watch over you and report back to the Vatican City anything out of the ordinary.

'I don't understand.'

'Two days ago, on Friday morning, His Eminence told me he had received a call from the Holy Father. The Holy Father told His Eminence an angel visited him in the early hours of the morning. The angel told the Holy Father that you have been spoken to and touched by God, so the Holy Father, as you can understand, wants me here. But you are by no means required to stay in the church or in my presence. In fact, the Holy Father forbade it. Whatever plan God has for you it is not within these walls. We advise you to get out and about, continue your life as normal, but do not mention any of this to anyone. As of now, two of my assistant priests will take over all your duties in the church, keep it immaculate for you, and carry out all Masses.'

Oliver sat down on the front pew and was lost for words. He felt the urge to tell the bishop about Jessica and her baby, but the whisper of the words 'Protect him' in the back of his mind stopped him. 'Did the angel say anything else?'

'Yes, but I'm not sure you'll want to hear it. Satan has declared his intention to wipe out all humanity. Which explains the hordes of demons causing havoc in London.'

'Demons?'

'The attacks last night, have you not heard?'

'Yes, I've heard, but I was told it was a virus of some sort.'

'They would say that, but I've done enough exorcisms to know a demon when I see one. All those poor people were possessed. I do not know what path God has planned for you, Father, but know this: no matter how dark or perilous it may be, I will be here by your side,' said the bishop, and placed his hand on Oliver's shoulder.

'Thank you, My Lord. I've never come across someone possessed before. How is it so many have become possessed all at once? Do you think it will happen to anyone else?'

Bishop Smith patted Oliver's back. 'I honestly do not know, to both questions. Do you know anything about exorcisms?'

'A little, I have read about how to identify demonic possession and I've been shown some rituals to expel demons, but I've never done one before, or been officially trained.'

'It may be worth reading up more about the subject. If we have a repeat of what happened last night, you may be forced to attempt one. We cannot allow the demons to act unchallenged, we must show defence. I would obviously prefer you to have had proper training, but unfortunately, I don't believe there is time for that now. Under these extremely rare circumstances, Father, I hereby give you permission to attempt an exorcism if these possessions continue, but please do not feel you are obliged. These rituals are dangerous, as you well know, and can harm you and the person possessed. So be sure before making your decision.'

'I will, My Lord, but hopefully it will not come to it. I understand the risks,' said Oliver, and let out a sigh. 'If only I'd known it was possession, I may have been able to save Vanessa. All the signs were there, but I was caught so off guard.'

'Vanessa?' Asked Bishop Smith.

'A waitress. She was serving me and a friend when she became possessed. We couldn't control her – she killed someone and was eventually hit by a lorry.'

'Poor child. It would seem that you and these events are most definitely connected. I pray it's over, but if it is not, promise me you will be careful.'

'I promise.'

'Thank you, Father Hall. You may stay if you wish, but if I were you, I'd take advantage of the free time. My bodyguard will give you his direct number on your way out. Please get in touch with me if anything happens.'

'I will, thank you, My Lord,' said Oliver, as he recovered his composure and stood up. 'I have a few friends I need to call. They need to know what's really going on – that's if they'll believe it.'

'It's been a pleasure to meet you, Father.'

'The pleasure is all mine,' said Oliver; he bowed his head. 'If I find out what's going on, I will come to you straight away. Thank you, My Lord, goodbye.' Oliver turned to leave the church.

'Goodbye, Father,' said Bishop Smith, then faced the crucifix to continue his prayers.

* * *

Alexander had not expected Oliver to leave the church so soon. He saw him making his way up the road after what looked like an exchange of numbers between him and one of the suited men.

'The priest is leaving – you two get your stuff,' said Alexander to the bearded man and a Chinese woman outside his door.

On the coffee table in the apartment's living room were two 9mm Uzis, three silenced pistols and two large combat knives. Alexander picked up one of the pistols and a combat knife; the bearded man and the Chinese woman picked up the rest. They filled the large inner pockets of their suits and headed out of the apartment.

* * *

Detective Constable Cole looked at his phone as it rang on the bedside table, but before he could reach for it, the slender blonde woman on top of him grabbed his face and kissed him.

'Leave it, it's your day off, you're all mine today,' said the woman, then kissed and pulled him closer.

Cole ignored the ringing and responded in kind. The woman smiled, apparently satisfied with her victory, and moaned a little, which enticed him even more.

The phone rang again, and Cole let out a loud sigh. 'Tasha.'

'Please don't stop.'

'I have to,' said Cole, and reached over to answer the phone.

Tasha jumped off the bed and violently pulled off the duvet, wrapped herself in it and stormed off into the en-suite bathroom. She slammed the door behind her.

'Tash!' Shouted Cole. He lay there naked and feeling guilty; it was not the first time his phone had interrupted them. The price of being CID, he thought, was always being obtainable. 'Hello.'

'Hi, DC Cole, it's Father Hall. I know you're probably busy, but is there any chance I can come and see you today? There's something I need to tell you.'

Cole sat on the side of his bed and looked for his clothes. 'Yeah, sure, Father. Can this not be discussed over the phone?' He asked whilst pulling up his boxers. 'I've been told to advise people to stay indoors if possible.'

'It seems okay outside at the moment, and I'd rather us have this conversation face to face. Just so you can see how serious I am about what I'm going to tell you. There's a chance you won't believe me.'

'Okay then. What time is good for you?'

'I'm five minutes away from my house. I'll get changed then I'll get a taxi straight to you, if that's okay?'

'That's fine, you may as well come to my house. I'll text you the address.'

'Thank you, Cole. I'll see you shortly.'

'See you soon,' said Cole and ended the call. After sending the message, he looked up at the closed bathroom door and sighed once again. He threw his phone on the bed and walked over to the door. 'Tash, please open the door. I'm sorry, but with everything that's happened in the last twenty-four hours, I had to answer the phone,' he said with his forehead pressed against the door. He paused. 'Tasha, please.'

The door unlocked and opened slowly. Tasha was standing there completely naked. The bed covers were on the floor beside her. 'So, was it important?' She asked, standing with her hand on her hip.

Cole was caught off guard; he took a step back, speechless, and coughed nervously.

'Well... does the important detective constable have nothing to say?'

'Father Hall, the priest I rang earlier, has something he needs to discuss with me. He's on his way here now,' said Cole, and admired the view.

'I'd best leave then,' said Tasha, and went to march past him.

'Oh no, you don't,' said Cole, and laughed as he picked her up at her hips and chucked her on the bed.

She let out a little scream as she landed. 'No, get off me,' she demanded and tried to push him away.

'But you're so cute when you're angry,' said Cole and kissed her repeatedly on the lips.

'No, just let me be angry for one more minute.'

It was futile; she pulled him closer and began kissing him back. Cole saw her spot the phone next to them on the bed; she grabbed it and threw it to the other side of the room. Cole laughed and took off his boxers, then threw them on the phone. She grabbed his face and kissed him deeply.

CHAPTER 5

As HE MADE his way through the cold damp tunnel, he was grateful for the thick robes and hood provided. The tunnel was narrow and the little light from the candles in their sconces glistened on the moist walls. As he neared his destination, he slowed his pace and his heart beat faster. He was afraid; even after years of learning to conquer his fear he considered running away, but he knew it would be pointless. All he could do was continue and attempt to hide his cowardice. He came to a wooden door and took a key from his pocket. He unlocked the door, slowly pushed it open and stepped inside, closing it behind him. The room was very dark, the only light coming from two candles on the floor to his left. Straight in front of him, hanging on the wall, was an inverted crucifix. The corner to his far right was in complete darkness, and it was here where his attention focused. As he stared into the darkness, it drew him in and hypnotised him. He leant forward and squinted his eyes as he tried to focus them better in the dark room. Something fell onto his hood and dropped to the floor. It was a huge black spider; he jumped backwards, and it scuttled into the darkness.

'So, what news do you bring?' A deep voice asked from within the dark corner.

The man regained his composure and stood straight. 'An angel visited The Holy Father. We tapped the phone of Cardinal Luvini of Westminster and listened in on an interesting conversation. A priest called Father Hall has been told a secret by God and has been given a divine power to protect that secret. I assume the Holy Father also knows of our intentions.'

A booming laugh filled the room. 'The old man knows nothing of our intentions. What else?'

'We have tracked down Father Hall and are in the process of bringing him in for questioning. Whatever secret he has we will get it out of him.'

'You don't have him yet? Disappointing,' said the voice from the darkness. The candles flickered, and one went out. The room became darker and the blackness in the corner started to move and expand as though it was alive. 'What else?' Demanded the voice.

The man sensed something terrible was about to happen. Having no more information for the evil entity, he panicked. 'Please, I've served Satan for years. I'm a loyal servant, just give me more time and I'll get you invaluable information.'

The darkness moved forward towards him. He took a few steps back and bumped into the door; he spun and tried desperately to open it, but somehow it was locked. He turned back to face his fate – the darkness had filled half the room. Inside it, he could see a figure. It looked like death himself, a ten-foot-tall figure in a cloak of darkness, with only blackness where a face should be.

'It is true, you're an archdemon,' said the man.

'I am Abaddon, and I can smell your fear – you reek of it, it's pouring out of you. Satan has no use for you,' said the archdemon, and laughed. 'Do you think you know fear? You know nothing of fear. I will show you fear.'

The last lit candle flickered again and went out. The room was covered in complete darkness. The only sound he could hear was his own heavy breathing. Then he burst into flames.

* * *

Oliver alighted from a taxi; he would have been completely unaware of being followed. Alexander told his bearded accomplice to park their car a few houses away from the priest's destination, then turned to face the Chinese woman on the back seat. 'Zing, is it?'

She looked at him, expressionless. 'Zhang, Zhang Cheng.'

'Zhang Cheng, why are you not finding out whose address that is? What am I actually paying you both for?' Alexander said, looking at the two of them. They did not reply.

Zhang opened her laptop, inserted her Wi-Fi dongle and investigated the address.

'So...' said Alexander, looking at the bearded man, 'you're obviously called Bear for your bearish looks.'

Bear looked at him, offended. 'I do not look like a bear.'

Alexander looked at Zhang, shocked. She seemed to be disguising a smile.

'It's a stage name from when I used to wrestle – my signature move was the bear hug. I never use my real name on assignments,' said Bear.

'How pleasant,' said Alexander. 'I feel sorry for any woman that wants to cuddle you.'

Bear gave Alexander a disapproving look.

'Any luck on the address, Zhang?' Asked Alexander as he peered at the house in question.

'It belongs to a Detective Constable Damien Cole, a twenty-eight-year-old male, no wife or children. There is nothing here to show how he knows the priest, but I have a photo,' replied Zhang, and showed Alexander the picture of Damien Cole.

'Okay. I must pay this Damien a visit, find out exactly how and why he knows the priest. When the priest leaves, you two follow him. I'll stay here and have a word with DC Cole.'

'Yes, boss,' said Bear.

* * *

Cole shook Oliver's hand and invited him into his house. 'Good to see you again, Father Hall, please come in.'

'Good to see you too, DC Cole. I hope I'm not being a pain coming to see you like this,' said Oliver.

'Not at all, you're welcome any time.'

Oliver smiled and stepped into the hallway, and Cole gestured for him to go into the living room.

'You have a beautiful home,' said Oliver, and walked into the big modern living room.

'Thanks. Please sit down. Would you like a drink?'

'I'm fine, thanks, I don't intend to stay long,' replied Oliver, and took a seat on the black leather sofa. 'Actually, could I have a glass of water please?'

'Yeah, sure. Tasha,' shouted Cole to the kitchen, 'can you bring us two glasses of water please?'

'Two minutes,' replied Tasha.

'Girlfriend?' Asked Oliver.

'Yeah, we've been seeing each other for a year now. We don't live together though, not yet. So, what is it you wanted to tell me?' Asked Cole, sitting down.

'Please have an open mind when I tell you this. I don't expect you to believe me, and you don't have to, but I just wanted to let you know what I was told.'

'Okay, I'm listening.'

Tasha walked in with two glasses of water.

'Thank you,' said Oliver as she handed his drink.

'Thanks, Tash,' said Cole and received his. 'Tasha, this is Father Hall. Father, this is Tasha.'

'Nice to meet you, Tasha,' said Oliver, and shook her hand.

'Nice to meet you too, Father. I'll leave you two to it,' she said, then leant over and gave Cole a kiss on the cheek. She left the room.

'Sorry, you were saying?' Said Cole.

'Remember, an open mind,' said Oliver, and Cole nodded in agreement. 'I've been talking to someone, someone who's had plenty of experience with what has been happening in London, namely these allegedly infected people.'

'He knows what the virus is?'

'Not exactly,' Oliver paused, 'he's the Auxiliary Bishop of Westminster and is adamant that those people are not infected by anything. He said demons have possessed them.' Oliver locked eyes with Cole to show his seriousness.

'Possessed?' Said Cole.

'Possessed.'

There was a long pause. Oliver could see from Cole's facial expressions that he wasn't quite convinced; his eyes rolled and his posture changed.

'Do you believe they have been possessed?' Cole asked, taking a sip of his water.

'It would most definitely explain a lot. I mean, look at what happened to Vanessa yesterday – only someone possessed would act in that manner. The bishop is one of the most respected and trustworthy people I know. So, yes, I believe they have been possessed. Though I must confess, I myself have never come across anyone possessed before.'

'I don't really believe in that sort of thing, but I'll keep an open mind. I won't ignore the possibility.'

Oliver nodded his head in appreciation. 'That's all I ask.'

'What do you suggest I do if I encounter someone in that state again?' Asked Cole.

'Try to secure them somehow, keep them from harming themselves and others. Detain them in a locked room and call me so I can attempt to help them. I will recite certain prayers and commands in the hope of driving out the demon. An exorcism. I must add that this is not my usual practice, but these are not usual events. I have had some insight into the ritual and I believe I may be able to save them. At least I must try.'

'Very well. Seeing as we have no idea what we're up against, if you believe you can prevent another death like Vanessa's, I'm on board. Hopefully, all this madness has ended, but if not, I'll be in touch for your help.'

'Thank you, DC Cole,' said Oliver and stood up. 'I'd better make a move. I've arranged to have a chat with Jessica too at her parents' house.'

Cole stood up too and they made their way to the front door. 'I appreciate you coming over, Father. I hope next time we meet it's under better circumstances. Please tell Jessica I said hello,' he said, and opened his front door.

'I hope so too,' said Oliver and patted Cole's back on his way out. 'Thanks for your time. I'll tell Jessica you said hi.'

'Thanks. Goodbye, Father.'

'Bye, DC Cole.'

They shook hands and Oliver walked back to his taxi, which he had instructed to wait.

* * *

As he saw Oliver leave Cole's house, Alexander prepared himself. He got out his pistol and tightened the silencer, checked the barrel to make sure it was loaded, and flicked off the safety. 'Whatever you do, do not lose him!' He demanded, and looked at Zhang and Bear. 'I'll be in touch when I'm finished with this detective constable.'

Alexander got out of the car, pulled up his scruffy black hood and made his way to Cole's house. He peeped through the front window; the detective appeared to be alone inside watching TV. Alexander thought it best to sneak around the back and make sure there was no one else around that could surprise him. He easily climbed over the six-foot gate at the side of the house and made his way to the rear. He crouched and peered through the kitchen window. It appeared the coast was clear. The window was open, but he gave the back door a try. Luck was on his side; the door was unlocked. He crept inside and slowly closed the door behind him. There was movement upstairs – a girlfriend, he assumed – he could hear a hairdryer. Pistol at the ready, he stood at the kitchen door. Cole was sitting with his back to him. He raised his pistol and aimed at Cole's head. Then he whistled.

Alexander watched the detective constable's head shoot around. They locked eyes and Cole jumped up, clearly startled, and raised his hands.

'Who the hell are you? What are you doing in my house?'

'Be quiet!' Alexander demanded.

'What do you want?'

Alexander shot the flat-screen TV. There was a pop and sparks sprayed out of the bullet hole. 'I said be quiet!' He demanded again and pointed the gun at Cole's chest.

Alexander knew his demands were now being taken seriously because Cole had stopped talking. 'I'm going to ask you some questions. Answer me truthfully and quietly, do you understand?' Cole nodded his head. 'Good. Who's upstairs?'

Cole looked petrified; Alexander could see that he was struggling to hold himself together.

'My girlfriend – she doesn't need to be involved in this.'

'So long as she stays upstairs she won't be. The man that just left here, who is he to you?'

'We only met yesterday. I know little about him other than he's a priest.'

'Why did he come here?'

'We were both involved in an incident yesterday which resulted in the death of a young woman. He believes a demon possessed her. He thinks the same for the attacks last night. He said the people were possessed by demons, not infected by a virus.'

'So, it has begun,' Alexander said.

'What has?' Asked Cole, looking confused.

'Where is he going now?' Alexander asked, ignoring Cole's question.

Cole was hesitant but then replied, 'To see another friend of his.'

Alexander knew he could press for more, but Bear and Zhang would find out anyway.

'Do you own any rings?' Alexander said.

'No,' replied Cole, looking even more confused, and showed his ringless fingers.

'Your phone and wallet, chuck them to me.'

Cole did not hesitate to do what was instructed. The phone and wallet landed by Alexander's feet and Cole re-raised his hands in the air.

'Don't move,' said Alexander as he picked up the items and put them in his pocket. 'Now, turn around and kneel with your hands behind your head.'

Cole did as he was told.

With his gun still raised, Alexander approached Cole and slowly pulled out a syringe from his inside pocket. The syringe was filled with a yellow liquid. Alexander placed his pistol on the floor, grabbed Cole, covered his mouth and injected him in the neck. Cole's attempt at fighting back was fruitless; within seconds his eyes rolled to the back of his head and he was unconscious. Alexander laid him on the floor, then very hastily and cautiously left via the front door.

CHAPTER 6

Steven stopped and gaped at Nicole's parents' house from the end of the footpath. The house was beautiful, painted white, and exceptionally large. Set back from the footpath the house was detached, and two pillars framed the thick double oak doors. The front garden and hedges had recently been neatly trimmed and there were flowering plants all over. Steven walked towards the astonishing house down the little stone path, climbed the three steps at the entrance and knocked on the door. There was a little wait but then Steven heard movement inside. He had taken more than a few hours longer than he had promised, and he braced himself for a telling off. The doors were unlocked and pulled open to reveal an extravagant hallway and staircase inside. Nicole ran and wrapped her arms around him.

'Where have you been, you idiot?' She said. 'I've been so worried.'

Steven pulled back a little and looked her in the eyes. 'Idiot?'

Nicole laughed, grabbed his face and gave him

a kiss. 'My mum has made you a roast dinner, come in.' She took his hand and pulled him inside, then closed the door and took him into the kitchen.

The modern black marble kitchen smelt beautiful, and Steven instantly realised he was famished. 'That smells so good, remind me to tell your mum I love her,' he said.

'I honestly believe she cooks the best roasts in the world, I'd put my life on it,' said Nicole, and put his food in the microwave.

'Where is she anyway?' Asked Steven.

'She's gone to see Nan at the retirement home. She's surprising her with a roast too.' Nicole smiled. 'On the subject of where people are, where have you been? You said one hour.'

'Yeah, sorry about that. I went home to do some checks and update some software. It only normally takes five minutes, but something came up on my routine checks.'

'Something so important you couldn't even call or text?'

'I don't know, to be honest. I was just looking for anything abnormal in the computer systems of some organisations. Then, just as I was about to finish, I spotted a couple of dozen highly encrypted emails being sent from one unknown IP address.'

Nicole looked at him, completely baffled, and the microwave beeped. She served his food, and he took a seat at the breakfast bar.

'I tried to trace the IP address of the sender, but it was coming up with different ridiculous addresses like the North Pole or the middle of the Atlantic. The encryption was way too advanced for my laptops to break so I had to improvise. The emails were sent to various organisations.

An electric company, the Metropolitan Police, an upmarket food chain, some top government authorities, and more. So, I hacked into the security systems of the food chain's head office. I got the IP address of the computer the email was sent to and, using their own cameras, I waited to watch someone open it. Sure enough, after a while, a man sat at the computer and opened the email,' said Steven between mouthfuls.

Nicole, still dumbfounded, just looked at him.

'Someone has sent a private email to a couple of dozen people. Being encrypted means no one else can see it, but by watching through a camera, I saw the email.'

'So why didn't you just say it like that? You and that geek lingo.'

Steven shook his head and continued to eat. 'Can I have a glass of water please?'

'Yeah, sure,' said Nicole, getting a glass out of the cupboard, 'So what did the email say?'

'"Meet tonight at 20.00 the usual house. The Bishops Avenue. Delete once read!"' said Steven as he received the water.

'I really don't think you should be getting involved in all this. These people you're snooping on will not take too kindly to you putting your nose in their business.'

'I know it could be dangerous because I don't know who these people are or what they're capable of, but I just can't help myself. They seem to have connections to everything and their computer skills are surreal. I have a feeling they're up to no good. If I can find out what and prevent it, I have to.'

'Okay, honey, but please be careful, you know I worry about you.'

'I know you do, babe, thanks. I will be careful,

I promise. Come here.' Steven opened his arms. Nicole complied and sat on his lap. 'If there's one thing you don't need to worry about, it's me being traced or caught on any sort of computer system. One, I'm too clever, and two, if I ever felt I could be traced or caught, I wouldn't even attempt it, okay?'

'Okay,' said Nicole and gave him a kiss. 'So, what are you going to do about the address in the email?' She asked, running her fingers through his hair.

'I'm not sure yet.'

'Well, while we have the house to ourselves, how about you forget about all this, finish your food and come up to my room, to... relax?' Nicole said with a cheeky smile.

'You know what's funny? I was just thinking how I could do with relaxing,' said Steven with a wink; he knew what she was getting at.

Nicole giggled, jumped off his lap and headed to her bedroom. 'Don't keep me waiting too long.'

'I'll be a couple of minutes,' said Steven, and stuffed his face as quickly as he could.

* * *

Cole tried to open his eyes but the searing pain in his head prevented him. He groaned and tried to sit up, but someone pushed him back down.

'It's okay, you're safe, don't waste your energy. He's awake – someone get the doctor,' said a female voice.

As he thought of nothing but the agony, Cole could not process who the voice belonged to. He rubbed and opened one eye. Tasha was sitting at his side and a police officer was standing by an open door. He looked around and slowly registered where he was. He was in a hospital bed hooked up to an electrocardiograph monitor and an IV drip. 'What happened?' He mumbled.

'Don't move, just wait until the doctor comes back,' said Tasha, and stopped Cole from sitting up again.

A second police officer entered the room, followed by a male doctor. The doctor's name tag read 'Dr Singh'.

'Damien. Let's see what we have here,' said Dr Singh, and pulled out a pocket torch. He shone it in Cole's eyes and checked the monitor. 'Do you know where you are?'

'A hospital. Why am I here?' Asked Cole.

'It appears someone has drugged you with a powerful tranquilliser. We'll know more once the blood tests come back, but you've been out for quite some time. How's your head?'

'It feels like I've been hit by a train.'

'High doses can have that effect. I'll get the nurse to bring you some pain relief. Do you have any pain anywhere else or any nausea?'

'No, I feel fine, it's just my head.'

'Okay, good. A little rest and you should feel back to normal. I would like to keep you here overnight though as a precaution. I'll send the nurse in now,' said Dr Singh, and left the room.

Tasha leant over Cole and gave him a squeeze. 'I'm so glad you're okay. I've never been so worried. What the hell is going on?'

'Wish I knew, my head is in bits. Someone drugged me?' Said Cole, confused.

Tasha sat back in her chair and one officer stepped forward. 'Hi, DC Cole. I'm PC McDonough and this is PC Sanders. We understand you're a little disorientated, but we would like to ask you some questions if you feel able?'

'I really don't think I'm capable, to be honest,' replied Cole, holding his head.

'I appreciate that, but you must understand the urgency. A firearm was discharged in your property and we need to apprehend whoever is responsible, especially if they pose a risk to the public.'

'A firearm?' Said Cole. 'The last thing I remember was watching the TV.'

'Honey, whoever it was shot your TV,' said Tasha.

Cole looked at Tasha through one eye, then at PC McDonough. He thought this was some joke and nearly burst out laughing, but the serious looks on all their faces made him hesitate. 'You're being serious?'

'Deadly serious,' said PC McDonough, and waited to let it sink in. 'Can you not remember what happened? Who had the gun? Why they were in your house? Where they might be heading?'

A nurse entered the room holding tablets and a plastic cup of water. 'Here you go, dear,' she said, and handed them to Cole. 'We're only supposed to give two tablets at a time, but Dr Singh said you may appreciate three.'

Grateful, Cole gave the best smile he could manage and downed all three tablets. The nurse took back the empty cup and turned to leave. 'If you need anything, just press the buzzer. I'm only down the hall. I'll leave you all to it,' she said, turning to leave.

'Thank you,' said Tasha.

Cole pushed the pain away for just a few seconds and tried to remember anything he could to help the officers. There was nothing after seeing

Oliver out and sitting to watch TV. Nothing.

'I'm sorry to be no help, guys, but I really don't remember anything. It's difficult to think with my head like this, but I will keep trying.'

The disappointment was clear on both officers' faces. 'Well, if you recall anything, no matter how trivial, please let me know. PC Sanders has to return to the station, but I'll be staying just outside your room,' said PC McDonough. 'Just a precaution until we know you're safe.'

Understanding, Cole nodded in agreement.

'Right, we'll leave you two alone. Get some rest. I hope you feel better soon. Bye now,' said PC McDonough.

'Bye, thank you so much for your help,' said Tasha.

The officers closed the door behind them. Tasha looked at Cole and he could tell she had something on her mind.

'What's up, Tash?'

'You really remember nothing?'

'I wouldn't lie, Tash.'

'I just need to know if I should be worried – if there's someone after you. I need to know if I'm safe.'

'Of course you're safe,' said Cole, sitting up. 'Look, no one is after me that I know of, but now it's apparent something's going on, I won't let my guard down. I'll make sure you're safe and I'll find out exactly what's going on.' He cupped her face with his hand and stroked her cheek with his thumb.

'Okay, I'm sorry. It was just so scary. I came into the living room to find you dead or unconscious with a blown-up TV. I thought you'd been electrocuted. It was the paramedics who noticed the bullet hole in the wall and needle puncture in your neck.'

'I can't believe some scumbag has shot my fifty-inch TV,' said Cole, devastated.

'How could you be thinking of the TV? They could have killed you.'

'Well, it's not your average TV – I love that TV,' said Cole defensively.

Tasha said nothing.

Cole lay back down and closed his eyes; he still felt drowsy. 'Do you have my phone?'

'Your phone and wallet are missing. They must have been taken. You can use mine if you want?' Said Tasha and pulled her mobile out of her bag.

Cole let out a sigh and rubbed his temples. 'Yes, please. I need to call Father Hall to make sure he's okay. This happened so soon after he left that I can't ignore the possibility they were following him.'

'Do you know his number?'

'Yeah, I had to write it down a few times on my paperwork yesterday. I still remember it. What hospital is this?'

'The Royal London,' said Tasha, and handed him the mobile. He dialled Oliver's number.

'Hello?'

'Father Hall, it's DC Cole.'

'Oh, hi, DC Cole, is everything okay?'

'Sort of, what are you up to?'

'I'm just with Jessica, she says hello, by the way.'

'Tell her I said hi. So, you two are okay?'

'Yeah, we're fine, thanks. We've had some food and I'm just about to leave.'

'Okay, that's good. Look, I need you to come to see me, but I don't want you to worry.'

'Worry? Why would I worry?'

'I'm in the Royal London Hospital. I'm okay, but I'd rather explain everything when you get here.'

'Okay, now I'm worried,' said Oliver. There was a slight pause while he passed the news to Jessica. 'We're on our way. Jessica insists she comes too.'

'No problem. Phone Tasha on this number when you arrive, she'll meet you at reception and bring you to me. Thanks, Father, and honestly you don't need to worry.'

'I'll try not to. We're leaving now, see you soon.'

Cole hung up and passed the phone back to Tasha. The tablets were taking effect. 'I'm going to try sleep this headache off, Tash, those pills are kicking in. Are you okay to meet Father Hall when he gets here?'

'Yeah, sure, you get some sleep,' said Tasha, and kissed him on the forehead.

Cole tried to reply but sleep took over and he drifted off before speaking.

* * *

Bear was driving so Zhang answered the phone to Alexander. 'Hello.'

'Zhang, how are you getting on pursuing the priest?'

'Fine, he is with a woman named Jessica West. They have just left a house in Wembley. We're about five cars behind and the traffic is calm, so it's been easy not to lose them.'

'Good, that's what I like to hear. The detective told me Father Hall was going to visit a friend, so that must be her. I want you to find out everything there is about her.'

'Already done. How did it go with DC Cole?'

'I got what I went in for. No one was hurt, but

he'll be waking up with a banging headache. I have his bank cards, driving licence, warrant card and mobile phone. I'm going back to the apartment now to do a thorough check on his whole life. I'll meet up with you once I'm finished. You two keep following him – any issues contact me asap.'

'No problem, boss.'

'Good,' said Alexander and hung up.

Zhang relaxed back in her seat and looked at Bear. 'What do you think of Alexander?'

'I think nothing of him. He's an employer... that's it,' replied Bear.

Zhang looked at him speculatively. 'Come on, so you don't think this is weird? He gives off a creepy psycho-killer vibe, yet we're following a priest. I've never had a job like this before. I usually have private military or politician contracts.'

'Yeah, I get that creepy vibe from him too. If it wasn't for the amount he will pay me, I would never have had accepted this job. I feel like there's something else going on that he's not telling us about. Something much bigger than this priest.'

'Good, so it's not just me that's feeling it.'

'No.'

'I tell you what, I'm better working alone, but if you have my back, I'll have yours. If things turn nasty, I'd rather have a bit of backup.'

Bear nodded in agreement and reached out to shake her hand. 'Deal.'

'Deal,' Zhang agreed and shook his hand.

When their attention was back on the road, they realised something had happened up ahead. A lorry had broken down and was taking up the two lanes. The taxi they were following had been in front of it and was now getting away from them.

'Dammit, this isn't good, can you not get

around?' Asked Zhang.

'Does it look like I can get around?' Said Bear patronisingly.

They both ducked as the roof of their car smashed in, the rear windows popped, and glass sprayed everywhere. Something had fallen on the car.

'What the hell was that?' Bear shouted. A second later there was movement.

'Quiet,' ordered Zhang.

The movement continued a few seconds more, then a man's face appeared over the top of the windscreen and looked at them with jet-black eyes.

'Look at his eyes – did the fall do that?' Said Bear.

There was another smash to their right; a woman had fallen from above and hit the bonnet of the car next to them. Two more bodies smashed down onto the car in front, and three people fled the car, screaming.

'What the hell is going on?' Said Zhang as she tried to see what was happening.

The man on their car started to headbutt and punch the windscreen as he tried desperately to get inside.

'Fuck this,' said Zhang, grabbing her laptop. 'I'm out of here.'

'What about the priest?' Said Bear.

'We'll have to try and catch up with him later. I'll hack his GPS and pinpoint his location.' She opened the door.

'Don't have to tell me twice,' said Bear, and they both climbed out of the car.

Zhang looked over the car and saw the woman, who had fallen from above, pounce on Bear. She slammed him against the car and tried to bite his neck and face; she settled for his right arm, biting deep into his bicep. He punched the woman's face hard but failed to get her off. 'Zhang!'

Zhang had problems of her own; the man on their car had got to his feet and his eyes were set on her. He jumped off the car and sprang towards her, but she was prepared. She grabbed him mid-air and threw him face first to the ground. Then she spun back around, pulled out her silenced pistol and shot the woman attacking Bear in the centre of her forehead. She dropped down dead and Bear was released from her relentless bite.

Bear put pressure on his wound and turned around to face Zhang. 'Thanks, I owe you.'

'Like we agreed, I got your back, you got mine,' said Zhang. 'Let's get out of here – there's more of them jumping from that building over there.'

Both looked towards the broken-down lorry as two men jumped onto it from a third-floor window.

'Yeah, let's get out of here,' said Bear.

CHAPTER 7

THE SUN WAS setting and there was a light breeze in the warm spring air as Jack Buckley drove with his window down. A line of ten expensive blacked-out vehicles was in front of him; he followed them to The Bishops Avenue. He looked ahead; a police officer had closed the road and was waving all the vehicles through a gap in the cones. As each one passed, it looked like the police officer was checking off a list on the clipboard he was holding. Buckley drove past the officer and gave him a wink as he did. In his rear-view mirror, he watched the officer close the gap with another cone before looking ahead again. The huge houses at this end of the street had long been abandoned by the billionaires who owned them, and Buckley wondered every time he came here why anyone would abandon such properties. Some looked derelict, but others he thought, still looked remarkable. Fortunately, he knew they were en route to one of the better properties. The gates were open. Buckley and all the other vehicles drove onto the huge driveway and parked. A man and a woman stood at the entrance of the mansion and were clearly waiting to welcome their guests. Buckley put on his mask and exited his vehicle. He counted twenty-three people on the driveway, all of whom wore different masquerade masks and were dressed exquisitely, the men in black suits and the women in long black dresses. The group made their way to the hosts at the entrance and formed a single-file queue. Buckley joined them.

'Welcome,' said the female host through her black cat mask, 'thank you for coming at such short notice. Please come inside.'

One by one the group entered and, following procedure, each showed an identical gold ring to the male host as proof of membership. Buckley looked at his ring, an eighteen-carat-yellow-gold ring emblazoned with the bold letter 'S', and thought of Satan.

The female host led them straight through the main hallway towards the kitchen. As they walked, their footsteps echoed throughout the dark empty mansion, and it was clear to Buckley the property was unfurnished and undecorated. He saw that cobwebs and dust covered most surfaces and it was being disturbed by their activity; he watched dust float like snowflakes down from the ceiling as they entered the kitchen. Candles illuminated the entire room; they flickered as a draught came in through the open back door. On the broad kitchen counter was a lavish buffet and a variety of drinks.

'If you require refreshments or the bathroom, now is the time. There will be no interruptions once we begin. When you are done, please join us

THE LIGHT

in the garden,' said the female host, then followed the male host outside.

Everyone in the group, except Buckley, indulged in the buffet and took the opportunity to chat and flirt amongst themselves. Buckley was in no mood to converse, so kept his distance from the others. A short while later they all made their way outside and joined the hosts in the garden. It was obvious the outside space had not been tended to in quite some time. The grass was overgrown, and weeds spread out in all directions. The bushes and hedges grew out of control, blocking the footpaths and passages, and the swimming pool was empty with brown slimy algae coating the bottom of the pool.

The hosts were at the far end of the swimming pool facing Buckley and the group.

'Can you all please spread out and stand on the pool's edge facing inwards?' Said the female host. 'Spread out so we cover the whole pool's edge.'

Buckley was the first to walk to the pool's edge; he waited there for further instruction as the others did the same. They spread themselves to surround the pool's edge, at arm's length from one another.

'Perfect,' said the female host, 'we can now begin.'

Silence filled the air, and they all bowed their heads. The silence lasted about a minute until a squawking bird disturbed it. Buckley looked up; a crow was flying in circles above them, squawking louder and more aggressively by the second. The crow took a nose dive towards the male host; it got just a few feet from its target when the man sprang to life. He snatched the crow from the air and with one quick swipe a blade in his hand decapitated the crow. Its head hit the floor and rolled away, whilst the man sprayed its blood into the empty pool. When the blood flow stopped, the crow's lifeless body was tossed aside. To Buckley's astonishment, the blood simmered as if the bottom of the pool was scorching hot. The blood spread across the bottom of the pool, moving like fast-flowing water. Moments later, the simmering became a boil and the blood turned black. It covered half the pool and thickened, like a rippling sheet. A large mound rose in the centre of it, followed by smaller mounds that bulged out all over it. They rolled over like bowling balls and revealed screaming faces, both male and female. Hands and arms joined the faces, reaching out as they tried to break through the black sheet. The central mound continued to rise until it was the depth of the pool and it formed a shape. A few seconds later the metamorphosis was complete; now, standing in the pool with a cloak of pure blackness, was an archdemon.

Buckley sensed the evil that now resided in the pool and could not look away. He stared into the black abyss of the archdemon's face and wondered why he was so mesmerised. It was either curiosity or just plain stupidity; he had no answer, yet as he looked he was not afraid. In fact, it was the most comfortable he had felt all night.

'You, take off your mask,' demanded the archdemon.

Everyone around the pool looked up to see who had been spoken to. Buckley took off his mask as instructed and threw it to the side. He stood there, silent and confident, a confidence he had gained over the years as a result of his flawless looks. So many men were jealous of him, and even more women lusted for him. He had been told in the past how his bright blue eyes shone; his symmetrical nose complemented his prominent cheekbones and his strong jaw appeared to have been chiselled by a master craftsman.

'What is your name?' Asked the archdemon.

'Jack Buckley,' replied Buckley.

'Do you know what I am, Jack?'

'You're an angel of hell.'

'I am the angel of the bottomless pit. My name is Abaddon. I rule over all the damned souls in hell – some of them you see in the pool with me now. Yet you show me no fear.'

Buckley had no response; he looked around at the group. Everyone was staring at him.

'Come here,' demanded Abaddon.

Buckley felt no fear, so he did as commanded without hesitation. He climbed into the pool and walked towards Abaddon. The damned souls parted and created a footpath leading to the archdemon, all desperately reaching out for him as he walked by. As he stood in front of Abaddon, Buckley looked into the black void that was its face and waited.

Abaddon turned to face the two hosts. 'Where is the priest?'

'We could not get his exact whereabouts. The priest's phone has a malicious virus within its GPS system – it took out several of our computers when we attempted to breach it. We did, however, manage to listen in on a recent phone call he had with a Detective Constable Cole. He has been the most frequently recurring contact recently and we believe the priest is on his way to see him as we speak,' said the female host.

'It would be very unwise to waste my time, so for your sake I hope you're right. Where is this Cole now?' Asked Abaddon.

'He's at the Royal London Hospital, in Whitechapel.'

'Jack Buckley and I will retrieve the priest. If you're wrong and he is not there, I will be returning. Now, carry on with your duties and understand this, the time to prove your loyalty has come. You will obey every command without question. Failure to do so will result in death. Satan will soon walk this Earth and only the strong and obedient will prosper,' said Abaddon, looking at each member of the group. 'For those of you that do not know, the church has been keeping a close eye on this priest, Oliver Hall. We believe it is because he has been spoken to by God, so we will extract any information he has on God's plan.'

There was silence while Abaddon's words sunk in.

'We hope this has settled any doubts about our upcoming tasks. The war we are fighting is real and soon the entire world will come to know about it. Continue your duties as you have been instructed and be ready for further instruction. You may all now leave,' said the female host. The group moved away slowly, talking amongst themselves. There was a sudden strong gust of wind. It blew through all the surrounding trees and Buckley had to fight against it to prevent being blown over. The ground beneath him became softer under his feet, and he, Abaddon, and the surrounding damned souls all spun into a vortex. Some kind of portal opened underneath them, and they were violently sucked into it. Everything went black.

* * *

Steven expertly landed his drone a few feet in front of him and turned off the HD monitor remote. Nicole took the remote from him and Steven retrieved the drone and switched it off.

'What the hell was that thing, Steve?' Asked Nicole.

'I have no idea. Let's get the recording back to mine and try to figure it out,' said Steven, putting the drone in the boot of Nicole's car.

Nicole put the remote next to the drone and closed the boot. They both got in and Nicole drove away. 'I'm so freaked out – that thing wasn't normal. You really have to stay away from those people, Steve, I have such a bad feeling.'

'Nic, we've been through this.'

'Yeah – that was before we saw some black alien thing appear out of the floor and disappear again, taking a man with it. Please, Steve, promise me you'll stop pursuing these people. I couldn't cope if anything happened to you.' She was on the verge of tears.

Steven put his head in his hands and sighed. 'Okay, I promise I'll stop pursuing them, but I just need to do one thing first.'

'No, you don't need to do anything. Just leave them to it and forget everything you've seen and found out so far,' said Nicole, her face flushed red with anger.

'I need to show the priest what we caught on camera. These people are after him. I don't know why, but they are – I need to warn him and show him the recording.'

'He will think you're a nut job. Why on Earth would he listen to you? What would you even say?'

Steven lost his patience; he wanted to dig deeper but she would clearly not allow it. Letting him do this one last thing was the least she could do.

'Look, I don't care if he thinks I'm a nut job. At least I will have tried. If he chooses not to believe me, then so be it. I'm going to his house and I'm telling him everything I know – ignoring this is not an option. If something bad happens to this innocent priest and we could have prevented it, I couldn't forgive myself. Could you?'

'I swear sometimes, Steve, I could...' Before she could finish a bright flash of light filled the car. 'What was that?'

The flash happened again.

Steven turned to look out of his window; there was a taxi beside them. 'It's just a taxi,' he said, but then with closer inspection he saw the priest inside with a red-haired woman. 'No way!'

'What?' Said Nicole.

Steven looked at Nicole, surprised. 'It's the priest, he's in that taxi.'

'Are you serious?' Said Nicole. 'That's crazy.'

'You see, fate wants us to tell him,' said Steven, and Nicole gave him a disapproving look. 'Follow him and I'll figure out what I'm going to say to him.'

'Okay, one last thing, Steve. After this we are done. No more getting involved in whatever this priest is mixed up in,' said Nicole sternly.

'I promise. Let's just do this and we'll go home.' He smiled and felt victorious.

'And you can take that smile off your face,' said Nicole, as a smile crept across hers. She pulled behind the taxi and began her pursuit.

* * *

Tasha struggled to stay awake as she sat in the warm room and watched Cole sleep. There was a TV she could turn on, but she did not want to risk waking Cole. I need coffee, she thought. Trying to make as little noise as possible, she got up and made her way out of the room.

PC McDonough was sitting on the chair outside the room and looked at her with hopeful eyes. 'Has he remembered anything?'

'No, sorry, he's still asleep. Hopefully, he'll remember something when he wakes up. I'm just trying to find some coffee; would you like one?' Said Tasha.

'You read my mind. I'd love one. White with two sugars, please. There's a nurse over there, she may be able to help,' said PC McDonough, and pointed to the nurse at her desk going through paperwork.

'Thanks,' said Tasha and made her way over.

'Hi, can I help you?'

'Yeah, sorry to bother you, but do you know where I can get me and the officer some coffee?' Asked Tasha.

'Just past the bathroom, the door on the left at the end of the hall. It's the kitchen for the patients on the ward,' said the nurse, and pointed.

'Thank you so much,' said Tasha with a smile.

The ward was quiet; no patients were wandering around and there were only two nurses as far as Tasha could see. The ward comprised of five single patient's rooms, the nurses' desk, a bathroom and a kitchen. Perks of being CID, she thought as she walked into the kitchen. The kitchen was small, like a converted storeroom. She switched on the light and stepped inside. There was a stool, a vending machine, a small fridge, a sink and a small countertop. The kettle and coffee were on the countertop. She flicked on the kettle and washed two cups that were in the sink. The kitchen light flickered as she dried the cups. The kettle clicked off and she made the coffee. The light flickered again more aggressively, this time with an electrical buzz. She looked up but was not too concerned, so she finished making the drinks, picked up the cups and went to leave. The light flickered again, and she stopped in her tracks. There was a loud squawk and she jumped, spilling both drinks.

'Shit,' she cursed, and turned to see a crow peeking through the open window.

She put the cups back on the counter and closed the window.

'Go away, you stupid bird,' she said, then banged the window to scare the crow away.

She got a tea towel to clean the mess on the floor. As she wiped up the coffee, the room temperature dropped drastically. It became freezing cold and she could see her breath as she exhaled. She stood up, left the towel on the floor and crossed her arms for warmth. She was scared stiff. Standing with her back to her, next to the vending machine, was a naked woman with long black hair. She was milk pale, with prominent veins visible all over her body, and her back was covered in scratches and bruises. She had her arms at her sides and was laughing, or crying, Tasha could not tell, but she thought this must be a patient from the ward. Confused, she asked, 'Are you okay?'

'Shhhhh,' replied the woman.

Tasha decided she'd better get a nurse. 'I will get someone, okay, just stay there.'

'Please, it wasn't me. Please tell him it wasn't me,' said the woman in a soft, broken voice.

The room became even colder and Tasha's body reacted with goosebumps. 'Tell who? Is someone hurting you?' Said Tasha as she approached the woman and reached for her shoulder.

The woman did not reply.

Tasha's hand was inches from her skin, but she hesitated; her hand felt ice cold and the silence in the room was daunting. 'Tell who?' She asked again; there was a pause, and the light went out.

'Me,' said a man's deep voice from behind her.

Tasha screamed so loud she thought her lungs would burst.

PC McDonough stormed into the room and tried to calm her down. 'What's wrong, what's happened?'

Tasha looked round frantically, but the kitchen was empty apart from the two of them. 'The woman, where did she go?' She asked, terrified. 'And there was someone else too.'

'Calm down – there's no one here, you're safe. You've obviously gone through a lot today,' said PC McDonough and took her by the arm. There was a crash as the crow smashed through the window and flew directly for his face. He jumped backwards, lost his footing and fell to the floor. Tasha screamed and ran out, leaving him behind.

* * *

The crow flew back out of the broken window and PC McDonough lay there trying to catch his breath. A black gooey substance dripped on him from above; he looked up at the ceiling and, hanging there like a spider, was a black-haired woman. Her neck was twisted round, and she stared at him with her jet-black eyes. She screamed at high pitch, then fell towards him. Instinctively, he put his hands forward and braced himself for impact. The woman landed on him and grabbed his throat with both hands, continuing to scream. Both his hands were unintentionally on her breasts; they felt strange, soft and doughy. His hands sank into her chest. He looked at her, petrified, and saw that her face was becoming soft too. The right side of it drooped so badly her eyeball looked ready to fall out. Her high-pitched scream became deeper and more like a moan as her body got softer and softer. His hands had completely sunk into her chest and he could feel something moving around his fingers. This sent him over the edge – he threw her aside and rolled away, watching in disbelief as she melted onto the floor until all that was left was a puddle of purple-pink liquid. He gasped for air, got up and ran to the sink to wash the liquid off his hands... something within it was moving, like hundreds of ants crawling in and over his fingers. Never in his entire life had he felt his heart beat so hard. Once his hands were clean, he leant on the kitchen counter to get his breath back. 'My God, what just happened?' He asked himself, looking down at the puddle.

There was a scream back on the ward. He took a deep breath and prepared himself the best he could, then ran out of the kitchen, baton in hand.

The nurse who had been at her desk earlier was being dragged across the ward by her hair by a male patient with jet-black eyes.

PC McDonough was full of adrenaline; he ran up to the man and pelted him full across the face with the baton. This was not his normal practice, but he believed the patient must have been infected. The force of the blow sent the patient head first into the window of Cole's private room, smashing it. Cole did not stir, but Tasha screamed and hid under the bed.

The patient loosened his grip on the nurse and went for PC McDonough, who was ferociously pounding him over the head. The blows were ineffective and forced PC McDonough to back away.

A female patient came out of her room to see what all the commotion was. PC McDonough pulled her out the way and shoulder barged the male patient into her room. He picked up a chair, jammed it under the handle and locked the man inside.

'Get out of here, both of you,' said PC McDonough to the nurse and the female patient, 'and get help.' He ignored the noise of the man's attempts to escape and scanned the area.

There was a whistling sound that seemed to come from all directions; it got louder, and an unnerving cold gust accompanied it.

What now? though McDonough. He held his truncheon in one hand and pepper spray in the other.

The whistling got louder, and the gust turned to a strong wind. McDonough was on the verge of plugging his ears and struggled against the piercing sound.

A black circle appeared on the floor in front of the nurse's desk. It drew the wind towards it as it sucked the air out of the ward. PC McDonough was being pulled towards it, and he had to use all his strength to stand his ground.

Dozens of shadows shot out of the black circle;

they went up the walls and across the ceiling. McDonough barely resisted the urge to run. He watched in a state of shock and tried to figure out what the shadows were. They were like large locusts, but with peculiar shaped heads and scorpion tails. He had already lost his nerve, so when a black mound started to rise from the black circle, he turned to run away; a man was standing right behind him. Before he had a chance to react, the man snatched his baton and hit him over the head with it, knocking him unconscious.

* * *

Cole felt cold from the wind that was circulating the ward and woke up. 'Tash, can you close the window, please?'

'Damien, get down here quick!' Tasha yelled.

'What, where are you?' Said Cole, then pulled up the sheet and looked under the bed.

'Just get down here now!'

He heard the genuine urgency in her voice and looked around to investigate what was going on. The window was broken and there was glass on the floor. He detached himself from the hospital apparatus and got out of bed. Then he looked out into the ward.

What he saw in the hallway shook him to the core; his rational mind knew it could not be real, but he could not dismiss what his eyes were seeing – he was looking at the grim reaper. The large personification of death was without its scythe and moved sluggishly with exaggerated shoulder movements through the ward. Its thick black cloak was soaked in black tar. It covered its entire body and dragged across the floor behind it. Attached to the back of the cloak were two large bat-like wings. They were folded in, at rest, and didn't look to be coming through the cloak, but rather a part of it, moulded into it. Fast-moving shadows circled the ward walls.

Cole dived under the bed with Tasha. The strong, athletic, alpha-male side of him was gone.

'What's going on out there?' Asked Tasha.

'Keep your voice down... you wouldn't believe what I've just seen,' whispered Cole.

'Was it the naked woman?'

'Naked woman? No, I don't know what it was. Have you got your phone?'

'Yes, it's in my bag just here,' said Tasha, and retrieved her phone.

'Text Father Hall and tell him not to come here.'

Tasha did as she was asked, then put her phone back in her bag. 'Done.'

There was a loud smash of what sounded like a window being put through in the room next door. Tasha grabbed Cole's arm and Cole grabbed hers. They held on to one another as something smashed through the remainder of the broken window in Cole's room and crashed onto the bed above them. Whatever it was – it sounded like a body – bounced off the bed and landed on the floor behind them.

Cole had to cover Tasha's mouth, so she did not scream.

The body moved around the bed heading for the door which blasted open. From under the bed, Cole could see someone's feet in the passageway. Their black, expensive-looking shoes marched into the room. There was a thud, then another smash of a window. Cole peered under the sheet and saw only one set of feet. Cole presumed the person with the nice shoes had kicked or thrown the other out of the window.

Cole and Tasha remained quiet as this person stepped to the bottom of the bed and stopped. They stayed there for a moment, then left the room. Cole's heart raced as he heard a slow dragging noise; he knew it was the thing he had seen earlier: death. It entered the room and moved like a snail, its cloak slithering along the floor.

The thing moved across the room, along the bottom of the bed. There was a whistling noise, followed by a loud roar and a wind that blew around the room, making the bed sheet flap. Cole took Tasha's hand. He thought they were going to die.

A huge gust of wind blew the sheet off the bed. Cole looked, and death was gone.

* * *

The taxi driver dropped Oliver and Jessica right outside the hospital entrance. They paid him, and he drove away. Oliver received a text message; he pulled out his phone and saw it was from Tasha. The message told him to stay away from the hospital.

'What's up?' Asked Jessica.

Before he could reply there was a smash from above. The pair looked up to see a male patient falling from a fourth-floor window.

'Oh no!' Screamed Jessica and covered her eyes.

Oliver grasped his crucifix as the patient hit the floor with a bone-shattering crunch. Jessica dared not look, but Oliver walked over to what he presumed was now a dead person. The patient was twitching on the floor and it looked as though he was still breathing.

'Jessica, I think he's still alive – we need to get

help,' said Oliver, looking at Jessica.

'Oliver, get back!' Shouted Jessica, and pointed towards the man.

Oliver turned back to see the patient, who had a badly broken arm, was now standing up. He was covered in blood and had jet-black eyes.

Oliver moved back to Jessica's side. 'He's possessed,' he said, as the man stumbled towards them.

'What do we do?' Asked Jessica.

Oliver clutched his crucifix and removed a small bottle of holy water from his pocket.

'Stand back,' said Oliver, and forced Jessica behind him. Then he sprayed the holy water in the air in the shape of a cross. 'I cast you out, unclean spirit, along with every Satanic power of the enemy, every spectre from hell, and all your fell companions, in the name of Jesus Christ.' He sprayed another cross in the air. 'Begone and stay far from this creature of God. For it is He who commands you.'

Unaffected by Oliver's words the man grabbed Oliver and lifted him into the air, screaming, 'Foolish priest.'

Oliver sprayed him in the face with the rest of the holy water. The patient's face burned as if it had been hit with acid. This filled him with rage and he went to bite Oliver's neck. Oliver pushed the patient's face away with his bare hand. Then he realised something was happening. His whole hand was tingling, and a bright light began to emanate from his palm.

The patient let out a high-pitched shriek as Oliver's hand gripped his face and the light from it intensified. When the shrieking stopped, the patient fell to the floor unconscious.

'What was that?' Said Jessica as she took two

steps back.

'I have no idea,' said Oliver, and looked at his hand, bewildered.

The collapsed patient coughed and gasped for air. Oliver bent down; the man no longer had jet-black eyes. 'Are you okay?' He asked and put a hand on the man's shoulder.

'My arm, what happened to my arm?' Asked the man.

Oliver helped the man to his feet and looked at Jessica astonished; Jessica returned the look.

A loud roar from the fourth floor drew everyone's attention. Demonic shadows were scurrying out of the broken window and making their way down the building.

'That does not look good,' said Oliver.

'We should get out of here,' said Jessica.

The patient supported his distorted arm and ran away. There was another roar and some sort of creature slowly emerged from the broken window.

'Lord, help us,' Oliver prayed.

'Oliver, watch out!' Jessica shouted, and pointed at two fireballs in the sky. They were falling at tremendous speed and looked to be coming right for them.

Oliver froze while Jessica covered her face. He expected an explosion when the fireballs hit, but there was nothing. The fireballs disappeared as they touched the ground and from them, to his utter disbelief, appeared two stunning angels. They stood either side of him with a superior ethereal presence. The one to his left was male, the other female; he gawked at them in awe, speechless.

'Oliver, you need to get Jessica and run,' ordered the female angel.

Oliver rubbed his eyes – he could not believe

what he was seeing.

'Oliver, run, now!' The angel repeated.

Oliver had so many questions but guessed this was not the time. 'Yes, sorry,' he said, then ran to Jessica's side and grabbed her hand. 'Let's get out of here.'

As they both ran a car stopped in front of them.

'Nicole, look, it's that thing again,' said the passenger as he leant out the window of the car, and pointed at the flying creature with its gigantic bat-like wings.

Oliver looked back to see the two angels, swords in hand, charge towards the demonic shadows now on the ground.

'We need to get out of here, can you help us?' Asked Jessica.

'Jump in,' said the passenger.

'Thank you,' said Jessica, and climbed into the rear of the vehicle. 'Oliver, get in.'

Oliver did so without argument and closed the door behind him. The wheels spun as the driver raced away from the hospital.

'Did you see that thing? What was that?' Asked Jessica, looking at Oliver.

'I don't know how it's walking the Earth, but I think that was the archdemon Abaddon, a demon leader of hell, and those shadows were its army of locusts. Jessica, I knew our meeting was no coincidence. Those angels knew our names – they told me to get you away,' said Oliver.

'Angels, what angels?'

'The two angels that landed next to me,' said Oliver, but Jessica just looked at him, confused. 'Could you not see them?'

'I saw the fireballs falling, but when they disappeared it was just you standing there.'

'Incredible.'

'I'm not sure incredible is the word I'd use – terrifying describes it more accurately.'

The front-seat passenger reached back and extended his hand. 'I'm Steven. This is Nicole, my girlfriend.'

Nicole waved. 'Nice to meet you.'

'Nice to meet you, too. I'm Father Hall. Thank you so much for getting us out of there,' said Oliver, and shook Steven's hand.

'Thanks again. I'm Jessica,' said Jessica, and shook his hand as well.

'Steven, when you pulled up did you say you had seen that thing before?' Asked Oliver.

Steven looked at Nicole for support; he didn't seem ready to answer the question. But neither had a chance to respond as a violent vibration rippled through the car. Nicole looked in the rear-view mirror. 'You mean that thing behind us,' she said, and everyone turned around to look.

Abaddon had gained on them. The archdemon flapped its wings ferociously in the early night sky.

'Get us out of here Nicole, quick,' ordered Steven.

'I'm trying... this car isn't exactly the fastest in the world,' said Nicole.

Another ripple of energy jolted the car, this time stronger than the last. The car swerved from side to side and Nicole nearly lost control.

'It's catching up... go faster,' screamed Jessica in panic.

'I can't go any faster,' said Nicole, and slammed on the brakes.

Abaddon flew right over them, and Nicole took

a swift right turn down a narrow side street.

'Yes, babe.' Steven cheered.

A cocky smile spread across her face; despite the surreal, scary situation, she looked like she was enjoying herself. She continued to the end of the street and turned left onto a main single carriageway. 'Have we lost it?' She asked.

'I think so,' said Oliver, inspecting the skies.

Nicole screamed and stopped the car in the middle of the carriageway. Abaddon was standing a couple of hundred yards in front of them.

'Back up, back up, back up!' Screamed Steven.

Nicole rammed the gear stick into reverse and drove as fast as the car would allow. She narrowly missed hitting other cars, dodging them as best she could.

'We're going to die,' said Jessica, gripping her seat like a vice.

Abaddon was flying towards them at a phenomenal speed; the gap between them closed rapidly and he landed on the car bonnet. He gripped the sides with his wings, then thrust his head through the roof. Everyone in the car screamed hysterically, but were soon muted as the void that was Abaddon's face let out a loud screeching whistle. It forced them all to wince in pain. All but Nicole desperately plugged their ears.

There was a bang, an explosion of light and Abaddon was gone. Out of the window, Oliver saw that the male angel from the hospital had him by the neck, and both were soaring through the air out of control. They smashed through an empty bus stop, rolled dozens of times, then slammed into a tree and knocked it down. Nicole was driving forwards again and was pulling away as the tree hit the ground.

'What have you got us into, Steve?' Said Nicole. 'I told you not to get involved with these people. Your stubbornness will get us killed. How am I going to explain this hole in the roof?'

'I'm so sorry,' said Oliver, and leant forward, 'if I'd known this would happen, I would never have got into your car and brought you into harm's way. I don't know why, but I have this horrible feeling that thing was after me.'

'It's alright, we wouldn't have left you there with that thing, would we, Nic?' Asked Steven.

'No, of course not,' said Nicole, and gave Steven a scolding look. 'I'm just glad we're all safe.'

'It's a miracle we are – that thing was serious. What just happened to it?' Asked Jessica and looked behind to see if Abaddon was gone.

'It was one of the angels – did any of you see it?' Said Oliver.

'I didn't see an angel. That light nearly blinded me though,' said Steven.

'Why am I the only one that can see them?' Said Oliver, but more to himself than anyone else.

'Maybe because you're a priest?' Suggested Jessica.

'Maybe,' said Oliver, and pinched his crucifix.

'Nicole, what did you mean by "getting involved with these people"? Were you referring to us?' Asked Jessica.

Before Nicole could answer, a familiar vibration rippled through the car.

'Shit,' said Nicole and looked in her rear-view mirror.

Abaddon was back in pursuit and closing in fast. Nicole turned onto Waterloo Bridge and put her foot to the floor. Fortunately, there wasn't much traffic, so she easily overtook the few cars in front of her.

'This thing just won't quit,' said Steven.

Abaddon had got within arm's length of the car when Oliver saw the angel launch into his side like a comet. They collided with such a thunderous smash that light illuminated the whole car. Both hurtled over the bridge and into the River Thames. Everyone in the car watched, amazed, as the water splashed a hundred feet into the air.

'I can't see it, Oliver, but there is definitely something helping us. That archdemon, or whatever you called it, just got wiped out,' said Jessica.

'Yeah, it did,' said Steven. 'Hopefully it will give up now.'

'I hope so. Let's get out of here and get to yours quick,' said Nicole, and kept her foot to the floor.

'Agreed,' said Steven.

* * *

Jade emerged from her portal and walked on the wonderfully white floors of heaven. Kleo was right behind her; she gave him a smile, satisfied with their success at sending Abaddon and his demonic pests back to hell.

Their smiles were short-lived. Michael landed in front of them, proud and majestic, anger written all over his face.

'What you two have just done was foolish and reckless. At what point did you decide that adhering to Father's warnings was unnecessary? When did you decide that you could confront an archdemon without consulting me first?' Demanded Michael.

Jade looked at Kleo and for a few seconds

neither responded.

'We... we thought—' said Kleo.

'You thought wrong. Never confront an archdemon without consulting me, especially at times when Satan is taking the souls of angels. Father has advised us not to go to Earth, but if Abaddon really had to be challenged, I would never have let you two go alone. Next time you feel the need to intervene, tell me. I may even join you,' said Michael.

It shocked Jade. They had never considered that Michael would ever entertain letting them go to Earth, let alone go with them.

'Yes, Michael,' said Kleo.

'Yes, Michael.'

'Good. Now, were there any complications?' Asked Michael.

'None. Satan may now have the power to open portals to Earth, but he has not managed to give his archdemons any more power than they usually possess. Abaddon was easily handled and retreated into a portal while we were underwater,' said Kleo.

Michael nodded. 'That is good.'

'There is one thing you should know, though,' said Jade. 'The priest, Oliver Hall. He could see us, without us allowing him to.'

The anger left Michael's face and was replaced by pure astonishment. 'Really?'

'Really. He was staring right at me and he could hear me too. I told him to run and he did – even though we hid our presence from all humans in the area. How is that possible?' Asked Jade.

'It's not possible,' replied Michael.

'And there's more. Just before we landed by him he exorcised a possessed with just the touch of his hand. I could not sense a hint of the demon afterwards within the human,' said Kleo.

Michael looked at Kleo as though he was lying or exaggerating. Kleo looked at Jade.

'It's true, Michael, he did,' confirmed Jade.

Michael seemed to believe them. 'It looks as if Oliver has a much bigger role to play in all this than I first anticipated. His abilities must have been given by Father for the protection of the saviour.'

'Or he is the saviour,' suggested Jade.

Michael briefly paused. 'Could it be that Satan intends to commence his attack so soon? If so, this would mean Oliver is the true saviour and there must be another purpose for the unborn child.'

'What will you have us do now?' Asked Kleo.

'Watch over them. If there are any changes, you come to me - certainly do not go there without seeing me. Understood?'

'Understood,' said Jade and Kleo together.

Michael's wings stretched out and he left just as quickly as he had arrived.

CHAPTER 8

Zhang and Bear walked into their apartment. Alexander was sitting in the living room with the television on, working on his laptop. The TV volume was low, but Zhang heard the reporter on the news say 'A patient at the Royal London Hospital lashed out at staff today and attempted suicide. The patient, who has not been named, was seen miraculously walking away after jumping from a fourth-floor window.'

'You're back,' said Alexander without taking his eyes off his laptop, 'and why are you not following the priest?'

The pair put all their gear onto the coffee table and threw their jackets over the opposite sofa.

'We were attacked,' said Zhang as she sat and opened her laptop.

'Attacked?' Asked Alexander and still did not look away from his laptop.

'Yes, attacked. Some freaky bitch nearly left a hole in my arm,' said Bear.

'I looked into it. Apparently, some virus is turning people insane – we had to fight them off. I will track the priest through his GPS now,' said Zhang, and turned on her laptop.

'Virus, that's hilarious.' Alexander sniggered. 'So, you failed. I shouldn't be surprised. Don't bother trying to hack his GPS, it will only destroy your laptop. It destroyed one of mine earlier. I'd be angry if I wasn't so impressed. Whoever protected his phone is very intelligent. I believe their IT skills may even surpass your own, Zhang.'

Zhang flushed red with anger; to call her a failure was one thing, but to also criticise her abilities was something else. She slammed her laptop shut and got up to storm out.

'You leave this apartment and you won't see a single penny of your payment. You see this through to the end, that was the deal,' said Alexander.

Zhang stopped at the front door and debated whether the money was worth it to put up with this insufferable arsehole. It was; after this she would never have to work again if she so chose. 'And when exactly is the end?' She asked.

'As soon as I know I will let you know. You know my word is good – you will get paid what you've been promised.'

Zhang turned back to face Alexander. 'Things have changed. You haven't told us anything about our mission, and if I'm to put up with your insolence, I will need half payment now.'

'Payment for failure.' Alexander chuckled. 'Okay, I'll transfer you both half payments now, but the details of the mission stay with me – you two just do as you're told. You wouldn't believe me if I told you anyway.'

Zhang looked at Bear and nodded; he gave her the thumbs up and nodded back. She felt victorious, and she felt her posture change to that of a strong, confident businesswoman. 'Good. I'd prefer to know more about the mission, but I suppose I can compromise.' She sat back down and opened her laptop; she wanted to see the money in her account before she did anything he wanted her to.

A few minutes passed, and Alexander hit the enter button extra hard. 'Done.'

Zhang logged into her account and her eyes widened; the money was there. She suddenly hated Alexander a hell of a lot less. 'Fabulous.'

'Yours is there too, Bear. Would you like to check?' Asked Alexander.

'No, it's fine, I believe you,' said Bear, who had been watching the transaction from over Alexander's shoulder.

'I've done a thorough check on DC Cole and he's clean. I thought he may have been a threat, but he's not. So now we need to find the priest. Any suggestions?' Asked Alexander.

'Jessica West,' said Zhang, 'the priest was with her. Let's see if her GPS has been tampered with.' Zhang bashed away at her keyboard and in no time at all got a location. 'They're in an office building on Clapham Road, Lambeth.'

'Get your things together, we're leaving now. There's another hire car out back. Bear, you're driving,' said Alexander, and chucked him the keys.

'Yes, boss,' said Bear, and caught them.

They all grabbed their gear and left the apartment.

* * *

Steven opened the entrance doors to the office building, turned on the lights and put in the alarm code to the security system. Once everyone was inside, he locked the doors behind them and headed towards the doors at the end of the hallway.

'What is this place?' Asked Jessica.

'It's an office building my cousin owns. The offices are for let but no businesses seem interested. I think he has the price too high, myself, but he won't budge. He lets me use an office on the second floor until someone decides to rent the space. I've been here for months now, it's great. There's no one here to bother me, so I can just get on with my work,' said Steven.

Nicole laughed. 'Work?'

'Well, it's more of a hobby, I suppose. Follow me.'

Steven opened the doors to the staircase, and the group made their way upstairs. The sound of their footsteps echoed loudly and shattered the silence in the building. When they reached the second floor, Steven took them through a set of double doors and switched on the lights.

'Here it is. Welcome to Steven Williams Enterprise,' said Steven, and bowed for effect.

The room was huge, an open-plan office with glass windows and suspended ceilings. Opposite the windows were three small private office cubicles, and at the far end was a computer set-up.

'Some place you have here, Steven,' said Oliver.

'It does the job,' said Steven, and winked. 'Come, check this out. It's my supercomputer – twenty multi-core processors.'

Steven sat at his desk and pressed the power button on his keyboard. All twelve computer monitors in front of them came to life. Each monitor looked to be displaying footage from cameras surrounding the building, all except for the main and largest monitor in the centre which displayed a desktop home screen.

'I've named her Rachel after my best friend. Like her, this computer is super-intelligent, hard-working, reliable, and has never let me down. Rachel, emails,' ordered Steven, and the powerful super-computer loaded up his online email inbox.

'Impressive,' said Oliver, genuinely impressed; he had always had a thing for computers and technology, 'but what exactly do you use this for?'

'That's classified, I'm afraid,' said Steven, smiling, as if he had always wanted to say that. 'There is a reason I brought you here though. There's something I need to share with you but promise me you won't freak out.'

'Why would I freak out?'

'I've kind of been spying on you.'

'Spying on me?'

'Yeah, kind of, but only so I could help you. Some people I believe to be very dangerous seem to be very interested in you. After you ignored my messages, I decided to protect your phone from any hackers. It seems to have worked.'

'Don't be ridiculous. Wait, you sent those messages?'

'Yeah, that was me, and before you think I'm crazy, look at this,' said Steven, and tapped away at his keyboard. He was on the Metropolitan Police website. He easily hacked his way inside, then gestured for Oliver to read.

'Oliver Hall, warrant for arrest, wanted for multiple sexual assaults,' Oliver read aloud, then looked at Steven. 'Is this some sort of joke?'

'No joke, that's the official Metropolitan Police website. I found out earlier they were at your church today looking for you.'

'I don't understand.'

'Like I said, people are after you. This is just one of their methods of trying to apprehend you. I wanted you to see it before I deleted it. Just one second,' said Steven, and deleted the file. 'Done. Also, it wasn't easy, but I cracked open an email that was sent to someone I know to be corrupt. Look at this.'

Steven opened another file on his desktop and Oliver read it aloud again. 'The Pope knows we are after the priest. He has sent his weapon to intervene, so stay vigilant. The capture of Oliver Hall, alive, is top priority above all else. Start the usual procedures for obtaining him.'

'I made it impossible for them to track you through your phone – they may have already got to you otherwise,' said Steven, leaning back in his chair with his hands behind his head.

Oliver took out his mobile phone and called the bishop's bodyguard.

After a few rings, he answered. 'Yes.'

'Hello, it's Father Hall. Can I speak to His Lordship, please?' Asked Oliver.

'One moment,' said the bodyguard. There was the sound of movement.

'Hello, Father, what can I do for you?'

'Hello, My Lord. This may seem like a strange question, but have the authorities been to the church today asking for me?'

'Yes, two officers were asking for you this afternoon. They made some ludicrous accusations, so I sent them on their way.'

Oliver looked at Steven, speechless. Then Steven stretched out his arms as if to say, 'I told you so.'

'Hello?' Said the bishop.

'Hello, sorry, I'm still here. A friend of mine has just informed me that some potentially dangerous people are after me, that this is one of their ways of acquiring me. He has also just shown me an email that talks about some sort of weapon the Holy Father has sent to intervene. Does this mean anything to you?' Asked Oliver.

There was a long pause. 'If that is true, then I fear for what is coming. The weapon is not an actual weapon, it is a. A man that the Holy Father would never have sent unless there is truly a very serious, evil threat here. I need to make some calls. Please keep me informed on anything else you find. Stay safe, Father. Goodbye.'

Oliver put his phone away and was speechless again.

'Now do you believe me?' Asked Steven.

'I do,' said Oliver.

'Good. So why are these people after you?'

'Your guess is as good as mine.'

'Sexual assault?' Asked Steven with a speculative look.

Oliver gave him a disapproving look.

'Sorry, I shouldn't joke. So, what are you going to do now? You obviously can't go home.'

'I could–' started Oliver, but was interrupted by the girls' loud laughter.

'They seem to get on,' said Steven.

'Sounds like it,' said Oliver, and looked over at the cubicle they had wandered off into. 'I could ask the bishop to help me find somewhere. He will know what to do.'

Oliver heard a helicopter approaching the office building, but neither he nor Steven took any notice.

'What about Jessica?' Asked Steven.

'Do you think Nicole would mind taking her home?' Asked Oliver. 'Until I know what's going on, I'd rather she was away from all of this.'

'I can't see that being a problem, I'll ask her now. I need to get her car keys anyway, I've left my drone in the boot of her car. You won't believe what I recorded with it,' said Steven, standing up and walking over to the cubicle.

The noise of the helicopter was directly above the office building. Steven ignored it and entered the cubicle as there was another outburst of laughter. Oliver went to follow him, but there was a flash of light in the corner of his eye. He turned around, but there was nothing there. Then he spotted movement on one of the monitors. He took a closer look; on the rooftop camera feed he saw what looked to be soldiers. They were abseiling down onto the building, equipped with what looked like specialist equipment, and all wearing black.

'Steve, I think you need to take a look at this,' shouted Oliver.

Steven walked back to his computer, putting the car keys in his pocket. 'What's the matter?'

'There,' said Oliver, and pointed to rooftop camera footage.

Steven transferred the feed from the monitor to the main screen. 'We need to go, now! Father, can you call the girls?'

There were eight soldiers in total in two groups of four. All were now on the rooftop and the helicopter flew away.

'Jessica, Nicole,' said Oliver as he watched Steven frantically type away at his keyboard.

'Rachel transfer C drive to location two and initiate program quick exit.'

A pop-up window came on the screen and Steven rapidly typed in the password.

'What's going on?' Asked Nicole, who was standing outside the cubicle with Jessica.

'We've got company. We need to get out of here now,' said Steven and walked towards them. He took Nicole's hand and broke into a run. At the entrance to the stairs, he looked back at the others and put his finger to his lips. 'We need to move quietly.' He slowly opened one of the double doors and entered the staircase.

They all followed his lead. Oliver let Jessica go first and was last to step into the stairwell; he leaned over the railing and peered up the stairs. The soldiers were in the building. They were at the top of the staircase and looked to be clearing the floors on their way down. There were several beams of light from torches and the faint sound of footsteps. Steven gestured for everyone to keep to the walls, then peered up the stairwell himself. He stepped back to the wall and they all silently tiptoed down the stairs.

* * *

Alexander and his team were parked a couple of hundred yards from the office building; they watched as the helicopter pulled away.

'Looks like we're not the only ones that tracked them,' said Zhang as a van pulled up to the building's entrance and four more specialist soldiers jumped out the back. Guns at the ready they made their way to the front doors, smashed the windows and broke their way inside.

'Let's go,' said Alexander, and got out of the car.

'What, to fight them? They're mercenaries,' warned Zhang.

Alexander stared at her; she looked at Bear, speechless, then she and Bear reluctantly followed as Alexander turned to continue quietly towards the building, pistol in hand. He reached the passenger side of the van where he could see a driver inside through the wing mirror. With one eye locked on the driver, he took out a tracking device from his inside pocket. He turned it on and placed it on the rear splash guard above the rear tyre. Then, with swift accuracy, and without hesitation, he stepped out and shot the driver in the head through the passenger window.

With the driver dead, Alexander knew he could sneak up behind the mercenaries in the building without them being alerted. He ran to the entrance and peered inside, just as Father Hall and three others, a male and two females, burst out of a door directly in front of the mercenaries.

'Don't move,' ordered the mercenary in front.

The group froze and put their hands in the air. The mercenaries moved to apprehend them as Alexander stepped into the building with his gun raised. He did not want to accidentally shoot through the lead soldier and hit Father Hall, so he pulled out his combat knife and flung it through the air. It went straight into the back of the mercenary's head. The other three mercenaries reacted instantly. They spun around and opened fire. Their bullets sprayed the hallway, popped windows and left holes in the walls and ceiling. Alexander ducked and dodged the barrage of bullets but did not fire back.

Father Hall and his group took the opportunity to flee and made for what looked like a rear fire exit.

Alexander took a single shot at one of the

mercenaries. The bullet passed straight through his neck and exploded on its exit. The mercenary's gun fired uncontrollably in the man's dead hand, shooting his comrade four times across the chest. His body armour was useless at such close range.

The last of the four mercenaries took a few more failed shots at Alexander, then ran to the open rear fire escape after the group. Alexander gave chase. The mercenary stepped out onto the rear car park, aimed at the group and fired a few rounds at the feet of the young woman at the rear. She let out a high-pitched scream and froze while the others continued towards a car.

The man with Father Hall opened the driver's door and looked up to see the mercenary had closed in on the young female. 'Nicole!' He shouted, then went to run for her but Father Hall stopped him.

'You won't make it, they'll get you too,' said Father Hall.

'So be it,' said the man, and pushed past Father Hall. He only managed two steps when a hail of bullets showered down from above and stopped him in his tracks.

'Steven, we need to get out of here,' said the other woman in a panicked tone.

Steven ran back to the car and they all jumped in. He started the engine and sped away.

The mercenary grabbed the girl called Nicole and easily chucked her over his shoulder. He ran around the side of the building and looked to be heading back to the van out front.

Zhang and Bear caught up to Alexander who was standing in the rear fire escape. He had not fired in case he missed the mercenary. All three watched as the priest and his friends got away.

'I'll get the car and we can catch up to them,' said Zhang.

'No,' said Alexander, and they looked at him, confused. 'I knew this group would come for the priest... they are the real target. I've placed a tracking device on their getaway vehicle. Let's get out of here and we'll find them again later.'

More mercenaries appeared out the stairwell on the ground floor and were making their way to the fire exit. Alexander opened fire. He clipped one in the arm before they all shot back at him.

Zhang and Bear ran outside to follow the mercenary with Nicole around the building to their car. Alexander fired a few more rounds and ran after them. When all three were back around the front, they saw the mercenary throw Nicole into the rear of the van and pull out the dead driver. The three of them ran to their car and got inside as the mercenaries chasing them came around the corner. They opened fire and punctured the bodywork with bullets. Bear started the engine and forcibly rammed the gear stick into reverse. He backed up as fast as the car would allow and spun it as soon as they were far enough away, accelerating through the gears as fast as he could. Before he could turn into a nearby junction, a bullet hit the rear windscreen, which shattered. He made the turn, put his foot to the floor, and left the mercenaries behind.

CHAPTER 9

Cole walked into Tasha's kitchen to see her standing in just his T-shirt making herself breakfast. He approached her from behind and softly grabbed her hips, then kissed her passionately on the neck.

'Morning,' said Cole.

'Morning,' she said, with a warm smile, 'why are you up so early?'

'I have work.'

Tasha turned to face him. 'You're not seriously going into work?'

'Why wouldn't I?'

'You could have been killed in your own home yesterday, and God knows what's going on around London at the moment. You can't just go into work like it's a normal day.'

'Look,' said Cole as he ran his fingers through her hair, 'I'd love nothing more than to whisk you back into bed and spend the day with you, but I have responsibilities I can't ignore. The world doesn't halt at every bit of madness.'

'Yesterday was not a bit of madness. It was full-blown, utter, colossal madness. You'd be out of your mind going in.'

Cole kissed her on the lips and backed away. 'I'll call you later once I've been to the office and got my new phone.'

Tasha crossed her arms in anger, yet the look of defeat was clear on her face.

Cole smiled, turned and walked away to leave the apartment.

Three hours later, Cole pulled up outside the scene of his newly assigned murder case. Dozens of officers were scurrying around, inside and outside a detached house. He parked his car and walked straight to the officer on the front lawn talking to the paparazzi. 'Sorry to interrupt, but can I speak to the officer in charge?' He asked.

The officer looked Cole up and down, but before he could inquire who he was, a superior called Cole over.

Cole passed under the police line without having to show his new warrant card.

'Inspector Newson, good morning,' said Cole, and shook Newson's hand.

'Good morning, Constable, it's been a while,' said Newson.

'It has. How's the family, sir?'

'Good, thanks. The girls are growing up way too fast. It only seems like yesterday when all they cared about were their dolls. Now it's make-up and boys,' said Newson, and shook his head in disapproval. 'Ruth is good, she was promoted to headteacher three months ago. It's more demanding but she seems to enjoy it.'

'That's great news. Tell her I said congratulations.'

'I will,' said Newson and started walking towards the house.

'So, what do we have here?' Asked Cole as he followed him.

'Double murder, a male and female killed in their sleep, and the couple's fifteen-year-old daughter seems to be missing.'

The pair walked into the house and the inspector led the way up the stairs. Forensic teams were all over, dusting for fingerprints and taking photos.

'So how did the killer get in?' Asked Cole as they reached the top of the stairs.

'There are no signs of forced entry, so the killer either had a key or was already in the house,' said Newson, and stepped into the master bedroom.

On the bed was a female lying on her back with a stab wound to the heart. On the floor was a male, face down, in a pool of blood.

'There's a laceration to the male's throat that projected blood onto the curtains and drapes. The woman next door spotted it when she was hanging out her washing and phoned the police. She also phoned the female victim's sister – she's the one who let us in. She's downstairs in the kitchen,' said Newson.

'How is she taking it, sir?' Asked Cole.

'As you'd expect.'

Cole nodded. 'Any suspects?'

'None as yet. Our main focus is finding the daughter, Claire. Hopefully she is alive and well, then she may be able to point us in the right direction.'

There was a bang and movement upstairs. Everyone in the room looked up.

'Sir, permission to check the loft?' Asked Cole.

Before Inspector Newson could answer, Cole was back out in the hallway searching for the loft entrance. He found it at the end of the hall; on the floor was a little stool, so he used it to reach the handle. It took one hard yank and a set of ladders slid down and hit the floor in front of him. He climbed the ladders two steps at a time; he stopped at the top and looked inside.

'Does anyone have a torch? I can't see a thing up here.'

Inspector Newson reached up and passed Cole a mini pocket torch from his chest pocket.

'Thanks,' said Cole, and shone the torch into the loft.

He moved the beam around and scanned the loft in a clockwise rotation. There was no noise or movement, but he sensed he was not alone. The loft was empty, just the odd box full of junk and a few dusty old suitcases. On one side was a brick wall with a rather large hole in it; he aimed the beam at the hole and he thought he saw movement inside. He stepped into the loft and cautiously walked towards the hole with the beam of light fixed on it.

'Claire, is that you?' He asked, and waited a few seconds for a response. 'I'm DC Cole. I'm with the police – you're safe now, you can come out.'

There was no reply; he approached the hole and looked inside. It was a small dark space covered in cobwebs and dust. The missing bricks were scattered on the floor and, sitting next to them, with her back to Cole, was a dark-haired girl.

'Claire, are you okay? You can come out now, you're safe. We're here to help. Your aunt is waiting for you downstairs. Just take my hand and I'll take you to her,' said Cole, and stretched his hand inside the hole, but then pulled it back when he spotted a bloody kitchen knife at her side. 'Claire, are you hurt?'

For a few seconds she did not respond, but then she turned. She kept her head down as she shuffled all the way around.

'That's it, good girl, let's get you out of here.'

She was dressed in scruffy grey, perhaps previously white pyjamas. Still with her head down, she faced Cole.

Cole put his hand out again for her to take, but her head snapped up unnaturally fast and she glared at him with jet-black eyes.

'Shit!' Said Cole, and he jumped back and lost grip of the torch. It bounced off the wooden floor and switched off, leaving them both in darkness.

'Constable, what's happening up there?' Shouted Inspector Newson.

Cole did not answer; he was concentrating on Claire coming for him and fell backwards with a bang.

Inspector Newson's voice came from below. 'You two – get up there, now.'

It's Claire – she's infected, thought Cole as she dived on top of him. They both fell through the ceiling and landed on the bed next to the dead woman.

Claire was face down under Cole, kicking and screaming as he held her hands behind her back.

'Help me control her, she's infected,' said Cole to the officers in the room.

An officer went to Cole's aid and held her legs down, and another officer took out his handcuffs.

'No, we can't use those, she'll rip her wrists to bits,' said Cole and looked around. 'Pass me the curtain tie-backs.'

The officer did as Cole asked, then tied her legs as Cole tied her arms.

'That's it,' said Cole, then pulled a pillowcase off a pillow and stuffed it in her mouth. 'That should stop her biting. Now we need to get her out of here.'

Cole climbed off and the two officers grabbed Claire under her arms and lifted her up.

'We've got her, we'll put her in the back of our car. Shall we take her to hospital, sir?' Asked one of the officers.

'No, she will only be a threat to the other patients. I'll have to speak to the chief and find out what he wants to do with her. For now, take her to the station and put her in one of the interview rooms. We'll be able to watch her properly in there,' said Newson.

'Yes, sir.'

The two officers carried her out of the room and Inspector Newson looked up at the hole in the ceiling, then at Cole. 'Are you alright?'

'Yes, sir, thankfully,' said Cole, dusting himself off. 'You should know, though, I think I found the murder weapon. She was up there sitting next to a bloody kitchen knife.'

'Do you think she did this to her own parents?' Said Inspector Newson.

'I don't know for sure, but if that's Claire it looks that way.'

'There's a family photo downstairs. That's definitely Claire. What sort of virus could cause someone to murder their own parents in their sleep? God help us if they don't stop this.'

'God help us,' repeated Cole, and paused to think for a moment. 'Inspector, if I could get permission from the aunt would you allow me to bring a priest to see Claire at the station?'

'A priest, why?'

'Because I made a promise to a priest I met. He believes he can help.'

Inspector Newson took a deep breath. 'I'm not sure how a priest plans to help with her condition, but I guess it may give the family a bit of hope. If you can get the consent, you have my permission to bring in the priest, but his safety is your responsibility. The aunt's name is Hayley.'

'Thank you, sir, I'll go speak to her now,' said Cole.

Hayley was at the front door being held back by an officer who had stopped her from following Claire and the two officers out of the house.

'Please, miss, stay inside, it's not safe to speak to your niece right now,' said the officer.

'I need to see her, just give me one minute, please,' said Hayley, but the officer would not budge.

Cole walked up to Hayley. She was taller than him, had a short mop of blonde hair and very large breasts. Cole was at eye level with them and failed to avert his eyes as she turned to face him.

She clicked her fingers twice and shot him an evil look. 'Up here, pervert.'

Great start, thought Cole, and looked her in the eyes. 'Hayley, I'm DC Cole. If you'd like to come with me, I'll take you to the station where they are taking Claire. It's not safe to speak to her right now, but once she is secure, I promise you can speak with her.'

Hayley's anger subsided. 'You promise?'

'You have my word, follow me. Excuse us, Constable,' said Cole as he passed the officer and made his way to his vehicle with Hayley close behind.

* * *

Oliver woke up on a floor; his neck ached and for a moment did not know where he was. After looking at his surroundings, he saw Steven focused on his computer. He remembered they were in Steven's best friend's house, upstairs in a converted loft. Jessica was on a bed in the corner and she was still fast asleep.

'Have you not slept?' Asked Oliver.

'Morning, Father, or should I say afternoon,' said Steven, and looked at his watch. 'I've not slept. I've been up all night trying to find Nicole.'

'Of course, Nicole,' said Oliver. He stood and stretched. 'Have you had any luck finding her?'

'As a matter of fact, I have. I believe she's being held at a nightclub on Gaunt Street.'

Oliver opened the skylight window for fresh air and turned to face Steven. 'How on Earth could you possibly know that?'

Steven pushed away from his computer and spun on his desk chair. 'It's a gift I have. I hope you're hungry, Rachel has cooked us all a full English.'

'I was hoping you'd say that – it smells so good.'

'Come down when you're ready. You should wake Jessica too,' said Steven, and tapped a button on the keyboard. He left the loft via the fold-out ladder.

Oliver watched as the super-computer, identical to the one left behind at the office building, shut itself down. 'Such a strange lad,' said Oliver to himself. 'Jessica... Jessica.'

'Oh no!' Said Jessica, then jumped up out of bed and raced down the ladder to the bathroom.

Oliver followed and knocked on the closed bathroom door. 'Are you ok?'

He heard Jessica vomiting.

'Rachel has made us breakfast. We'll be downstairs if you fancy it,' said Oliver, and made his way downstairs to the sound of Jessica vomiting more.

Oliver reached the bottom of the stairs and his mobile rang; it was a number he did not recognise. He stopped and contemplated ignoring it, but a gut feeling made him answer. 'Hello.'

'Hello,' replied Cole.

'Cole, it's so good to hear from you. I've been so worried since the hospital. Are you okay?' Oliver walked into the kitchen.

'Thank you for your concern, I'm fine. I'm back at work on a case and I think I may have something you'll be interested in.'

'What's that?' Asked Oliver and took a seat at the breakfast bar with Steven eyeing him with curiosity.

'I'm sitting here with the aunt of a young woman who has unfortunately become infected. She has given us, well, you, consent to visit. The family is Catholic so you being there for Claire will be a comfort. She is being held at Lavender Hill Police Station. I've been given permission to let you see her in a secure room to help her in any way you can.'

'Just one moment, Cole,' said Oliver, and muted the mic on his mobile. 'Steven, do you think I can go into a police station after what happened with that warrant?'

Steven thought about it for a second, then replied, 'I don't see why not. The document has been deleted so you won't be flagged. Why?'

'I'll explain in a sec,' said Oliver, and unmuted the mic. 'Sorry about that, Cole. So how soon can I see her?'

'As soon as you like, I'm just pulling in to the station now. Shall I get her prepared?'

'Yes, please do, I'm just having some food and I'll be on my way. I should be no longer than an hour.'

'Okay, I'll get things set up here then. See you soon, buddy.'

'Thanks, Cole, see you soon,' said Oliver, and hung up the phone.

Rachel put Oliver's breakfast in front of him, followed by a cup of coffee. She was very attractive with a fit, athletic body, and her clear golden complexion shone. Steven had mentioned that her parents were Jamaican, but she was born and raised in England, hence her strong English accent.

'There you go. Enjoy,' said Rachel.

'I'm sure I will, thank you very much,' said Oliver, and picked up his knife and fork.

'So, what was all that about?' Asked Steven, looking at Oliver.

'I asked a friend of mine in CID to call me if he managed to secure someone infected. I believe they are actually possessed, and I want to help them with prayers. He has a young woman for me now at Lavender Hill Police Station.'

'You really believe they're possessed?' Said Steven.

'I do, and hopefully an hour from now I'll prove it,' said Oliver.

'Well, good luck with that.'

'Thanks,' said Oliver, and started on his food.

* * *

Nicole woke up in a pitch-black room, damp, frozen and petrified. Her head hurt where she'd been knocked out the previous night and she was in a small steel cage. Stretching her legs was impossible, so she lay in a foetal position and prayed cramp did not set in.

I'll kill Steve for not listening to me. We should have stayed well away from whoever these people are. That's if they don't kill me first, she thought, and a tear trickled down her face.

The door at the other end of the room burst open and a large man entered. He switched on the lights and walked towards Nicole. He had sleeve tattoos on both arms, stood around six feet tall and had a goatee and topknot.

Nicole wiped the tear from her face and tested the cage for weakness; there was none, though she discovered it was on wheels.

The man disappeared behind her and pushed the cage.

'What's going on, where are you taking me?' Said Nicole over her shoulder; she was too constricted to turn around.

The man did not respond and continued to push her out of the room, which Nicole could now see was a beer cellar. There were dozens of beer barrels and cold air was being pumped in from the air conditioning. *No wonder it's so cold.*

The man pushed her out of the beer cellar and along a narrow hallway until they came to a staircase. He picked up the cage, held it to his built chest and made his way up the stairs. At the top, he put the cage back down and pushed again. They went around three corners, up more stairs and down a long corridor before they got to their destination: a room which, according to the sign, was the manager's office. Someone inside must have heard them and opened the door as they approached – a fierce-looking bald man dressed in a sharp black suit. Sitting behind the manager's desk was another man in a well-tailored black suit.

'Come inside, young woman, don't be shy,' he said and waved them in.

Nicole was pushed inside; she had never felt more terrified. She was surrounded by three menacing men and felt completely vulnerable. To her own surprise she did not break down in tears or even plead with her captors.

'So, enlighten me, little girl, what is your name?' Asked the man behind the desk.

For some reason she had the urge to rebel and not answer, but she considered her current position and decided against it. 'Nicole.'

'What a lovely name, Nicole, I'm Jack Buckley. The bald guy is Mr Campbell and topknot is Mr Wells. Now, straight to the point, what the fuck are you doing in my office?'

'You brought me here,' she replied, confused.

'Wrong answer,' said Buckley, and Campbell booted the cage.

Nicole did not understand what to say and panicked.

'You've been helping that priest, Father Hall, and have caused me quite the inconvenience. That is why you are here.'

'I told Steve not to get us involved. I want nothing to do with all this. I just want to go home,' she said, and could feel herself about to break down; a few tears escaped her eyes.

'There's no need to cry, dear, we've been nothing but hospitable, and so long as you tell us the truth it will remain that way,' he said, then leant forward and looked her in the eyes. 'Who's Steve?'

'My boyfriend – he's a computer geek and too bloody nosey for his own good.'

'So, he's the one who has upset me. Where is he?'

'I don't know, we got separated.'

Buckley sat back and looked away. Wells stepped up to the cage.

'I don't know, I swear,' she said.

Wells picked up the cage, flipped it upside down and dropped it to the floor.

The crash jolted every bone in Nicole's body. She bit the inside of her mouth and her head crashed on the steel bars. She was so shocked she hardly felt it when the cage was flipped back onto its wheels.

'Shall we try that again? Where is he?' Said Buckley.

Wells pulled out a large hunting knife and tapped it on the cage right by her face.

'I suggest you think of something before my friend here starts putting holes in you. You have ten seconds,' said Buckley and looked at his watch.

'You bastards,' said Nicole, and another tear escaped her. She was petrified of knives. They reminded her of a few years ago when she had witnessed a teenage boy being fatally stabbed right in front of her. The experience had not only left her with a morbid fear of knives but, in her mind, to be killed by a knife would be the worst way to die. Her thoughts became frantic, panic set in, and all she wanted was the knife gone. The consequences of answering Buckley truthfully did not really come to mind. She knew it was morally wrong, but her fear was in control. She tried to remember if Steven mentioned where they would head next, but she was sure he hadn't. Then it hit her... she'd heard him shout 'Transfer all C drive to location two' at his computer back at the office building. Location two was in Rachel's loft; she had known that for some time.

'He went to his friend's house in Clapham Common – her name is Rachel, now move the knife, please!' Nicole begged, and instantly felt sick to her stomach. *How could I give them up like that?* She thought.

'You see how easy that was? All you have to do is comply. This Rachel, is she the redhead that was with you?'

There was a flash of light in front of Nicole, just like the one she had seen in her car the night before. No one else in the room seemed to have seen it, even though it was so bright. She focused her eyes in its direction and spotted the word 'lie' scratched into Buckley's desk. The word was tiny, and if it had not been for the flash, she would never have even noticed it.

'Yes,' she lied, clenched her fist and hoped he would accept her answer.

'Okay, and now for the main question. What is the priest hiding?'

Nicole's relief was short-lived. She had spoken little with Father Hall and most definitely knew nothing about what he was hiding.

'Please don't hurt me, I hardly spoke to the priest. I was with Rachel. Steve was showing him his computer, so I left them to it... please, I swear. Please,' she begged, and fresh tears streamed down her face.

Buckley sat back in his seat and put his hands on his head. After some deliberation, he slammed his hands on the desk and made everyone jump.

'I believe you. Campbell, get her out of that cage. Wells, go get her some food and water and be quick about it,' he said, and the two obeyed.

A wave of relief washed over her; she could not handle another toss in that cage or that knife's point near her any longer. The cage opened and she finally got to stretch; bones cracked, but the feeling was wonderful. She stood up, stretched more and faced Buckley.

'Now, write down this Rachel's address and take a seat,' said Buckley, and handed her a pen and some paper.

Nicole did as she was asked, then sat by the window.

Buckley passed the paper to Campbell then looked Nicole in the eyes. 'If she's lying, you phone me, and I'll kill her,' he said without breaking eye contact.

'Yes, sir,' said Campbell, and left the room wearing a disturbing grin.

* * *

Oliver walked into the main reception of Lavender Hill Police Station where Cole was waiting for him.

'Father, so good to see you,' said Cole, shaking his hand.

'You too, Cole. Glad you're okay,' said Oliver.

'Thanks, I'm fine, just still stumped by what I saw in that hospital. Please follow me.'

'You saw it too, then, the archdemon?' Asked Oliver as the pair made their way through the station. It was a busy corridor with staff running around oblivious to their presence.

'I don't know what it was, but I knew I wasn't getting involved with it. Tash and I were hiding under the hospital bed when it took off out the window.'

'Yeah, that's when we saw it. Jessica and I were outside.'

Cole stopped and looked at Oliver astonished. 'So that was you getting into that car. I looked out to make sure it was gone and watched it chase you. What happened?'

'Angels saved us,' replied Oliver.

'Now how did I not see that coming? Of course you were,' said Cole, rolled his eyes and continued walking.

'I swear to you; two angels flew down and saved us. Though I was the only one who could see them,' protested Oliver.

'I tell you what, if you somehow miraculously help this girl, I'll believe all your stories of angels and demons.'

'Well, if that's what it takes for you to finally have faith, then I truly do hope I save her,' said Oliver. Cole took him down a second corridor which was less hectic.

They approached a room which had a sign reading 'Viewing Room 1' on the door. They stepped inside, and Cole closed the door behind them.

Hayley was inside and was looking at Claire through the mirror glass. Claire was still tied up and was struggling to free herself in the interview room.

'Father, this is Hayley,' said Cole.

'Nice to meet you, and thank you for allowing me to be here,' said Oliver, and shook her hand. 'Is that Claire?'

'Yes, that's her,' said Hayley, and Oliver walked up to the glass for a better look.

'Will you need any assistance when you go in?' Asked Cole.

'It would be helpful if you could hold her down while I say some prayers. I don't want her to hurt herself if she resists,' replied Oliver.

'I'm grateful you're here for us, Father, but how do you suppose prayers will help her?' Asked Hayley, sounding desperate.

'My hope is with a few carefully chosen words, God will give her the strength she needs to fight this awful infliction. Failing that, I hope my words can somehow soothe her, make her feel more at peace and calm. That would at least make it less likely she'll hurt herself.'

'Thank you, Father,' said Hayley.

'Can you feel that?' Said Oliver, feeling bewildered.

'Feel what?' Asked Hayley.

'The heat coming from that room,' said Oliver.

'I don't feel anything,' said Cole.

A tingling sensation began in Oliver's fingertips and in seconds it spread all over his hands. Claire had stopped struggling and stood staring in Oliver's direction. The tint in the mirrored glass gave the illusion of even blacker eyes.

'I can feel it,' said Oliver, focused on Claire.

'Feel what?' Asked Cole.

'The evil presence inside her... I can feel it,' he replied. Cole and Hayley looked at him, confused.

Oliver placed both his hands onto the mirror glass and focused on the evil presence inside Claire. The tingling intensified, and light shone from both his palms. Claire cursed through her gag and was clearly agitated by what he was doing. Not entirely sure what he was doing himself, Oliver just went with it. He put pressure on the glass and pushed against an invisible force he could feel in his hands. Claire let out an inhuman scream and convulsed violently. Oliver knew this was the demon inside her fighting back; it did not want to give up its host.

'My God,' said Hayley, and backed away from Oliver. He was dimly aware of Cole watching in amazement.

'I've got it,' said Oliver.

Claire froze and looked at him pleadingly. Oliver paid no attention and thrust his arms apart, which removed the demon from her body. Claire fell to the floor, unconscious, and the light from Oliver's hands disappeared.

'Claire!' Shouted Hayley and ran to the room.

Oliver and Cole followed her; once inside Cole took the gag from Claire's mouth so she could breathe, then fanned her with his hand.

'Is she okay?' Asked Hayley as Claire opened her eyes. She regained consciousness and inhaled deeply, desperate for air. Her eyes shot to the surrounding people, uncomprehending.

'Hayley, what's going on, where am I?' She asked.

Hayley burst into tears and took her hand. 'It's okay, darling, you're okay now, everything is going to be alright.'

Oliver was standing in the doorway of the interview room and looked at them, speechless.

'You did it, you saved her,' said Hayley, tears pouring down her face.

Cole stood and looked at Oliver, astounded. 'I don't know how or what you just did, but I think I'm ready to hear those stories.'

Feeling utterly bewildered himself, Oliver just looked at Claire, mystified. He walked away to find somewhere to collect his thoughts.

* * *

Jessica climbed up the fold-out ladder to see Steven busy at his computer. He was so engrossed in what he was doing that he didn't hear her enter the loft. She quietly sneaked up behind him to give him a fright.

'What are you doing!' She shouted, slamming her hands on his shoulders.

'Jesus!' Screamed Steven and nearly fell off his chair.

Jessica stepped back, howling with laughter. 'I'm so sorry, I couldn't help myself.'

'I nearly had a heart attack – how long have you been there?'

'I've only just come in. You really zone out on that thing, don't you?' Said Jessica, and laughed.

Steven straightened up and shifted himself back to his computer. 'That's because it requires my undivided attention. One slip up and I can lose hours of progress – or worse, get caught.'

'I'm really sorry, it won't happen again,' said Jessica, and held back her laughter. 'What are you doing anyway?'

'I'm trying to find out who was after us last night. So far, I've had no luck. I know they are a group of some sort, but that's about it. The members all seem to be in positions of power but have no similarity to one other. It's extremely difficult to find out who's involved,' said Steven as Jessica looked over his shoulder to his computer screen.

'What is all that?' Asked Jessica.

'That's just code, don't worry about that. It'll just give you a headache,' he replied and shut down the computer. He spun around in his chair to face Jessica and stood up. 'I have, however, found places this group seem to be interested in,' he said, and made his way down from the loft.

'Places they're interested in?' Asked Jessica as she followed him.

'Yeah, like that nightclub where I believe Nicole to be. That's one place I found. Then there's Wembley Stadium, RAF Marham, the Royal Artillery Barracks, Woolwich and the weirdest one, an area in the middle of the Sahara Desert.'

They both made their way downstairs and into Rachel's living room, where she was sitting watching TV.

'The Sahara Desert? Why would they be interested in the Sahara Desert, or any of those places, thinking about it?' Asked Jessica.

'Beats me,' said Steven and shrugged his shoulders. 'Rach, have you seen Nicole's car keys?'

'They're on the side in the kitchen, dear,' replied Rachel, not moving her eyes from the TV.

Steven made his way into the kitchen with Jessica close behind.

'Wait a minute, my father is a major at the Woolwich barracks. Do you think he's in danger?' Asked Jessica.

'I think if your father's a major you have nothing to worry about. He'll be able to look after himself,' replied Steven.

'Yeah, but those soldiers last night.'

Steven picked up the car keys and looked Jessica in the eyes. 'Jessica, your father will have scores of soldiers like that at his command. You really don't need to worry. Now, are you ready to go?'

'Go where?'

'I'm taking you home, then I need to get Father Hall and take him to his church,' he said as he walked towards the front door.

'Yes, I'm ready, but can you take me to my parents' instead? I'd rather not go home alone.'

Steven opened the front door. 'Of course, no problem. You'll be fine though. I've protected your phone and, to be truthful, I believe those guys were after me, not you.'

Jessica stepped outside first. 'Maybe, but I'd still feel much better being there. Bye, Rachel, thanks for having us.'

'Bye, love, any time,' shouted Rachel.

'To your parents' then. Bye, Rach, thanks again,' said Steven.

'Bye, babe,' shouted Rachel as Steven closed the door behind him.

* * *

Rachel knew she should really be cleaning, but she was too engrossed in the TV show she was watching. *There's no rush*, she thought, and snuggled deeper into her sofa.

Ten seconds went by, then there was a loud knock on her front door.

'Bloody hell, Steve, I just got cosy,' she said, getting up and storming to her front door. She was seriously annoyed that Steven had forgotten something. 'What is it,' she said as she opened the door.

A bald man wearing a suit was standing on her footpath with his hands in his pockets. 'Sorry to disturb you, miss, but does Rachel live here?'

Rachel looked at him suspiciously. 'Yes, I'm Rachel, can I help you?'

The bald man gave her a big smile and walked towards her. 'Yes, I think you can.'

CHAPTER 10

Unsure as to why he had been called to see Lieutenant General Winters, Major James West hesitantly knocked on his office door.

'Enter,' said a stern voice from inside.

Major West entered and closed the door behind him. 'Sir,' he said as he saluted, 'you wished to see me.'

'Take a seat,' replied Winters as he finished some paperwork.

Major West did as instructed and sat rigidly in his seat. Lieutenant General Winters opened a drawer in his desk and pulled out a folder with the word 'Classified' stamped across it. He dropped it on the desk and slid it to Major West.

'What's this, sir?' Asked West as he picked up the folder.

'Open it,' ordered Winters, and West did so.

The folder had a document inside and written on the top was 'Archaeological Find from the Sahara Desert'. Clipped to the document was a photo of a black marble-like ball, roughly the size of a tennis ball, with red symbols inscribed all over it. Major West guessed the symbols were words, but in all his years had never seen such a language.

'A team of British archaeologists secretly did some excavating in the Sahara Desert in 2011. They found items dating back between CE 1 and 500. They found the usual stuff like paintings, pots, bowls and coins, but also that black ball,' said Winters, pointing at the document.

'I take it this object is not part of the usual findings?' Said West.

'Far from it. It gained our attention when one of the archaeologists was demonstrating, to an ex-military colleague of his, how the object is indestructible. We were soon notified, and we confiscated the item. We've had some of the top minds in the world analyse it, and each agrees that this object is not of this world. The symbols and the material it's made of are unknown, and it truly is indestructible. Not so much as a scratch can be made on it.'

Major West looked more closely at the picture, amazed. 'What does it do?'

'Nothing that we know of. Up until two days ago it just seemed to be a useless black ball.'

Major West looked up at Lieutenant General Winters. 'What happened two days ago?'

'For some unknown reason it went from weighing fifteen pounds, say your average bowling ball, to weighing thirty long tons. It ripped through a research desk and two floors below before it hit the concrete ground floor. Luckily no one was injured, but unfortunately a researcher received serious burns to his hand when he decided to touch it. The object now has a temperature of one hundred degrees Celsius, whereas before it was twenty-three Celsius.'

'Remarkable,' said West, and closed the folder. 'What would you like me to do with it?'

'I require you to gather as many men as you need and transport it to one of our secret underground bomb shelters. As a precaution, it is to be under complete lockdown. You and your men will guard it until further notice. A team have already contained and loaded it onto a heavy equipment transporter at Transport Squadron, Surrey. You'll be leaving tomorrow morning at 0600 hours and you alone will know the contents of the container. Is that understood?'

Major West stood and saluted again. 'Understood, sir. Permission to go home and get my things in order?'

Lieutenant General Winters took back the folder. 'Permission granted.'

'Thank you, sir,' said West, and turned and left the room.

* * *

After Steven had taken Jessica to her parents' he had collected Oliver from the police station and driven them to the church. Oliver was worried about the church being watched, so decided to enter through the rear. Bishop Smith was waiting for them and opened the door upon their arrival. 'Quickly, come inside,' he said, and beckoned them in. He locked the door after them.

'Thank you, My Lord. This is my friend Steven who I spoke to you about on the phone,' said Oliver.

'Nice to meet you, Steven. I'm Bishop Christopher Smith.'

Steven put his drone remote in his left hand and shook the bishop's hand. 'Nice to meet you too.'

'Follow me. We'll go somewhere more comfortable to talk,' said the bishop, and led them down a stone corridor, through an old wooden door into the main hall of the church.

Oliver closed the door behind them and Bishop Smith walked over to the font, dipped the first three fingers of his right hand in and blessed himself. Oliver did the same, then followed the bishop to take a seat on the front row. Steven did not want to offend, so he blessed himself too, making the bishop chuckle.

'So, Steven. Father Hall tells me you have something to show me.'

Steven walked over to the pair and knelt in front of them. 'I do. It's a video recording I took with my drone the other night. These are the people I believe are after Father Hall, for what reason I do not know, but watch what happens.'

Steven played the recording on the remote's mini-screen and passed it to the bishop, who watched in silence with Oliver. The video showed a group gathered around an empty pool. A crow flew in and moments later they watched as Abaddon formed in the pool. The pair watched wide-eyed as the drone drifted around and showed Abaddon in high clarity.

'You truly recorded this?' Asked the bishop, sceptical.

'I can vouch for that thing's existence. I've seen it. I believe it to be Abaddon,' said Oliver, and the bishop looked at him, intrigued.

Oliver looked at Steven, then explained. 'Steven and his girlfriend Nicole were kind enough to help my friend Jessica and I escape it. Though it was difficult. That thing was intent on catching us, and if it hadn't been for an angel, it may have succeeded.'

'An angel?' Asked Bishop Smith.

'Well, two, to be precise. They flew down and stopped it, though only I could see them,' said Oliver.

'I can't really doubt you, this footage is highly convincing,' said the bishop as Abaddon disappeared from the pool on the video. 'Can it be true – an archdemon is really walking the Earth?'

Oliver stood and paced back and forth. 'I believe so, and that's not all.'

'There's more?' Asked the bishop as he passed the remote back to Steven.

'You were right about the people being possessed.'

'You performed an exorcism?'

'Not exactly, I attempted and failed, but something else happened. I touched one of the possessed with my hand and the demon was instantly exorcised. Also, earlier today I could feel the presence of a demon inside a young girl. I exorcised that one too, though I could not tell you how. I don't know myself,' said Oliver and walked to the font to splash his face. 'I feel like I'm going insane!'

'It's not unheard of – holy people have been known to feel the presence of evil within a host. Though an exorcism by touch I have not heard of. That is something I would most definitely like to see.'

There was a sudden gust of cold air and the few candles that were lit went out, as did the electricity. The sun had just gone down so there was still a little light, but their eyes had to adjust. The main doors of the church opened and three of the bishop's guards walked in, two more entering from a side door.

'What's happening, Mario?' Bishop Smith asked the main guard as he stood up.

Mario signalled for the other guards to spread out around the hall. 'There's been a blackout. This is just a precaution, My Lord. Please remain where you are until we give you the all-clear.'

The guards held positions around the hall with their hands on their taser guns. Everyone stood in silence and waited for something to happen, but nothing did.

'Little jumpy, aren't they,' said the bishop.

Footsteps sounded outside the main door. The two guards at the door pulled out their tasers and aimed at the entrance. Mario stood not far behind them in the centre of the nave.

All five guards were focused on the front doors as the handles went down and the doors slowly opened. A petite woman and a rather large man, both smartly dressed, entered.

'Don't come any closer,' shouted Mario. 'Leave and close the doors. The church is closed.'

A strange roar of some sort from down the street interrupted them. The intruders glanced in the general direction of the sound, but ignored it and the woman took a step into the church.

'We just want to say a prayer, why the animosity?' She asked.

'Don't you dare take another step,' replied Mario, and moved towards them with his taser raised.

'I wouldn't do that if I were you,' warned another man who had appeared from nowhere and had the bishop around the neck with a pistol to his head. 'Tell your men to lower their weapons.'

'Lower your weapons,' ordered Mario, and they all obeyed.

The first pair of intruders made their way inside and closed the doors behind them. The tension in the air was fierce, but Bishop Smith abruptly started laughing.

The third man let him go and put his weapon away. 'I've missed you, My Lord.'

Bishop Christopher Smith spread his arms and gave him a huge welcoming hug. 'Alexander, must you always make a dramatic entrance,' he said, and kissed him on both cheeks. 'Don't worry, everyone. Alexander is an old friend with a wicked sense of humour. You can relax.'

'My Lord, these are my associates, Zhang and Bear,' said Alexander, and gestured towards the two intruders.

There was another ominous roar outside, though this time it was closer and accompanied by the sound of scattered footsteps.

'Unfortunately, we will have to catch up later, old friend. Have you received my package?' Asked Alexander.

Oliver heard something climb up the outside of the church, over the stained-glass windows, and up onto the roof.

'Block those doors now!' Shouted Alexander to Zhang and Bear. They nodded and quickly used a small bench to barricade the doors.

'Yes, I have the package,' replied Bishop Smith.

'Please bring it to me,' said Alexander, and the bishop went to retrieve something from behind a pillar.

'What's going on? Who is that outside?' Asked Mario.

'It's not who's outside, it's what's outside. Light some candles and get your men ready. We're about to have some company,' said Alexander as the bishop passed him the package.

Oliver could hear more of the whatever it was outside clambering the church to the roof. Alexander eagerly opened his package. He tore at the outer wrapping and revealed a long, narrow, light wooden case with a keyhole dead centre. He reached into his pocket and took out a small key, then opened the case. Inside was a long sword and a leather scabbard.

Alexander put on the scabbard, sheathed the sword, and approached his crew.

'What are those things out there?' Asked Bear as he looked at the silhouettes through the stained-glass windows.

'Would you believe me if I told you they are hellspawn? Hell-born minions of Satan.'

Bear sniggered. 'Funny.'

Alexander's hard-line expression spoke volumes.

Bear looked at the silhouettes, then back at Alexander. 'What, as in Satan Satan?'

Alexander pointed to the ceiling as he looked Bear in the eyes. 'They will find a weakness in that roof very soon and break their way in. They'll move fast and spread out from one another in different directions, so please, don't shoot anyone. That goes for you too, Zhang. Now get ready and take cover.'

Though they still didn't seem entirely sure what was happening, Bear and Zhang took out their Uzis and hid behind pillars at opposite sides of the hall. Mario and his men were also dispersed around the hall and hidden behind cover.

Alexander spoke to the bishop, Steven and Oliver. 'You three get behind the altar and keep down. I'll stay in front of it and protect you.' He pulled out his silenced pistol and unsheathed his sword as they ducked behind the altar, Oliver watching through a gap in the altar cloth.

A few seconds later there was a loud scratching noise above. All eyes focused on the ceiling. The scratches became faster and more erratic. Then bits of the ceiling and dust fell from the top left corner.

'There!' Shouted Alexander and pointed with his sword, 'they'll enter there.'

A hole appeared. Then a thin jet-black arm with enormous claws reached through and scratched at the ceiling. It left three deep gouges, then ripped the hole wide enough for its large head to peek through. Like its arm, the hellspawn's head was also jet black, shaped like a human adult's, but smooth and without facial features. Alexander shot it, and it disappeared back out of the hole. Another hellspawn instantly took its place and smashed the hole big enough for its long thin body to fit through. It entered and scampered across the ceiling on all fours. Bear panicked at the sight of it and sprayed the ceiling with bullets, but each one completely missed. Alexander aimed and shot one bullet into the top of its head. It was a fatal shot and the hellspawn exploded into black ash, which rained down to the floor. Two more were inside, moving fast in opposite directions.

Zhang stepped out of her cover and fired a few rounds across the back of one, which made it lose its grip. It fell and landed awkwardly on one of the pews. The pew smashed to bits and splinters were sent into the air. The hellspawn got onto all fours. Zhang quickly pulled out her silenced pistol and shot it through the top of the head. It also burst into ash. The other hellspawn moved across the ceiling and down a pillar as four more followed through the hole. It leapt and landed next to Alexander. Without even looking, Alexander slashed his sword upwards and took off its head. Then he shot two others on the ceiling in their backs. They fell and wrecked another two pews. Both hellspawn recuperated fast and darted for targets. One went for Bear and the other for one of the bishop's guards. Bear jumped back and sprayed his Uzi again. He missed the hellspawn going for him but accidentally killed another on a pillar. The hellspawn approached him at speed, grabbed him by the shoulders and slammed him into a wall, then thrust its smooth jet-black head right up to his face. From what Oliver could see, its head had opened to form a wide mouth that opened at the crown of the head. It let out a deep roar and spat pink saliva onto Bear's face. Bear struggled, but managed to aim his Uzi inside and pull the trigger. The hellspawn let go, stumbled back and burst into ash. Bear wiped his face and reloaded his weapon. The bishop's guard had unsuccessfully tasered the other hellspawn. The taser had shot out and stuck in its target, but was ineffective. The hellspawn opened its mouth and leapt head first onto the guard's arm. It clamped on halfway up. The guard screamed and tried to pull his arm free. Mario came up behind the hellspawn and shot another taser into its back, with no effect. He chucked it aside and booted the hellspawn between the legs. It had no genitalia, so the blow was useless. It kicked back into Mario's stomach and sent him flying, straight into a statue of Mary the mother of Jesus.

'You,' called Alexander and looked at Steven, 'take this and shoot anything that comes this way.' He chucked his pistol into Steven's clumsy hands.

'But I've never used a gun before,' said Steven.

'Aim and pull the trigger, you'll be fine. Now, keep these two safe until I get back,' said Alexander and ran for the guard in trouble with his sword still drawn. He mounted the front pew with ninja-like balance and ran across the front four rows. He leapt onto the hellspawn's back and thrust his sword down into its upper back. It made a deep moaning noise and released the guard. Alexander pulled out his sword and cut off its head. It exploded into ash and Alexander landed gracefully on his feet, then looked around to make sure he was clear. 'Are you okay?' He asked, looking at the man's wound.

'That thing nearly took my arm off,' said the guard, gripping his bleeding arm.

Bear came to the guard's side and undid his belt. 'Here, let me tie this for pressure.' The guard held out his arm.

Oliver heard two hushed pops to his side. He spun around and saw the last hellspawn trying to grab Steven. He had shot it and the two bullets had hit its chest, but only temporarily wounded it – the holes were healing themselves.

'Oh shit!' Shouted Steven as the hellspawn grabbed him with one arm and lifted him into the air. It spat it's tongue out and wrapped it around his neck, then pulled Steven's head towards its mouth.

Alexander dashed to help, but Zhang was already on its flank with her pistol aimed at its mouth.

'Help!' Screamed Steven as he gazed into the mouth of hell.

Zhang took the shot. The bullet narrowly missed Steven's face and went straight down the hellspawn's throat. It burst into ash and Steven fell to the floor. The pistol bounced out of his hands and landed at Alexander's feet.

'Sorry, I forgot to mention bullets can only destroy them if you shoot them in the mouth, dead centre at the top of their heads. Body shots just get absorbed and do minimal damage. You did hit it though – not bad for your first time using a gun,' said Alexander, picking up his pistol and sheathing his sword.

Zhang pulled Steven to his feet. 'Are you okay?'

'Yeah, I'm fine thanks, just a bit shaken up. How did you know where to shoot it?' Asked Steven as he dusted himself off.

'I'm very observant. I noticed how Alexander and Bear killed theirs,' replied Zhang.

'How dare those foul creatures enter here,' said the bishop furiously as he and Oliver emerged from behind the altar.

Two more hellspawn jumped through the hole in the ceiling and landed on the floor. Everyone's attention was on them.

'Get back!' Shouted Alexander to the whole group.

'Wait,' said Oliver and walked forward.

'What are you doing?' Asked Bishop Smith.

'I can feel them,' said Oliver.

The hellspawn ran towards the group with clearly vicious intent. They ripped away at the pews as they approached. Alexander and Zhang drew their weapons but, before they could act, Oliver stepped forward, raised his illuminated hands and stopped both hellspawn in their tracks. He did not understand how it was possible, but he could reach out with the energy he felt within his hands and grab evil. Everyone watched him wide-eyed as he threw his arms apart and slammed the hellspawn into pillars. They roared and fought with all their might to escape the invisible force that held them, but failed.

Oliver then slammed his hands together and the hellspawn collided into one another at high speed. They roared one last time as Oliver squeezed his hands and twisted his wrists; both were torn in half and turned to ash. Everyone in the room watched with utter disbelief.

'What is happening to me?' whispered Oliver as he fell to his knees and stared at his hands. He glanced up at the bishop as Alexander and Zhang put their weapons away. Bishop Smith looked totally perplexed.

'I think that's the last of them,' said Alexander.

The power cut ended. The electricity came back on and so did the street lamps outside.

'Great, the power's back on,' said Steven.

'My Lord,' called Mario, 'I must get Enzo to the hospital. Are you okay here? I'll leave all my other men.'

'I'm more than safe with Alexander. Hurry, get him seen to, Mario,' replied the bishop, and waved them out of the church.

Bear helped them unblock the main doors and the two guards left. He made his way back to the group at the altar. 'So, hellspawn are real. I'll never sleep again.'

'You and me both,' said Zhang.

'Only twice before have I been unfortunate enough to encounter them. Both times they were after something. My guess, they're after you. Do you care to explain?' Said Alexander and pointed at Oliver.

The thought of Jessica and the secret of her baby flashed through Oliver's mind. 'Me?'

'Yes, you. What on earth was that you just did and why are they after you?'

'I don't know. I've come here hoping His Lordship can help me understand what's happening to me,' said Oliver, and stood to face the group.

'It is true, Alexander, he knows nothing of what's happening to him or why there's an interest in him. You should see this. Steven, would you mind showing Alexander what you captured on your drone?' Said the bishop.

'No, not at all,' said Steven, and picked his remote up off the floor. He pressed play and Alexander, Bear and Zhang all watched in silence.

Bishop Smith took the opportunity to speak to Oliver alone and pulled him to one side.

'I'm sorry that I brought this into the church, My Lord. Please forgive me,' said Oliver.

'It is not your fault. I'm just grateful we're all alive and more so we're not harmed. When you said you could feel their presence I did not think you meant it in that sort of way. Feeling an evil presence, yes, but to actually feel it so strongly you can manipulate it, that's unheard of. Can you think of any reason why or how you could have gained such an ability?'

'None whatsoever, it just came out of nowhere. Though I must confess, it feels like it's getting stronger. Claire, the young possessed girl at the police station, took all my energy to control. Those two just then were easy. In fact, I believe I could have tackled more than two.'

'Well, let's pray you never have to,' said Bishop Smith, and patted Oliver on the back. 'Just one more thing – if you have anything you'd like to share with either me or Alexander, I can assure you one hundred per cent we will both support you in any way we can.'

'Thank you, My Lord, that means a lot,' said Oliver and moved in closer to the bishop's ear. 'I don't know for sure, but I believe I may know why they are after me. Telling anyone will only cause confusion and doubt, so I beg you, please don't press me. If true, this information will only put you and others in grave danger.'

'I understand,' said the bishop with his arm around Oliver. 'Let's get back to the others.'

Alexander passed the remote back to Steven and looked at Bishop Smith. 'This situation is worse than I could ever have anticipated. I've never come across anything like that.'

'We have,' said Steven, and looked at Oliver, 'we escaped it, then a group of soldiers kidnapped my girlfriend Nicole. They have her at a nightclub on Gaunt Street, but I have no way of getting her. I can't trust the authorities, so I'm stuck.'

'Well, it would seem you're in luck. We're on our way there now,' said Zhang.

'You are?' Said Steven.

'Yes. I've been watching and waiting for such a group to show themselves. They work for a secret organisation known as the Natas – Satan spelt backwards. Each member of the Natas is a dedicated votary to Satan, and each possesses a solid gold ring marked with the letter S. These soldiers that took your girlfriend have led me to that nightclub. We're going to pay them a little visit and my hope is one of the Natas will be there. I'll make sure we bring Nicole back to you safe,' said Alexander.

'Thank you,' said Steven, sounding excited, 'can I help? I've been through the plans of the entire building. I know it like the back of my hand. I breached their security system earlier today, I can easily do it again. I was able to see and control all their cameras and alarms.'

Alexander looked at Steven, astounded. 'Really? So, are you the one who planted the virus in Father Hall's phone?'

'Yes, why?' Asked Steven, looking worried.

'Pure genius! You can come and run our communications. You'll be in constant contact with all three of us via earpiece and you will be our eyes. Watch all the cameras and when you see trouble you let us know. Do you think you can handle that?'

'Definitely! It's what I do. I won't let you down.'

'Good, welcome to the team,' said Alexander, and shook Steven's hand, as did Zhang and Bear. 'We must be leaving now, My Lord. Here's the key to my apartment across the road. You and Father Hall should go there and wait for me. You'll be safer there than here,' he said, and passed the key to the bishop.

'We'll head there now. Thank you, Alexander,' said Bishop Smith, and put the key in his pocket.

'Let's go,' said Alexander, and his team followed him out of the church. The bishop, his guards and Oliver followed close behind.

* * *

THE LIGHT

Major James West walked into his house and dropped his bag on the floor. He took a moment to take in the warm homely feeling he always experienced when he returned from the barracks, then closed the door behind him. The familiar scent of his family overwhelmed him with happiness, and he realised just how much he missed being home. Thick white carpet ran throughout the house, so he took off his boots and placed them on the shoe rack to his side. All the lights were on and he could hear the television from the living room. He made his way there and inside Jessica was sprawled out on the long sofa. At her side was their grey cat, Misty.

'Jessy, what are you doing here?' Asked West, smiling.

'Dad,' said Jessica with excitement and jumped up to hug her father, 'I've missed you so much.'

'I've missed you too, sweetheart,' said West, and squeezed her tightly. 'Where's your mother and Aaron?'

'Aaron's in bed and Mum's making us a cup of tea. You should go and see her, I'm sure she'll make you one too,' said Jessica, smiling as she let her father go. She slouched back on the sofa with the cat.

'I'll do just that,' said West and made his way to the kitchen.

Charlotte West was pouring boiled water into the cups when West walked through the door. 'James!' She shouted, surprised, and put the kettle down. 'I thought you weren't back until next weekend?' She walked over to her husband and wrapped her arms around his broad shoulders.

'Hello, gorgeous,' said West, and kissed her on the lips. 'I've been allowed home to get my things in order. I'm transporting some goods tomorrow and they're not sure how long I'll be gone for.'

'I got excited then, thinking you'd be home for a while,' said Charlotte and frowned.

'I'm sorry. It is only national transport though, so I won't be leaving the country,' said West, trying to soften the blow.

'It's okay,' said Charlotte and kissed him again, 'I'm just happy you're here now. Would you like a cup of tea?'

'I'd love one,' said West and let her go. 'I'm just going to see Aaron and I'll be back down.'

'Okay, but don't wake him. I'll take your tea into the living room.'

West left the kitchen and made his way upstairs. The three-bedroomed house was larger than average, and Aaron was now in Jessica's old room. West laughed to himself as he thought about Jessica sleeping in Aaron's old infant decorated room. He quietly opened Aaron's door and entered without making a noise. Aaron was fast asleep and had left his curtains wide open. West went over and viewed his large garden from the window, then pulled the curtains together. He walked over to his son and stroked his hair. Aaron did not wake, so he gave him a kiss on the forehead. 'Missed you, little man.' He left the room, closed the door quietly behind him and made his way back downstairs.

Charlotte and Jessica were sharing the sofa, so West sat in his single recliner. He reached for his tea and sat back to relax.

'So, Dad, how's work been?' Asked Jessica.

'Alright, to be honest. I've been doing a lot of training in the last few weeks, but it's been fun. There're some really promising new recruits that

I'm proud to say are a part of the force. I believe they'll go far in their careers.'

'That's nice, glad you're enjoying it. Have you had any issues with that virus that's going around?'

'Fortunately, not, but we have all been put on alert. If the crisis worsens, the military will be forced to take to the streets to keep everyone under control, including the infected. We don't want mass panic and we must prevent any rioting or looting that could occur.'

'"Keep the infected under control", do you mean kill them?'

'All non-lethal methods will be employed first before we consider any lethal force, but it is a possibility. It's understood these individuals are not in their right frame of mind, but the military's primary concern is the lives of the uninfected.'

'I can understand that, I suppose, but they need to remember the people infected need to be cured, not killed. I saw the sweetest waitress turn and it was awful. She didn't deserve what happened to her.'

'Does anyone know what it is yet or where it's come from?' Asked Charlotte.

'No one has a clue, it's a mystery, though it's believed the virus must attack parts of the brain that deal with reasoning and aggression. There are people working around the clock trying to figure it out.'

'This whole situation is so scary. I wish you weren't going away tomorrow, James,' said Charlotte.

West sat forward and put his tea back on the coffee table. 'Listen, I may be away, but if you, Jessica or Aaron are in any danger, I'm just a phone call away. I can get soldiers here within ten minutes, and they will watch you until I can return myself. Okay? You have nothing to worry about, I promise.'

'Okay, darling, but you can't blame me for worrying. No one even knows what it is... what if it infects one of us?'

West stood up to go to the bathroom. 'Just stay positive and we'll be fine. I'm sure they'll figure out what's going on soon enough.' He left the room and headed upstairs. At the top of the stairs he noticed his bedroom door was slightly open, and from the corner of his eye he caught something move in the room.

'Aaron, is that you?'

There was no reply, so he went to his room to investigate. He pushed the door fully open and flicked on the light switch. The light bulb popped and made him jump.

'Fuck!' He looked around the dark room, but he could not see his son. 'Aaron, are you in here?'

West went all the way into his room and closed the door behind him. He thought if there was an intruder they were about to feel the full force of a fully trained Tae Kwon Do instructor. He cautiously searched the room, looked under the bed, inside the huge wardrobe and behind the curtains. Yet there was no one; the room was empty beside himself.

'Strange,' he said; he decided he must have been seeing things.

A crow flew past his bedroom window and squawked, but he thought nothing of it and went to leave the room. He pulled down the handle, but the door would not budge.

'Huh?' He said and tried the door again with no success. He was extremely confused – there was not even a lock on the door – and he stepped back, bewildered.

More crows flew past his window and the temperature in the room dropped to below zero.

West stood speechless and eyed the room for some sort of explanation. His hairs stood on end and it felt like his body was going into defensive mode. Yet as there was no visible threat, he could not understand why he had the feelings he was experiencing. His mind raced, and he was hit by a wave of panic as claustrophobia set in. There was something in the room with him. He could not see it, but he could feel it; it felt as though he was being hunted. He broke out into a sweat and started to breathe heavily as his mind went into fight-or-flight mode. He thought jumping out the window was an option, but he knew his pride would not allow such cowardice. So, he chose fight, and stood ready and firm. Then he saw it... it was difficult to see in the dark room, but he could just make it out. It was a transparent apparition, and it was standing in front of his wardrobe. It was a camouflage West would never have thought possible. Though it was not perfect; it refracted light so when he looked through it, at the objects behind, they were slightly blurred, which made it detectable.

West went for the attack, but the apparition was quicker. It spun out of West's grasp and pushed him against the wardrobe. West quickly bounced back to fight, but the apparition grabbed his face and shoved both its thumbs into his eyes. The searing pain and heat were unbearable, but no matter how hard West tried to scream, he could not make a noise. He was somehow muted. The apparition was entering his body through his eyes and he could feel it taking over his mind – he was going to lose consciousness. West backed up to the bedroom door and tried desperately to open it.

* * *

Aaron walked out of the bathroom and heard someone trying to get out of his parents' bedroom. 'Mum?' He said and walked towards the room.

The door was banging, and the handle was viciously going up and down.

'Mum, are you okay?' Asked Aaron and started to worry; he approached and raised his hand to open the door. His fingertips brushed the handle and the door flew open.

His father stood there motionless, looking at him with jet-black eyes, and Aaron jumped back.

'Dad, you scared me – what's happened to your eyes?' Asked Aaron, pointing at them.

His father blinked three times and his eyes went back to normal. 'Sorry, son, just trying some new contacts. Now, let's get you back to bed before your mother hears you're up.' His dad picked him up and carried him back to his room.

CHAPTER 11

They pulled onto Gaunt Street and parked a few car spaces down from the club's main entrance. It was student night and a group of drunken students were still hanging around outside, waiting to be admitted.

'We're really going to stand out inside there with that crowd,' said Zhang.

'Which is why we must move quick. Remember what we discussed. We climb the fence and sneak around the back, then we break into the beer cellar through the cellar door. We make our way up into the club, go across the dance floor and head up into the VIP area. It's here I expect us to face some trouble. We'll deal with that, then head behind the bar and into the corridor that leads to the manager's office. I don't know how much resistance there will be, but we don't stop until we get whoever is in charge. Do you understand?' Said Alexander as he looked at his team. They all nodded in agreement. 'Good. Steve, you'll loop the camera feeds, so we can get through unnoticed and communicate to us if anyone approaches our position.'

'Understood,' said Steven and opened his laptop.

'Let's do this,' said Alexander, and he, Zhang and Bear exited the vehicle.

The three walked alongside the queue of students towards the entrance. The four bouncers on the door paid no attention to them as they passed. Just past the entrance was the target five-foot fence. Alexander looked back to make sure they were not being watched, then quickly jumped over. Zhang also easily cleared the fence, but Bear struggled; he flipped over and landed on his back hard. Zhang had to hold her mouth to stop herself from laughing out loud, whilst Alexander helped him back to his feet.

'You're not the most agile, are you, Bear,' said Alexander.

'Climbing isn't one of my strong points,' said Bear and dusted himself off.

'Clearly,' said Zhang, and held back laughter.

With Alexander in the lead, the three made their way down the side of the club to the rear. Alexander peered around the corner and spotted a camera pointed directly at the beer cellar door, and another on the rear exit door.

'Steve, we're ready to approach the rear cameras, is the loop in place?' Asked Alexander through his earpiece.

'Just one moment,' said Steven. A few seconds passed. 'Done, you're clear to go.'

They walked out and Bear pulled out a small pair of bolt cutters.

* * *

Nicole was back in the beer cellar in her steel cage. It must only have been a couple of hours, but to her, constricted as she was, it felt like two days. The door in front of her opened and Mr Wells walked in holding a very large knife. He closed the door behind him and walked towards her, slapping the flat of the blade on the palm of his hand.

'Someone has been telling lies,' said Wells, still slapping the knife on his palm. 'We have Rachel upstairs and she's not the redhead like you said she was.'

Past the point of being scared, Nicole's anger took over; she could not understand how a person could put another human being through this. 'Fuck you, arsehole.'

'Fuck me?' Said Wells and laughed. 'How about fuck you? You lied to the boss and now he wants you taken care of. I was going to make this quick, but now I think I'll take my time.'

'Such a big man threatening a helpless girl in a cage. I'd say that your mother must be proud, but how could she be proud of producing a turd. I mean, what's with the fucking hair?'

Wells flushed red and stopped slapping the knife. 'Let's see how many holes I've got to poke in you before I get an apology. I'm going to say one, because this first one will be deep.' He marched towards her and raised his knife.

Nicole braced herself and closed her eyes.

* * *

Alexander jumped into the cellar and had a quick look around for any staff. It appeared to be clear, so he called the others down. Once all three were inside, Bear reached up and closed the doors. The beer cellar was well lit, and the music thumped above, though it was not deafening. Alexander knew the camera loop had worked outside, otherwise a bunch of bouncers would have already stormed in. 'Well done, Steve, we're inside,' he said into his earpiece. 'Is there anyone in the corridor outside the beer cellar?'

'No, the corridor is clear, and the loop out there is already playing. There are two bar staff at the top of the stairs at the end of that corridor though.'

'They won't be an issue... we'll tell them we're new security staff if they ask. We're heading out of here now.'

'Help me!'

All three moved forward cautiously and saw a girl in a steel cage.

'Oh my God,' said Zhang.

'Please help me, he's going to kill me,' said the girl, panicked.

'Who's going to kill you?' Asked Alexander.

A man with a topknot ran out from behind some boxes and went for Alexander. Alexander hit the knife out of the man's hand, but was caught too off guard to do anything else. Topknot grabbed him and headbutted him straight in the face, then tossed him over the cage. Zhang punched him in the face to no effect; he grabbed her by the neck and lifted her into the air.

'Bear, a little help,' said Zhang, trying to loosen the grip of her attacker.

Bear came up behind Topknot and got him in a chokehold. Topknot released Zhang and then tried desperately to get Bear off; Bear just smiled and patiently waited for the other man to fall unconscious. After a minute of fighting, he gave in and passed out, and Bear dropped him to the floor. 'Well, that was fun,' said Bear.

'Was it?' Said Alexander, wiping the blood trickling out of his nose. 'Get her out of there.'

Bear pulled out the bolt cutters and cut them through the cage's lock. Zhang took the girl's hand and helped her to get out; the girl's bones cracked, and she struggled to stand.

'How long have you been in there?' Asked Zhang.

'Hours,' the girl replied and fell forward. Zhang caught her and supported her until the feeling came back in her legs.

'Are you Nicole?' Asked Alexander.

'Yes, how did you know?'

'Steve told us. We're here to get you out, he's outside now waiting for you. Zhang, do you think you can get her back to the car?'

'Yeah, no problem. Will you two be okay without me?'

'We'll be fine – just get her out of here.'

'Wait!' Exclaimed Nicole. 'They have our friend Rachel too. I think she'll be with Jack Buckley in the manager's office. Buckley's the one in charge. Please save her. It's my fault she's here... I led them to her. If anything was to happen...'

'I'll find her, don't worry. How many guards does this Jack Buckley have?' Asked Alexander.

'Just the two bodyguards I know of – this one on the floor and a bald guy in a black suit called Campbell.'

'Okay, that's good. Now you two need to make a move,' said Alexander, as Zhang helped Nicole towards the exit. 'Steve, Zhang is bringing Nicole to you. Let me know when they get there.'

'Is she okay?' Asked Steven.

'She's fine, but they also have your friend Rachel, we will try to find her now.'

'They have Rachel? How's that possible?'

'Nicole will explain. We need to keep moving. Don't forget to tell me when Zhang gets to you.'

'I won't. Thank you, Alexander.'

Alexander led the way out of the beer cellar. He slowly opened the door, checked the corridor was clear, and he and Bear made their way to the stairs. They climbed the stairs to the bar and the music became exceptionally loud. At the top, two young barmaids were busy serving drinks. Alexander and Bear walked into the bar area and out into the club unnoticed. The club was packed; lights and lasers were moving to the electronic dance music, and artificial smoke filled the air. The men crossed the dance floor and forced their way through the busy crowd of drunk students. An attractive brunette clawed at Alexander's chest and pinched his bum on his way through; not the slightest bit interested, he continued.

At the bottom of the stairs leading up to the VIP area, Alexander pulled Bear closer to him. 'Now, this is the difficult bit. I'll be moving fast so stay sharp and stay as close to me as you can. No weapons until we are well clear of all this lot, understood?'

'Understood,' said Bear, nodding.

Alexander led the way up the stairs and advanced on the bouncer standing at the VIP rope barrier.

'Can I help you two?' Asked the bouncer and looked them up and down suspiciously.

'We're here to see Jack,' said Alexander.

The bouncer's posture changed; he straightened his back and stood more firmly. 'There's no Jack here. Now do one.'

'What do you mean? He's right there,' said Alexander, and pointed behind the bouncer.

The bouncer turned; a couple were sitting chatting with each other. He turned back to face Alexander, saying, 'It's time for you to leave.'

Alexander took the opportunity to punch the bouncer hard on the chin, which knocked him unconscious. Alexander opened the rope barrier, stepped over the bouncer and walked towards the VIP bar. The sole bartender there was talking to another bouncer and pointing at Alexander, who spoke into his radio, then ran for Alexander and Bear.

Alexander stood ready; the bouncer threw a punch, and Alexander dodged it with ease. He threw another and missed again. Alexander grabbed his arm and pushed him to Bear. With one swift punch to the side of the jaw, Bear knocked him out and into the laps of two drunken women. The bartender looked petrified as the men walked round the bar and through the 'staff only' door. Bear downed a shot off the bar and winked as he passed.

They were inside a long corridor, only about three feet wide. Alexander assessed the man at the other end who was wearing knuckledusters on both hands and was scrutinising Alexander. *That must be our Mr Campbell*, he thought, looking at the man's shaved head.

'Stay here and stop anyone that comes through that door,' said Alexander, gesturing to the door they had just come through.

'No problem,' said Bear, and clenched his fist.

Alexander and Campbell walked to one another quickly, then ran. As they neared each other, Alexander kicked himself up off the wall to his left, then off the wall to his right and tried to punch his opponent on his way down. Campbell grabbed his arm, spun him and hurled him to the floor. Alexander landed on his arse but quickly recuperated and got to his feet. Campbell was on him instantly. Alexander dodged his first punch, jabbed him in his right side, then left-hooked him in the face. Campbell kicked out at Alexander's front leg and sent him off balance, then right-hooked him in the face. The knuckleduster broke the skin, but Alexander still managed to grab Campbell's right arm, gain his balance and headbutt him full force on the nose. Blood sprayed out as it broke, and Campbell stumbled backwards as he shook off the daze. Alexander gave him two hard punches to the stomach and a rapid right hook to the chin which sent blood up the wall. Campbell somehow stayed conscious; he grasped Alexander's hair and smashed the side of his face into the wall. He kicked him in the stomach, then rained punches on him, which Alexander parried expertly. Alexander returned some punches of his own, but they were also deflected. He took a quick glance at Bear and saw he was fighting with another three bouncers. If he did not finish Campbell soon, they'd lose this fight. He threw more punches, faster and harder, waiting for a gap. It came. Campbell could not keep up, and Alexander seized the moment to jab him hard in the throat. The blow stunned him; he froze and gasped for air. After two more fast punches to the face and another swift hard jab to the throat, he buckled and fell to his knees. Alexander jumped and brought his elbow down like a sledgehammer onto his shoulder. Campbell screamed in pain. He fell into a sitting position and clutched his shoulder. Then, with one powerful boot to the face, Alexander finished him.

Now that Campbell was unconscious Alexander could finish off the bouncers with Bear. One had already been dealt with so the remaining two gave them one each. The bouncers were seriously outmatched; the fight with Campbell had just warmed Alexander up. He went in brutal and strong, and within seconds his opponent was knocked out. Bear threw an almighty right hook to the last bouncer and sent him into Alexander's chokehold. With a vice-like grip, he squeezed and squeezed until the bouncer finally collapsed to the floor and passed out.

'Do you think that's all of them?' Said Bear.

'Just one more,' said Alexander, and went to run down the corridor but stopped instantly.

A man, Alexander assumed to be Jack Buckley, was standing outside the office door holding a woman with a knife to her throat. Tears ran down the woman's face, and Buckley's hand covered her mouth.

'I see you took out my main guy,' said Buckley, and looked at Campbell unconscious on the floor. 'I'm impressed. I've never known him to lose a fight.'

'Let the girl go,' demanded Alexander as he eyed Buckley's gold ring showing the letter 'S.'

'I'll let her go, but first tell me who you are, and why the fuck you have taken out all my men.'

'You know who I am, and you know why I'm here. Now, let the girl go. She has nothing to do with any of this.'

Buckley looked at Alexander, wide-eyed. 'It's you... you're the weapon. So, the stories are true. What a privilege it is to be in your presence. Say hello, Rachel, don't be rude. Do you know who this man is?'

Rachel mumbled something, and more tears streamed down her face.

Alexander took a few steps forward. 'I will not ask again.'

Buckley shot Alexander a vicious look and pushed the knife harder against Rachel's skin. 'The stories about you state you are quite the fighter, unmatched in hand to hand and deadly with a sword. Yet there was one other thing I remember, what was it now? Oh yes, I remember, your compassion for the innocent.'

'No!' Shouted Alexander and reached for his pistol.

Buckley slit Rachel's throat. Blood sprayed out in front of her and poured down her chest. Alexander shot three times but missed Buckley as he ran down the corridor to his right towards a window; he jumped straight through it.

'Zhang, there's a white male in a black suit running to the street, stop him!' Ordered Alexander into his earpiece as he ran to Rachel's side.

She lay on the floor struggling to breathe as blood filled her mouth. Alexander knew her artery had been cut; there was nothing he could do to save her, but he still put pressure on her neck.

'I see him,' said Zhang through the earpiece, 'I'm going after him.'

'Be careful – he has a knife,' said Alexander.

'I know, we watched on the camera feed. I'm going to kill this son of a bitch,' said Zhang.

Rachel tried to talk but just spat out more blood.

'Don't talk. Keep your energy and stay calm, you will be okay. Help is on the way, you will be fine,' said Alexander, trying to keep her as calm as possible.

'What can I do to help?' Asked Bear.

'Just give her room, she's going to be fine,' said Alexander. He looked into her eyes; life was slipping away from her. 'You're going to be okay.'

Her eyes widened; she gripped Alexander's arm and squeezed. He looked at her, helpless, and wanted to say 'sorry', but he could not speak. She exhaled one last time and died in his arms. There was a long silence before Bear patted Alexander on his back. When he did, a tear ran down Alexander's face. Even after all the innocents he had witnessed die over the years, it still hurt him to his core. He used his sleeve to wipe the tear away, then he wiped his bloody hands on his trousers. He closed Rachel's eyes and stood to face Bear.

'You okay, boss?' Asked Bear.

'I'm fine. Let's get in that office and see what he's been hiding.'

The pair walked in and went straight to the desk. There was useless nightclub paperwork on top, so Alexander ransacked the drawers. After throwing lots of paperwork aside, he came across something of interest: a picture of a black ball with some sort of writing in a strange language inscribed on it, and what looked to be a list of names and addresses. He took every bit of paperwork that was with the picture in the drawer, stuffed it into his pocket and went to leave.

'Is that what we came for?' Asked Bear.

'I hope so. Now let's get out of here. I expect the police will be here shortly,' said Alexander. They ran and headed for the exit.

'He got away. A vehicle picked him up at the bottom of the street. I've got the number plate so I will find out who the owner is,' said Zhang through the earpiece, out of breath.

'No need. It was probably stolen, and we will never see that car again anyway. Just head back to Steve and Nicole, we'll be with you in a minute,' said Alexander.

When they reached the car Nicole and Steven were in the back comforting each other and Zhang was in the driving seat. Alexander got in the front and Bear squeezed in the back; as soon as the doors closed Zhang drove away. 'Back to the apartment?' She asked.

'Yes, I must speak with Bishop Christopher,' said Alexander. He looked back at Nicole and Steven. 'I'm sorry about your friend.'

Nicole started bawling louder into Steven's chest. He had her in his arms and all he could manage was to nod at Alexander as tears poured down his face. Zhang raced through the gears, and they completed the rest of the journey in silence.

* * *

Oliver opened the apartment door to the group and it was obvious something terrible had happened. The look of defeat was clear on all their faces, and clearly Steven and Nicole had been crying.

'Nicole, you're okay,' said Oliver, and hugged her. 'We've been so worried. What happened?'

'Thank you, Father, I'm fine – these guys will fill you in. I just need to get some rest,' replied Nicole.

'Of course. There's a bedroom straight through there,' said Oliver, and pointed at the door behind him. 'I'm so happy you're back safe.'

She gave him a small smile and went to the bedroom.

Oliver hugged Steven. 'Please excuse us, Father, we just can't talk right now,' Steven said.

'No problem at all, Steve. Go get some rest. We'll talk tomorrow,' said Oliver with a smile. Steven half smiled back, then followed Nicole.

Alexander went straight to the coffee table and spread out all the paperwork he had acquired.

'What is all this?' Asked Bishop Smith, looking over Alexander's shoulder.

'I'm not sure yet. I was hoping you may be able to tell me,' said Alexander, and moved aside.

The bishop took a seat in front of the coffee table and started going through the papers. After disregarding most, he focused on a piece of paper with a picture of a black ball.

'Do you know what that is?' Asked Alexander.

The bishop dropped the piece of paper back onto the table and put his face in his hands. 'I do.'

The group looked at each other, puzzled, and waited for him to go into more detail. The bishop's guards, who were standing in the kitchen chatting amongst themselves, were completely uninterested.

Bishop Smith stood and paced around the room with his hands still to his face. 'For thousands of years, the location and knowledge of that black orb have been kept secret, a secret that passes down from Pope to Pope. Its discovery a few years ago forced the Holy Father to make a few privileged cardinals privy to its existence. Cardinal Alberto Luvini was one of them. Before sending me here, His Eminence shared this information with me.'

'What is it?' Asked Oliver, and picked up the piece of paper, intrigued.

'I was sworn to secrecy, but, seeing as the enemy now knows it has been unearthed, and is more than likely trying to obtain it, the secret is no longer logical or practical. It makes more sense now to let you know what you're dealing with. Though whether you choose to believe it is another question,' said the bishop, then turned to face everyone and put his hands to his sides. 'That black orb is a holy relic and was crafted in heaven itself. Every angel possesses one, but they are usually white. Satan's was once white, but it turned black when he was cast out of heaven. It is said to contain all his power, energy and strength, which was stripped from him when he was banished to hell. It has been hidden on Earth for thousands of years. The belief is that if Satan were to somehow reach his shadowy spirit out of hell and take hold of it while surrounded by bloodshed, he will gain his full strength and walk the Earth whole again. I believe the world's future after that would be very short indeed.'

The mention of Satan's shadow hit Oliver so hard it took his breath away, forcing him to collapse onto the sofa. The image of the black misty figure from his dreams was vivid in his mind, along with the fear that accompanied it. He must protect Jessica's baby from Satan, he thought; how could he possibly accomplish such a task being only a priest? 'I don't understand... reach out of hell, how?' Asked Oliver in a shaky voice.

'Certain sacrificial rituals and the deaths of thousands at one moment have been known to draw out his presence, or his astral projection, some would say. If the orb were to be present at such a time, it would be the end,' replied the bishop with a lugubrious look.

'Where is the orb now? If we destroy it, would that not solve the problem?' Asked Alexander.

'Unfortunately not, it is indestructible. It is currently in the possession of the British Army. We believed their strict policies on classified items would have kept the orb hidden, but it seems they may have been infiltrated. We had our own people undercover watching it too, but obviously it wasn't enough. The enemy now knows it has been found,' said the bishop, sounding defeated. He sat down opposite Oliver.

Oliver's eyes scrolled the list of names and addresses on the same piece of paper as the black orb picture. He stopped on one: it was Jessica's parents' address, and next to it was her father's name, James West. 'I know this address, and this is the name of my friend's father who lives there. He is a major in the British Army,' said Oliver, and pointed out the name. 'Why would his details be on here?'

'I believe that all the people on that list are either in grave danger, or they are an enemy of the church,' answered Bishop Smith.

'I have to phone Jessica,' said Oliver. He pulled out his mobile phone and called her, but it went straight to voicemail.

'No luck?' Asked Alexander.

'She must be asleep. Her phone is off.'

Alexander picked up the piece of paper, folded it, and put it back in his pocket. 'Father Hall, you're coming with me. Hopefully, this Major West will be home and I can ask him a few questions about this picture. Zhang, dig around in the military's computer systems and find out the whereabouts of this thing.'

'No chance of that happening – my laptop is nowhere near capable of doing that,' said Zhang.

Oliver stood and looked at Zhang. 'Steve has a computer that you may be able to use. It's at his friend Rachel's house. I'm sure if you ask he'll have no problem letting you use it.'

Zhang rubbed her head and Alexander and Bear sighed in the background.

'What?' Asked Oliver after a few moments of silence.

'Father, Rachel is dead,' said Zhang.

'Dead, I don't understand… what do you mean, she's dead?'

'The person who held Nicole captive at the club also got a hold of Rachel. His name is Jack Buckley and he is a member of the Natas. He is the club owner and was interrogating them both for information about Steven and you. He murdered Rachel and then escaped,' said Zhang.

Oliver's mouth dropped open and he looked at Alexander, who nodded to validate. Then he looked back at Zhang. 'She's dead? That lovely young woman has been killed?'

'Yes, and to make it worse, both Nicole and Steven witnessed it. It was awful,' said Zhang.

Being no stranger to grief himself or the effects of it, Oliver was overwhelmed with empathy for them. 'I see now why they couldn't talk… this is dreadful news. Why did he do it? She was harmless.'

'It was a means to escape. He knew it was the only way I would not give chase. I've crossed paths with men like him before. He has no regard for human life and will crush anyone who stands in his way. Next time I see him, I will put him down,' said Alexander.

'And what of your regard for human life, Alexander? He is still human, is he not?' Asked Bishop Smith with his arms crossed.

Alexander was clearly hiding his pain as he faced the bishop. 'It's no secret that many of you disagree with my ways, old friend, but you know as well as they do that I do this with a heavy heart. I may have to beg forgiveness every day for my sins, but I will never have to ask forgiveness for being a bystander. I will not watch while these monsters abuse and murder innocent people. If I have to take them down, so be it.'

'I will never be able to see it as you do, Alexander, but you are a good man. I will pray for you and your soul.'

Alexander walked to the apartment's front door, ready to leave. 'We will never see eye to eye, My Lord. Yet I am ready to answer to God, my friend. I just pray he can give me answers and truly make me understand the things I've seen and endured. Maybe then I'll find peace and understand the world as you do.'

'I pray you do, Alexander.'

Alexander opened the front door. 'Father, we should be going. Zhang, speak to Steve and use his computer. I need the orb's location. Bear, you stay here with His Lordship and his guards and keep him safe. I'll be in touch with you all soon.'

Oliver walked out of the apartment followed by Alexander, who closed the door.

CHAPTER 12

THE JAMES WEST who came out of his bedroom and stood at the top of his staircase must have looked proud of himself, though internally his mind was at war. He was no longer in control of his own body and could only watch in horror, moments ago, as the evil spirit that dominated him strangled his wife to death in her sleep. West was broken and screamed inside, but no sounds or words would leave his mouth; he could not even shed a single tear. The evil spirit that had control of his body fed off his despair and laughed as it mentally tormented him. West unintentionally thought of his children; an image flashed unbidden across his mind that excited the demon. The thought of them helpless and asleep was too delicious. It deliberated the time available and decided to go for Jessica in Aaron's old bedroom.

No, God, please no, thought West, and was once again terrorised by taunting laughter. He looked through his own eyes, but it was as though he was watching a movie he had no control over.

He walked to the bedroom door and reached for the handle. The door opened and for a second he thought he'd regained some control, but it was false hope. His fight was futile, and he knew it, yet he refused to give in.

Jessica was asleep, curled up with her back to him and totally unaware of the approaching danger. As the demon moved towards her, it visualised the murder to come. Its lust and internal laughter intensified. West's determination managed to slow its progress, but its advance was unstoppable. There was movement to his right. A cat... Misty... jumped from a wall shelf with her claws open, latched on to his face and sent him back out onto the landing. He desperately tried to yank the cat off, but her claws only sank deeper into his face. They wrestled with each other and West backed into the landing bannister and nearly toppled over it. Misty let out a long hiss, and some demonic noises, then slashed his face twice. West's grip loosened. Misty dropped to the floor and raced back into the bedroom. West ran down the stairs, clutching his bleeding face. His boots were still on the shoe rack where he'd left them; without tying his laces, he pulled them on and ran out the house.

* * *

Jessica woke to the sound of the front door banging shut and Misty's growls at the bottom of the bed. 'Quiet,' she said; she stretched and rolled over. The bedroom door was wide open. She sat up and rubbed her eyes of sleep. Misty growled some more, and Jessica patted her head. 'Hey, calm down, what's wrong with you?'

Misty jumped off the bed, ran out of the room and went downstairs. Jessica followed slowly behind, still half asleep and yawning, and made her way into the kitchen to make breakfast. Misty chased her in and hovered around her empty bowl patiently, looking up with needy eyes. Unable to deny the stare of those precious marbles, Jessica put off preparing her own cereal and opened a can of cat food.

Once they both had food, Jessica went to the living room, eating on the way. She turned on the TV, sat down and switched straight to the news. She hoped to see things had calmed down in London.

The news reporter was talking about a football final happening that Saturday between two big teams at Wembley Stadium. Jessica was uninterested and continued to eat her breakfast.

Then there was a report of a young woman found murdered in a London nightclub. They showed a picture of the man wanted in connection with the killing. This got Jessica's attention and she turned up the volume.

'We have Inspector Newson at the scene. Inspector Newson, can you please explain to our viewers the situation here?'

'Yes, Ronda. A few hours ago, our officers were called to a nightclub on Gaunt Street. Initially, the police were contacted because of a brawl between two unknown males and security staff. Upon the officers' arrival, a woman's body was discovered in the staff area on the upper level of the club. Details of the cause of death and identity of the victim cannot be shared at this time until the next of kin have been notified. We are looking for three people in connection with the murder: the two unknown men and the owner of the club who has been missing since the incident.'

There was a knock at the front door. Jessica froze for a moment while she tried to think who would knock this early. Then she thought her father must have returned for something he had forgotten. She put her bowl down and went to answer the door. *Well, he didn't forget his boots*, she thought as she looked at the empty space on the shoe rack. She opened the door and was surprised to see Oliver, and another man she did not recognise, on her doorstep. 'Hello, Oliver, is everything okay?' She asked, and looked at the stranger dubiously.

'Hi, Jess, sorry to disturb you so early, but I couldn't get through to you on your phone. This is Alexander, he's a friend. Alexander, this is Jessica,' said Oliver. Alexander bowed his head. 'Everything is not okay. I have some terrible news and we need to speak with your father.'

'My father, why?'

'May we come inside?'

'Yes, of course, sorry. Come in.'

'Thank you,' said Oliver. Jessica directed them into the living room and closed the door.

'Please, have a seat,' said Jessica. She sat on the one-seater recliner and waited to hear what Oliver had to say.

'Is your father here now?' Asked Oliver.

'No, he had to leave early for work. He's transporting some goods and may be away for a while.'

'It's being moved,' said Alexander, and Oliver nodded in agreement.

'What's being moved?' Asked Jessica.

'A very powerful and dangerous item. The British Army has it in their possession, and I believe your father may have knowledge of its whereabouts. It's a black orb, a holy relic, and until recently its existence has only been known of by a select few over the millennia. Did your father mention where he was going?' Asked Oliver.

'He only said he wouldn't be leaving the country. He never gives us full details of his work, to be honest.'

'Well, if he is moving the orb, as I think he is, he can give us its location. The church has a responsibility to keep it hidden so we will be taking it from them.'

Jessica let a laugh slip and covered her mouth. 'If you think my father would hand over anything he'd been assigned to guard, you'd be mistaken. I'm sorry to break the news to you, but he will never disobey his superiors. Most likely any information on this orb is classified, so he'd just deny its existence. You wasted your time coming here hoping for that.'

'In all honesty we knew that, though I was hopeful. The other reason we came was to warn him. There's a good chance your father's in some very serious danger. The same people that sent that military team, or mercenaries, to Steve's office building are also after the orb. They will stop at nothing to get it and they will kill anyone who stands in their way.'

Jessica now grasped the severity of the conversation and sat forward, all smiles gone. 'What else should I know about this orb?'

'It's a black ball with writing in an ancient language inscribed on it. On its own it just looks like a piece of junk, but if it gets into the wrong hands, all hell will break loose, literally.'

'I don't understand. How can a simple black ball be worth worrying over?'

Alexander seemed to be getting impatient. 'Look, all you need to know is we need it, otherwise some bad shit will happen. How or why is irrelevant. Father, let's go, it's too late to help her father. As for the orb, I will know where it is soon enough.'

Alexander made his way out of the house and Oliver stood. 'Sorry, Jessica, we must go. Again, I apologise for coming so early.'

'Wait, Oliver. If my fathers involved, I'm coming with you.' She rushed to Oliver and grabbed his arm.

'Jessica, I'm sorry, but I can't allow it. The things that have happened today you really would not believe,' he replied.

'I don't care, you can't stop me from being there for my father. I'll find him and go alone if I have to.'

'Jess, Rachel got murdered today. She's dead.'

Jessica let go of his arm and stood back a step. 'Steve's Rachel? How?'

'A man involved in all this slit her throat in a nightclub where Nicole was being held. Nicole was lucky and got away safely.'

'Oh my God,' said Jessica, and looked at the TV. 'I just saw it on the news. I can't believe that was Rachel.'

'So now do you understand why you can't come?'

Jessica stood strong and held back tears that were about to escape her eyes. 'No. I have to let my dad know what's going on – he will only believe it if it comes from me. He will listen to me and then he can't be caught by surprise. Please, Oliver, I must come.'

Oliver looked at the front door that Alexander had left wide open. 'Alexander will not like this.'

'I don't care. Stay here while I quickly get

changed out of these pyjamas,' said Jessica, and ran upstairs to the bedroom.

After a short while she came trotting back down the stairs fully dressed. There was a notepad and pen on the table by the front door. She wrote a note for her mother explaining that she had gone out with a friend.

'Ready?' Asked Oliver as she dropped the pen.

'Ready,' she said, and they both left the house.

* * *

Cole returned home from Rachel's murder scene and caught Tasha just as she was about to leave. He opened the front door; she was in his hallway putting on a cardigan.

'Honey, there you are. What happened? I woke up and you were gone,' said Tasha.

'I got called into work, a young woman was murdered. I didn't want to disturb you, so I snuck out,' replied Cole.

'Poor girl. Please don't tell me about it, it'll just upset me. I seriously don't know how you do your job. To see the things you do and be called out of bed – you must be knackered. Are you going back to bed?'

'I'm wide awake, no chance of me sleeping just yet. Where are you off to?'

'I'm going shopping, doing a bit of retail therapy. You interested?'

Cole rolled his eyes. 'Of course you are. Yeah, I'll come, I need a distraction.'

Cole stood to the side and held the door open for her to lead the way. Tasha jumped with excitement, kissed him on the lips and skipped out the house smiling. She waited for him at the end of the path while he locked the door. She grabbed his hand and they made their way down the street.

It was a beautiful day, blue sky, not a single cloud in sight, and the temperature was rising. Cole could already feel his tension slipping away. He looked at Tasha and her smile was entrancing; he squeezed her hand and she kissed him in response. She was happy, and it made Cole feel warm inside. They walked to the end of the road and turned onto the high street. As always, it was buzzing with people whizzing in and out of the variety of stores up and down the road. A coffee shop's queue was so long it spilled out onto the street, an outdoor pig roast stand outside a butcher's was serving pork baps with apple sauce, masses of people were streaming in and out of the underground station, and two drunken men were singing loudly outside the pub.

'So, are you looking for anything in particular?' Asked Cole.

'No, not really. I'm just going to browse and see if anything catches my eye. Do you need to grab anything?' Asked Tasha.

'I think I'm okay, thanks,' he replied.

Ahead of them was a scruffy-looking, ungroomed man. He was shouting at the crowds of people that passed him by. There was something in his hand – a bible.

'The end is near. You must beg the Lord for forgiveness before it's too late. The damned walk the Earth disguised, but I see them. More will come, a great evil is approaching,' said the man, and made eye contact with Cole. The man stepped in front of Tasha and waved the bible in the air with his eyes still locked on Cole. 'They will use our loved ones against us. Faith is our only defence.'

Cole would have usually ignored this man, but after what had happened at the police station with Oliver and Claire, he paused. 'What do you mean, more will come?'

The man looked shocked; someone had actually acknowledged his existence. 'The damned, more are coming. We've had just a taste of what's coming. More will die unless they repent.'

Tasha moved around the man and dragged Cole hard. 'Get away from us, you lunatic.'

'Repent,' shouted the man in a crazed, panicked sort of way.

'What the hell were you doing talking to that madman?' Said Tasha as they weaved through the crowd.

'Something happened yesterday at work, and I don't think he's all that mad,' Cole said.

Tasha stopped and gave him the one-eye-brow-raised look again.

'Don't look at me like that,' said Cole.

There was a scream from across the road; a man had snatched an elderly woman's handbag. He ran, jumped over cars and headed straight for Cole.

'My bag!' Shouted the elderly woman.

'Damien, watch out,' warned Tasha, and reached for his arm as the man charged towards him.

Cole forcefully stretched out his free arm and clotheslined the man hard, sending him into a backflip, and he landed face down with a thud. Cole picked up the bag and booted the man in his leg. 'Get out of here, you piece of shit.'

The man looked at Cole and instantly knew he was outmatched; without argument, he got up and ran away.

Cole took Tasha's hand and crossed the road to hand the bag back. The elderly woman was stunned, but she soon looked overjoyed when Cole approached her with her handbag.

'Oh dear, thank you so much. I'm sorry, it's my fault. I shouldn't have been so stupid. I only put it down for a second to get a better grip of my shopping,' she said.

Cole helped put the handbag over her shoulder and stepped back. 'It's my pleasure, and it was not your fault. That scumbag took advantage.'

'Yes, but if I'd just kept hold of it...'

'No buts! It was not your fault,' stressed Cole.

The woman smiled and pinched Cole's cheek. 'You're such a gentleman, if only they were all like you.'

'Are you okay?' Asked Tasha.

'I'm more than okay now, lovely. You keep a hold of this one, you hear me?' Said the elderly woman.

'I intend to,' replied Tasha. She took his hand and gazed at him.

'Look at you two... to be young and in love, so beautiful.'

'Thanks,' said Cole, 'are you sure you're okay?'

'I'm sure, and I'm going to leave you two to it, I have a bus to catch. Thank you again,' said the elderly woman, and blew Cole a kiss.

'No problem, stay safe,' said Cole and waved goodbye, as did Tasha.

'Bye,' said Tasha. 'What a lovely woman.'

'I know, I'm just glad I could help her.'

'You didn't even hesitate, it was so sexy.'

'Really?' Replied Cole with a raised eyebrow.

Tasha squeezed his bicep. 'You were so strong.' She reached into her handbag and pulled out two tickets.

'What are those?' Asked Cole.

'Two tickets to the game this Saturday at Wembley.'

'No way! How?' Asked Cole and snatched them out of her hand to inspect them more closely.

'Let's just say I have connections. I was going to surprise you later with them, but after what you just did, I think you deserve them now.'

'Yes, babe!' Shouted Cole, and lifted her up into the air. When he brought her back down, he grabbed her face and kissed her as hard as he could. 'I love you.'

'I love you too,' replied Tasha.

Cole tucked the tickets into his rear pocket and put his arm over Tasha's shoulders. She slid her arm around his waist, and they continued with their day.

CHAPTER 13

THE MOST DIFFICULT and risky part of the journey was done. The roadblocks through London had worked effectively; they caused severe traffic jams, but the eleven-vehicle convoy had gotten through with no issues and was now travelling down a country lane in Sidlow, Surrey. The Apache helicopter overhead protected the airspace and kept a close eye on the five Jackals, four Mastiffs, a heavy equipment transporter, and a Panther Command Vehicle below. Major James West was in the Panther. He sat silently, eyeing the container on the transporter in front. The evil spirit within him was trying to devise a plan to steal the black orb inside.

The convoy moved for another half an hour and was well away from urban civilisation. Fields stretched out as far as the eye could see, and in the distance were hills covered in forests.

'Major West, we're approaching our destination,' said the soldier driving the Panther.

West looked out of the window at the solar

panels in the rapeseed field outside. It was a sun farm occupying fifty acres of land.

'Good,' replied West.

'All of that power for one bomb shelter?' Said the driver.

'It has been significantly modified and extended since its construction. The bomb shelter is just a safe room in a much larger complex,' replied West.

The convoy turned onto a dirt track and drove for half a mile before it came to a barrier guarded by two armed soldiers; the barrier was lifted, and the convoy was waved in.

The demon in control of West's body spotted there were cameras on posts all over the place. Every square inch of this area was being watched; he would never get the transporter out unnoticed. After another half a mile, the convoy came to a halt at the entrance to the mini-base. Hangar-style doors had been built into the hillside and were big enough for an aeroplane to pass through. They opened horizontally from the middle, and a dozen armed soldiers ran out and took up defensive positions.

The Apache pilots lined up the helicopter to the helipad a hundred yards away and descended as three suited men exited the base. They made their way to the Panther and West got out to meet them. He had to cover his face while doing so because of the dust and blades of grass being blown around.

'Major West, right on time. I'm Agent Charles,' shouted the obvious lead agent over the noise of the Apache. He shook West's hand. 'Get your vehicles inside.'

West whistled and gave hand signals to the convoy. In a single file, all but two Mastiffs entered the 155,000-square-yard facility and parked in an orderly fashion against the far side. The entrance doors began to close and the soldiers that had covered the vehicles' entry retreated into the building.

Inside, West stood with the three agents. He watched as his soldiers left their vehicles and a heavy-duty forklift drove up to the container on the transporter. 'It must be taken straight to the bomb shelter and put under lockdown,' he said.

'Of course. As ordered, we will store it in the vault with our other sensitive items,' said Agent Charles with a look of concern on his face.

West glanced at him, and a smile nearly escaped him. 'Is there a problem, Agent?'

'Well, it's just that we have concerns. The urgent requirement of the shelter has some of us believing the cargo may explode. Is this the case?'

One of the agents behind Charles received a communication through his earpiece and plugged his other ear with a finger to hear better.

'Charles, something has triggered multiple motion detectors on site,' said the agent, and paused as more information came through. 'And the lights and camera feeds are down. We're under attack.'

West could not restrain his smile any longer. 'Whether or not that container explodes is the least of your worries.'

All three agents looked puzzled and were caught totally off guard when West pulled out his pistol and opened fire.

'We've been compromised,' shouted West, and he shot the three agents through their chests, killing them.

Confusion rapidly swept through the room. One of Charles's soldiers opened fire on West. It sparked a fierce firefight and soldiers were hit on both sides, three fatally. Using the vehicles as cover, West's soldiers sent relentless gunfire towards Charles's soldiers, allowing four of their men to run out and get West to safety. West looked at Charles's dead body on the floor, apparently having a seizure; he was excreting thick black liquid and a foggy mist from every orifice.

'Major West, why are we firing on our own men?' Asked one of the sergeants once they were safely behind the cover of a Mastiff.

'I'm not sure. It was radioed through that the base is under attack, then Agent Charles pulled a gun on me. I defended myself and took him out first. This site has been compromised - we need to initiate an escape and take the container to site B immediately. I'll drive the transporter... you get the doors open,' said West, and pointed at the entrance.

'Understood,' said the sergeant, then went to find soldiers to accompany him. West eagerly made his way to the transporter.

* * *

'Hold your fire, hold your bloody fire!' Shouted one of Charles's soldiers from behind the poor cover of a wooden crate. All the gunfire ceased. 'This is Sergeant O'Keeffe. I demand to talk to the commanding officer.'

The sergeant that was carrying out West's orders stepped out from the cover of a Jackal. 'Sergeant O'Keeffe, this is Sergeant Ward. Tell your men to drop their weapons.'

'Sergeant Ward, you are not the commanding officer. Why did he kill those government agents?

There will be severe repercussions for this.'

'It was self-defence. Now make the order, or we will be forced to keep defending ourselves. Those wooden crates will not protect you and your men for long.'

'I cannot make that order. From our point of view, you have come here and attacked us. I will open the doors and you will leave. Order your men to hold their fire so I can come out.'

'Hold your fire, soldiers, that's an order. Sergeant O'Keeffe, don't try anything stupid. Drop your weapon and make your way to the door controls with your hands in the air. I assure you none of these men will open fire on you.'

O'Keeffe reluctantly followed Ward's instructions and threw his rifle to one side; he raised his hands, stood up and cautiously walked towards the door control point.

'Sergeant, look over there, what is that?' Asked the soldier next to Ward, pointing at Agent Charles, who was now standing. Black tentacles extended out from his body.

Ward eyed Charles, feeling utterly confused, and did not reply.

'Sarge?' Said the soldier.

Ward snapped out of his momentary paralysis and rapidly aimed his light gun at Charles. He paid no attention to the soldier and took cover at the rear of a Jackal. The soldier followed his lead and did the same.

More people were noticing Agent Charles, and many from both sides fixed their guns on him. His black tentacles and the puddle he was standing in were growing larger, and profuse amounts of black liquid gushed out and streamed down his face and body.

There was a short loud bleep followed by orange flashing lights as the entrance doors prepared to open. Seconds later they did so, and a powerful gust of cold air rushed into the base accompanied by a flock of squawking crows, which flew directly above Charles and circled him at an unnatural speed.

The soldiers outside were shouting and running around the Mastiffs as their mounted heavy machine guns opened fire on something outside.

'Fuck this,' said Ward, and shot at Charles; every other soldier with their sights on him instantly did the same.

Every bullet that hit Charles was absorbed: no hole, no blood. His body was like dough. Completely unfazed by the attack, he walked towards Sergeant Ward and his soldiers. Two of the soldiers ran out in front of Charles and emptied an entire magazine into him to no avail, though they did destroy his suit. His legs were visible, and his jacket and shirt fell to the floor, which left him naked from the waist up. The black liquid was clearly pumping through his bloodstream – black veins visibly covered his torso and arms.

The two soldiers, struck with panic and disbelief, froze as two of the black tentacles whipped them across the face. Both collapsed, screaming on the floor and writhing in pain. Moments later, as their comrades watched in horror, they burst into flames.

Next to the Jackal that Sergeant Ward was using as cover was a Mastiff. Ward got into the Mastiff's rear and manned the heavy machine gun on top.

The gunfire outside had intensified. Ward took a quick glance and saw soldiers were being attacked and flung through the air by jet-black creatures. They swarmed their way into the base, and a couple moved in on Sergeant O'Keeffe and his men.

Ward ignored all that chaos and focused on the target that was advancing on his position: Agent Charles. Ward aimed the gun and pumped large 12.7mm bullets into Charles's chest. Charles was sent back two steps, but still managed to whip another three soldiers with a tentacle; all three of them burst into flames. The bullets had slowed his pace, but they did not stop it. He made it to the Jackal and tossed it out of his way like a toy car. Ward stopped his fire from the Mastiff – it was obviously useless. Then he had another look around to assess the situation. The soldiers outside had been completely overrun and were desperately trying to escape. The black creatures were using their tremendously long tongues as nooses. They lashed them out and snared the soldiers, then pulled them in to gorge on their heads. Both heavy machine guns outside the base had stopped firing.

Inside there were now dozens of the black creatures attacking both groups of soldiers. Sergeant O'Keeffe was backed against a side wall but held his ground. Black ash and mist floated around him. Ward then witnessed him destroy one creature with a shot into its mouth.

'Head shots to the mouth, kill them with head shots to the mouth,' shouted Ward, then spun the heavy machine gun towards the entrance and opened fire.

Agent Charles neared the Mastiff, but Sergeant Ward ignored him and continued to take out several more black creatures that tried to enter.

Charles's tentacles were touching the vehicle and crept up the sides towards Ward. A soldier ran out and tried to defend him. Ward watched him fire a few rounds off and then stop as a tentacle entered his mouth and shot down his throat. He dropped his weapon and stood rigid as if thousands of volts of electricity pulsed through his body. He burst into flames and was lifted into the air and slammed down on top of the Mastiff, right next to Ward, who instinctively ducked down into the vehicle.

'Shit, that was close,' said Ward and wiped the sweat off his forehead.

There was a bang and the Mastiff shook. Ward had no time to react as the vehicle was violently flipped over onto its roof. He bounced around inside and smashed his face when he landed. The collision was painful; his nose bled, and his eyes closed as he absorbed the pain. Once it settled down, he wiped the blood from his face and looked out of the rear exit of the Mastiff. The Apache pilot was starting up the helicopter outside and two soldiers were with him defending it. Ward had a clear run right to them. If he ignored everything around him and ran as fast as he could, he would make it. He pushed himself up, prepared his feet and legs for take-off, then someone blocked his exit. Charles had stepped in his way and peered into the vehicle. Ward's heart stopped; he did not want to die burning from the inside out like the others, but this thing was unstoppable, and it had him pinned. He thought he may be able to escape out of the front doors of the Mastiff. He looked behind, but two of the black tentacles had already entered through the broken front windows. Charles gave the most sinister smile and stepped into the vehicle. As he did, Ward was overwhelmed with feelings of anxiety. He felt surrounded by a presence of pure evil and cowered, helpless, waiting for this monster to close in.

There was a sudden crack and a flash of light that filled the Mastiff. Ward looked up, and whatever the light was, it knocked Charles out of the way. Ward wasted no time and got up to look outside the vehicle. The black creatures had stopped their assault and were instead roaring and slashing the air at nothing.

There were random flashes of light which appeared and disappeared, both inside and outside the base. When one was near a black creature, it exploded into black ash.

The crows dispersed and flew away in all directions as Ward took the opportunity to run for the helicopter. He had to dodge the heavy equipment transporter as Major West reversed it from parking and drove away.

The rotors started on the Apache and the noise attracted the attention of the soldiers that remained. Ward made eye contact with Sergeant O'Keeffe, who left his last few men to defend the base and made his way to the Apache. He was moving fast, aiming down his sights, with the butt of his gun pressed firmly into his shoulder. The gun was pointed directly at Ward, and he knew O'Keeffe was coming for answers.

'Get this in the air. When we draw that thing out you blow it to fucking hell!' Shouted Ward to the two pilots, who both gave a thumbs up and closed the cockpit.

'Sergeant Ward,' called Sergeant O'Keeffe.

'I'm a little too busy for chit-chat,' said Sergeant Ward as he gestured for the two soldiers that were defending the helicopter to follow him.

'Okay, well, let me help you. Then we talk,' said O'Keeffe, and reloaded his weapon.

After seeing first-hand what O'Keeffe was capable of, Ward was happy to have him by his side. He paused briefly as he made his assessment, then replied, 'Follow me.'

* * *

Michael, Kleo and Jade had Agent Charles pinned to the floor; he was laughing hysterically, and black liquid was bubbling out of his mouth. All his tentacles had been severed. Jade firmly held both his legs, Kleo stood on his forehead and Michael was on his chest holding down his arms. Michael's face was a foot away from Charles's and he looked deep into those jet-black eyes without blinking. The hysterical laughter stopped, and the two became locked in a silent stare so intense the atmospheric pressure around them seemed to change dramatically.

'Satan,' said Michael in a tone of disgust.

'So now you show your face, Michael, after all this time,' said Satan.

'And yet it has still not been long enough. Why are you here?'

'You know why I am here.'

'We will never allow you to walk this Earth.'

'And how do you presume to stop me? Humankind is swayed way too easily to sin and hell is bursting at the seams. You do not have the numbers to prevent what is to come.'

'Was being cast out of heaven not enough to prove just how weak you are? True power comes from good, love and forgiveness, not evil, hate and greed. We may or may not have the numbers, but our strength will always surpass anything you could ever hope to gain.'

'We shall see,' said Satan and kicked his legs, sending Jade spinning through the air and across the floor.

Kleo was launched up towards the ceiling by an invisible force. Michael felt Satan begin to rise from the floor. He flew elegantly back onto his feet and drew his two swords.

Five other angels, completely covered in armour, joined Michael; they had finished destroying the hellspawn and now surrounded Satan in a circle. Each one was in an attack stance with their swords raised.

'You will not win this,' warned Michael.

Satan was eying the white orbs on the angels' gold belts and smirked. 'Not yet, but soon.'

Michael picked up on what Satan was implying and remembered the contents of the container. 'Jade, retrieve the orb.'

Jade jumped up from the floor and without hesitation flew out of the base, heading for the heavy equipment transporter. As fast as lightning Satan was in pursuit; he barged through two angels and charged after Jade. His advance on her was rapid, but Michael was right behind him. When within reaching distance, Satan went to grab Jade's ankle and rip her from the air. Michael could have intervened, but he wanted the humans to have the victory. Two sergeants were in a vehicle about to crash into the possessed agent. Michael had listened in on their plan as they were approaching and calculated every possible scenario. He knew they would succeed. The army vehicle smashed into Satan's side and sent him hurtling through the air. He landed with a crash and rolled multiple times before coming to a stop some distance from the base. Michael focused on the helicopter. He heard the machine's lock-on system whining. Moments later, two rockets were sawing through the air towards Satan. They hit with precision and blew up the entire area. The explosion was spectacular, and fire roared towards the sky as eight smaller missiles also shot in and obliterated the same area. Michael saw that Jade had gained more height and was some distance away. Kleo was not far behind her; he must have flown after her during the explosion. There was no movement in the fire. Michael and the others waited to make sure Satan had indeed left the possessed body. Cheers erupted around them from the soldiers as the remaining few hellspawn retreated; they sank into the floor and left behind a black, sticky residue.

'Is it over?' Asked one angel next to Michael. Knowing it was far from over and that another encounter with Satan was bound to happen again soon, Michael shook his head. 'It is not over, but we are done here.' He unsheathed a sword and sliced a portal to heaven in the space beside him. 'Thank you all for your bravery. Go back and I will return once the black orb is retrieved and under safeguard.'

Each angel bowed their head to Michael before one by one entering the portal. Once all were inside, it closed, and Michael took off into the air after Jade and Kleo.

* * *

'Sergeant Ward to Apache One, over.'

'This is Apache One receiving, over.'

'Great shooting, Apache One, we have a confirmed kill, over.'

'Thank you, Sergeant, how would you like us to proceed? Over.'

'Sweep the area and confirm we have the all-clear, over.'

'Affirmative, over and out.'

Sergeant Ward approached Sergeant O'Keeffe from behind and patted him on the back. 'We did it. Whatever that thing was, it's blown to hell now.'

'And that's where it needs to stay. We have lost some good soldiers and those creatures have severely wounded a lot of the others. We need to report this attack to our superiors as soon possible and get a much higher security level to protect the contents of that container,' said Sergeant O'Keeffe.

'The container is being transported to another classified location and our major has gone dark, as part of protocol, so it may be difficult to implement that higher security level. For now, let's just focus on getting the wounded seen too and then we'll speak to our superiors.'

'Okay,' said Sergeant O'Keeffe. They shook hands and went to aid their wounded soldiers.

CHAPTER 14

'Oliver... Oliver...' called a distant female voice.

Too tired to respond, Oliver tried to go back to sleep.

'Oliver... wake up.'

Reluctantly Oliver opened his eyes. He struggled at first from the brightness, but once his eyes adjusted, he could see clearly and vividly. Apart from his footwear he was fully clothed and lay on his front inside a bright white empty room, no bigger than the average living room, with no windows or doors.

'Hello,' replied Oliver, confused, 'is someone there?'

Only an eerie silence filled the room; he was alone. He pushed himself up off the floor and wandered around looking for an exit. Hoping to find a hollow point, he tapped along the solid wall. It was ice cold, and for a second, he feared he may be trapped inside a large freezer, but then dismissed the thought. He tried to recall what he had been doing prior to being in this room, but after giving it some serious thought he realised he did not know where he had been, or who he had been with before he had awoken. It felt like a brick wall had been placed in his mind, completely blocking him from accessing memories he knew were there. Then something came through; he could not visualise it completely, but it was there. A silhouette in the shape of a man, a shadow on smoke or dry ice, and it was looking for him.

There was a noise behind him, and Oliver turned to see a crack in the wall. Knowing it had not been there before he went for a closer inspection. The crack was three inches long and not wide enough to see through. As if drawn to it somehow, he reached out and touched it, and instantly it grew. Within seconds, the crack had spread to the floor and ceiling, and the room began to rumble.

Taking a few steps back, Oliver watched as jet-black vines like tree roots shot out of the crack and spread across the walls, ceiling and floor at ridiculous speed. It was not long before they covered the entire room. The vines thickened and pulsated, as though a liquid was flowing through them.

In a panic Oliver stepped back onto a bulging vine and it popped, gushing blood all over his bare feet. He fell to the floor and the vines wrapped around him, holding him in place. Other bulging vines began to pop and spray blood all over the room, completely covering the white that was once there with red.

Oliver tried to pull free of the vines, but they only tightened the more he fought. The rumble intensified, and there were loud cracking noises from the cracked wall. Moments later it shattered to the floor and the vines attached to it came down with it.

Oliver froze and stared in horror at the tunnel of fire that was behind the wall. It was like the inside of a large pipe and went as far as the eye could see. It was ringed by fire in a complete circle.

The cold in the room was now gone, and Oliver broke into a sweat from the rapidly increasing temperature. The vines were pulling him towards the fire and there was nothing he could do to stop it; the more he resisted, the faster they went.

A figure appeared within the tunnel; it was coming towards him and Oliver could see it was the silhouette he had envisaged earlier. At that moment, he knew in his mind and soul that this was Satan.

'Oliver!' Came a deep, booming voice that filled the room.

The fear that was consuming Oliver was like nothing he had ever experienced, or even knew existed.

'Oliver... Oliver, wake up,' called the female voice again.

Oliver recognised the voice that was calling and tried to only focus on that, even though Satan was now stepping into the room.

'Oliver...'

Satan was so close, but Oliver closed his eyes and concentrated; he knew all he had to do was remember who the voice belonged to.

'Jessica,' he said out loud, then flew forwards and smashed into something hard. He opened his eyes and he was in the passenger seat of a car.

Alexander had slammed on the brakes, and he had hit the dashboard.

'Are you okay, Oliver? You were having a nightmare,' Jessica said from the back seat.

Oliver was soaking wet with sweat and was having to calm his breathing to slow his heart rate down. 'Why did you brake so hard?' Oliver asked and looked at Alexander.

'Well, you wouldn't wake up for her, so I had a better idea. Plus, you really should be wearing a seatbelt,' said Alexander, sounding unremorseful.

Oliver reached around and fastened his seatbelt, then fell back in his seat with his eyes closed, panting.

Jessica placed a hand on his shoulder. 'Are you okay?'

'It was just a bad dream, all I need is some air,' said Oliver, and wound down his window.

'That was some bad dream. The way you were talking to yourself and jumping around in your seat, we thought you were being possessed,' said Alexander.

'If that's what it feels like to be possessed, I pray that I never am,' Oliver said, leaning his head out of the window to cool himself off. 'How long was I out?'

'About an hour. Zhang has been in touch. She's been having fun on Steve's computer at Rachel's. Her exact words were "absolutely phenomenal",' said Alexander.

'Has she located the orb?' Asked Oliver.

'She has, there's a—' Alexander started, but was interrupted by Jessica grabbing his shoulder and pointing out of the front window.

'That's my dad,' said Jessica as an army truck carrying a large steel container passed them going in the opposite direction.

Alexander skidded the car and spun it around in the narrow country lane. Caught by surprise, the car behind went up the grass verge to avoid a collision, and the woman inside blasted her horn. Alexander ignored it and began following James West at a steady pace some distance behind.

Oliver saw the angel that had spoken to him at the hospital fly over them and land on the container, but was so overwhelmed by everything that had happened he didn't mention it to the others. He watched in awe as the angel raised a sword and went to break the lock sealing the container.

The army truck violently swerved from side to side; it looked as though West was attempting to shake the angel off. From a field next to the road, three hellspawn jumped onto the container. The angel stopped trying to open the container to deal with them.

Oliver watched, wide-eyed, gripping his seat as the angel easily took care of the three hellspawn. He looked at Alexander and Jessica, who were deep in conversation, then looked back to see the second angel from the hospital fly in and land on the container. The urge to tell the others was so strong, but Oliver felt he was losing his mind, so he remained silent.

The transporter swerved again. This time it sent a small car on the opposite side of the road straight into a tree. The angels seemed to be unaffected by the motion, as though glued to the container, and did not budge an inch. Four more hellspawn leapt up next to them. The female angel ignored them and cracked the lock with her sword. It exploded into a dozen pieces and the thick steel door swung open.

'Shit, what is going on over there?' Said Alexander, pointing at the hellspawn.

'What the hell are those things?' Asked Jessica as she pulled herself forward for a better look.

'Hellspawn,' replied Alexander, and gripped the steering wheel hard.

'Oh my God, we've got to get my dad out of there.'

'Your father could be a part of all this – we need to approach with caution,' said Alexander.

'Don't be ridiculous. My father has nothing to do with any of this.'

'Then explain to me where his soldiers are and why he's out here alone, driving a vehicle covered in hellspawn?'

Jessica did not answer.

'And I bet on my life the black orb is inside there,' said Alexander, and pointed at the open container. 'We'll follow him to wherever he's going and then assess whether it's safe to approach him.' Alexander slowed the car and created a bit of distance between them.

* * *

Michael joined Jade and Kleo. He was flying above them, listening and observing their current situation. There was a lot of activity underneath him, but the first thing that caught his attention was the mental state of James West. Michael could not only listen to the man's thoughts, but he could also feel his despair. West was at war with a demon, and he was losing. If Michael did not intervene soon, West would lose his mind permanently to fear and insanity. Michael felt some comfort though as he knew West had found hope in the realisation that angels existed. He knew this because the demon in his mind could see them, which meant he could too. West could see them now in his side mirror battling with the hellspawn. Michael could feel West's relief as he took solace in the hope that he would see his wife again in heaven, though Michael knew this boost in morale would not be enough to defeat this particular demon possessing him.

Michael's attention switched to Kleo, who was spinning his two swords in his hands, waiting for the hellspawn to attack. The tongue of one shot out, trying to disarm him, but Kleo was faster and sliced off the tip. There was a chilling shriek as the hellspawn swiftly sucked its tongue back in. In a fit of rage, it ran at Kleo. He jumped into the air like an acrobat, spun and chopped off the hellspawn's head as it passed under him. He landed gracefully with both swords pointing in the air and his back to the remaining three hellspawn. Two leapt for him, seeing an opportunity, but Kleo anticipated their motion and backflipped, then took off both their heads as he did so. The final hellspawn gave out a monstrous roar and dug its claws into the container, preparing itself to pounce. Kleo was ready, but Michael came down from above and took off its head before it even knew he was there. Just like the others, it burst into black ash.

'Michael,' said Kleo with a bow of the head. 'Jade is inside with the orb.'

Michael nodded. The top of the container exploded; a fireball blazed upwards and smothered them both in flame as they fell inside, landing on their feet. They stood in the fire unharmed and once the flames cleared they saw Jade with her hand on the orb. She was not moving and appeared frozen solid. The orb had turned her to a block of ice. Michael knew her fight against it was what had caused the explosion.

Standing next to her was Abaddon. The archdemon took Jade's frozen body by the throat and lifted her into the air.

'Put her down, now!' Demanded Michael, and Abaddon turned to face him.

'If you insist,' said Abaddon, and threw her out of the container.

Kleo was after her in a flash and caught her mid-air before she hit the road.

Hellspawn came in over the side of the container and surrounded Michael. He weighed up the situation, as he always did, but there was nothing for him to worry about other than the orb. Jade had obviously touched it, which had caused the explosion. That meant that Satan's power must have reactivated it. Only Satan and his followers could handle it now, he knew. 'You realise all your efforts are for nothing,' he said, without so much as a flinch despite the hellspawn creeping in around him.

'If you could stop us, you would have done so already, Michael,' said Abaddon in a tone of disgust, and spat out thick black tar-like sputum.

Michael took a step forward; the hellspawn froze and growled whilst Abaddon took a step back, ready to defend himself.

'Time to put you back in your hole,' said Michael.

Abaddon ignored him and went to spit once more, but before he had a chance, all four hellspawn roared in agony. They fell to the floor of the container and writhed in pain as the midsection of their torsos started to tear. The wounds opened into deep cuts and spread, widening into huge gashes. The screams echoed through the container as the remaining few inches of flesh tore off, then they were ash.

A twinkle of light in the distance behind Abaddon caught Michael's attention. The ordinary human eye would not have seen it, but Michael's exceptional eyesight could see right into the car it came from. Three people were inside, one of whom was the priest, Oliver Hall. His hands were alight with divine power.

'What do you hope to do now, Michael?' Asked Abaddon. 'You cannot touch the orb and if you send me back, more will come.'

Abaddon was right, but Michael still had options. Destroying the archdemon and flying off with the entire transporter was one, but Michael felt something else had to happen. The presence of the priest meant Father had another plan, but leaving the orb here with Abaddon felt wrong and against his instincts. Another twinkle of light from the car made his decision; he would have faith in Father and sit this one out. There was obviously a lot more to this Oliver Hall than he had first thought. Michael's wings outstretched and without so much as a word to Abaddon, he flew to James West. He reached through the open driver's side window and touched his face, sending the demon in him back to hell. Then he took off after Kleo and Jade. The laughter that escaped Abaddon as Michael flew away was booming and sinister.

* * *

Oliver dusted off his hands and could hardly believe that he had been able to reach out over a distance and kill the hellspawn on the army vehicle. 'I did it.'

'That was incredible,' said Alexander.

'What about that other thing? Wait a minute, that's the thing from the hospital. Please, we've got to help my dad before he gets killed,' said Jessica, panicked.

'That's the archdemon from Steven's recording,' said Alexander.

Oliver's hands were still emitting light, and for a moment they distracted Alexander. He drifted over a lane and was heading towards oncoming traffic.

'Watch out!' Yelped Jessica just in time for him to steer away before they hit a tractor. 'Are you trying to kill us?' She shouted.

'Sorry. Seeing his hands like that is not something you can get used to.'

'It's getting stronger... whatever this is, it's somehow progressing. You should know there were angels over there too,' said Oliver, and looked at his hands. 'I can feel the archdemon. I think I could deal with it the same as the hellspawn.'

The only thing that delayed him was his worry of whether he could do it fast enough, and without giving Abaddon a chance to fly at their car and kill them.

'The angels have flown away,' said Oliver. 'Shall I still try to take it out?'

'Do it,' said Alexander, 'tear that thing a new arsehole.'

'No. If you can't, it will kill us, then God knows what will happen to my father and the orb,' Jessica said hysterically.

'And what's saying it will even sense it's coming from him, Jessica? It didn't with the others,' argued Alexander.

'I can't believe we're even debating this. Father,

you said the angels have flown away, yes?' Said Jessica.

'Yes, all three.'

'Then please don't do this – that archdemon thing is obviously a lot stronger than you realise, it's not worth the risk.'

The risk was high, and Oliver knew it, but something deep inside him believed Jessica's worries about her father may be influencing her feelings. In a different scenario, she may well agree with Alexander, he thought.

'Father,' said Alexander, getting frustrated, 'you have been given a gift by God, a gift that allows you to send these monsters back to hell. You need to have faith that you can do this. I don't believe you would be presented with this opportunity if you couldn't. Do you believe you can?'

'Yes, I do,' said Oliver, full of confidence.

'Well get to it, before I drive this car straight at it and leave you no choice.'

'This is a mistake, please,' moaned Jessica.

Oliver rolled up his sleeves, rubbed his illuminated hands together and focused. 'I'm sorry, Jessica, but I must try. I'm a soldier of the Lord. I cannot sit back and allow this thing to walk the Earth, not whilst I have a way to stop it.'

'I understand, you must have these abilities for a reason. I just don't like this situation at all. Do what feels right to you, but please, don't get us all killed.'

Abaddon was standing over the black orb, facing their vehicle. Oliver concentrated his energy and focused on the archdemon. Then Abaddon's wings expanded out. He picked up the orb and with one stroke he bolted high into the air, the second stroke sending him like a missile across the sky.

'Damn it,' said Oliver as Abaddon got away. 'I would have had him.'

'There's no point even trying to pursue him, he's way too fast,' said Alexander, as the transporter veered off the road.

'Dad!' Shouted Jessica.

It tore through bushes before it came to a halt in a deep ditch after tipping onto its side. Alexander stopped the car with a skid and Jessica was the first to jump out. All three ran to see if West was okay. Jessica ran even faster when smoke began rising from under the engine.

West stumbled out on his own and fell to his knees on the ground.

'Dad!' Shouted Jessica again.

'Jessie?' Asked West in disbelief.

Jessica knelt beside her father and hugged him hard.

'It's me, Dad, are you hurt?'

'Oh, Jessie,' said West, then burst into tears and returned the tight hug.

'You're okay now, we're here.'

'You don't understand, Jess,' said West, and held her out at arm's length. 'It's your mother – she's dead. I killed her.'

Jessica's expression instantly became blank. She stared at him, hollow-eyed, then stepped away towards Oliver. 'What do you mean, she's dead?'

'I was possessed. Whatever it was in me made me watch... I had no control.' West sobbed.

Jessica took out her mobile phone and walked back towards Alexander's car.

'Jessie, please, you must believe me... I wasn't in control. Jess!' Shouted West, but Jessica ignored his calls.

'You're not possessed now, though, I'd feel it.

What happened?' Asked Oliver.

West wiped his eyes and, as if hit by a wave of adrenaline, stood up firm with certainty. 'I don't know how or why that evil spirit left me, but I know where it was going.'

'You mean you know where they've taken the orb?' Asked Alexander.

'Yes, I know where they're taking it. The spirit who controlled me loved to talk and boast way too much.'

'What else did it speak about?' Asked Oliver, intrigued to learn more.

'I will tell you more on the way. Right now, I need to make a call to get my son picked up. Then I need to get a team together and hunt these fuckers down. You two are taking me, and you can explain who you are and why you're with my daughter.'

There was a wail behind them. Jessica had collapsed on the ground, sobbing; whoever she had spoken to on the phone must have confirmed her father's news.

'Oh no,' said West, and ran to her.

Oliver went to follow, but Alexander grabbed his shoulder. 'Give them a moment.'

'Of course,' said Oliver; he stepped back and watched from a short distance.

West sat next to his daughter and took her into his arms; she wailed loudly again, and they both cried into each other's shoulders.

'She can't be Daddy, she can't be dead. Please,' said Jessica through her tears.

'I'm sorry baby, I'm so sorry,' said West, burying his face into her.

Alexander and Oliver listened and observed West's reactions in silence. Police sirens sounded in the distance.

'We should probably get out of here... we don't have time to be answering police questions,' said Alexander.

'Yes, we'd best make a move,' said Oliver, and walked towards the car. 'Do you think he's telling the truth, about being possessed?'

'I don't know,' said Alexander, looking at West. 'We don't know who's involved. This could be a trick, so I'll be staying cautious. Though I must say, his mannerisms do not look like those of a liar – he looks genuinely distraught.'

'Agreed. I wish I could help them... this is awful.'

'Indeed, it is,' said Alexander, looking grim.

* * *

Lesa Stevens, sister of Charlotte West, finished her call with Jessica and returned to speaking with DC Cole in Charlotte's living room.

'That was my niece, Jessica, Charlotte's daughter. She said she's with her father and wanted to speak to her mother. I didn't want to tell her over the phone, but it was as though she already knew,' said Lesa, black mascara running down her face from crying.

'I could really do with speaking to her and her father. Did you say his name was James West?' Asked Cole, looking at his notepad.

'Yes, that's right. He and Charlotte were fantastic together, they're literally soulmates. There's not a chance he has done this, no way. I don't care how it looks.'

'I'm sure that's the case, but I still need to speak with him. The sooner we can eliminate them both as suspects, the sooner we can put all our resources into finding the actual murderer. Let's go over your statement one more time, then, if you wouldn't mind, could you get back in contact with them for me?'

'Okay, sure, I'll try,' said Lesa.

'So, you came here at 9 a.m. to spend the day with Charlotte and Aaron. The plan was to have breakfast here, then go to the town centre to find Aaron some new school trousers. When you arrived here, you knocked on the door, and there was no answer. After knocking another two times you were finally greeted by Aaron who had obviously just woken up. Surprised as to why Charlotte did not answer the door and why Aaron was not ready, you went inside to investigate. After calling her name several times and checking all the rooms downstairs, you decided to go and search upstairs. You called Charlotte's name one last time before entering her bedroom and finding her lying on her back, not breathing, with strangulation marks around her neck. Aaron tried to follow you in, but you held him back and asked him to wait downstairs. You asked Charlotte again if she was okay, but after no response you immediately phoned 999,' said Cole.

'That's correct,' replied Lesa.

'And there were no signs of forced entry when you arrived?'

'No, nothing. All the windows in the house were closed and all the doors were locked. The only thing I found was that note I showed you from Jessica telling Charlotte she'd left.'

'Okay, that's great.' Cole paused for a moment. 'Wait, your niece's name is Jessica?'

'Yes, Jessica, why?' Asked Lesa.

Cole was thinking hard. 'Jessica West?'

'Yes, Jessica West. Is there a problem?' Asked Lesa, sounding worried.

'No problem, I just know a Jessica West, that's all. I don't suppose there's a picture lying around is there?'

'Next to the TV there,' said Lesa, and pointed at the small family photo next to the television.

Cole got up off the sofa and picked up the photo. 'This is her, Jessica. I met her a couple of days ago with a priest, Father Hall. I can't believe she's part of another investigation. Poor girl has had a rough few days. Is this her father next to her, James?'

'Yes, that's James. I can't seem to get through to her now. Either she has no signal, or her phone has died,' said Lesa, taking her mobile away from her ear.

'I'll try Father Hall. Hopefully, he's with her or can get in touch,' said Cole, and placed the photo back down. There was a knock on the front door. 'That'll be the ambulance. I think it's best I deal with this. Would you like to take over from the officer watching your nephew in the kitchen?'

'Yes, sure, thank you,' said Lesa, and wiped her runny nose. She made her way to the kitchen.

Cole waited until the kitchen door closed behind her before he opened the front door. Two men in black uniforms stood on the doorstep. Their black ambulance was parked behind them; Cole invited them in.

'The body is upstairs, room on the right. The forensic team will be out of your way any minute now,' said Cole.

'And the family?' Asked the smart-looking male in front.

'In the kitchen. They're keeping out the way until you're done.'

'Great, we'll get started then.' Cole stepped aside and watched the men make their way upstairs;

as they reached the top, the forensics team of six were leaving the room. They came down the stairs, and each said goodbye to Cole as they left the house.

'Thanks for your work, guys. I'll be in touch for the results,' said Cole.

Leaving the front door open, Cole went to the kitchen to check on the others. He opened the door and popped his head inside. 'Everything okay?'

A female police officer, Lesa, and Aaron all looked up at him from the kitchen table. Aaron had been excitedly explaining what his father did in the army.

'He shoots baddies, keeps our country safe and protects the queen.'

'We're fine, thanks,' said the female officer to Cole. Turning back to Aaron, she said, 'Does he really? Your daddy sounds like a hero.'

'He is a hero. When I grow up I'm going to be in the army just like him.'

'Well, you'd better eat all that sandwich I made you. You must get big and strong like your father,' said Lesa, and pointed at his half-eaten cheese sandwich.

Aaron grabbed his sandwich and eagerly finished it; the female officer and Lesa laughed.

There was movement upstairs and Cole turned to see the ambulance crew heading downstairs with Charlotte's body, which was now inside a black body bag. He closed the kitchen door and stood at the bottom, waiting. They cautiously got her body down the stairs and safely out of the house. Cole followed them to their vehicle and opened the rear doors for them. Charlotte's body was gently placed inside, and the doors were securely closed.

'Job done. Goodbye, officer,' said the smart-looking male.

'Goodbye, and thanks for your help.'

The ambulance crew got in their vehicle and pulled away. Cole watched them drive to the end of the street and turn the corner, just as two blacked-out cars turned that same corner, heading towards him.

'Oh shit.' Cole sensed there was about to be trouble.

The two vehicles charged down the street and pulled up violently in front of the house. Their brakes shrieked as they came to a halt, and soldiers leapt out of the rears. Several of them instantly circled Cole.

'Is everything okay?' Said Cole, but got no reply. He watched, confused, as a woman in a suit exited one of the cars and headed to the house with the other soldiers. They let themselves inside. Soon after was loud, incoherent shouting. The woman in the suit came back out first; she had Aaron's hand and was leading him back towards the cars. The soldiers came out next, holding back Lesa and the police officer.

'What do you think you're doing? He's only a child. Do you know who his father is?' Shouted Lesa, trying to fight off two soldiers. 'Kiss your jobs goodbye – he'll strip your ranks for this!'

'Just a minute, what do you think you're doing?' Said Cole to the woman, trying to edge forward.

The woman raised her hand and signalled for Cole to stop. 'We are under instructions from Major West to secure and escort his son back to our base. Anyone trying to stop us will be regarded as a threat, so I suggest you all keep calm and do not intervene. No one needs to get hurt here.'

'And barging in with no explanation or proof was the best way to do this?' Asked the police officer angrily.

'Let him go!' Screamed Lesa. 'No, you're not taking him. Help! Someone stop them.'

'We are taking him and that's final. Aaron is in safe hands, I assure you all. So, I'll say again, calm down. Aaron, come with me, honey. I'm taking you to your father.'

The woman walked Aaron to the car and he waved back at his worried aunt. The group looked at each other. None of them spoke as the woman and all the soldiers re-entered their vehicles with Aaron.

'Lesa!' Shouted Aaron, poking his head out of the rear window.

'It's okay, baby, don't be scared, they're taking you to your father,' said Lesa through her tears.

Lesa fell into the female officer's arms as the vehicles drove away. Wasting no time, Cole darted for his car and did not even look at the others, let alone offer an explanation. He followed the vehicles at speed. He had to speak with James West, and they would lead him straight to him.

CHAPTER 15

THE INSTRUCTIONS WERE strict and clear: if the safe house had to be used, Jack Buckley must arrive alone, and have no one following him. This was why he was now on foot, rushing through the streets of Mayfair with his head down low. He couldn't be sure, but he assumed the police were looking for him and had probably shown his face on the news.

After walking some distance and assuring himself he was not being followed, Buckley walked up to the brown front door of an Edwardian terraced town house. He reached for the knocker and banged it hard three times while looking over his shoulder.

After a wait of what felt a lifetime, someone unlocked the door. It creaked open slowly to reveal a craggy-faced butler, who was easily in his seventies. He first looked at Buckley, then poked his head out further to peer up and down the street.

'Can I help you, sir?' Asked the butler in a weak, cracked voice.

Buckley was impatient. 'I require refuge. Is this the house of Demantay Florence?'

'And his middle name, sir?'

Buckley was unsure for a second, but then remembered this was the code word for entry. 'Natas.'

The butler opened the door and stepped aside, allowing Buckley into the superb entrance hall. The high ceilings were embellished with two wonderful chandeliers, and Buckley could not help but notice the exceptionally soft and thick red velvet carpet beneath his feet. 'Some place,' he said, nodding his head approvingly.

'Mr Florence has a taste for the finer things, young man. Would you be so kind as to remove your footwear? We work very hard to keep the carpet as immaculate as possible.' The butler closed the front door.

'Of course,' agreed Buckley, and placed his shoes on the shoe rack to the side, replacing them with the red guest slippers provided.

'If you'd like to follow me upstairs, I'll take you to see Mr Florence,' said the butler, and made his way to a staircase at the end of the hall. The red velvet carpet covered the entirety of the stairs, but the floor on the landing was black and white chequered marble.

On the first-floor landing Buckley stood mesmerised by the gleaming white walls and the stunning paintings of various sizes that covered them. Against the landing rail was a marble-topped table upon which a marble sculpture was displayed, but Buckley could not make out what it was supposed to depict.

'If you'd like to go inside, sir, Mr Florence awaits you.' The butler waved Buckley into the spectacular drawing room.

Buckley entered the voluminous room, which was no less extraordinary than the rest of the house. Once again there were high ceilings, exquisite artwork and sculptures, beautiful antique furniture, and French doors leading onto a Juliet balcony.

Sitting next to the fireplace, in a crocodile-skin armchair, was a man dressed in casual but highly fashionable clothes; this had to be Demantay Florence. He was a dark-skinned man with a rough complexion, but still somehow good looking, with his Afro and tidy moustache.

Two very attractive black-haired women with olive skin were sitting on the floor in front of him, clutching his legs, naked apart from their black G-strings.

Demantay raised his whisky glass, took a swig of his drink and remotely switched off the TV in the corner which had been showing a camera feed of the front door.

'Welcome, Jack. Would you like a drink?' Asked Demantay in a very deep yet warm, soothing voice.

'Yes, and make it large,' answered Buckley, and took a seat on the armchair opposite.

One of the women stood up and walked provocatively over to the open dumbwaiter in the wall; inside was a bottle of the finest Scotch, a whisky glass and a bucket of ice. As she poured Buckley a drink, the firm and perfect shape of her backside hypnotised him. She turned and caught him staring, but only smiled as she seductively took a big gulp from the bottle, then poured some over her voluptuous breasts. Buckley's smile broadened as she put down the bottle and slowly made her way towards him. He relaxed back into his chair and rubbed his hands together in anticipation. The woman's shoulders were back, her arms swung loosely, and her hips moved seductively from side to side. She reached Buckley, handed him his drink, then, with both hands on the arms of the chair, leant forward and thrust her wet tits into his face. Buckley pushed into them, licked her cleavage and got a burst of sweet and fruity flavours from the alcohol and her perfume.

'Jack, meet the lovely Adalia. She's quite something, is she not? This here is Isabella.' Demantay stroked Isabella's hair. 'They will both keep you entertained for your stay. Anything you require, just ask, and they will be more than willing to assist.'

'Marvellous,' said Buckley with a smile, and playfully pulled Adalia onto his lap.

Adalia wrapped her arm around him and grasped his face, pulling him in for a kiss. 'I like this one,' she said after removing her tongue from his mouth and biting his upper lip.

'You'll have plenty of time to play later, Adalia. Right now, Buckley and I must talk,' said Demantay, making Adalia frown.

Buckley sipped his whisky and leant forward. 'Indeed, we must. Can you tell me more about the man who took out all my security staff, including my two best men? All I've heard are stories. I didn't believe them, so I didn't pay much attention.'

'I can. His name is Alexander. Controversially, he fights for the church.'

'Controversially?' Questioned Buckley.

'Everything he does is to protect the church and the innocent, yet his actions have been scrutinised by Catholics who know of his existence, including the Pope himself.'

'And what actions are those?' Asked Buckley, finishing his drink in one large gulp. Adalia took his glass to get him another.

'He has and will kill to uphold his devotion, but some believe his behaviour should not be condoned.'

'Then why is it?' Asked Buckley, once again admiring Adalia's behind.

'Because he gets results. He has never failed a mission they have tasked him with and countless times has prevented our advances against the church. You should not underestimate this man.'

'Fuck him!' Said Buckley and grabbed his drink from Adalia as she sat back on his lap.

'You have been warned. Now, there's the matter of the priest. You've failed to acquire him, and how do you suppose you'll be able to do that now? You're all over the news and the authorities are looking for you.'

'I would not be in this situation if the mercenaries, sent by someone you spoke highly of on the phone I might add, had done their job right to begin with. They brought back some useless little bitch instead of the priest, and it was probably them who led this Alexander straight to me. So please forgive me for my lack of concern.' Buckley necked his whisky in one.

'Nevertheless, the necessity of his capture cannot be stressed enough. There are concerns he knows some way of sabotaging Satan's rise, but none of us knows for sure. We must interrogate him and extract everything he knows, otherwise you and I may be hunted next, and by worse things than mercenaries.'

'Adalia, be a babe and bring that bottle here. I'm going to need more than a few shots,' said Buckley. Adalia did as instructed. Demantay raised his own glass for a refill; she obliged, then returned to Buckley's lap with the bottle.

'What do you suggest we do? How do we go about finding this priest?' Asked Buckley while filling his glass.

'I have a guest arriving shortly who apparently knows of his whereabouts. When he gets here, you must excuse us and take these lovely two women upstairs until he leaves. He's very particular about who he allows to know his identity. If only he knew you were taken to hell by Abaddon.'

Buckley smiled and swigged his drink. 'You were at the pool party? Funny, you'd have thought I'd remember the Afro.'

'Ha, yeah, you'd think, yet I assure you I was there. So, what happened?' Asked Demantay, captivated.

'The moment we left I was unconscious, dreaming. I dreamt I was in a white room with no way out, and soon the room filled with blood and fire. There was someone in there with me, but I couldn't see their face. I remember an inner voice screaming at me to wake, but I chose not to... pride and intrigue, I guess. Then there were images of the things I most desired. I smiled with yearning and filled with joy, but then I felt overwhelmed or consumed, I couldn't tell the difference. Then I woke up on the floor at the Royal London Hospital.'

'Sounds to me like you sold your soul. I've

known others to speak of this white room. My guess is it's the inner self, locked deep within all our minds. Do you feel different?'

'Only more agitated than usual. An old man stepped out in front of me on my way here, and I've never been so close to ripping a man's head off for such a trivial thing. Even now there is a boiling in my stomach that I can't put a reason to.'

'Well then, I'd say it's probably about time these ladies took you upstairs to help you relax. Adalia, Isabella, please escort our guest to the master bedroom. This is a very important man and I want both of you to treat him extra, extra special,' ordered Demantay.

'Oh, we will,' said Adalia, and licked the inside of Buckley's ear.

Isabella stood and walked over to Buckley, grabbed his arm, and she and Adalia pulled him up. Without another word, they playfully escorted him out of the room.

* * *

There was a knock at the front door. Demantay had a quick look at the camera feed to see that his next guest had arrived. He went to his dumbwaiter and lowered it for another bottle of Scotch, then switched the camera feed off. In no time at all the dumbwaiter was raised again with a fresh new bottle, ice and two glasses. He made two drinks, placed one on the coffee table and sat down to patiently wait.

The butler entered. 'You have another visitor, sir.'

'Send him in, Alastair,' said Demantay.

'Right away, sir.'

Seconds later, Lieutenant General Winters entered. He was casually dressed in a plain black

T-shirt and straight denim jeans.

'Winters! Please take a seat. The whisky is for you if you're in the mood,' said Demantay.

Winters sat, emptied his glass of ice and downed the drink.

'Thirsty?' Asked Demantay, looking him in the eye and rubbing his index finger around the rim of his glass.

'These last few days have been very stressful. How our plans keep falling apart is beyond me. First failing to capture the priest, including the mercenaries' failure to do so, which still baffles me. That team have never let me or any of my associates down. Then the plan to hold the orb at our bunker base and have it extracted later without detection. Instead, I'm having to deal with what I've been told was a war zone. I have two sergeants demanding explanations, and a major dead set on attacking the location where he believes the orb has been taken. Alexander and the priest are with this major now, en route to see me at the barracks.'

'It's almost as if they're being protected by some divine power,' said Demantay sarcastically, and Winters glared at him with disapproving eyes. 'Look, we all knew our tasks would not be easy, but buckling under them will not help us. Satan himself attacked your bunker base, and because of that we now have the orb in our possession. So that part was not a failure, just a change of plan. Now we need you to send your men to attack the location where the orb supposedly is. It will be a trap and a diversion. The orb will be nowhere near where they believe it to be. A demon planted a fake location in the weak mind of the major coming to see you. So, do not stress. Alexander will most definitely want to get involved with the attack. It is your choice to let him if you need him out of the way, I'll leave that up to you. When all their attentions are on the orb you will be able to snatch the priest and bring him to me at this address.' Demantay pulled a pen and a piece of paper from his pocket.

After scribbling down an address, he passed the paper to Winters, who pocketed it and stood up.

'One more for the road?' Asked Demantay.

'No, I'm fine now, thank you. Just make sure I receive my payment. I'll get your priest.'

'That's the attitude, Lieutenant General. Until we meet again,' said Demantay, and smiled. Winters nodded, then left the room.

* * *

While Nicole was out with Rachel's family, trying to come to terms with her murder, Steven and Zhang were attempting to discover what was so important about RAF Marham and Wembley Stadium. A recent phone call with Alexander had now led them to believe it was Major James West who was of importance at the Royal Artillery Barracks in Woolwich.

'I can't find anything out of the ordinary in either RAF Marham or Wembley Stadium. Both are running as usual – the Marham base still has its Tornado GR4 jets at high readiness, and Wembley is preparing for a sold-out final this Saturday,' said Zhang while typing at Steven's computer in Rachel's loft.

Steven was sitting on a beanbag in a corner of the room and looked up from his mobile. 'Sold out... that's got to be around ninety thousand people, surely?'

'Yeah, that's about right, give or take,' agreed Zhang.

Steven got up and stood beside her. 'May I?'

'Sure,' said Zhang, and allowed him to take her seat.

Steven started bashing away at the keyboard and was rapidly opening and closing browsers.

'What is it you're trying to find?' Asked Zhang, looking over his shoulder.

'I want to know what's happening on that base on the day of the game, also if they'll have any aircraft flying over London during the game. After hearing what happened to Jessica's father, I'm a little nervous knowing the firepower they're packing at the base, and there being ninety thousand people crammed together in one place,' said Steven.

'I see, you're worried in case a pilot gets possessed and they attack the stadium. Surely that wouldn't be possible?'

'I don't know, but Jessica's father could drive a truck when a demon controlled him. If somehow when in possession of a person the demon can use their learnt abilities, what's saying they couldn't fly a jet if they took over a pilot?'

'I understand your logic, but driving a truck and flying a fighter jet are two entirely different things. I highly doubt it's possible. Plus, if a pilot was to go rogue, they'll have procedures in place to take them out. We don't need to be worrying about that. I think we're missing something else.'

'Maybe, but it doesn't hurt to look into it. I'm going to find out all the backgrounds of the pilots working on the day and, though a little more difficult, check the flight paths of any of their aircraft that may be passing over London.'

'You're wasting your time with the flight paths. I was offered a substantial amount of money to get the flight path of an army helicopter not so long ago, and it's pretty much impossible.'

'Well, with that sort of attitude it would be,' said Steven, smirking.

'Ha, you'll see,' said Zhang. 'Wait! What was that? Go back two pages.'

Steven clicked back twice on the browser bar to the RAF news page.

'That's it,' said Zhang.

'It reads, "Two experienced Tornado GR4 pilots have been drafted for overseas conflict, making room for two newly ranked pilots to join the squadron. Their initiation takes place this week at Marham, where they will be introduced to the base and team. They will have the opportunity to get a feel of their new aircraft with a flight over the base, a traditional exercise for pilots starting at Marham",' Steven read out.

Zhang looked at Steven, eyebrows raised. As though reading her mind, he started researching every detail of these two new pilots.

Zhang watched in amazement as he acquired every aspect of their lives: medical history, criminal record, education, work history, training, financial documents and personnel documents including their family trees.

'I think Alexander may have been right - your skills do surpass my own!' Said Zhang.

'Wasn't enough to keep Rachel from being killed though,' replied Steven sadly, and Zhang placed a hand on his shoulder.

'We'll make him pay for what he did, Steve, and all the others we find to be involved.'

'Thanks, I hope so,' said Steven, then tapped the enter key one last time. 'Flight Lieutenant Holland, first name Luke, and Flight Lieutenant Cutts, first name Vincent. I have their current address. They're staying together in a private detached two-bed house in Swaffham until they move into their new accommodation on Marham base. What do you say... shall we pay them a visit?'

Zhang smiled. 'Definitely.'

'I knew you'd want to. Rachel, save and shut down,' said Steven.

* * *

It had been an hour since the two blacked-out cars, one of which was carrying Aaron, had entered the Royal Artillery Barracks. Cole had waited in his car the whole time, trying to devise a good enough reason to ask the guard if Major James West was present inside. As of yet he had not come up with one, but he decided to just go for it. He got out of his car and began a slow jog over to the guard hut at the entrance. The guard inside was dressed in a well-kept red military guard tunic with a spotless black bearskin and had his rifle tight to his side. Determined to get an audience with James West and inquire about the murder of his wife, Cole confidently approached the guard. 'Excuse me, would it be possible to speak to Major James West?'

'Are you booked to see Major West, sir?' Asked the guard.

'No, I don't have an appointment,' replied Cole.

'Are you a friend or family member?'

'Neither.'

'Then I'm afraid you will only be able to see Major West by appointment, sir. I can however pass a message onto him if you'd like?'

'Could you please give him this business card and ask him to get in contact with me as soon as possible. It's regarding an investigation involving his wife.' Cole pulled out a business card from his inner pocket, which the guard took.

'I'll make sure he gets the message,' replied the guard, inspecting the business card.

'Thank you,' said Cole, and turned to walk away.

A car full of people pulled up to the barrier at Cole's side. Unable to help himself, Cole peered inside and to his surprise saw Jessica and Father Hall.

The passenger window came down and Father Hall looked at Cole, astonished. 'DC Cole, what are you doing here?'

'I could ask you the same question,' replied Cole, bending down to see who else was in the vehicle. He spotted West, recognising him from the family photo back at his home, and knew he needed to get in this car. Then he saw the driver. The memories of this man breaking into his home, holding him at gunpoint and shooting his TV came flooding back. He tried to hide his anguish, but was momentarily speechless.

Jessica wound down the rear window and waved Cole inside. 'Get in. You're a witness to some things we're about to explain to my dad's superior.'

Hesitating slightly, Cole did as instructed and climbed in next to Jessica. 'Hi, everyone, DC Cole for those that don't know me.'

'Major West,' said West and shook his hand.

'Alexander, pleasure to meet you,' said Alexander, but he neither shook Cole's hand nor looked at him.

West passed his ID card to Oliver, who in turn passed it to the guard, who glanced at it, looked at West to confirm his identity and opened the barrier. They drove through and Alexander did not so much as peep at Cole, so he was completely oblivious to Cole's eyes burning a hole in the back of his head.

Further inside, what looked to be a Lieutenant General was standing in the entrance of a building and Cole guessed he was awaiting Major West's arrival. Alexander parked the car near him, and everyone got out to meet him.

'Lieutenant General Winters,' said West, and saluted, 'this is my daughter Jessica, and these are her friends. All have had similar experiences to the one our soldiers and I went through at the bomb shelter. They can vouch for what I'm going to tell you.'

'Very well, West, but let's make this quick. I'm on an extremely tight schedule today. Follow me.' Winters led the group into the building.

Cole caught up to Winters as he entered and held the door open for the others. He made sure to stare Alexander in the eyes and make his presence known. Alexander just smiled and continued inside.

They were led down a long narrow corridor, passing plenty of rooms on both sides, and eventually reached their destination: Lieutenant General Winters' office.

Already inside were two sergeants. Both were standing in salute at Winters' desk as the group crammed inside. Jessica and Oliver took two seats on the far wall whilst everyone else stood.

Winters entered last and closed the door behind everyone. He looked at the sergeants individually as he spoke. 'Sergeant Ward, Sergeant O'Keeffe, at ease.' He sat down behind his desk. 'So, where do we begin?'

'Maybe Major West can explain to us why he opened fire on Agent Charles back at the bomb shelter, causing a firefight which left us with dead and wounded on both sides, sir?' Suggested Sergeant O'Keeffe.

'As I explained to the Lieutenant General on the phone, I was not in control of myself. Those incidents that have been occurring around London with people being infected. The same sort of thing happened to me, but it was only temporary. In half a day I not only caused that chaos and managed to lose the sensitive cargo, but I also watched as whatever was in control of me killed my wife. You cannot even begin to understand the pain I have had to endure today,' said West, with an expression of pure agony.

'Charlotte's dead?' Said Sergeant Ward. Jessica got up and left the room, the wound obviously too fresh for her to hear the conversation.

'Yes... even saying it now it does not feel real, but it's true. This threat we face is serious and if we don't find a way to stop it soon, things will only get worse.'

'There are people working around the clock trying to figure out what this virus is with no success. What exactly do you think we can do?' Said Winters.

'I don't know yet, but I assure you I'll be taking steps to make sure my family are protected. Do you know if Aaron has arrived yet?'

'Yes, he's here and safe playing in the sports hall,' said Winters.

'Great. I'd like to see him once we're done here,'

said West, and Winters nodded.

'So, are we just supposed to accept you weren't in your right frame of mind and forget the fact you have killed and got people killed... sir?' Said Sergeant O'Keeffe.

'I will face any consequences necessary for my actions, but first we need to recover the item we were transporting. I've come to learn that the item was a holy relic, known as the black orb, and is considered a very valuable artefact to a secret group of people who are in possession of it right now. It's unclear who these people are as yet, but I know exactly where they're holding it. If we don't act quickly, we could lose it permanently,' said West, mainly to Winters.

'The fact you managed to lose it in the first place is a cause for concern, West, but we can come back to that after you help us find it. Once you give us the address, I'll set up a raid team,' said Winters.

'And what if he loses control again?' Said Sergeant O'Keeffe, looking at West. 'I'm not comfortable having you around knowing that any second you could try to shoot me, sir.'

'He is right,' agreed Winters.

'I suppose you can't fully trust me, but if I show any sign of not being myself you have full permission to take me out in any way possible. I will not have any more innocent lives on my hands,' replied West.

'If you show me any sign that you are not yourself I will be first in line to take you out, sir,' said Sergeant O'Keeffe, sounding totally serious.

'I'm happy with that, but I believe we should keep a close eye on everyone. We do not understand how or why people turn... it can happen to any of us. What do you think, sir?' West asked Winters.

'As much as I want you to be involved in the raid, West, I'm afraid until we understand more about this virus and can prove your innocence, you will have to remain under military arrest,' said Winters. 'This is a job for the special forces. If the orb is there, they'll retrieve it. I'll get in touch with the local police and instruct them to ignore any civilian phone calls reporting any disturbance at the target building. The special forces will infiltrate in the early hours of tomorrow morning. An investigation into what has happened to you, West, can be undertaken post-retrieval. Where is the target location?'

West looked frustrated and wanted to argue with Winters, but instead he answered the question. 'An abandoned building on Dundee Street in Wapping.'

'Thank you. Now I think we all need to discuss these things you had to fend off at the bomb shelter. You can speak freely in front of the company. Major West informed me earlier that you have all witnessed them too. Do any of you know what they were? I've only seen video footage, but I can honestly say I've seen no such creature in my life,' said Winters.

'Hellspawn,' said Oliver, and everyone turned to look at him.

Lieutenant General Winters laughed. 'And who are you?'

'I'm Father Hall, a priest and a friend of Jessica. Those creatures were hellspawn and West was not himself because a demon possessed him. We are facing Satan himself and things are most definitely going to get worse.'

Winters scanned the expressions of everyone

in the room then replied politely, 'I am a man who believes in the Lord so I'll be as respectful as possible when I say this: I doubt very much that this has anything to do with Satan.'

'You're wrong. It has everything to do with Satan, and if you believe it was a virus that infected those people, you are mistaken again. They were all possessed. I've already tested this and successfully exorcised a demon from two such people.'

'It's true,' said Cole. 'I'm DC Damien Cole, also a friend of Jessica's, and I witnessed Father Hall exorcise a young girl. She was so out of her mind she murdered both her parents in their sleep. After Father Hall did what he did, she was completely back to normal but had no memory of what she had done.'

At this moment, Jessica came back into the room and sat back down next to Oliver; he put a supportive arm around her.

'I've got to be honest here – those things that attacked us were not of this world. As crazy as it sounds, them being hellspawn I could completely agree with. The wounds they left on some of the soldiers were like nothing I've ever seen, and the way they moved was so unnatural. Also, that thing Agent Charles turned into, how do you explain that?' Said Sergeant Ward, and looked at Sergeant O'Keeffe, but no one answered.

Alexander stood quietly, looking out of the window. Then he coughed. Everyone's attention was now on him, and he turned to face them.

'I'm sorry, I didn't catch your name. Do you have something you'd like to share?' Said Winters.

'No, please continue,' replied Alexander, and went to look back out of the window.

'Still didn't get your name.'

'Alexander,' he replied as if it pained him to say it.

'And what do you know of these creatures, Alexander?'

'Nothing I'm at liberty to discuss with you.'

The sergeants and the major gave Alexander a quizzical look.

'Why is that?' Asked Winters, interlocking his fingers.

'It's not yet apparent I can trust you. I'm also under instruction not to speak about such matters. So, if you wouldn't mind, could we please move along.'

'Alexander, if you have any information to help, please tell them. This is too important,' pleaded Oliver.

Alexander seemed to think about this for a while, then stood next to Sergeant Ward. 'If I tell you what I know, I want to be a part of the raid and assigned to one of the teams.'

'Impossible,' said Winters.

'I'll speak to the person I work for and get them to contact you directly. Once you hear what they have to say, and they tell you who I am and the training I've received, you'll have no issues with me joining one of your teams,' said Alexander.

'Who exactly are you?' Asked O'Keeffe, sounding confused.

Alexander smiled but did not reply.

'If you're so confident I'll have no issues. Tell me something you believe can help us,' said Winters.

'What I'll tell you now is that it'll be a trap. They will be fully expecting a retrieval team to go in and will have taken measures to guarantee no one gets near the orb. Those creatures you were fighting can be killed by internal damage. Their mouths are smack bang in the middle of the top of their heads. Bullets will not pass through their skin, so it must be head shots into their mouth to kill them. Decapitation and explosions will also get the job done. There will be a lot of them to deal with as well as people in a possessed state. Therefore, I'd recommend using all non-lethal methods first to subdue the possessed, then bring them back to Father Hall. He can then prove to you they are indeed possessed and attempt to help them.'

'Anything else?' Asked Winters.

'For now, no,' replied Alexander.

'Okay, thank you all for the information you've shared... but now I'm afraid you all need to be detained. You have all been in contact with these creatures, so I cannot allow you out into the general population. You pose too high a risk. If any of you were to turn like Major West did and kill someone, their blood would be on my hands. Guards!' Shouted Winters. The door to his office burst open and ten soldiers armed with assault rifles poured inside.

'Sir?' Said Sergeant Ward.

'Sir, this really isn't necessary. I assure you whatever was inside me is long gone – and what sort of threat do you believe my daughter and the priest to be?' Asked West, as the soldiers handcuffed him and the others.

'Dad?' Said Jessica with a slight tone of panic.

'It's okay, my dear, just do as they say.'

'I'm sorry, everyone, but I see no other option. Until we better understand what's happening, you'll remain here detained and under constant surveillance. Any attempts to escape will be presumed an attack on the citizens outside this base and we'll be forced to use lethal force. Take them all to lock-up,' ordered Lieutenant General Winters. One by one they were escorted out of the room, protesting.

'Surely this is some sort of joke? You can't do this. I'm in the middle of several investigations, I don't have time for this farce,' said Cole and resisted. He looked at the stern faces on the soldiers and it became evident this was serious. It gave him an unsettling feeling of butterflies in the stomach; he was nervous. His hands became clammy as he continued to resist. 'No, you can't do this.' His words fell on deaf ears.

* * *

Taking hours longer than they should have because of a serious accident on the motorway, Steven and Zhang arrived in Swaffham late evening. Steven drove past Luke Holland and Vincent Cutts' house as both men were getting into a car on their drive. Both were average height but completely different in features. Luke was tanned with wavy black hair and had a smooth face; Vincent was very pale with ginger hair and a short beard.

Steven continued down the road a little, then pulled Nicole's new courtesy car onto the kerb and switched off the engine. He and Zhang looked out of the rear window and waited for the men to drive away.

'So which one is which?' Asked Zhang.

'The ginger guy is Vincent and the other is Luke. Where do you think they're going?'

'Could be anywhere, but hopefully they're gone long enough for us to search their house and see if they're hiding anything. We can then come back to the car and await their return. If we do find something, I'll confront them and if we don't, I'll approach them anyway and ask them some questions, see how they react,' said Zhang.

'Will you be able to get us in?'

Zhang looked at him in disbelief without responding.

'Silly me, of course you can,' said Steven, feeling stupid, and watched as Luke and Vincent drove away.

'Right, let's do this. We need to get in from the back so no one on the street or the other houses can see us. Make it quick getting over that garden gate, Steve. People in this sort of area are nosey and will phone the police for any suspicious behaviour,' said Zhang, getting out of the car.

'No problem,' replied Steven.

Fortunately, it was dark, so the street was empty and most of the surrounding homes had drawn curtains. The pair walked as casually as possible up the street until they reached the house, then quickly darted across the drive and over the garden gate, which seemed a lot smaller up close. Though it was difficult to see in the dark, the garden seemed clear. Zhang crouched and moved towards the back door; Steven was right behind her. She took out an advanced lock-picking tool from her jacket.

Steven stood from his crouched position, but this activated the motion-detector light above the back door. Zhang now had to act fast. She rapidly fiddled with the back-door lock. It was no match for her entry-breaking skills, and in mere seconds the door was flung open before the light had even gone out. They entered the kitchen, and Steven closed the door quietly behind them.

Zhang flicked a little switch on her lock-pick tool and the tiny built-in torch came on. She pointed it around the room, but there appeared to be nothing out of the ordinary.

'Where do we start?' whispered Steven.

'I'll start upstairs and search through their bedrooms. You wait in the front room and keep an eye outside. If they come back, call me so we can get out of here.'

'Okay.' Steven followed Zhang out of the kitchen into the hallway.

At the front door Zhang went right and up the staircase. Steven went left and opened the door into the living room. His eyes adjusted to the darkness, and so he avoided hitting any furniture on his way through. He sat on the TV stand and kept watch out of the front window; no cars or people were on the street. He felt himself becoming increasingly tired. It had been a long day and he was unable to suppress a yawn; he rubbed his eyes and visualised being in bed. The thought depressed him – he knew it would not be any time soon.

A car came towards the house and snatched away all his dreams of sleep. He tried to make out whether it was the car Luke and Vincent had left in. He stood and watched as the car slowed to turn into the drive and realised it was.

'Shit!' He said and scrambled out of the room to warn Zhang. At the bottom of the stairs he called up louder than he would have liked. 'Zhang, Zhang they're back.' There was no reply or sound to suggest she had heard him, so he went up a few steps. 'Zhang, we need to go, now!'

Answered only by silence, Steven froze; he was

in two minds whether to run and leave Zhang behind. He could hear the men were approaching the front door as their voices were getting louder. Steven could hear their keys jingling and knew they would be inside very shortly. He wasted no more time and sprinted up the stairs to find Zhang. The house was not very large and there were three rooms in the compact upstairs, one of which had its door wide open. He assumed Zhang must be inside and ran for it as the front door was being unlocked. The room was dark and as expected she was inside. She was flicking through paperwork and letters on a cabinet surface with her lock-pick torch in her mouth.

'Zhang, what are you doing, didn't you hear me call?' Said Steven as quietly as he possibly could; she replied with incoherent mumbling.

'Sorry about this, mate, can't believe I forgot my wallet,' came a voice from one of the men downstairs.

'Don't worry about it. We've still got plenty of time. I'm just going to have a quick piss while we're here,' said the other and turned on the lights. The front door closed, and he walked upstairs.

'Fuck!' Said Steven, then hid under the bed.

Zhang quickly pocketed a curious-looking red-enveloped letter and also dived under the bed.

'The torch,' warned Steven and Zhang quickly switched it off.

Which of the two flight lieutenants had come upstairs was unclear, but whoever it was went straight into the toilet without closing the door and urinated.

'Vince,' Shouted the other from downstairs.

'Yes, mate,' answered Vincent while he peed.

'We closed the living room door on the way

out, didn't we?'

'I think so, not too sure though. Why?'

'It's open,' said Luke.

'Maybe we have a ghost.' Vincent flushed the toilet.

Steven heard Vincent walk out onto the landing, but he did not go down the stairs. He was unable to see outside the bedroom from his position so had to acutely listen. There was no movement or any further communication between the men, just silence.

Zhang slowly took out her silenced pistol, which only amplified Steven's anxiety. He guessed the pistol was just a precaution, a means for escape. It unnerved him, nonetheless.

Vincent finally moved; he walked into the room and switched on the light.

'Come on, Vince, we got to go,' shouted Luke.

'I definitely closed my door... didn't I?' Said Vincent to himself. He turned off the light, closed the door properly and went back downstairs.

The remaining lights went out and the pair left the house.

'That was close,' said Steven, his heart beating hard in his chest.

'Just a little,' said Zhang, and tucked away her weapon.

'Shall we get out of here?'

'Not yet. We should have time now to search around some more. You can go wait in the car if you're uneasy.'

'No, no, I'm fine, I'll help you look,' said Steven, letting his pride take over.

'Okay, but stay with me this time just in case,' said Zhang, and was about to turn her torch back on when Steven felt something stand on the bed above them; it pushed the mattress down with slow, hair-raising creaks.

They looked at each other and stopped breathing; Steven tried to figure out what was on the bed. Zhang very cautiously went to reach for her gun again. Steven did not want her to move – he was anxious about any noise being made – he shook his head, mouthing 'No'.

In an instant Zhang was viciously ripped from under the bed and up towards the ceiling. Steven shot out from under the bed; Zhang was floating horizontally in the air. Just as quickly as she was pulled from under the bed, she was launched through the window with incredible force. She plummeted into the back garden along with all the shattered glass.

Steven missed most of the steps on his way down the stairs and ran to get to Zhang faster than he had ever run in his life. He opened the back door and found her bloodied, in the foetal position, and struggling to breathe. 'Zhang, are you okay?' He asked, and realised it was a ridiculous question as she was visibly not.

Unable to respond, she just passed Steven her gun. He took it from her, and with his other arm tried to help her rise. 'We need to move... what the hell was that? There was nothing there.'

The neighbours on both sides of the house were peeking out of drawn curtains, clearly desperate to see what was happening.

Steven thought he saw something move in Vincent's room but could not be sure because the garden light was blinding him. Adrenaline pumped through his veins – he did not care who was watching. The protection of his fallen friend was the only thing that mattered. He raised the gun and took three shots into the upstairs room.

Zhang managed to get to her feet with Steven's help and took a few deep breaths. 'We can't go back to the car, we've drawn too much attention.'

'So where are we supposed to go?' Asked Steven. He walked her away from the house and towards the back fence, his eyes still fixed on Vincent's room.

'Over this fence and just run. I'll get Bear to find us when we're away from here,' she said.

'Can you get over?' Asked Steven. In response, she pulled away from him and climbed the fence.

Steven covered her while she went over and landed on the other side, the gun aimed upstairs the whole time. A crow flew past his line of sight and perched itself on the window ledge he was aiming at. The back door burst open. In a fit of fear, he recklessly started shooting at the house, taking out the kitchen window as he did. The gun was quickly out of bullets, so he clumsily scarpered over the fence after Zhang. Thinking something may grab his legs on the way over, he didn't plan his landing and just dropped hard on his side. Zhang was already some distance ahead, limping as fast as she could across a large open field. Steven got to his feet and sprinted after her. She was about halfway across the moonlit field as he gained on her. She did not look back once and continued to run towards the thick treeline ahead.

'Where are we going?' Said Steven as a loud blast sounded behind them. He turned to see that the fence had exploded into bits and a wind was blowing the pieces around.

'Just get into those trees – whatever that was, it's coming for us,' said Zhang, and ran faster.

Steven looked back again. The wind was

heading for them. It was blowing the grass flat as it moved at speed. 'Oh crap, you're right... there's something coming.'

'Keep moving, we have no chance of losing it in the open like this.'

Steven caught up to Zhang near the woods. They were about a hundred yards from them, but it was too dark inside for them to see through. The wind behind them had caught up considerably and was now halfway across the field. They reached the trees and without hesitation plunged in, making their way deeper in the woods for better cover. The moonlight scarcely penetrated the leaves and branches. As they struggled to see, they had to slow down to ensure they didn't trip over anything concealed in the dark. In the corner of Steven's eye there was a little flash of light; trying to focus his eyes in that direction, he saw nothing. Zhang grabbed him by the wrist and pulled him behind a tree that had snapped a quarter of the way up – the top piece was lying on the ground in front of them. With their backs to the tree trunk, they caught their breath. Once again, a flash of light got Steven's attention; it was way ahead of them, and he couldn't understand what was making it.

'I don't think we're alone in here,' said Zhang and crouched down, pulling Steven with her.

'What do you mean? Something other than that behind us? I did see a couple of flashes down there, straight in front of us,' said Steven, and Zhang looked in the direction he indicated.

'Be quiet a second,' she said. She seemed to sense danger.

There was an odd feel to these cold woods. The darkness and quiet gave them an evil, sinister atmosphere. The approaching mysterious wind that had been on their tail soon broke the silence. It snaked its way through the trees towards them, blowing broken branches and leaves into the air as it moved.

'There,' said Zhang, and pointed to three shadows just barely visible crawling in their direction.

'Are they what I think they are?' Asked Steven, knowing the answer already.

'Hellspawn,' replied Zhang, nodding.

'What are we going to do? They're going to find us.'

'Just stay close to me. Let me reload that gun for you,' said Zhang, and Steven passed her the pistol; she reloaded it, handed it back and took out her Uzi for herself.

The leaves around their feet were disturbed as the wind came in and surrounded them. They held onto each other and fought against it as it formed a mini-tornado.

'Zhang, if you have another plan I'm listening,' said Steven at the top of his voice, struggling to be heard over the rushing wind; he spotted another crow on a tree branch above. Zhang was concentrating on the hellspawn ahead, her hair wildly blowing into her eyes. 'Zhang!' He shouted, feeling himself losing grip of her.

Zhang aimed and was about to fire at the hellspawn when Steven's grip finally gave way and he was catapulted high off to the left; he bounced off a tree and was flung into a bush.

'Steve!' Shouted Zhang.

The impact of the tree knocked the wind out of him. He rocked from side to side on the ground, desperate for air. When it eventually came to him, his body would only allow small amounts. He suckled for oxygen like a baby on a dummy. In the distance he could hear the roar of a hellspawn and the sound of rushing footsteps. He needed to recuperate fast. He rolled onto his front and tried to push himself up. A pair of feet ran up next to him: Zhang.

'Stay down,' she said.

Steven lay flat on his stomach and Zhang did the same beside him.

'Steven, thank God, are you okay? You have a cut on your face.'

'I'm fine,' Steven assured her, and pointed forward through the bush at the two hellspawn sniffing around for them.

'Where's the third?' Asked Zhang, and Steven shrugged his shoulders. 'We won't last long hidden here, I will distract them. I'll draw their attention to me and run as far away from you as I can. When you feel it's safe, run as fast as you can in the opposite direction.'

'I'm not leaving you to these monsters. We can take them,' argued Steven.

'No, Steve. I took a risk bringing you with me and I will not have you being killed, even if I must risk my life to get you away safe. Do you understand?'

'Okay... but for the record, I still think we would have them.'

A branch snapped behind them and both rolled onto their backs. The third hellspawn had sneaked up on them. It grabbed Zhang's ankle and lifted her into the air, standing on its back two legs. The roar it then let out was so deep and loud it filled the entire woods, scaring all the wildlife within and making dozens of birds fly off into the night. Hanging helplessly, Zhang rocked back and forth trying to break free of its grip, but her efforts were fruitless. It raised its other arm and showed her its razor-sharp claws, which were ready to strike and tear away at her flesh.

Steven shot it three times in the chest to no avail, other than to anger it. It looked down at him and roared once again. He replied with two precise shots inside its hideous mouth; it burst into black ash. Zhang fell to the ground but was quickly back on her feet and running away from Steven just as she had said she would. The remaining hellspawn fell for the diversion and went after her at breakneck speed, while Steven stayed hidden in the bush.

* * *

The whirlwind and hellspawn were after Zhang, but she smiled to herself for a split second, knowing Steven could escape. She could see a lot better now her eyes had fully adjusted to the dark, so she was able to run faster without stumbling. She even had the confidence to look back to see if they were gaining on her. She saw that the two hellspawn had separated and were on her left and right flanks. They jumped on and off the trees like huge black panthers desperate to catch their prey. Not wanting to waste a single bullet Zhang held off firing at them for now and just focused on running. There was a roar from her right; she turned just in time to duck as the hellspawn flew over her, claws drawn, and smashed into a tree on her other side. The tree went down as the hellspawn's claws ripped through it like butter and the second hellspawn came in to pounce. Anticipating its movements, she ran directly for a tree; it jumped for her just as she reached it. She ran vertically up the tree, pushed off and did a backflip. The hellspawn went under her and hit the tree with a hard thump, folding itself around it. Zhang landed perfectly, held her Uzi out with both hands and blasted the hellspawn's head and mouth full of bullets. The flashes from the shots lit up the surrounding area, and the bangs sounded ten times louder in the quiet woods.

She noticed too late that the other hellspawn was back on her. It swiped her legs and spun her sideways in the air. She landed nastily on her side and smashed her head off a rock. The ringing in her ears was so deafening it travelled through her whole skull and brought immense pain with it. She held the side of her head with her eyes closed and tried to sit up, but could not. Blood covered her hand and she could feel a gash on her head, but she knew the hellspawn would not stop, so she blindly fired in a clockwise circle, hoping for a fluke shot into its mouth.

After emptying the clip, she shook off her disorientation and sat up, then reloaded the Uzi. A wet splash hit her leg. Then another. Some sort of liquid was dripping on her lap from above. She looked up to see the hellspawn dangling above her from its feet. Its protruding tongue was raining saliva onto her. It let go of the branch it was hanging from and fell towards her.

Zhang pointed her Uzi skyward with her eyes closed and clamped on the trigger. There was no avoiding the succession of bullets on the hellspawn's descent; all it could do was a roar in defeat as they entered its mouth one by one and burst it from the inside into black ash. The ash showered over Zhang as she used her forearms to brace herself, expecting to be crushed. After a tense moment she realised she was not going to be and opened her eyes, laughing in disbelief. The wind encircled her once again; her hair ferociously flapped about, whipping at her face and neck. Dust and dirt were thrust up into her eyes. She covered her face with her arm and screamed in frustration.

* * *

Steven saw it again, though he could not say if it was the same one; a crow was perched on the branch directly above Zhang. He found it odd – the reappearance of this bird accompanying the wind. He went with his gut. After aiming down the barrel of the gun he took the shot, and to his surprise hit it the first time. Nothing but feathers remained, and they glided their way down, swaying side to side. The wind dissipated the instant the crow was taken out, and Steven ran to make sure Zhang was okay. Clutching her head, she got up and stumbled a few steps.

'You're bleeding,' said Steven, and grabbed her before she collapsed.

'I'm okay,' said Zhang, falling into him.

'I've got you, don't worry.' Steven supported her weight.

'What happened, did you stop it?' Asked Zhang.

'Yes, I think so, I'm not sure. There was this weird crow. I shot it and it stopped.'

'You shot a crow?'

'It seemed like the right thing to do at the time, and it obviously was, because it worked.'

'I hope you're right. We should get out of here before anything else attacks us. We need to get as far away from here as possible and find a place to hide until Bear can get to us,' said Zhang. 'The police will be all over the area after they see the state of that house.'

'You're right. What do you suggest we do?'

'If my memory serves me correctly, there's a farm on one side of these woods. I saw it on our drive in. There'll be somewhere we can hide there.'

Steven took out his mobile and checked his signal. 'I've just about got internet here. I'll check where we are and get us heading in the right direction.'

'Great, the sooner we're out of here, the better. This place is giving me the creeps,' said Zhang, gripping her Uzi.

'That way,' said Steven, and pointed off to their left.

'Good work, Steve,' said Zhang, and they both walked in that direction.

CHAPTER 16

THE FEW PEOPLE that were awake, either driving or walking, paid no attention to the two 3.5 ton Royal Mail vans that passed them by. They made their way down Wapping High Street drawing no attention and continued until they reached the junction with Dundee Street. They both turned into Dundee Street, drove fifty yards, and pulled into the rear car park of a block of maisonettes. The engine on each van was cut and for a few minutes nothing happened.

A hooded man came out of the alleyway from Reardon Path and walked past the inconspicuous Royal Mail vans with no concern. When he was some distance away, the rear roller shutter on both vehicles lifted. Four male special forces, equipped with MP5SDs, jumped out of each and in single file approached the low wall that circled the abandoned building.

All eight were wearing black lightweight stealth clothing, balaclavas, helmets with built-in radio earpieces, and gloves. The leaders of the two teams had crowbars and head cameras which were sending live footage back to their superiors. The first team jumped over the wall from the car park, while the second team went around the side of the building and jumped over the wall from the street.

'Alpha 2, stack up,' ordered the leader of the first team into his earpiece; his three men lined up against the wall next to a flimsy metal cover that sealed the window. They huddled together in single file holding the shoulder of the man in front, guns raised.

'Bravo 2, stack up,' said the leader of the second team. His three men lined up against the wall next to a metal security door, which looked to have already been tampered with as it was hanging off its hinges.

'Alpha 1, 2, 3 and 4 in position,' said Alpha 1, after positioning himself to breach and be last to enter.

'Bravo 1, 2, 3 and 4 in position,' said Bravo 1, also positioning himself to be last to enter.

All members of both teams switched on mini-torches, attached them to their guns and awaited the next order.

'Remember, proceed with caution. You may have to face the creatures that attacked our base. We're calling them lamprey, owing to the similarities reported about the structural layout of their mouth and teeth. The main objective which you have all been briefed on, is the retrieval of the black orb. Once the orb is located, extract it and yourselves immediately,' a voice said in all their earpieces.

Using hand signals only it was confirmed the mission was a go, and both teams went into action.

Alpha 1 breached the window; he jammed his crowbar behind the metal cover and ripped it off with one hard yank. Alphas 2, 3 and 4 jumped inside and took up their positions, clearing the room as they did so. Alpha 1 entered last and noted they were not being followed and that no civilians had spotted them in the process. The dark, damp room they had entered was very large, with weeds, bushes and trees growing out of control. The ceiling had collapsed from the second floor, and rubble was scattered all over. Dirty water leaked from above, even though it was not raining outside.

'Room clear,' shouted Alpha 4. 'Alpha 1, stack up.'

Alpha 1 took point at the one door that led to another room. Alphas 2 and 3 were right behind him, hands on shoulders and guns raised. Alpha 4 would now breach and would be the last to enter the second room. There was no need for the crowbar; he just stood beside the door and pushed it open. Then just as swiftly as before the men went in.

Bravos 1 and 2 ripped off the metal security door and began their breach. Bravo team stormed in and cleared the room, just as disciplined as Alpha team. The room was small, a storage room with junk-like clothes, toys, cleaning equipment and broken cabinets. There were two other doors in the room, excluding the one they had entered through, and one of them was completely barricaded. Bravo team squeezed in the best they could with all guns aimed at the one clear doorway, which was missing an actual door.

'Stack up,' ordered Bravo 1 again, and they did so in the same order as before.

Alpha 1 aimed his gun and scanned the entire area for anything out of the ordinary. The second room they breached was all clear, but their path was blocked because the next door had collapsed. Once convinced they were safe, they cautiously approached a large hole in a crumbled wall and aimed their guns inside. They lit up the adjoining room, which was in a similar state to the first room, but the ceiling was intact. Alpha 1 gestured for his men to follow and climbed through. Two rats bolted into his path, and with super-sharp reflexes his gun was on them. Dismissing them instantly, he continued to secure another perimeter whilst the others came through the hole and did the same.

Bravo team moved out of the first room and proceeded into the second. It was a hallway with an open doorway directly opposite, a staircase next to that, and three closed doors to their right at the end of the corridor. They worked fast and in synchronised rhythm. They went in a clockwise direction and cleared every room on the ground floor in that section of the building. All the rooms they breached were dry and free of any wild growth, but had undoubtedly been deserted for some time. The team made their way around with exceptional speed and brute force. Their training and experience kicked in and was speeding up the process. Within a couple of minutes, they had cleared eight rooms and were now back in the hallway, stacked up against a wall at the bottom of the staircase. With Bravo 1 in the lead, they prepared to climb and clear the floor above.

Alpha team had intensively scoured the current room for the orb, and for anything that would suggest hostiles were in the building.

There was nothing out of the ordinary in the room. There were two other ways in and out of this room, other than the hole in the wall they had come through: a rotten door with no handle and a crumbled doorway with no door at all. This led out to what looked to be a garden but was actually a badly decayed large room. It was heavily consumed by greenery due to the lack of a roof, which exposed it to the elements, with huge overgrowth of moss, weeds and vines completely covering the crumbling walls.

Alphas 2 and 3 did a quick sweep and cleared the room, then re-joined Alphas 1 and 4 at the rotten door.

'Alpha 2, stack up,' Alpha 1 ordered, and Alphas 3 and 4 got behind Alpha 2 ready for the breach.

Alpha 1 booted the door so hard it burst from its hinges, fell forward and landed on its front. The whole team ran over it as they entered. Inside was a long dark hallway, empty except for some rubble, with a hollow doorway to their left. Without breaking momentum, they continued through the doorway and cleared all adjacent rooms. They returned to the hallway to clear rooms further along. Once the whole ground level was cleared, Alpha team stacked up at the foot of a staircase and was ready, like Bravo team, to rise to the next level. All four had their weapons aimed to the top of the staircase as they climbed. Every step creaked as they made their way. They got halfway up and heard a louder creak above. All four stood motionless, and they eyed the landing above for the source. Alpha 1 signalled for Alphas 3 and 4 to hold their position on the staircase and provide cover. He continued the ascent with Alpha 2. The pair crept up to the last step and had a peek of the first floor. Alpha 1 looked to the left and Alpha 2 looked right. The floor was not clear. To the right was a dead end, but to the left stood a man. He had his back to them at the very end of the poorly lit corridor. Alpha 1 beckoned his team and readied himself to deal with the unknown person. He got cable ties out of his pocket and took two deep breaths, stepped onto the landing and moved towards the man with his gun raised.

'Down, get down now!' Shouted Alpha 1 with his team just behind him.

The man did not move a muscle and seemed oblivious to the force that was approaching him.

'I said down, now!' Shouted Alpha 1 again, but still the man did not comply.

Choosing to take him down alone, Alpha 1 signalled for his men to wait and went ahead solo. His intention was to be quick; the man had to be subdued before they could clear the floor. He wasted no time; he ran up behind the man and raised his gun to hit him to the floor. In the rush to do so, he missed the crow standing on the man's shoulder. It squawked and flew straight at his face. It sent him stumbling backwards and down onto his back. The bird was shot down with a single bullet from one of his team and the instant the bird was hit, the man came to life.

First the man's back snapped, then he bent backwards onto his hands, crab-like. His neck cracked as his head spun a hundred and eighty degrees to face the wrong way for his body, then he vomited a thick black liquid onto the floor. His left eye had been pecked at by the crow and hung out of its socket; it dangled down and swung like a hypnotist's watch.

Alpha 1 got to his feet, dropped the cable ties and aimed his gun at the mangled man. From the light of the attached torch, he noticed movement behind the man. He took his aim away and moved the torch beam upwards. Behind the man was a high black silky wall that reached the ceiling. It was moving, and upon closer scrutiny he realised it was a wall of crows, dozens of them, all fidgeting and cramped together.

'What the f–' started Alpha 1, but the mangled man dived on him.

As the pair crashed to the floor, Alpha 1 opened fire and hit the birds. The crows burst into flight. They rapidly swarmed towards Alpha 1 and rushed down the corridor to the other three men. Alpha 2 ran forward into the flock to help Alpha 1, but Alphas 3 and 4 were too perplexed to react. They stumbled backwards into one another, tripped and fell down the stairs. Intertwined they rolled to the bottom, hit with a hard thud and lay sprawled out in pain, hesitant to move in case they discovered a major injury.

Alpha 2 pushed through the endless flock of birds with effort. They pelted and pecked him from every direction, and he had to lash out at some to get them away. His endeavour paid off when he finally reached Alpha 1 and was able to shoot the mangled man off him, putting a stop to the assault. Alpha 1 had been punched in the face numerous times, but other than that he was okay. Alpha 2 lifted him to his feet, held him by the arm and tried to lead him back to the stairs, through the black sea of crows.

Alpha 1's earpiece was making a noise; he assumed it was Bravo team so hastily tried to communicate and relay their current situation.

After a few failed attempts, he gave up as the connection was broken.

'We should get out of here,' suggested Alpha 2 as the pair battled through the crows.

'No, we aren't leaving without getting what we came for. Let's regroup and assess our options,' said Alpha 1 as they reached the staircase and made their way down.

The crows flew down the stairs and scattered frantically around the ground floor. Alphas 3 and 4 were now back on their feet dusting themselves off; both had escaped any serious injury.

'All of you on me. We need to re-establish a connection with Bravo team,' Alpha 1 ordered. They followed his lead back the way they had entered the building. In numerical order they re-entered the room they had climbed into earlier through the hole in the wall. Alpha 4 walked backwards and covered their rear the whole time.

Bravo 1 moved as silently as a predator approaching its prey. He crept up the stairs and each of his team replicated his exact movements. On the last step, Bravo 2 stood beside Bravo 1. They silently mouthed a countdown together from three, then both leant out in opposite directions to clear the landing before stepping up onto it. The silence in the fragile building was unnerving, yet somehow on this floor it felt even more so. To their left were many rooms along the corridor. They chose the route to the right with the fewest rooms to clear. There were four rooms to their right and all four were breached and cleared in very little time. They returned to the top of the staircase and began to clear the rooms off to the left. The first room, just like the previous ones, was empty. They doubted whether the orb was on the premises at all.

Bravo 1 stepped back out into the corridor and headed for the room directly opposite. There was a flash of light to his right; he looked, and a door was closing seemingly by itself. Without a word to his team, Bravo 1 rushed to investigate. The others sensed his concern and immediately followed him to assist. He approached the rotten door and wasted no time booting it open. He hoped to use surprise as his advantage. Something crossed his line of sight, moving too quickly for him to make out what it was, but it was big. There was a bang as it crashed into something. The whole team stormed the room ready to kill. They tried to discover what was moving in the room, but it was difficult. A small window allowed a little moonlight to enter, but it did not help. It was a struggle for them to see and manoeuvre around the high stacks of tables and chairs inside. They stood still, shoulder to shoulder, and frantically shone their torches around, hoping to spot the cause of their alarm.

The door they had come through slammed shut on its own. All four jumped and aimed at it. There was nothing there, but before any had the chance to realise the distraction was intentional, there was a wet thud. It sounded like a soaked flannel hitting a hard surface. Bravo 4 now had a hollow pipe protruding from his stomach. He dropped to his knees, flopped to the floor and died.

There was movement again between two stacks of chairs; without hesitation, the remaining three opened fire. Two stools were obliterated, and the room was lit with strobe flashes. But whatever had attacked them was gone. They ceased their fire, and Bravos 1 and 3 moved in for closer inspection. They pushed over tables and chairs but found nothing. There was a ruckus behind them. Their reflexes, having been sharpened from intense training, made them react instantly. Both spun, knelt and aimed their guns at the jet-black lamprey holding Bravo 2 in the air by the throat.

Bravo 1 instantly reported to Alpha team that they had made contact; he held the button on his earpiece and described the hostile.

The sight of it stunned Bravo 3, causing him to forget the instructions to shoot it through the mouth. Instead, Bravo 3 emptied a full magazine of bullets into its back.

The lamprey's response was merciless and swift. It snapped Bravo 2's neck and tossed his limp, lifeless body with absurd and inhuman force at Bravo 3. The impact broke Bravo 3's arm and he screamed as he looked at his arm's deformity. The lamprey crawled over to him and took hold of both his arms, then slammed him to the floor and pinned him in position.

Bravo 3 was in agonising pain and screamed for help. Bravo 1 ran to him and attempted to intervene but was kicked away and sent straight through the door they had entered.

The creature opened its mouth to gorge on Bravo 3's head. Its three parallel rows of teeth rotated, then it clamped on like a leech to a host. After a short but violent convulsion Bravo 3's head was ripped from his body and blood gushed all over the floor.

Bravo 1 got to his feet and looked back into the room. The lamprey spat Bravo 3's head through the broken door at Bravo 1's chest. It fell to his feet and bounced around his ankles, eyes wide open. Bravo 1 had seen enough in his time to know when he was out of his depth. He took off down the corridor as fast as his legs would allow.

The lamprey burst out from the room and pursued, taking a huge chunk of the doorway with it.

Bravo 1 reached the top of the staircase, ready to jump down four steps at a time. Three more lampreys were making their way up. He looked behind and fired off a few shots at the one pursuing him, which was advancing on him along the wall. The bullets did nothing, so he continued to run down the corridor looking for a way to escape. He ignored all the rooms he passed either side of him and went for the one straight ahead with a shoulder barge. It flew open easily enough but after two steps inside he had to stop quickly: there was no floor; it had collapsed to ground level. Close to going over the edge, he managed to stop on his tiptoes and balance himself before turning and going back out into the corridor. The adrenaline already pumping through his system increased tenfold at the sight of the four creatures racing up the corridor towards him. He clumsily attempted to open a door to his left, but it was locked, then he booted open the door to his right. It shot open and he got inside just as two of the creatures lunged for him. They toppled over one another, rolled into the room with no floor and fell over the edge to the ground below. The other two went straight for him and got stuck in the doorway as they fought with one another to get in. This gave him the vital time he needed to figure out where to go next. The room was bigger than any of the other rooms he had been in so far and was the most cluttered. Broken appliances and discarded furniture blocked the only other two doors in the room, which left only the windows as a means of escape. He shone the torch from his gun and scanned for an alternative route to jumping out of a window with no certainty of where he would land.

In the dead centre of the room the ceiling had collapsed, and directly under it were two disco speakers, each about three feet tall. Bravo 1 quickly got on top of one and turned to unload his bullets at the lamprey still jammed in the doorway. The magazine emptied rapidly, but no damage was inflicted to them as they finally got inside. Bravo 1 flung his gun, which miraculously diverted their attention... only for a moment, but it gave him the time he needed to jump and grab what was left of the ceiling above. He effortlessly pulled himself up but was still close to being yanked back down – a lamprey had nearly snatched his foot. He was now on the second floor looking down at the lamprey. They had knocked the speakers away and were just shy of reaching the edge of the collapsed floor when they jumped. There was no doubt in his mind that they would eventually make it, so he ran for the closest door of three and cautiously took hold of the handle. He pressed it down slowly and carefully pushed the door open. The room looked clear. He entered undaunted, then closed the door behind him. He watched all flanks as he made his way to another door directly in front of him. Even more cautiously than before he pushed the door open, though this time it required more force as there was an obstruction the other side.

Bravo 1 heard a chilling roar as he squeezed into the room. It confirmed to him the creatures were now on his level, but he knew they had not seen which way he had gone. Without delay he barricaded the door again with the battered sofa that had obstructed it, doubtful it would stop them. He backed away from the door and kept his eyes on it, expecting it to burst open any second.

The room was very dark despite the moonlight that shone through the two large windows. Bravo 1's eyes were adjusting as he took a few blind steps backwards. He bumped into something, and it moved. It was soft and tall enough to hit his shoulders when they collided. He spun around and was taken aback by what he saw. It was a man, and he was not alone. Twenty to thirty men and women were in the room with him. All were facing away from him, and not one made a single noise or moved. It was unclear to him whether these individuals were hostile, so as a precaution he took out his holstered pistol and approached them stealthily.

After inspecting the male he had bumped into, it was apparent the man was unresponsive; his eyes were jet black with black liquid leaking from them. Bravo 1 quietly and slowly weaved between the people – they were all in the same state. They stared blankly ahead, as if transfixed by something. He waved a hand in front of the faces of some and even poked some with the pistol; none reacted in the slightest.

'How bizarre,' said Bravo 1 to himself. He spoke into his earpiece. 'Alpha 1, if you're reading me I'm on the second floor and urgently need assistance. Bravos 2, 3 and 4 are all KIA and I'm currently having to retreat from hostiles. Are you receiving?'

A few seconds went by and it seemed Alpha 1 was trying to reply, but there was interference with the connection. Only broken, unintelligible, hysterical shouting came through with static.

'Alpha team, are you receiving?' Asked Bravo 1 again, but only received static. 'Piece of shit!'

It was clear he would have to escape alone. He took out his earpiece and eyed the room for alternative routes out, other than the way he had entered. He sensed something else was in the room. There was a noise... at first, he was not sure what it was, but as it got louder, he thought it sounded like the crackling sound of wood on fire. He glanced around and realised there was a red glow coming from the other side of the room; this was what all the zombified people were staring at. He pushed two men aside for a better view. On top of a fragile-looking table was the black orb he had been tasked to retrieve. The red inscriptions on the ball were aglow with red light, and each time it pulsated it got brighter. He felt as if he was being drawn towards it, a feeling that intensified with every flash, and even though warning signals were going off in his mind, its allure was too strong. He placed his pistol down next to it, reached out and cupped it with both hands, then lifted it from the table. It continued to crackle and chips of it flaked away, falling to the table like bits of charcoal until nothing remained in his hands but specks of black. Open-mouthed, he dusted them off. This was a booby trap.

It was not the genuine orb and Bravo 1 knew he was in danger. He turned around fast to face the crowd behind him. Two of the lifeless males in the room had come alive. They had silently closed in on him and were now at close proximity, staring menacingly. Before he had any time to react, they pushed him powerfully onto the delicate table. It broke apart like it was held together with tape and he hit the floor, which was just as flimsy. The floorboards gave way and he was free-falling through the air. He plummeted past the collapsed first floor and screamed for just a second before smashing headfirst onto the concrete ground floor. It killed him instantly.

Once all four of the Alpha team had climbed back through the hole into the second room they had breached, Alpha 1 tried to reach Bravo team again. 'It's no use, I'm getting nothing but fuzz.'

'What do we next? What if they need backup?' Asked Alpha 3.

'We'll go find them. We'll have to trace their steps from their entry point. Follow me,' replied Alpha 1, and headed back towards their original entry point in the next room.

As he stepped into the room, there was a crash from above. Bravo 1 fell through the high ceiling of the first floor to his death not ten yards from Alpha 1's position. The ceiling continued to collapse, which made it impossible for Alpha team to check on Bravo 1. Then bodies began to fall with the rubble.

At first Alpha team feared it was the rest of Bravo team and held their breath as each body hit the floor, but then they came to realise there were too many.

Men, women and debris crashed down, and the room quickly filled with dust, making it very difficult to see. Alpha team didn't believe their eyes when the people that had fallen began to stand up.

'No way have they survived that fall,' exclaimed Alpha 4.

'We're not staying here to find out how... quick, get back through that hole,' Alpha 1 ordered, backing up and raising his weapon.

Alpha 2 was the first to climb back through the hole, closely followed by Alpha 3. Then through the thick cloud of dust the zombie-like people charged for Alpha 1. He held off firing his weapon until they fully emerged from the cloud. When they revealed their grotesque faces, he killed each one with a single bullet to the forehead. The bodies came at him quickly, but he dropped them faster. Yet he knew there were too many to hold back. Alpha 4 saw this and shot some down himself.

'Go, I've got this!' Alpha 1 ordered as a man grabbed his arm. He got the man by the throat, pulled out his combat knife and stabbed him through the left temple. He went down with it still inserted and Alpha 1 carried on shooting the others.

'Get over here,' Alpha 4 ordered; he was now the other side of the hole with Alphas 2 and 3.

Alpha 1 made a run for it just as a large group tried to get at him.

'Hurry!' Shouted Alpha 4 and provided cover fire.

Without looking back, Alpha 1 dived headfirst through the hole. The group chasing him ran into the hole and jammed each other, desperately reaching through.

With the help of his team, Alpha 1 got to his feet and all four stood side by side and opened fire. The zombie-like men and women dropped like flies; only a couple managed to climb through and get into the room, but they were quickly shot down. Alpha team felt they had the upper hand, which led Alpha 4 to take his eyes off his targets and scan the room. Two lampreys were in the doorway to the room with the overgrowth. Alpha 4 was so shocked he could only watch as they began their attack.

Alpha 3 was the first to be hit. A lamprey smacked him so hard from behind that he flew across the room and through the hole like a dummy out of a crash test car. He was pounced on and dragged away by the remaining zombie-like people.

Alpha 2 shot at the lamprey while Alpha 1 reloaded. His reload was clumsy, but he managed it. The lamprey stood over him, beat on its own chest, then backhanded him through the air. The blow broke several of his ribs, and when he landed he coughed up blood.

Alpha 2's ammo clip emptied and after seeing it was ineffective he began backing away, only to see more lamprey coming into the room from the two doorways behind them. Several of them entered fast and going in different directions; some crawled across the walls while others went across the ceiling and floor. They encircled Alpha team and closed in on them. They clearly had no intention of letting anyone out alive.

'What do we do?' Said Alpha 4, sweating and panicked.

Alpha 2 did not respond; he slowly walked backwards towards Alpha 1, who had propped himself up against a wall and was gasping for air.

'What do we do?' Asked Alpha 4 again, this time at the top of his voice, but was ignored again.

Alpha 2 was silent because he knew there was nothing they could do. He had accepted they would not survive the attack and would comfort Alpha 1 until it was over.

In denial, Alpha 4 threw his weapon to the floor and legged it for the hole in the wall, attempting to escape. Two of the lampreys leapt on him from above before he was even halfway to the hole. They fought for ownership in a ferocious game of tug of war. Then tossed him violently all the way into the overgrown room. He screamed, and both lampreys instantly gave chase to finish him off.

'What's the damage, Georgie?' Asked Alpha 2, and put a hand on Alpha 1's shoulder.

'Marson, what are you still doing here? My ribs are bust,' replied Georgie in agony.

'I'd ask if you're capable of running, but I doubt we'd get very far,' said Marson, and sat beside his comrade.

'I'll distract them... you still have a chance,' said Georgie, and wincing with effort he pulled out his side pistol.

'Don't be daft, we die together, brother. I wouldn't leave any of us to die alone to these things, or any enemy come to think of it,' replied Marson, and pulled out his pistol. 'I'll save us a bullet each – beats being ripped apart alive.'

'For fuck's sake, Marson, you should have got out – now I feel guilty to die, you arsehole.'

Marson burst out laughing. 'So you bloody should. I'll be expecting a few pints waiting on the other side.'

'You never get the rounds in here and you're already trying to swerve them in the afterlife. You make me laugh,' said Georgie, and tried to laugh, but it hurt too much. 'Let's just shoot the fuckers already!'

'No need to tell me twice,' said Marson, and raised his weapon.

* * *

Gabriel flew as fast as his wings would allow. Below him was the abandoned building with the special forces inside. He dived straight down, smashed through the roof and entered the building, landing directly in front of two humans who were pinned down by the hellspawn.

Gabriel knew Georgie and Marson were unable to see him. He stood facing the hellspawn, unconcerned for the moment about the humans' distress after he had brought the ceiling down around them.

The hellspawn were no longer interested in the humans and switched their attention to Gabriel. Each arched its back, dug its claws into the floor and growled in anger.

Gabriel's golden trumpet was in his right hand. A few of the hellspawn took a step back at the sight of it, then a couple more when he smiled and raised it to his lips. Some were reckless enough to attack and went at him, roaring loudly as he blew the trumpet. The sound that came out was so thunderous and powerful the entire building vibrated; it shook the room so violently it was close to falling apart. The attacking hellspawn were stopped in their tracks by the intense wind that accompanied the booming sound. They gripped the floor and held on desperately as the sound rattled their bodies.

The two humans behind Gabriel watched the hellspawn's discomfort in confusion. All they would hear would be harmonious sounds, and the ferocious vibrations would be pleasant, comforting rumbles that gave a feeling of well-being.

Gabriel took a quick breath and four of the hellspawn attempted to flee. Gabriel blew again, but harder and more intensely than before. The sound the trumpet produced was so deafening and fierce it muted all the hellspawn cries. One by one they disintegrated to pieces of black ash under the blazing white light that poured out of the trumpet and filled the room. With one last deep blow from Gabriel, the light filled the room and spread throughout the entire building. It burnt away all the hellspawn inside and rendered all the possessed humans unconscious. The building was now empty of any evil presence, and Gabriel felt it. He had vanquished them all. Without so much as a glance at the two men behind him, he spread his wings and flew away.

* * *

'What on Earth was that?' Asked Marson, his weapon now on the floor beside him.

'I have no idea, but that light, wow. Did you feel it?' Said Georgie.

'I did, I never wanted it to end.'

'Me too, it was unbelievable... and them things, they're gone.'

'They are. We should get out of here, can you walk?' Asked Marson, getting to his feet.

'I think so, but what about the orb?' Said Georgie, and with the help of Marson he stood up.

'No way is that here. This has been a trap from the beginning... they knew we were coming. Let's get back and report what's happened. Then they can decide how they will clean this up and retrieve the bodies.'

'Okay, but take it easy. I'm in agony,' said Georgie, and they headed for the exit.

They left the building and trudged up to one of the Royal Mail vans waiting for them. They ignored the open shutter at the back and went straight for the front passenger side door. Both got in and within seconds of closing the door the van drove away up the street.

DEAN JONES

CHAPTER 17

Zhang peered out of the bushes to see Bear pull into the pitch-black narrow country lane as she had instructed. He was driving slowly and had turned on the car's high beam. She and Steven burst out of their hiding place, and the car squealed to a halt. Steven slapped his hands on the bonnet and looked at Bear appreciatively.

'Bloody hell, I nearly ran you over,' complained Bear from his open window. 'Come on, get in.'

Zhang got in the passenger side while Steven got in the back. 'We need to move fast... the police are everywhere. It's a miracle we've been able to avoid them this long,' she said, looking through the window into the bushes.

'No problem,' said Bear, as he spun the car around.

As they left the country lane and joined the main road with several other vehicles, a police helicopter flew over them with its spotlight on, searching the woodland area they had just escaped from.

'That was too close,' said Steven, looking out of the rear window.

'You're telling me.' Zhang checked the time on her watch. 'You made good time, B.'

'Yeah, lucky for you I was already on the way out of central London and the roads were pretty clear,' said Bear.

'It's a good job – that chopper would have had us in no time. Thanks,' said Zhang.

'Any time. Why were you out here for anyway, and what's with all the heat?'

'We wanted to find out if there was anything fishy with two new pilots who are joining RAF Marham. There definitely is – they're being protected. Something attacked us in their house and we had to fight off hellspawn in the woods. That reminds me,' said Zhang, and pulled out the red envelope she had found with the other letters in Vincent's room.

'What's that?' Asked Bear.

'I'm not sure yet... it could be nothing, but it stood out from the rest, so I swiped it.' Zhang opened the letter and read out the handwritten message. '"As promised, the agreed funds have been deposited into your offshore account. If everything goes as planned, a generous bonus payment will also be made to you – gratitude for the successful completion of the difficult task at hand. Once you've executed your orders, eject out at sea in the area we discussed. There will be a sea crew waiting to pick you up and transport you out of the country. You will never have to work another day in your life; keep that in mind if you begin to falter. This will be the last communication between you and me. I'm confident you won't let us down. Burn this message once read."'

Zhang placed the A4 piece of paper back inside the envelope and pocketed it.

'What do you think he's being paid to do?' Asked Steven.

'Nothing good, that's for sure, and soon he'll have one of the RAF's most powerful aircraft in his possession,' said Zhang.

'Do you think they're both involved?'

'No idea, but the aircraft they'll be assigned to requires a two-man crew, so presumably they are.'

Steven sat back and looked out the window. 'Surely... surely, they're not being paid to attack Wembley Stadium on Saturday... that would be a suicide mission, wouldn't it?' He said.

They fell silent; no one seemed to have any answers. Zhang's mind was racing, considering such a scenario. Bear continued to drive.

* * *

Oliver stretched his arms and yawned as he awoke from what felt like a decent sleep. He took his time and sat up, stretched once more and opened his eyes to find himself back in the white room.

It shocked him wide awake and he jumped to his feet. 'Not again!'

Like last time, it was freezing cold and a crack appeared on one of the walls, which began to spread. Black vines once again emerged from the crack and spread around the room at speed. He remembered the next events and out of pure fear took hold of his crucifix, closed his eyes and prayed under his breath.

He heard a rustling sound and squinted with one eye. The vines were retracting quickly back into the crack which completely sealed itself.

Oliver felt his fear subside; he opened his eyes and was relieved to see the room was back to its original state. 'Thank God.'

He walked to where the crack was and stroked the wall; it was solid with no evidence of a crack ever being there. Then, feeling a gust of wind behind him, he turned. He was no longer inside the white room but was standing in the middle of the football pitch at what appeared to be Wembley Stadium. The white walls had disappeared, and he looked around the stadium in disbelief. There were no players on the pitch with him, the stands were all empty, and not even a bird flew over him in the night sky above. He was completely alone. He took an uncertain step forward, but the ground beneath him began to rumble and undulate. Afraid, he retreated and paced backwards as fast as he could. The rumbling increased, and where he had first stood the ground began to break apart and fall in, forming a sinkhole of unknown depth. The circular hole grew larger, expanding outwards, forcing Oliver to turn and run. It chased him at his heels and a few times nearly swallowed him whole. As he reached the penalty box on one end of the pitch, it stopped its growth, allowing Oliver to catch his breath and peer inside the mouth of this gigantic sinkhole. Huge chunks of mud and rock broke away from the sides and fell into what appeared to be a bottomless pit.

'I need to get out of here... this is insane,' said Oliver, and turned to do so; he froze. Jessica was standing in front of him on the goal line. She wore the clothes she had worn the day they had first met; Oliver stared at her, puzzled – she looked terrified. 'Jessica, what's happening? Are you okay?' He asked and moved towards her slowly.

Looking through him, Jessica ignored his question and continued to stare blankly forward. Then, as if something had appeared in her gaze, her eyes grew wide and she started screaming without a sound, as if something muted her. Her hands came up in front of her, like she was bracing for some sort of impact, and a flood of tears flowed down her face.

Oliver tried to close the gap between them, to comfort his friend and assure her she was safe. But every step he took left him in the same position; the ground was like a treadmill, preventing him from getting any closer to her.

'Jessica!' Shouted Oliver in frustration.

A boiling black puddle began bubbling up out of the grass between them. Thick black steam rose from it, which moved as though it was alive, dancing in the air and getting thicker with every second.

Oliver had seen this before, and just as he expected, it formed the shape of a large man.

'Jessica, run!' Shouted Oliver as she backed into the net of the goal.

The black ghost-like figure advanced on her; it took a few steps and grabbed her by the throat, pulled her from the goal and lifted her into the air. The look of horror on her face was nothing compared to her expression when the apparition thrust its free arm into her stomach.

'No!' Shouted Oliver, still running but unable to move forward.

After rummaging around inside her, the dark apparition took out its arm and held in its hand a bright ball of white light. Jessica stared at it, her lips trembling and tears dripping from her chin. The evil entity disposed of the ball of light by flinging it over its shoulder into the sinkhole. As it disappeared into the darkness, the apparition decided it was finished with Jessica. It snapped her neck and threw her bloodied body to the ground, the sight of which stunned Oliver so much he stepped back with both hands on top of his head. He lost his footing on the edge of the sinkhole. The ground gave way beneath his feet and he fell inside, screaming. The darkness consumed him as he plummeted, and his screams got louder. He felt the heat first before he saw anything. Then a red glow appeared below. It got brighter and hotter until it was everywhere.

New ground was approaching him; it was as though he was falling from the sky of a world inside the Earth. Below him were huge black volcanoes and mountains. Fire and lava erupted everywhere, red rivers spread for as far as the eye could see, and on the landscape below were hellspawn, millions of them. The heat in the air was scorching and got hotter the closer he fell to the rocky ground. It was approaching fast; he covered his eyes with his right arm and yelled out as his clothes, hair and skin ignited. Breathing was beyond difficult. His every breath felt as though he was inhaling fire... it burned his airways and spread throughout his body. Just as he longed to die, to escape from the unbearable pain, the ground answered his wish and he hit it with incredible force.

Oliver sprang up from his sleep into a sitting position, out of breath, red hot and sweating immensely. He ripped off his top, and steam rose from his skin.

'Oliver, are you okay?' Asked Jessica, and put a hand on his shoulder. 'My God, you're burning up.' She picked up a plastic cup of water beside him and passed it to him.

In just a few gulps he downed the lot and gave it back, desperate for more. Jessica refilled it and handed it back. He snatched it from her and drank fast, most of it pouring down his face.

'Seriously, are you okay?' Asked Jessica again.

Oliver dropped the empty cup onto the bed and caught his breath. 'I'm fine, it was just a bad dream.'

'A bad dream? Look at the steam coming off you. You're burning away your own sweat, you're so hot,' said Alexander, who was sitting against a wall on the cell's floor.

'Surely a dream couldn't make you go like that. What was it about?' Asked Jessica, sounding more concerned.

'I can't remember, I just know it was bad. I'm so thirsty,' Oliver lied, the full vivid memory of the dream still clear in his mind.

'Let me get you some more water,' said Jessica, and filled the plastic cup again.

Alexander got to his feet and paced around the windowless cell. The small room and lack of fresh air were clearly making him agitated.

'How long can they keep us in here? This is ridiculous,' said Jessica.

'They have no right holding us at all - keeping us here is an utter farce,' said Alexander, and booted the locked cell door.

'I want to see my son, I was told I can see my son!' Shouted West from the cell opposite that contained him, Cole, Sergeant Ward and Sergeant O'Keeffe.

'Pipe down the lot of you,' demanded a military police guard from outside the cells.

'This is bullshit,' said Alexander, continuing to pace around.

Having cooled down, Oliver got back into his top and stood to shake off his tremors. As he did, there was a clanging of keys outside the cell, and the door was unlocked. It swung open and on the other side were three military police officers and Lieutenant General Winters.

'Have you come to your senses?' Asked Alexander, glowing red with anger.

'Father Hall, come with us. We need to talk,' said Lieutenant General Winters.

'Me?' Said Oliver.

Alexander stepped in front of Oliver.

'You can come out peacefully or we can come in and drag you out. Either way, you'll be coming with me,' replied Winters.

'It's okay, Alex, I'll be fine. There's no need for there to be violence,' said Oliver, and pushed past to leave the cell. Alexander did nothing to stop him, and the cell was locked again.

'Winters, let me see my son!' Shouted West again, but was ignored as the five men walked away. 'Winters!'

After taking one last look over his shoulder at the cells he was leaving, Oliver put his hands in his pockets and kept close behind Lieutenant General Winters. The corridors they walked down were long, and they had to turn many corners. They passed dozens of rooms, but Oliver paid none of them any attention. Eventually they came to a thick grey metal door with a keypad. Lieutenant General Winters entered a code, and the door opened. They entered what looked like an indoor Royal Mail van car park. There were easily twenty to twenty-five Royal Mail vans inside, all parked parallel to one another, and as Oliver looked at them, puzzled, another drove inside from an entrance opposite them. He could see that the entrance was an underground tunnel. They continued to walk down a flight of metal stairs and onto a metal platform. All the Royal Mail vans were backed up to the platform with their rear shutters open.

They stopped at the back of the first vehicle and Lieutenant General Winters turned to face Oliver, then nodded his head to the side. 'In there!'

'In the back of that, why? And what about the others?' Asked Oliver, panicking a little.

'Don't you worry about the others, now get inside before I lose my patience,' Winters demanded, and one of the officers prodded Oliver in the back with his rifle.

Not having a choice in the matter, Oliver obeyed and went inside. He realised it wasn't a typical Royal Mail van. There were computers along one side and lockers with weapons and clothing on the other. Choosing the far spinning stool, one of six bolted to the van's floor, Oliver sat. One of the military police officers followed him in and stood guard at the shutter entrance, not speaking a single word the entire time.

'Make sure he doesn't escape and contact me the moment he's been delivered,' Winters ordered; the guard answered with just a nod of the head.

Lieutenant General Winters pulled the rear shutter down with one hard tug and left both men in darkness inside. As the vehicle was started the internal lights came on, as did all the computers.

Oliver looked behind him, but there was no window or any way to see the driver. Concluding it must be the second military police guard he thought nothing more of it. The van pulled away and they began their journey to wherever they were taking him. It was strange; Oliver knew he should feel anxious about the situation, but somehow, he did not. Compared to the fear he had felt in his recent nightmares, this was nothing. He shuffled to get himself more comfortable and looked at the equipment, curious what it was all used for.

* * *

Cole was slouched back on the cell bed against the wall plotting to himself how he would unleash the full force of the law onto Lieutenant General Winters for this unlawful imprisonment. Flicking his thumbnail off his top teeth and staring at the ceiling, he barely heard the conversation of the others.

'You're saying it's all true... heaven, hell, all of it, it's all real?' Asked Sergeant Ward. Sergeant O'Keeffe stood at his side. Both had their arms crossed and looked down at West, who was sitting on the floor against the door.

'For the tenth time, yes. Look, whatever possessed me, its thoughts were hell-bent on torturing me. It didn't give me any answers to the questions we'd all love to know. But I can tell you one thing I know for certain: it's undeniable knowledge of the existence of God and Satan. It didn't believe or have faith, it knew. And its knowing was so real that it made me know too, they exist. You both saw those things attack the base. What are your guesses as to what they could have been?' Asked West; the sergeants looked at each other, then back at West.

'At first we had no clue – panic took over and we just shot them – but once we'd calmed down and thought with rational minds, we thought maybe a militarised mutant animal,' answered Sergeant O'Keeffe.

'But then Agent Charles and those flashes of light that were taking out those things... we can't come to a logical explanation for them. I don't know, maybe what you say is true, it just seems so far-fetched and I find it hard to believe. Especially as I still don't trust you, sir. I think I will put a hold on the hellspawn theory for now. I'm sure a much more plausible explanation will arise once there's been an investigation,' said Sergeant Ward, and Sergeant O'Keeffe nodded.

'I understand,' said West. He took his mobile out of his pocket and glanced at it. 'I'm surprised they didn't bother confiscating our phones. They must have decided it was unnecessary because of the signal blockers.'

The lights in the cell went out.

Cole's attention was quickly switched to this new situation. 'Any clue why that's happened?' He asked as his eyes adjusted.

'None at all,' said Sergeant O'Keeffe.

With no sounds of keys or personnel, the cell door unlocked itself and slowly opened.

'Jessica,' said West, and ran to her cell.

'Dad, how did you open the door?' Asked Jessica as her father walked in and went to her.

'I didn't, they opened on their own. Must be a power cut,' said West, as he gripped his daughter.

'These doors aren't electronic, they need keys to unlock them,' said Alexander, inspecting the door.

'Who cares? Let's go,' said Cole, and raced out of the cell, the others following.

'Wait, are you sure this is a good idea? You heard what Winters said he'd do if we tried to leave, and what about Oliver?' Said Jessica.

'There's no way we'd get shot, especially as we're unarmed. It's just a scare tactic to get us to do as we're told. It's not likely we'll make it out anyway, but I'm not hanging around here to be thrown back in there,' said West, and as he did the door they were heading for opened.

The military-police guard left behind to watch over them stepped through and caught them. He took a step back, surprised, but then raised his weapon and went to confront the group.

Disheartened from not even having the chance to attempt to leave the base, the group raised their hands in defeat.

'How did you get out?' Asked the guard.

The lights going out had made the block dark; it was light enough to see, but none of them were ready for the sudden emergence of a blinding white sphere of light in front of the guard's face. It was the size of an average football and bright enough to make the group turn away from it, but just as suddenly as it had appeared, it disappeared. When the group looked back and reopened their eyes, the guard was unconscious on the floor. Perplexed, no one except Alexander moved; he ran forward and booted the guard's weapon away, then checked his pulse.

'Is he alive?' Asked Cole.

'Yes,' said Alexander, and stood, 'we should make a move while he's out.'

'What was that thing?' Cole said.

'I don't know, but seems to me something is helping us escape,' said Alexander.

'I've seen something like it before when we were being chased in Nicole's car with Father Hall and Steven,' said Jessica.

'So have we, back at the base when all hell

broke loose,' said Sergeant Ward.

'Well, so long as it continues to act in our favour, I can live with that. We should make a move though before anyone else comes,' said Alexander. They all nodded.

'We're going to stay here. Being held like this may be extremely unorthodox, but going AWOL is out of the question. You guys go, and we'll try and make up some story about how you got out,' said Sergeant O'Keeffe.

'I have to find my son and then I'll decide what I'm doing once I have him. Going AWOL is not what I want, but I may not have a choice. I either leave, or I stay and confront Winters to convince him that this is not the way to deal with the situation. I can also try to find out where he has taken Father Hall. Jessica, you go with your friends and as soon as I've found Aaron I'll contact you and let you know what I'm doing next,' said West. Jessica nodded in acceptance, then hugged her father goodbye.

'It's clear out here,' said Cole, peering round the door leading out.

'Well, after you then, Cole,' Alexander said, and Cole led the way out.

'Be careful, Dad, I'll speak to you soon,' said Jessica as West left in the opposite direction.

* * *

After what felt like an hour, the van escorting Oliver came to a halt, and the driver banged twice on the partition, presumably to confirm their arrival to the guard watching him. In response the military-police guard opened the rear shutter and told Oliver to get out of the vehicle. He pushed him out, flung him to the ground, then before he had time to complain, closed the shutter again. Another two bangs were exchanged between the guard and the driver. Then the Royal Mail van drove off and left Oliver alone in a dark alleyway surrounded by tall buildings.

Oliver got to his feet and cursed at the grazes on his palms. He looked around, hoping to figure out where he was. Ten seconds into his exploration, he was interrupted by a door opening at the base of one of the buildings. A light from inside prevented him from seeing the features of the person who stepped out, but it was clear from the silhouette it was a man with an Afro hairstyle.

Oliver stopped and waited for the individual to say something, but all he did was turn around and walk back into the building, leaving the door open.

After looking around and not seeing any better options, Oliver made his way to the open door to follow the man inside. He stepped into the building and as soon as he did the door closed behind him and locked.

Oliver did not bother to try the handle. He took in his surroundings and watched as the man he was following stepped into an old vintage cage lift and beckoned him to follow. He guessed this building used to be a hotel, long left abandoned by its owners and empty of any guests. There were six rooms in the hallway in front of him leading to the lift, three either side mirroring one another. The carpet was dull and lacking in colour, as was the wallpaper, which was peeling away from the wall. Strangely, electricity still ran through the building – the lights were lit – but for what reason Oliver did not know. He walked towards the lift, and on passing tried two of the doors to discover they were locked.

'You'd find nothing of interest inside any of those rooms, I assure you,' said the man, and checked his watch.

'Really? And why is it you assume to know what I find of interest?' Asked Oliver with a bit of a bite; the situation was annoying him.

'Well, if rotting furniture, dust and cobwebs are your thing, then go ahead and break in, Oliver. Otherwise, please follow me. We have much to discuss, you and I.'

'How do you know my...' Oliver started, but fatigued after the day's events and thinking the knowledge of his name must have come from Winters, he decided not to question. He walked to the lift as requested. 'So, who are you?' He asked as he got into the lift.

'My name is Demantay,' the man replied.

Demantay tugged the scissor gate closed and pulled back on the handle in the mounted cylindrical container beside him, and the lift descended. The peculiar noises the elevator produced made Oliver doubt its safety, but unable to do anything about it, he travelled quietly. They went down two floors before Demantay brought the lift to a halt, and when he did, he opened the scissor gate straight away. He allowed Oliver to step out first. Oliver once again took in his surroundings. Immediately it was obvious this part of the building was nothing to do with the rest of the hotel, but was a hidden level most likely built after the hotel was closed. 'Wow,' he said in fascination.

'Were you expecting some grotty basement?' Asked Demantay as he too left the lift.

'Actually, yes,' Oliver confirmed, shocked by the beauty of the luxurious hallway.

There was only one way to go once out of the lift and that was straight ahead to the wooden double doors at the end of the hall, a good thirty yards away from them.

Several portraits of well-dressed men and women adorned the walls, as well as decorative gold candle holders with each candle alight, casting warm flickering rays throughout the hallway.

'Follow me,' said Demantay, and walked towards the doors.

Oliver followed warily, leaving a gap between them; the doors were pushed wide open and Demantay strolled in head high, full of confidence.

'Ladies and gentlemen allow me to introduce Father Hall, the elusive priest.' A group of ten or so people, all finely dressed, were drinking and conversing within the room. The chatter died down and the people all set their eyes on Oliver, who had stopped in the doorway looking into the red-lit room. It was a room for relaxing, like the lounge area of a tropical beach bar, but indoors. The seats had huge red cushions big enough to lie on. The canopy beds were covered with rose petals, feathers and white fluffy pillows and surrounded by filmy white transparent voile that moved gently in the warm air that circulated the room from air vents on the low ceiling.

Oliver stepped further inside; there was mist and a sweet fragrance to the air. It made his head feel dizzy the more he breathed it in.

'The head rush is normal. There's a little something I put into the ventilation... it heightens one's feeling of pleasure. It won't harm you, I assure you. Come inside, say hello to everyone,' Demantay said to Oliver.

The people who were seated got to their feet and joined the others around Demantay. Oliver counted eleven people in total, including Demantay. He decided against any customary greetings and remained silent.

Demantay clicked his fingers and a waiter appeared from a door that appeared in the wall. If it had not been opened Oliver would never have known, it was there. The waiter carried a tray of full champagne glasses. Some of the group replaced their empty glasses with a full one. Demantay took two. He handed the second drink to Oliver, who was happy to accept it from him. The events of the day had more than scrambled his mind, so the drink was not only welcomed but swallowed in one.

'Thirsty?' Asked Demantay with a suspicious grin.

'You could say that,' replied Oliver, and exchanged his glass for another. Just like the first, he necked the drink in one and placed the glass back on the tray. The waiter bowed his head and headed back to the secret door. 'So, would you like to explain why I'm here? I assume you are the people behind the lies in the police database, and the mercenaries that tried to capture me and my friends,' said Oliver, who was feeling uncomfortably hot from breathing in whatever substance was in the air.

After a few giggles from the group, a petite woman in a red dress stepped up to Oliver, and with the back of her right hand stroked his right cheek. The woman was stunningly beautiful, with silky soft long brown hair, captivating grey eyes and a dark olive skin tone.

'You are here because we need you to answer some questions,' said the woman, and continued to stroke his ear and the side of his neck.

'That's all? All of this just to ask me questions? You could have just visited me at my church to do that. Not that I know anything of interest. Are you sure you have the right priest?'

'Oh, you are the right priest,' said the woman, smiling. She stepped even closer to him while fiddling with his clothing.

The woman's perfume was even more intoxicating than the air. Oliver took in deep breaths of it and his whole body warmed, especially between his legs. *What was in that drink?* The mist in the room thickened, and everything around him was blurred. His breathing got deeper, and his pulse rose. The woman ran her left hand through his hair and looked up into his eyes, grabbed the back of his head and pulled his face towards hers.

Oliver resisted and pulled his head back, although it was not easy; the urges that were building up inside him were unlike anything he had ever felt before. He was fully erect, and thoughts of pure lust flooded his mind. *This is a trap, I must stay focused.*

He was aware that his arousal and lustful thoughts were the effect of what was in the air; he had to stay in control.

Two more women came up behind him and began touching and stroking his body. The rest of the group were invisible to him now, blurred out from his fuzzy mind by the thickening mist in the room.

Oliver spoke directly to the woman in front of him. 'Who are you?'

'Vedrana,' whispered the woman into his ear, then looked at him with a cheeky smile and a provocative gaze.

Oliver looked at her, suspicious, then the girls behind him caressed him again. He did not struggle, and he could not understand why. They pulled him back and threw him onto a canopy bed. When he landed, it felt as though time had slowed down; he was extremely dizzy, and it worried him that something was wrong. As he lay on his back, the three women approached him in slow motion. He waved his hand in front of his eyes and saw twelve fingers and three thumbs. The other people and the surrounding room had disappeared. A wall of red mist encircled him. Only the bed he was on and the three women enticing him existed. They stood at his feet at the bottom of the bed, and none of them spoke a word. *What a fool I was to have taken those drinks!*

'What have you done to me?' Asked Oliver, who now felt like he had been on a heavy drinking session.

'He's yours now, Vedrana,' whispered one of the women.

'Where're the others?' Said Oliver, his head swaying from side to side.

'Don't worry about them, all you need to focus on is me,' said Vedrana; the other two women backed away into the mist and disappeared like the others.

'Vedrana? What is happening, did you drug me?' Asked Oliver as Vedrana's face blurred. She roughed up her hair, flicked it around and crawled up the bed over him.

Oliver shook his head and refused her advance as she crawled over him like a cat. She whipped her hair around again and grabbed the bottom of her dress. She pulled it up over her hips and torso, then removed it completely and discarded it to the floor. She sat back onto his crotch in red lingerie and ran her hands from his stomach to his chest.

'Stop!' Oliver demanded; he grabbed her hands and removed them from his body. The drug was now fully in his system and disrupting his brain processes.

Vedrana pulled her hands free and placed them back onto his chest, then leant down, getting her face close to his. 'I know you want me,' she said, and kissed his cheek again.

Oliver pushed her away. 'Please, stop.'

'Why,' said Vedrana and put his hands onto her breasts.

Oliver took his hands away instantly. 'No, I've been drugged, I need to leave.'

Vedrana ignored him.

'Do you remember your secret?' Asked Vedrana, who was now fondling her own breasts.

'What do you mean?' Replied Oliver.

'You have a secret, one that no one can know... do you remember it?'

Oliver did not understand what was happening to him or where he was. With the little brainpower he had left, he tried to remember any secrets he knew. Jessica's baby sprang to mind above all else, accompanied by the voice urging him to protect the baby. 'A secret?'

'Yes, do you remember your secret? You told them, Oliver. They know all about it. How could you?' Vedrana was now stroking his body again.

'I never told anyone.'

'It was you, Oliver. I can't believe you told them. Why did you do it?'

'No, it wasn't me. I would never have told them about Jessica's...' *Stop!*

Oliver had a moment of lucidity, then slipped back into disorientation. *I mustn't speak of the baby, not feeling like this. I'm so confused.*

'Jessica's what?' Asked Vedrana.

The voice echoed again through his mind loudly.

'What were you going to say?' Vedrana's nails pressed into him.

'Thank God,' replied Oliver with a smile; he felt himself drifting away. He closed his eyes and waited for sleep to take him, take him far away from this madness. It was so close.

'Jessica's what? Father, Jessica's what? Are you awake? Oliver?' Asked Vedrana and slapped him hard across the face. He did not react; sleep nearly had him.

He heard a few more muffled words from Vedrana, then he was gone.

* * *

Alexander, Cole and Jessica sneaked out of a fire door which led out to the side of the military building.

'Follow me,' said Alexander and crept along the side of the building to reach the front.

'There's our car,' said Jessica, indicating that it was still where they left it.

'It doesn't look like anyone is around. We should get it and speed out of here,' said Cole.

'That'll be risky with that armed guard at the entrance. I tell you what, you two get in the car, get ready, and wait for me to deal with him and wave you over when it's safe,' said Alexander.

'Be careful,' Jessica said.

Alexander gave a wink with a smile, then went for the guard hut. Hidden by the shadows of trees, he ran crouching across some grass. He got to the guard hut unseen and stealthily sneaked up on the lone guard inside. Giving him no chance to fight back, Alexander got him in a tight sleeper hold from behind. The guard struggled and kicked off the side, slamming Alexander into the hut, but he did not let go; he held him hard, and after a short while the guard passed out. Alexander laid the unconscious man on the floor and pressed a button on the wall which raised the exit barrier. He left the guard hut to wave his friends over.

As Cole pulled up next to Alexander, there were shouts directed at them from three guards who had run out from the main building.

'Floor it!' Said Alexander as he got in the back of the car.

Cole put his foot down and they sped out of the base, leaving the soldiers behind. Overtaking cars and running through red lights, Cole got as far away from the base as possible as fast as he could.

'Head to the rear of my apartment, Cole, there's a place we can hide the car if they come looking for us,' said Alexander. Cole nodded.

'Looks like our phones have signal again now we're out of that place,' said Jessica who had her phone in her hand.

Alexander got his own phone out and dialled a number. 'Hello, Zhang, where are you? Are you okay? Really? Okay, well, head back to the apartment. You can fill us in there, we'll be arriving shortly. No problem see you soon,' he said and ended the call.

'Everything cool?' Asked Jessica.

'We weren't the only ones to have an eventful night. Zhang and Steve were in a bit of trouble earlier, but they're okay now. They'll fill us in when we get back,' said Alexander, then dialled another number. 'Hello, it's Alexander. can you put His Lordship on, please? He's asleep? Where is he asleep? Why does that man never listen to what I say? I suppose he'll never change. Okay, well, make sure you get him to phone me as soon as he wakes. Any trouble you ring me straight away. Thank you, bye.' He ended the call.

'Let me guess, Bishop Christopher has left the apartment,' said Jessica.

'Yes, he's gone back to his own house. He has never been a man to be told what to do. Especially when others believe it's for his best interests. Only he knows what's best for his own interests, so he'll just do as he pleases regardless of any danger surrounding him. He must believe himself to be invincible or something.' Alexander sat back in his seat.

'Bless him, he's cute.' Jessica smiled.

'We're here. Where shall I park the car?' Asked Cole.

'Just inside that open garage there,' said Alexander, pointing out of the front window.

'I see it. I tell you what, after all this I could do with a hot cuppa,' said Cole, and pulled into the garage.

'Same here. I'll treat you both to one in the apartment,' said Jessica.

'Deal.' Cole turned off the car engine.

* * *

As it was the early hours of the morning, James West got around a lot of the base with no confrontation. After a long search, he finally found his son Aaron asleep on a worn sofa in the TV room. Two soldiers asleep on another sofa were guarding him, so West had to creep into the room and move silently to get his son.

'Aaron, Aaron, it's Daddy.' West pushed his arms under Aaron to pick him up.

'Dad,' said Aaron, confused and half asleep with his eyes still closed.

'Yes, son, it's me. I need you to be quiet,' whispered West, and picked up his son.

'Where were you, Dad?' Asked Aaron, clinging on to his father.

'Shh, just be quiet for a second, son.' Aaron complied.

West carried him to the door and left the TV room without waking either of the two soldiers. Once outside the room, he put Aaron down on his feet to walk.

'I'm sorry to wake you, son, but we need to leave. I need you to keep up with me, do you understand?' Said West while Aaron wiped the sleep from his eyes.

'Where are we going?' Asked Aaron.

'Just out of here, now let's move, stay close to me,' said West; he held Aaron's hand and they jogged down the corridor.

The pair made their way down corridor after corridor until they reached a thick grey metal door. West entered the access code into the keypad and the door opened, allowing him and his son to enter. They stepped inside then froze immediately; three men were just leaving. All three stopped and looked at West and Aaron.

West put himself between the men and his son, then shuffled Aaron behind him and held him there.

'Major West, I thought you were detained?' Said one of the men who was being supported on his feet by the other two.

'Georgie, I was, but fortunately people came to their senses and let me out. What's happened?' Asked West, seeing that Georgie was injured.

'Infiltrate and extract failed badly. Me, Marson, and the drivers are the only survivors of two teams. My ribs are broken. We're heading to medical now.'

'I knew it was a mistake, Lieutenant General Winters sending you. He should have listened to me... he doesn't know what he's dealing with. What happened?'

'We're not sure exactly what happened to Bravo team, but we were ambushed by... well, we don't know what we were ambushed by, but bullets had no effect and we didn't stand a chance,' said Georgie, just as an alarm sounded around the base.

'You were let out, you say?' Asked Marson.

'Look, I'm leaving with my son, getting him to safety. Then I will find out where these things are coming from and eliminate them. Winters has ordered I step down, but I can't, I must help stop what's coming. Something bad is coming and Winters just doesn't see it. Marson, I need you to come with me – your skills are invaluable, and it'll give you the chance to avenge your team. Georgie, you get to medical and when Winters asks why I was able to leave, you tell him I had a gun and threatened to kill you.' There was a very tense, silent moment before Marson nodded his head in agreement and took his arm from around Georgie.

'Go kill them bastards for the others, brother,' said Georgie to Marson, and pushed him towards West.

'Will you be okay from here?' Asked Marson.

'Yeah, I'm good, just get going.'

'Okay, but take it easy. Major West, we can use the van we just came back in, it's still running,' said Marson, and he, West and Aaron ran for a Royal Mail van.

Once all three were inside, Marson spun the van around and drove straight for the underground tunnel that led to the public roads outside the base.

CHAPTER 18

After spending most of the early hours discussing what they had gone through the previous night, they woke up in the afternoon and went to visit Bishop Smith at Oliver's church. They went on foot and arrived at the church to find the doors open. Inside, the church was full of people, some sitting and others standing, either praying or demanding time with the bishop.

Alexander led them through the crowd of people and pushed his way to the front where Bishop Smith was trying to calm down a group of individuals screaming at him.

'Why is this happening? Is God punishing us?' Shouted a woman.

'Please can we all just calm down. I don't have any answers, but we must all have faith that God will guide us through these troubling times,' said the bishop, who spotted Alexander approaching him.

'Last night I watched as my wife repeatedly smashed her face into our bathroom mirror. She was too strong to be stopped... she flung me to the floor with ease, then slit her own wrists in front of me. Tell me why God would allow this to happen? We must be being punished,' shouted a man covered in dried blood seated on the front pew.

'What's going on, Your Lordship?' Asked Alexander over all the voices.

'Don't you know?' Said the bishop, and Alexander shook his head. 'Last night, all around London, hundreds, maybe thousands of people have been affected. So many have died.'

'It's the virus – it's turning people insane,' came a voice from near the back of the hall.

'Virus, ha, it's no virus. The vile things my five-year-old daughter was saying to me would never have come from her. She doesn't even know half the words she used. It was a demon in her. I looked in her eyes and I could see it, pure evil. It was not my daughter,' said a woman standing next to the bishop, pointing to a little girl sitting on the floor. 'There she is now perfectly normal, as if nothing had happened. I brought her here this morning and His Lordship exorcised the monster that was in her.'

Everyone started chatting amongst themselves, debating the woman's story and examining the daughter.

'Alexander, come with me. Everyone, I will be back shortly. I must speak with my friends. Please make yourselves comfortable. There is juice and water by the front doors. And please keep calm... I'm sure the worst is over.' Bishop Smith led Alexander and the others through to the back of the church and into a large room with a wooden desk and chairs. 'Sorry, there are only a few seats, but make yourselves at home.'

Jessica, Zhang and Steven sat down, leaving Alexander, Cole and Bear to stand. The bishop sat at the desk.

'So, what news do you bring?' Asked Bishop Smith, both his palms flat on the desk.

'I won't bore you with all the details from last night, but from everything that has happened to us all, we have a theory. We believe it's likely something terrible will happen at Wembley Stadium on Saturday during the final,' said Alexander. He slowly paced around the room with his hands in his pockets.

'Go on,' said the bishop, sitting back with his arms crossed.

'You said before that certain rituals or mass death can summon an astral projection of Satan.'

'Yes, supposedly – not his entire being, only his spirit or energy can be brought forth.'

'And if this astral projection was to encounter the black orb?'

'Satan would regain his full power, break his bonds to hell and walk the Earth whole.'

'That's what I feared. Steven found evidence that the same people who now have the orb are also interested in Wembley Stadium. For what reason we don't really know, but we believe it could be because they intend to murder all the eighty thousand football fans in attendance. Assuming we are correct, the orb will be somewhere in Wembley Stadium when the match begins. We must find it and get it out of there before any harm is done,' said Alexander.

'I've never known you to be wrong on a hunch, Alexander, so I'd urge you to act on this. You have full support from the church. Anything you need from me, just ask,' replied the bishop.

'Thank you, My Lord, that means a lot. Okay, so we'll go ahead as though our theory is fact. We will need to find the black orb and protect every person there from any potential threats. Your Lordship, we'll need entry into Wembley Stadium and unquestionable security clearance at the highest level to allow free roaming of every section of the building.'

'Done,' replied Bishop Smith without hesitation.

'We will need more eyes around the stadium. Can you supply us with more bodies, so we can cover the entire stadium?'

'Consider it done. I'll make some phone calls.'

'Great, we will need priests on site too in case people become possessed. Jessica, when your father gets in touch let him know of our plans and get him to meet us at Wembley Stadium on Saturday. I'll give you an exact time and meeting point closer to the time. Cole, go to the game as planned with your girlfriend, but keep a close lookout for anything suspicious. Notify me of anything out of the ordinary and leave immediately if you see trouble. Bear, Zhang, you're with me. Steven, I need you to investigate Demantay Florence's involvement in all this, and to find Father Hall. There must be a way to trace where he has been taken – if there is you're the best person to find it.'

'What's happened to Father Hall?' Asked Bishop Smith, sounding concerned.

'We don't know. He was taken from us when we were locked up on an army base. It's a long story, but we won't stop until he's found,' said Alexander, throwing the red-enveloped letter Zhang had found in Vincent's bedroom to the bishop. 'The handwriting in that letter belongs to Demantay Florence. I'd recognise it anywhere. The day I catch up with him again, I will not let him live.'

'Surely that's unnecessary, Alexander,' said the bishop. Alexander was already on his way out of the room, ignoring any objection and preventing any debate of his decision.

* * *

After stepping into his home, West let go of Aaron's hand so he could reunite with his aunt. Lesa dropped to her knees as Aaron ran to her with arms open; he slammed into her, and they squeezed each other in a long affectionate hug. Tears ran down her face and a fresh wave of guilt hit West deep in his stomach.

'Aaron, I'm so sorry, are you okay? Did they hurt you?' Said Lesa.

'I'm fine, it was Dad who told that woman to take me, he did it to keep me safe,' said Aaron.

'You were safe with me, they should never have taken you. You're back now, that's all that matters,' said Lesa, wiping the tears from her face. She stood up.

'Lesa, I know I promised to speak to you and explain what's going on, but I just can't do it yet. There are things going on that you won't understand, but once it is all dealt with, I swear I will explain everything to you.'

'No, James, you need to speak to me now. I need to know what happened to Charlotte. You are avoiding me, which is only convincing me it was you who killed her.'

'Lesa, please, I will tell you everything once this is all over. Just get yourself and Aaron to his grandparents' as we discussed. Don't stop for anything, and when I get in touch with Jessica, I'll get her to come to you too.'

'James, don't do this. I need to know why my sister is dead,' said Lesa, weeping uncontrollably.

'I'm sorry. I love you, Aaron. Goodbye, Lesa,' said West. He left the house, closing the door behind him, and got into the car where Marson was waiting. 'Everything okay, sir?' Asked Marson.

'No,' said West, then dialled a number from his mobile. After a short silence, the phone connected. 'Jess, it's Dad.'

'Dad, thank God, are you okay? Did you find Aaron?'

'I'm okay, thanks, and yes, I got Aaron. He's with Lesa now, en route to your grandparents'. You need to get yourself over there and help them look after your brother.'

'Dad, no, I want to help you and Alexander.'

'This isn't up for debate, Jessica, you're going to your grandparents'. Head there now and I'll call later to check up on you, do you hear me?'

'I hear you, Dad.' Jessica sounded annoyed.

'Good! Now, what does Alexander have planned? Did he mention anything to you?'

'Yes, he said to tell you to meet him before the game on Saturday, on the corner of Royal Route, at Wembley Stadium. He'll be in a minibus. He believes the orb will be somewhere in the stadium. Shall I let him know I've passed on the message?' Asked Jessica.

'Yes, please. Thanks, Jess. Now get to your brother. I'll speak to you later. Love you.'

'I love you too, Dad.' They both hung up.

* * *

Looking in his side mirror Alexander spotted James West park the Royal Mail van he and another man had arrived in. They both walked up to Alexander's minibus, which was parked on the corner of Royal Route and Wembley Hill Road. Bear slid the side door open for them to enter.

'Thank you,' said West, and shut the door behind them after letting the other man step in and take a seat first. 'Everyone, this is Marson, one of the best of Her Majesty's Special Forces. He and another are the only two survivors from the failed locate and extract of the orb Winters sent in. Not only does he know first-hand what we are up against, but he's also determined to achieve some form of justice for his murdered teammates,' said West.

'If it's justice you want it's Winters you should be going after. He sent you and your team into that building knowing full well the orb wasn't there, and that you'd most likely die trying to find it. I can't prove it yet, but I know he's involved in this... his complete uninterest in our input and our unlawful detainment says it all. But welcome, Marson, and you too, West. My two associates back there with you are Zhang and Bear. We believe the orb is inside the stadium in the hands of the Natas. They are the ones who stole it from the army. I hope we're wrong and they're not here, but if they are, we're all in for a serious fight,' said Alexander from the driver's seat, switching on the ignition as he spoke.

The weather could not have been any better for a football final: not a single cloud in the sky and twenty-nine degrees, with a blissful breeze cooling all it touched. Thousands were already surrounding the stadium, and thousands more were still travelling in. The area was heaving with fans of the two big teams, and on top of the usual police presence was a heavy military deployment. Army vehicles were parked all around the stadium, and armed soldiers were patrolling the area. Yet despite this the atmosphere was still happy and vibrant.

The minibus made its way down Royal Route heading towards the West Service Gate. Trying his best not to mow down the crowds of supporters, Alexander blasted the horn and shouted out of the window for people to move. Neither worked very well, and when someone did acknowledge him, it was only to give him the middle finger.

'Imbeciles!' He shouted, hitting the horn again.

'So, what's in the box?' West asked Zhang, who had a long and slim aluminium case on her lap.

Zhang popped open the two clips and revealed the contents: guns, and a black nylon case with Velcro straps.

'Surely those aren't getting through security?' Said West.

'We have our own people all over the stadium, including security. We won't even be checked – they know we have the weapons. It was a difficult decision to bring them. There're so many innocent people we'll be putting at risk, but if hellspawn show up, there's no other way we can put them down.'

'You mean those black creatures? The major told me they're hellspawn too. Do you actually believe that?' Asked Marson.

'Do you think they could have come from anywhere else other than hell? I mean, look at them,' said Zhang.

'I see what you mean. Well, I definitely want in. If I can kill just one, it will be a little payback for my fallen team,' said Marson.

The minibus approached the West Service Gate, and Alexander looked for the two security men he'd been instructed to check in with.

'There, they're our guys. Only two wearing shades,' said Alexander, and pointed to the two security men waving in his minibus.

Zhang clipped the box shut again and the vehicle slowly made its way into the stadium. Alexander gave a thumbs up to the security guards; they returned the gesture, then pointed ahead for Alexander to continue further inside.

There were three men ahead, one of whom was Mario, Bishop Smith's head of security. Alexander pulled the van up next to them and knocked off the engine.

'We're here. Follow me,' said Alexander, and got out of the minibus.

The rest followed and huddled around Mario and his two men.

'Good to see you again, Mario,' said Alexander, and they shook hands.

'You too, Alexander. Please, all of you, come with me. We have a room where we can discuss the plan of action for today.' Mario led the group through some double doors into a long corridor.

After passing only a few doors, they entered a room that looked to be an unused changing room. Wooden benches lined the walls and a big fold-out table stood in the centre. On top of the table were ID passes and the schematics of Wembley Stadium, drawn on which were the positions and patrol paths of all Mario's men. Everyone stood in a circle around the table except Zhang, who went to place the box of weapons down on a bench, then popped open the lid and sat next to it.

'This shows where all my men are positioned and what patrol paths they are taking around the stadium. They've all been issued with a photograph of the orb, so they know what they're looking for. They've also all been instructed to keep an eye out for anything out of the ordinary and to challenge any individuals acting or coming across strangely. If the Natas are here, we'll find them. All my men are dressed casually so to identify them they'll be wearing sunglasses and earpieces in their left ears,' said Mario, pointing at the schematics.

Alexander studied the patrol paths and spotted two areas not covered by Mario's men. 'Can you get any men to patrol here and here?' He asked, showing the areas of concern.

'No problem. You two, get to those areas asap. Any trouble, radio through. Decide between yourselves who's on which point, it makes no odds,' Mario ordered, and the two men nodded and left.

'Do you have any more earpieces for us, so we can stay in contact?' Asked Alexander.

'I only have two left, I'm afraid, but you're welcome to have them.' Mario got them out of his pocket.

'Great, two will be fine – we'll just split into two groups. I'll take one and have West with me. Zhang, you take the other and have Bear and Marson with you.' Alexander and Mario gave them the earpieces.

'You'll all need these passes too. They have the highest security level and these will grant you access to any part of the stadium, unquestioned,' said Mario, and gave out ID passes on lanyards to everyone in the room from the pile on the table.

As each of them put on their passes, Zhang handed out the weapons. She and Bear had an Uzi and a silenced pistol each, while West and Marson had a silenced pistol each. Zhang picked up the nylon case and handed it to Alexander, who put his arm through the straps and threw it over his shoulder, resting it on his back.

'What are you packing in there?' Asked West.

'My sword,' said Alexander.

'Looks more like you're carrying a trumpet or something with that case,' said West.

'That's what I was going for, an instrument case. Still out of place in here, but better than people thinking I'm carrying a weapon.'

'I think that's everything. What areas will you be searching?' Asked Mario.

'All the public restricted areas. If West and I go clockwise around the stadium, Zhang, Bear and Marson can go anticlockwise until we meet up on the other side. If we see anyone somewhere they shouldn't be or acting anxious or out of the ordinary we confront them and make sure they aren't carrying the orb, or have any knowledge of its whereabouts,' said Alexander to everyone in the room.

'Good plan. While you do that, I'll do rounds checking up on all my men and keep an eye out on the crowds, see if I spot anything fishy. No doubt if the orb is here one of us will find it soon enough, and if we do we need to radio the location through to everyone. Same goes for any trouble – radio through for backup straight away – and if there's a single threat to the public, make it known and we'll assess whether we need to evacuate,' said Mario, and walked to the door.

'Understood. Let's get on with it then. Good luck, everyone,' said Alexander, and everyone got up to leave.

* * *

Oliver was slowly beginning to wake up and come out of the drug-induced coma state. He was in total darkness, sitting in some type of chair. His head and eyes rolled as he gained more awareness. He was not bound, gagged or blindfolded, but the drugs still flowing through his system prevented any major movement or coherent speech. There were muffled voices from people in close proximity, but he was unable to decipher what was being said, or who was talking. Then directly in front of him two doors were opened outwards, letting in the light he needed to see where he was, which seemed to be the back of a transit van. His eyes hurt, and he had to squint, but once they adjusted to the sudden light, he saw it was Vedrana who had opened the doors, and she was now attaching a ramp to the back of the van. Behind her were Demantay and another man; both stood watching as she got in with Oliver, walked behind him and unlocked the brakes to the wheelchair he was sitting in. She wheeled him out of the van, down the ramp and over to Demantay and the other man.

Still lacking any real control, Oliver sat looking at the pair with his head slumped to one side and drool leaking uncontrollably from his mouth.

'I'm impressed. You got us in with no questions asked,' the stranger said to Demantay.

'You'd be surprised the things I'm capable of, Buckley. My part is done – now be sure not to fail on your part like last time,' said Demantay.

'Don't worry, I won't,' the man called Buckley replied sharply.

Oliver tried to speak, but he only mumbled, and more drool came out his mouth.

'What do you think he's trying to say?' Said Buckley, laughing.

'It doesn't matter. He'll be dead soon anyway,' said Demantay. He removed the ramps from the van, threw them inside, closed the doors and walked towards the driver's door. 'You know where I'll be once this is done.'

As soon as Demantay had driven away, Vedrana pushed Oliver's wheelchair towards Buckley.

'Follow me. Demantay sorted us an empty room just through here.' Buckley led them forward into a corridor.

At the fifth door on the right, they entered a room that was clearly a cleaner's room. The room was relatively large and full of mops, buckets, and towel bins. Vedrana closed the door behind them and pushed Oliver, who was now starting to feel the drugs wear off a bit, further inside.

'What are you going to do to me?' Oliver managed to ask.

'Us? We're not going to do anything to you,' said Buckley.

'Then who?' Asked Oliver.

'You'll find out soon enough, so sit tight. Unless you'd prefer to leave? Go on, try to walk, we won't stop you.' Buckley laughed.

A double knock on the door shut Buckley up and both captors became tense. The door was pushed open and a man with an earpiece in his ear walked in.

Buckley and Vedrana ignored the man and acted as though they were in conversation. Oliver tried to ask the man for help, but only managed to blow a raspberry.

'What are you three doing in here?' Asked the man, pushing the door shut behind him.

'Oh, sorry, we took a wrong turn. We're trying to find the disabled toilets,' Buckley said.

'Well, they're not in here, and there aren't any nearby. So please tell me how you ended up here?'

'We were having a meet and greet with the players and got lost looking for the loo. We'll just head back. We won't be a bother.' Buckley edged closer to the man.

'I will have to report this,' said the man, reaching for the button on his earpiece.

'Now there's no need for that, my friend, just point us in the right direction,' said Buckley, getting himself into arm's reach of the man. He punched him full force in the throat.

The man stumbled back and gasped for air. Buckley quickly got behind him, gripped his head with his left arm, snapped his neck and dropped his body to the floor. Acting fast, Vedrana emptied a towel bin of dirty towels. Buckley picked up the dead man and placed him inside the bin, and Vedrana covered the body with towels.

'They know we're here,' said Buckley.

'Does that change anything?' Asked Vedrana.

'No,' said Buckley, 'just makes it more fun.'

'What happens now?' Asked Vedrana.

Buckley looked at his watch. 'It's still thirty minutes till kick off – that's when we'll make our move. Demantay will electronically hack and disrupt the exit barriers, making it difficult for anyone to exit the stadium, and we will activate the orb to draw in the hellspawn. The Natas here with us will then be notified to take up their positions around the stadium. We will all then cut an inverted cross into our foreheads with our blades. This will allow the hellspawn to tell us apart, so we can witness the massacre. Demantay's link in the army will order his men to surround the stadium and stall everyone trying to escape. Two RAF pilots will fire at the stadium and cause more terror. All the death and fear will speed up the summoning of Satan. Until all this begins we must remain undiscovered, so we need to move from here. There'll be a patrol sent to find out where this guy has disappeared to.'

The pair left the room with Oliver.

* * *

Jessica had no issues at the ticket office; the queue moved fast, and they accepted her identification just as Steven had said they would. She had got Steven to work his magic and provide her with a ticket for the final, completely going against her father's orders. *I've been involved in all this from the beginning. I'm not hiding away now. They need as many people as they can get in that stadium looking for the orb. I'll mingle in with the crowd and they won't even know I'm there. If I spot it, I'll let Alexander know, then I'll get my arse out. They'll appreciate an extra set of eyes, even if they don't know it yet*. She tucked the ticket into her back pocket and paced around the outside of the stadium, looking for her designated entry gate.

'Jessica!'

She turned to see a hand waving above the heads of the crowd. It was Cole with a young woman. Waving back, Jessica smiled and went over to the couple.

'Hey, Jess. I didn't know you'd be here too,' said Cole.

'Yeah, I thought I'd come and be an extra set of eyes. The stadium is huge and the orb could be anywhere, if it is in fact inside,' said Jessica, smiling at Tasha who looked confused.

'Do the others know you're here?' Asked Cole.

'Of course,' replied Jessica with what she knew was an unconvincing grin.

'Okay then. This is Tasha. Tasha, meet Jessica... she was involved in the incident at the cafe I told you about.' They shook hands and exchanged pleasantries.

'Are you on your way to the ticket office?' Asked Cole.

'No, I'm trying to find Gate F,' said Jessica after looking at her ticket.

'That's fortunate – we're heading to Gate G. We can find them together,' suggested Cole.

'Sounds good. I'm sure it's over this way.' Jessica continued in the direction she was going before she'd stopped.

'After you then, Jess,' said Cole, and took Tasha by her hand. 'You know, we have two empty seats next to us if you'd like to sit with us, Jess? Tash's friend and her boyfriend couldn't make it so one's yours if you wish. We even have their tickets here if you need to show anyone.'

'I wouldn't want to intrude... you two should go ahead without me.'

'Don't be silly, it's fine, come with us. Football isn't my thing so if it gets too much at least we can get to know each other a little better,' said Tasha.

'I don't know... you really don't mind?' Said Jessica.

'Of course not, please come with us.' Tasha nudged Cole in his side.

'You're coming with us, that's final,' said Cole.

Jessica laughed and knew she had no choice but to give in. 'Okay, you've twisted my arm.'

The three continued walking, Jess and Cole keeping an eye open for the orb. Before too long they reached the gate and the queue was reasonable. They got in line and chatted until they were inside.

'If you girls want to carry on, I'll go grab us some food and drinks. Three hot dogs and three Cokes okay?' Said Cole.

'Yes, please,' said Tasha.

'Perfect,' said Jessica, and Cole nodded and disappeared into the crowd.

Walking with the flow of loud supporters, Jessica and Tasha followed the signs to their row and eventually found their seats. They were in a good position, about a quarter of the way up, midfield and close to the stairs.

'Great seats,' said Jessica.

'Yeah, we did well, didn't we?'

While they chatted, Jessica scoped the area for anything out of the ordinary, and for anyone that would recognise her, like her father, so she could stay out of sight. A few rows down she spotted a man who looked weirdly out of place. He was sweating and didn't look comfortable at all. Zoning out from what Tasha was saying, she focused her attention to the man, but then a young boy ran up to him and into his arms. The man was clearly the boy's father. Jessica guessed the man was probably uncomfortable because of some form of anxiety at being in a big crowd; she concluded he was not a threat.

Cole arrived with their refreshments and took a seat next to Tasha. 'Babe, I still can't believe I'm here. Thank you so much for doing this,' he said, and kissed her on the lips.

'Any time, gorgeous.' Tasha smiled.

'Guys, I'm going to go and find the toilet. I should have gone on my way in but didn't think.' Jessica had no intention of going to the toilet but would be on the lookout for the orb.

'Okay, don't be long – you don't want to miss kick-off,' said Cole.

'I won't, don't worry. I'll see you in a minute,' said Jessica, and left the couple.

The stadium roared with the booming voices of the crowd. Their singing and chants made the walls vibrate, and excitement spread like a contagion. It was clear the players would soon make their appearance to start the game.

Jessica had made it to the top of some stairs that led down to the front rows; she looked at the pitch and decided to go down for a closer look.

'Excuse me,' she repeated to each person she had to push past on the narrow stairs.

Once at the bottom she walked along the front row of seats, squeezing her way through, the whole time looking for anything or anyone suspicious. Nothing seemed out of place. Everything was normal, and she was thinking maybe they were wrong. Then she saw him. Oliver was slumped in a wheelchair at the end of the row on the other side of the barrier. He was very close to the pitch with a man and woman standing beside him. From what Jessica had seen of Jack Buckley on the news, she believed him to be this man. Trying not to look too panicked, she picked up her pace and headed towards them.

* * *

Alexander and James West were moving rapidly through rooms, checking inside them and questioning many people about their reasons for being there. Occasionally they had to show the pass given by Mario, but each time it was accepted without any issues. So far, they had come across nothing out of the ordinary. Alexander phoned Steven, who was hacked into the stadium's camera feeds. 'Have you found anything, Steve?'

'Nothing, everything looks good at the moment.'

'Okay. Keep looking and call me straight away if you spot anything.' Alexander hung up.

Before he had a chance to pocket his phone, a text message came through from Cole. He was inside as planned with Tasha, but had also picked up Jessica from outside the stadium.

'Jessica is here, did you know?' Said Alexander.

'My Jessica? I told her to go to her grandparents'. Are you sure?' Said West.

'According to Cole, she's with him now.' Alexander showed West the message.

'I specifically told her not to come here,' said West angrily.

'As did I. She'll be safe with Cole... if there's trouble he'll get her out.'

'I hope so. Where to next?' Asked West.

'Let's check on the players, they should still be in the changing room just down here.' Alexander led West down the hallway.

There was a security guard at the changing room door. Alexander approached the man and flashed his pass. 'Everything okay down here?'

'Yep, same old shit, different day. The players

will be out shortly. Do you mind standing to the side?' Said the security guard.

'No problem. So, nothing out of the ordinary, no one hanging around acting peculiar?'

'No, well, I don't think so. Is there something going on I should know about?' Asked the security guard, looking concerned.

'No, not at all, we're just making sure, can never be too careful. Keep up the good work, we're sorry to have bothered you,' said Alexander.

The players burst from the room. Alexander and West were pressed up against the wall, allowing the players to pass. As they did, Alexander looked through the flow of footballers at a woman directly in front of him at the other end of the corridor. He could not say why, but she gave him an odd feeling in his stomach, a gut feeling that something was off. She watched the players going by, then spotted Alexander looking at her. After staring back for a short while, she turned and walked away.

Alexander tapped West on the arm and pointed in the direction the woman had gone.

The pair battled through the players, then had a slow jog up the corridor to where the woman was walking. About fifty yards ahead of them they saw her turn down another corridor out of sight. Alexander ran; they were in pursuit.

The two men went for her full sprint, shouting for her to stop. She ignored them and barged passed a group of people as she ran.

'Stop her!' Shouted Alexander, but the group were caught too off guard to react.

They chased her for a few minutes, dodging and jumping over the obstacles she flung behind her in an attempt to slow them down. She darted into a room, slammed the door behind her and lodged it shut somehow.

'It's jammed,' said West, who tried the door first.

'Watch out.' Alexander stood back and booted the door open.

The woman was backing away from them as they came through the door. A broken broom was on the floor in front of her. She backed into a towel bin, toppling it and herself over. The towels and a body spilled out onto the floor. Kicking and screaming, the woman pushed the body away with her feet and tried desperately to get up. Alexander helped by grabbing her by her top and pulling her up while West inspected the body.

'Who are you and what are you doing here?' Asked Alexander, but the woman did not answer.

'This is one of Mario's men,' said West, and retrieved the earpiece from the corpse.

Alexander got the woman by her throat and slammed her against the wall. 'Who are you?' He squeezed her windpipe.

The woman tried to get Alexander's hand off her throat. Using both hands she fought against his grip, but he just gripped tighter until he spotted the ring on her finger: a gold ring embossed with a capital 'S'. He let go of her neck and ripped the ring from her finger. Leaving the woman where she was, Alexander walked away, inspecting the ring. West came up beside him and looked at it as well.

'S?' Asked West.

'Satan,' replied Alexander, and pressed his earpiece. 'Mario, it's Alexander. I have confirmation the Natas are here. Can you send a team down to the first cleaner's room on my patrol path?

We have a woman here who needs interrogating, and we've found the body of one of your men. It wasn't the woman who did it, though – there are definitely others in the stadium. Tell your men to look out for anyone wearing a gold ring with the letter S on it. Anyone connected to all this will be wearing this ring.'

'Alexander, you carry on ahead. I'll stay here till Mario's men come and I'll get whatever I can out of her till they arrive,' said West.

'I was going to suggest the same. If she gives you the location of the orb, contact me straight away. Thanks, James,' said Alexander, and patted him on the shoulder.

West clenched his fists, walked over to the woman and rolled up his sleeves.

Alexander left the room and returned to the tunnel that the players had used earlier. He walked towards the pitch at the midfield point, and a childhood dream of being a footballer reignited inside him. The sensation that went through him as he approached the pitch was surreal, and it caught him by surprise, but not as much as the smile he felt slowly creeping across his face. He walked out into the open and did a slow three-hundred-and-sixty-degree spin. He took in all his surroundings and for the first time in a long time let himself feel joy. West called him through his earpiece, and as quickly as the joy had filled him, it left.

'James.'

'She's a tough cookie, this one,' said West, a little out of breath.

'And has she given you anything?'

'Nothing. The only thing that came out of her mouth was that the Natas are here, and there are many of them. They are here to witness the rise of Satan.'

'Okay, well, keep trying to get us an exact location. The orb must be here, but it could be anywhere.'

'If she breaks I will let you know straight away. Out.'

Alexander pulled out his phone and rang Steven as he walked alongside the pitch. 'Steven, please say you've found something. I don't think we have much time,' said Alexander with a finger plugging his other ear.

'Nothing from the stadium, no, but our two RAF pilots have just disappeared off radar in a fighter jet. Strange thing is, they have raised no alarms. It's as if no one knows or it's been approved, I don't know,' said Steven, and, as if on cue, a Tornado jet flew over Alexander and the stadium.

'You hear that? That's a jet flying over... it must be them. Is there any way you can raise the alarm, claiming this is a rogue jet?' Asked Alexander.

'Give me a second.' Alexander heard frantic typing on Steven's keyboard. 'Right, I've sent an untraceable alert to the RAF's Quick Reaction Alert Station in Coningsby. If they take it seriously we should hopefully see them in around eight minutes.'

'Good work. Now find me something to go with here. I don't think we have much time,' Alexander repeated.

'It would help if I knew what to look for.'

The jet flew over again, and the sound of it roared through the stadium.

'Wait, is that...?' Said Steven.

'What? Where?' Replied Alexander, who was standing next to a linesman who looked at him like he shouldn't be there. Alexander backed away a bit.

'It's Jessica, and there's Father Hall... oh shit, it's him. The one that killed Rachel,' said Steven.

'Where, tell me where?' Alexander demanded loudly, and the linesman waved for security.

'They're at one of the corners. Father Hall is in a wheelchair and Jessica is standing directly behind him.'

Alexander looked at the corner opposite him on his half of the pitch: nothing. Then he looked at the far corner and, just as Steven said, there they were. Two security guards arrived next to Alexander; he didn't have time to explain, so he ran for the corner, straight onto the pitch. The security guards gave chase and the crowd started roaring at the sight of a man invading the pitch with his musical instrument bag bouncing off his back.

CHAPTER 19

Lieutenant General Winters stepped out of his escort vehicle onto one of Wembley Stadium's car parks. Four army trucks accompanied him, and the fifty soldiers in them jumped out onto the car park too. Leading the way, Winters walked towards the stadium with his eye on the circling jet above.

'Sergeant!' Called Winters to the male beside him.

'Yes, sir,' answered the sergeant, and got closer to him.

'Give the order to surround the stadium. I want every gate entrance covered. No one gets in or out. Pass the message to the others already patrolling the area and get them to surround it as well. Make sure everyone is on high alert... there is an imminent threat. Then wait for me to radio through more orders. Under no circumstance take orders from anyone else. Do you understand?'

'Understood, Lieutenant General, sir.' The sergeant gathered the soldiers together for a briefing.

The flashing headlights of a van just in front caught Lieutenant General Winters' attention. He walked over to the driver's side and the window came down.

'Demantay, I didn't expect to see you here,' said Winters, looking around to make sure no one was close enough to hear the conversation.

'I'll be leaving shortly. I just wanted to tell you in person that I have made your payment, and with a healthy bonus on top for your consistent good results. I expect you'll be giving us the same results now when it all begins,' said Demantay.

'You can be sure of it. The stadium is being surrounded as we speak. I won't be able to completely stop the flow of people leaving, but I will slow their escape as agreed. How will I know when it's begun?'

Demantay started his vehicle and gave Winters a sinister look and smile. 'When the screaming starts.'

Lieutenant General Winters backed away from the van as Demantay drove off, then headed towards the stadium to take up position.

* * *

'It's time,' said Buckley, and reached into his pocket.

Vedrana left his side and approached Oliver, her proximity bothering him. She reached under the wheelchair to a hidden space and pulled out the orb. Oliver grabbed her arm tightly and looked her sternly in the eye.

'Oh, nice of you to join us. We were worried you'd sleep through all the fun. Can't have you causing any trouble though,' said Vedrana, and reached deeper into the space under the wheelchair. She pulled out a syringe.

After placing the orb on Oliver's lap, she stood up, pulled his head to the side and plunged the syringe into his neck.

'Only a mild sedative to keep you under control. Wouldn't want you sleeping on us again,' said Vedrana with a wicked smile.

Buckley joined them and took the orb from Oliver's lap. 'Any last words? No? Good, I'm not one for speeches.' Buckley pulled a knife from his pocket.

'No!' Came a female voice Oliver recognised. Jessica jumped the barrier onto the pitch and ran towards them, but Buckley only smiled.

With no apparent remorse or hesitation, Buckley stabbed Oliver deep in his abdomen. It surprised him to find the sedative also had an anaesthetising effect and he barely noticed it.

'You bastard!' Shouted Jessica. 'Leave him alone!'

Vedrana successfully intercepted her. Buckley pushed the orb against the wound and covered it in Oliver's blood. The inscriptions on it lit up in bright red and heat radiated from it as the blood activated something inside.

Jessica fought to escape Vedrana, but she wasn't strong enough. Buckley smiled, turned away and threw the orb high into the air and onto the pitch. As the black orb left his fingers, someone rugby tackled him hard. Both slammed into the floor and skidded a few yards before the man started pounding Buckley's face with punches. Oliver realised it was Alexander. With each blow Buckley just smiled and laughed louder, even as his blood sprayed from his nose, cuts and lips. Like a madman, he laughed hysterically. 'You're too late. It's already begun.'

Alexander took the case from around his neck,

removed a sword and threw the case to the side. 'What's begun?' He shouted and pressed the sword into Buckley's throat.

A tremor in the ground was the only response, and it intensified.

Alexander kept the sword to Buckley's throat and turned his head to look at the playing field. Oliver did the same. The players were no longer competing; they were fighting to keep their balance as what felt like an earthquake threatened to throw them all to the floor. Then the ground broke away, almost dead centre of the pitch... a sinkhole, and it took two players with it. The crowd's screams spread faster than any ever had for a goal, but these were screams of terror, not joy. The sinkhole grew as more of the ground crumbled away and fell into it. The players fell as well. One by one the gaping hole consumed them. It ate away at half the pitch before stopping, leaving both ends and penalty areas untouched.

* * *

A whirlwind developed at the main entrance, and a black portal opened in the floor. Abaddon rose out of it and stood, huge and menacing. Bystanders watched as the surrounding soldiers opened fire at the archdemon without hesitation. They emptied their clips and screamed for reinforcements via radio.

The jet above zoomed across the sky and the pilots inside spotted Abaddon. They did a swift U-turn and flew back towards the stadium. Lieutenant General Winters watched their approach with a sly smile, then readied his radio to communicate with the soldiers surrounding the stadium.

The jet aligned with the stadium's main entrance and aimed for the archdemon. It fired a Brimstone missile directly at it, which soared through the air towards its target, skimmed the Bobby Moore statue outside, blew up the main entrance doors, but missed Abaddon.

People and rubble flew out in all directions as the explosion destroyed the entrance. The Bobby Moore statue was undamaged from the blast, but was now covered in dust and debris.

Abaddon flew off unscathed to another part of the stadium.

'This is Lieutenant General Winters. The stadium is now a quarantine zone. Infected are inside and we've contacted an unknown enemy. We are now on highest alert. Strictly only military can enter the stadium and civilians can only leave once it's clear they're not infected. Every individual must be inspected before being allowed to leave. That's an order. Weapons free. I repeat, weapons free.'

The stadium was completely encircled with soldiers and every entrance was blocked by a wall of them with guns at the ready. People began spilling out, and the soldier's shouts and demands to stop were ignored. After a few scare shots into the air and more shouting, the fans began to obey and slowed down, preventing a potential stampede. The soldiers allowed the crowds out in pairs, forming an orderly line around and away from the stadium. They inspected everyone for infection as they passed, yet the whole process still moved smoothly. Then there was another explosion from a Brimstone missile.

The crowds ran for their lives out of pure panic, and the soldiers struggled to keep them all under control.

* * *

Buckley's female accomplice looked interested only in the events in front of her, and she let go of Jessica and watched, transfixed. Jessica wasted no time and leapt for Oliver, who was trying to stand up from the wheelchair. 'It's okay, don't move, I'll get you out of here,' she said, pushing Oliver back into his seat before wheeling him away.

'What have you done?' Alexander turned his attention back to Buckley, who was still pinned under him.

'It doesn't matter, you're too late... there's nothing you can do now.' Buckley smiled and broke out into laughter.

Alexander wanted to cut his throat there and then, but contained himself. Then the air fell cold; a rumble developed deep within the ground and dark clouds appeared above, followed by a flock of loud squawking crows that covered the sky. People's screams were coming from everywhere as a stampede of terrified fans frantically tried to escape the stadium. But what concerned Alexander more were the sporadic explosions and gunshots outside. Overwhelmed by a gut-wrenching panic in the pit of his stomach, Alexander released Buckley and stood to face the sinkhole. Something was coming.

Buckley got to his feet and scampered away as fast as he could.

The rumble under Alexander's feet intensified, and he realised now what was causing it. Hellspawn. Hundreds of them. Ferocious roars were exploding out of the hole and he had no doubt it was them. He gripped his sword and readied himself for a battle he knew he could not win. One came out the hole, then another, then three more, followed by ten. The hellspawn scurried out the sinkhole at incredible speed. Their numbers became uncountable as they went for the thousands of people still inside the stadium.

Buckley's female accomplice walked forward with her arms outstretched, apparently mesmerised by the hideous creatures feasting on their helpless prey. She was smiling as one mounted her. It latched on to her head, taking the whole of it in its mouth, then ripped it from her torso. Her lifeless body collapsed to the floor, spilling a pool of warm, steaming blood onto the pitch.

Alexander's first challenger approached. Fast and with murderous intent, the hellspawn charged. Keeping his composure, Alexander stood completely still until the monster was nearly upon him. The hellspawn dived and Alexander ducked underneath it, swiped his sword up and cut the hellspawn in half at its abdomen. The two halves broke out into spasms on the floor, involuntary convulsions like a chicken without a head. Alexander stepped up to this now pitiful-looking creature and removed its head.

Two more emerged from the abyss, but Alexander was quick to react. He gave them no chance to get the better of him and decapitated the two in swift succession. But now he was surrounded by four. They had encircled him whilst he fought and now they stood growling, salivating drool at the thought of the kill.

'Shit!' Said Alexander and clenched his fist around his sword.

* * *

Jessica was leading them to a staff exit at the opposite side of the pitch; she pushed Oliver past the front of the goalpost and the wheelchair hit a huge crack in the ground. Oliver went flying onto the pitch and Jessica toppled over. Both crashed hard and they had to help one another up. Oliver was able to stand and put pressure on his wound. It hurt and was bleeding, but he believed it had pierced nothing vital. He also felt like he had come around from the drug substantially. 'Are you okay?' He asked, holding Jessica's arm.

'I'm alright. Sorry, I didn't see the crack,' said Jessica.

'It's okay, don't worry. I feel like I can probably walk now,' said Oliver, then fell back to the ground.

'Of course you can. Here, let me help you,' said Jessica, and picked him up, then supported him to help him stand, 'we need to get out of here.'

It was only at that moment that Oliver realised where he was and what was happening around him. His heart stopped. The only thing missing from this picture was Satan's astral projection, the dark shadow that emerged from the hole in his dream – the one that killed Jessica and her baby. 'Jessica, you need to run,' he said.

'What do you mean? I'm not leaving you, we'll get out of here together,' she replied.

'You don't understand, you need to go now! I dreamt this, you were...'

'I was what?' Asked Jessica.

'Do you trust me?' Said Oliver, staring at her sternly.

'I do.'

'Then run, don't look back – just run. Don't worry about me, I'll be fine,' Oliver said, applying pressure to his stab wound.

'I can't just leave you.'

'Jessica, go! Get out of here!' Oliver demanded, and he pushed her away from him.

She looked at him, ready to resist and put up a fight, but then her face cleared. She put her faith in him, gave him her trust, nodded and ran away.

Now feeling a lot more like his normal self, Oliver walked towards the sinkhole. His senses were coming back to him and his hands began glowing as he felt the presence of all the hellspawn around him. It was not their presence that worried him, though; it was the feeling of terror he experienced in all his dreams that had him on edge. Something was climbing out of that hole and he could feel it. Satan. He stood a few yards from the edge and waited, ignoring all the sounds of gunshots, explosions and hellspawn. He was going to face this evil no matter the outcome. He would not allow it to kill Jessica and her baby like it had in his dream.

An arm reached out over the side and gripped onto the pitch. The arm was pure black and looked like liquid black tar encased in an invisible skin. Black smoke was swirling around it as if its temperature was scorching, and it held on while the other arm reached out and grabbed the pitch. Together the arms pulled and out from the pit emerged the horror that had tormented Oliver's dreams for weeks: Satan. This black smoky astral projection of Satan would stop at nothing to encounter the black orb which would free his real body from hell and allow him to walk the Earth. Oliver knew he had to prevent this.

Oliver watched, horror-struck, as the lanky black figure climbed out the sinkhole directly in front of him. It took all his willpower not to run away.

Alexander's scream stole his attention. He was fighting hellspawn and one had slashed his back. Oliver reached out his glowing hand and with his power snapped the necks of two of the hellspawn. He ran closer to help defeat the others. Alexander took out one himself, decapitating the monster, and Oliver broke the back of another.

'The orb. We need to get it out of here!' Shouted Alexander and pointed to it.

Oliver agreed and left Alexander to defeat the remaining hellspawn around him alone. He ran to the orb, pulled down his sleeves to cover his hands and attempted to lift it. The ball was impossible to lift and roasting hot in temperature.

'It won't budge. It's like it has a mind of its own... this thing was light as a feather for Buckley and Vedrana. I think it wants to be reunited with Satan. We'll never get it out of here,' said Oliver.

Alexander finished off the hellspawn around him and ran to Oliver. 'Then we must fight and stop them reuniting.'

They both turned to face Satan's astral projection. The sinister-looking thing had a smirk across its face that said nothing would get in its way.

Alexander went first and charged for it with his sword pointed out to his side. It casually walked towards him as if the threat did not exist, grinning the whole time. Alexander struck, swiping through its torso. The sword passed through the body without leaving so much as a scratch. There was no physical body to connect with, but the thing somehow made itself physical enough to slap Alexander like he was a mere mosquito. He went flying backwards and hit the ground with such force it knocked him unconscious.

Oliver felt no presence within it like he did with the hellspawn, so his power was useless, but he wondered whether actual physical contact would make a difference. He mustered up all his courage and walked towards it. As he walked, he looked up and saw meteors falling from the sky - balls of fire, hundreds of them, all coming for the stadium. The apocalyptic scene made him think this might be the end of the world.

He picked up his pace and stretched his hands out in front of him, ready to grab this inhuman thing. But it grabbed Oliver first, clutched him by the throat and lifted him into the air. Oliver clutched his hands frantically at its arms, hoping his power would put it down somehow, but it did not. Its grip just got tighter around his throat.

'There is no point in fighting, priest, I cannot be stopped. I will destroy this world, and once I am done, I will come back for you. You will sing that little secret of yours to me in the hope of mercy, but there will be none,' said Satan as he looked deep into Oliver's eyes. He opened his mouth and pulled Oliver closer.

Oliver felt a tug inside him, a weird, uncomfortable sensation from deep within. Satan was taking his soul. Oliver tried to fight, but it was futile. His life force was leaving him, he could feel it. He felt cold and overwhelmed. The black liquid-like substance from the creature's hand spread around Oliver's face and body; like water it ran into every orifice, consuming him. Oliver's mouth was open, trying to scream, but something muted his vocal cords. No sound left him as a ball of white light came up through his throat and left out of his mouth to float in the air.

* * *

One of the falling fireballs landed right behind Oliver. It disappeared with a blinding flash of white light, but no explosion. It was Michael; he stood armoured with a sword in each hand and his wings folded behind his back.

'Just one of many souls hell shall receive tonight, Michael. Maybe the next will be yours?' Said Satan after tossing the ball of light into the pit and dropping Oliver's body.

'Push them back!' Shouted Michael to the dozens of angels that now surrounded the remainder of the pitch.

The angels, though outnumbered ten to one, battled with the swarm of hellspawn. The two forces clashed with one another ferociously as reinforcements for both sides came flooding in, an army of angels from the heavens and a legion of hellspawn from the pit. In the middle of it all were petrified humans, whose rational minds could not comprehend the supernatural events taking place. They could not see the angels, just flashes of light, but their panic and fear were clear as they tried to escape.

Along the arch and the rooftop of the stadium stood angels holding golden bows. Michael raised his sword and they all raised their bows in unison; they drew their bowstrings and a solid gold arrow appeared nocked on each. Michael pointed his sword to the astral projection and they loosed the arrows. Countless crows flew in and acted as a shield, sacrificing themselves to block or deflect the hail of arrows from their target. The hellspawn quickly blocked any that managed to slip through on the ground. Only one got close enough to scrape the face of Satan. It left a scratch that seeped black ooze.

Satan's anger could be felt in the air; he clenched his fists and charged forward to take out Michael, the only thing between him and the black orb.

* * *

The exit gates and the corridors leading up to them were crammed with fans trying to escape. Marson, Zhang and Bear had pushed right through up to a gate. They saw that the problem was the exit barriers; they were locked so people were having to jump over them to get outside. The soldiers were also holding people back, forcing them to leave calmly.

Marson rushed ahead and barged his way through the tightly packed crowd. He jumped the barrier and got outside to assess the situation. A monster unlike the so-called hellspawn he had seen flew down from above and landed by his side. The sight of the creature was enough to make his knees buckle, but he managed to stand firm and looked up to watch the jet aligning itself on their position.

The jet got closer and Marson knew they were now in its firing range. He went to run, but then out of nowhere, a second jet swooped in from the side and crossed its flight path. It sent the attacking jet away from the stadium and two more jets flew in chasing after it.

The three new jets were Typhoons on quick reaction alert from Coningsby. Marson had seen them before and had never felt so relieved.

The monster gave a roar of rage and burst into the air after the interfering jets.

'I think we should get back inside,' said Zhang.

'Agreed,' said Bear, and Marson nodded in agreement.

'Zhang!' Shouted a female voice from behind them.

The three of them turned to see a girl fighting her way out of the stadium; she was waving her hand in the air, so they would spot her.

'Jessica, what are you doing here?' Asked Zhang as Jessica made her way to them.

'I'll tell you later... right now Father Hall needs your help. He's in there on the pitch and there's this thing that climbed out of the hole.'

'Hole?' Said Bear.

'The pitch, it fell away. There's a massive hole and hellspawn are coming out of it. Please, you must go help him,' said Jessica, panic-stricken and distraught.

'Sounds dangerous. If we go back in there's a chance we won't come back out,' said Bear more to Zhang and Marson than Jessica.

'Those monsters are the reason I'm here. Even if I only take down one, it'll be worth it. I'm going back in. Where is this Father Hall?' Said Marson.

'Go back in here and turn right, head for the goalposts down the second staircase on the left. He's directly in front of them on the pitch.'

'This is a little above our pay grade, Zhang, wouldn't you say?' Said Bear.

'Yes, I would,' said Zhang, looking thoughtful.

'Getting paid as well as we are is pointless if we're dead,' said Bear.

'I know, but then again if this really is the end of the world it'll be pretty pointless then, too,' said Zhang.

'You can't seriously be worried about money right now?' Said Jessica.

'Screw the money. This is bigger than money. We need to get back in there and into the fight.'

'I was hoping you'd say that,' said Bear.

'Yes!' Said Jessica.

'Okay, let's do this. If your friend Father Hall needs help, we probably don't have much time,' said Marson eagerly.

'After you then, Marson. Jessica, you stay here, or even better, head back to the church. I'll get everyone to regroup there if we survive this,' said Zhang, and let Marson lead the way back into the stadium.

'Ok, sure, I'll head to the church. Thank you all.'

They jumped the barrier again, and as they got to the other side, screams broke out ahead of them.

'They're infected!' Shouted several people from within the crowd.

Marson and the others looked through the crowd to see people being attacked by other people who looked crazed and were clearly possessed, with black liquid seeping out of their faces.

'Oh no,' said Zhang, and a commotion stirred behind them outside.

'Go, go, go!' Shouted a soldier, and a squad of five jumped the barrier and stormed ahead towards the possessed.

'Get back, they're infected!' Shouted another soldier, and all five opened fire.

Shooting in bursts, they hit every intended target – head shots to each one. But for everyone they put down, two more people would turn. They were quickly outnumbered, with an easy twenty possessed people now surrounding them.

'We need to stay out of this... there's no stopping them,' said Marson as even louder screams broke out around them and people started to stampede.

'Agreed. There are priests here to deal with this anyway. Quick, follow me into the stand, down these steps,' said Zhang; they followed her down to the pitch.

* * *

Cole had Tasha gripped firmly by the wrist as he struggled with the crowd to get out of the stadium. They were still in the stands on the narrow stairs, pushing their way up to get out.

People were climbing over the seats to escape, and Cole had to contain himself from lashing out as they barged ahead with total disregard for others.

'This is madness – people are getting crushed,' shouted Tasha, holding on to Cole for dear life.

'We'll be okay, just don't let go of me.'

After a very tight squeeze at the bottleneck of the stand exit they made it out and looked around for the nearest gate exit. There was the sound of a bottle smashing, followed by harrowing shrieks of several people in pain. Cole turned; people had been set on fire. Two men just ahead of him had petrol bombs and were at that moment lighting another three.

To Cole's utter disbelief, he recognised one of the men: Jack Buckley. Buckley's head was dripping with blood from a freshly cut cross shape that had been carved into it. It made him look even more insane than usual and, with the flickering flames from the petrol bombs, no one dared approach.

The pair launched petrol bombs into the crowd in opposite directions. The bottles smashed, and the flames spread like wildfire from person to person.

Cole instinctively went for Buckley, but Tasha pulled hard and held him back.

'What are you doing?' She asked.

'I've got to stop them.'

'Are you mad? They'll kill you. No, we're going this way, we can get out just down here.'

'Tash.'

'I mean it, Damien, we're getting the fuck out of here. It's not your job to deal with them – you're CID, not armed response.'

'I am a detective constable, and that man is the main suspect in one of my cases. It's my duty to bring him in. Look, take my phone and call my contact Alexander. He's in here somewhere with people that can help. Tell him I've found Buckley and to get here asap.' Cole handed her his mobile.

'Please, Damien, don't do this.'

'I love you,' said Cole, blowing her a kiss and turning to run towards Buckley.

Tasha cried, but still did as she was asked and ran in the opposite direction.

Not having a real plan in place, Cole hesitated at first, but then spotted a bin up against a wall. He went for it, and luckily it was not attached to the floor. He lifted it above his head, aimed for the two attackers and threw it as hard as he could. It smashed into them, and the last petrol bomb slipped from Buckley's hands and shattered at the feet of his accomplice. The flames wrapped around his lower body and quickly spread their way upwards. He flapped around screaming in agony, speeding up its growth as the fire burned away at his clothing through to his flesh.

Buckley looked furious. He pulled out his knife and waved it for everyone to see.

It was not the first time Cole had faced a knife-wielding madman; he kept his cool and focused on remembering his self-defence training.

'You should have got out while you had a chance, because now I'm going to kill you!' Cried Buckley, and ran for Cole.

Cole had his weight on his back leg and both his fists up in front like a boxer. When Buckley was close enough, Cole grabbed his arm and used his own weight against him to spin him around and trip him up. Buckley fell to the floor and slid, but kept hold of the knife. Cole stepped back and prepared for another advance. Buckley sprung to his feet and waved the knife around frantically at the spectators surrounding them, keeping them at a distance. He went for Cole again, but this time with more caution. They circled each other, eyes locked, both waiting for the other to slip up, so they could take advantage. Buckley jabbed forward with the knife, testing Cole's reflexes; they were sharp, but he was forced backwards. A few more jabs and Cole went back further, placing him right over the smouldering body of Buckley's accomplice.

'Put the knife down, Jack. You will not get away with what you've done... all you're doing is making things worse for yourself.'

'You know my name? I should have guessed. None of these scared little sheep would have challenged me. Off-duty cop, I take it?' Said Buckley.

'CID,' replied Cole.

'Oh, CID, how lovely for you. I'm guessing you've had to find the balls to come up to me because I'm a prime suspect in your case? Well, here I am!' Buckley lunged forward with the knife.

Cole jumped back and tripped on the body

on the floor, sending him down hard on his arse. Buckley was on top of him in no time, two hands on his knife pressing down towards Cole's chest. Cole reached forward and grabbed Buckley's forearms. It was difficult, but he held Buckley back. Buckley pushed down with all his strength, but Cole was stronger. With a loud outburst, Cole began pushing Buckley off.

'Not so fast,' said Buckley, and kneed Cole in the balls.

Cole's resistance gave way and the knife slipped into his shoulder. There was no pain to begin with, but Cole was filled with rage, nonetheless. He punched Buckley in the side of the face, a blow so shattering he lost a tooth, and a considerable amount of blood. Cole hit him again, this time knocking him off. Buckley crumbled to the floor in agony beside Cole. Cole rolled away and got himself up, then removed the knife as he got to his feet and chucked it out of reach. People from the crowd now gathered around to back him up, forming a mob intent on justice.

Buckley laughed to himself on the floor and spat a ball of blood in Cole's direction. 'You're all fools. None of you are leaving here alive.'

'Get up, Jack, I'm taking you in,' said Cole.

'I'd like to see you try. Do you hear that? That's the sound of cleansing,' said Buckley as screams and shouts rose from the stands.

The noise escalated, and people started to stampede again.

'Run, they're coming, run!' Shouted a voice from within the crowd.

From the stand exits, hellspawn burst into the corridor. First half a dozen, then a dozen, then two dozen. Everyone was screaming, and

Buckley took advantage of the distraction to get away. He got up off the floor, picked up his knife, and blended in with the running crowd to escape.

'Tasha,' said Cole to himself, running after her in the direction she had gone earlier.

The hellspawn were killing everyone, and Cole had to run right past as they ripped people apart. Being only a couple of yards away, he had to be careful not to get killed himself. He barged his way through the crowds and lied to himself that it was not living people he was running over. Then he saw the first person turn. Their head and arms convulsed from side to side, they drooled black liquid and their eyes went jet black.

'Fuck!' Said Cole and ran faster to reach Tasha.

CHAPTER 20

Warmth filled the air. A continuous gentle breeze brushed past, and upon it rode the delightful songs of birds from afar. Overwhelming scents of fresh grass and bloomed flowers pervaded everywhere. Then Oliver heard his voice. A voice not composed of words but expressed through visions, emotions and feelings. The voice rippled through him like waves hitting cliffs along the shore, and its charge vibrated his very soul. It was God's voice, and Oliver had never felt more at peace. Flashes and images flickered across Oliver's mind. He watched in full clarity the past events of his life. The family he grew up with, his friends, and then there was Jessica. Though this vision of Jessica was not one from his past, it was a moment that had never occurred. A moment that was either yet to happen, or could now never happen, Oliver did not know. They were in his church and Jessica was standing with both arms behind her back, hiding something. After focusing more, Oliver could see that behind her was a shy child. She pulled him out for Oliver to see and the boy cowered, tucking himself into her side. Then the boy who was around four years of age, recognised Oliver and his whole attitude changed. He ran towards him, excited, with his arms outstretched for a hug. The boy, Oliver somehow knew, was Jessica's unborn baby. So, he embraced him and hugged the boy with nothing but love, like that of a father.

Then God spoke. The child was no ordinary child; he was born with a purpose. A purpose that would decide the fate of the Earth.

Oliver watched the child's life unfold before his eyes. His first day at school, his first kiss, his eighteenth birthday party, his first love, his grandparents' deaths, the birth of his children, his own death, and then beyond his death. Now in heaven after living a human life on Earth, Jessica's child stood as a new archangel with Michael, Gabriel and Raphael. His whole life he had viewed the world through the eyes of a human being. He lived and died as one, truly believed he was human. However, he was really an archangel secretly sent by God to live with and assess humans and their actions with a totally unbiased viewpoint. This was unknown to him his entire life, as it was to every human on the planet, but now he stood as a judge after his death. He, and he alone, faced a decision as to whether life on Earth should continue for a while longer, or whether it should end and the second coming of Jesus should commence.

No other archangel could make this decision because they had not lived as a human. None of them but this new archangel could truly understand how precious and fragile life on Earth was. He stood forward, looked up at God and gave his verdict. As he did, the vision disappeared. The images in Oliver's mind turned to smoke and fizzled away to leave him in nothing but darkness. The air became cold and he felt considerably numb. He had no heartbeat, and the warmth from the usual movement of blood in his veins did not exist. He was an empty vessel, with only just enough feeling to be able to move. He sat up and he ached all over; his entire being burned and felt fearfully fragile.

Oliver knew he was dead, and he knew this must be hell. Nowhere else could produce such a repulsive stench - a smell so intense it took great effort to breathe; it singed his nostrils and brought bile to his mouth. It opened lacerations in his throat, causing him to heave and add blood to the pool of sick beside him. A splitting headache erupted dead centre of his forehead. He leant forward and let out a gurgling groan of discomfort, then threw up again, twice as much as before.

After a few minutes of pure misery, he calmed himself somewhat. He rocked back and forth, gasping for air that was not available, but his vomiting halted. He wiped the tears from his eyes, and for the first time took in his surroundings. He was in his childhood bedroom. The only difference was that every square yard was charred, as though a fierce fire had ripped straight through the room. He looked around in disbelief, but it was undoubtedly the room he had grown up in.

He stood and leant against the wardrobe for support. It was fragile, and a large charred piece fell from the door. What it revealed took Oliver by surprise. Instead of wood, the wardrobe seemed to be made of a red lava substance, held in place by some invisible membrane. It radiated warmth and after looking closer it looked to be moving inside as liquid magma would. The charred outer layer was just a skin, a cover that disguised the true body of the room.

Oliver tore away at different parts: the bed frame, the floor, the wall and even the charred toys on the floor. Under it all was the encased lava – the whole room and all its contents were made of lava.

'This is crazy,' said Oliver, and pushed his palm against this strange phenomenon.

It was soft, like play dough. The imprint left behind faded slowly and Oliver stared, puzzled.

Three loud bangs on the bedroom door broke Oliver from his thoughts and petrified him.

'Oliver, get downstairs, your dinner's ready.' It was a female voice.

'Mum,' said Oliver under his breath, confused, 'it can't be.'

He shook off the fear and went to open the bedroom door, which although made of lava, still opened like a door. He stepped outside the bizarre room and entered the hallway at the top of the stairs of his childhood home. Everything was exactly as it had been, even down to the large cheese plant outside his parents' bedroom. But all was charred like everything else he had encountered so far.

'Oliver, I won't tell you again,' shouted the female voice from downstairs.

Standing on the top step, Oliver peered down the dark burnt-out staircase and felt too terrified to go down. His mother was alive and well, he knew, so whatever it was calling him, with her voice, he did not know.

'Don't make me come up there, young man.'

Oliver took a step back and as he did, he noticed the darkness at the bottom of the stairs expand. It spread like a fog, thickening as it moved until he could see nothing down there at all, just a black hole.

The bottom step creaked, followed by the second... the slow footsteps of whatever was lurking below.

Oliver stepped back again, but this time his foot sank into the floor. He threw his arms backwards, looking for the wall to stop him falling, but they sank into the wall like his foot, up to the elbows. As if trapping him on purpose, the floor and wall solidified around his three limbs and held him in place.

'Bollocks,' said Oliver, and tried to free himself.

The third step creaked, and the darkness was working its way up the walls.

'What have I told you about cursing, young man,' said the voice, but this time it sounded nothing like his mother; it sounded non-human.

Oliver's eyes were fixed on the staircase; he desperately tried to escape, but nothing would budge. He pushed hard with his free leg, trying to get himself out, but it was no good. He was trapped and completely at the mercy of whatever was coming up the stairs. Oliver felt fear in the place he had always felt safe – and he knew this was what the voice wanted. Fear far worse than any he had felt in his worst nightmares: this was true terror. Expecting something to jump out the darkness Oliver braced himself, but to his surprise nothing happened. No movement, no noise, nothing. Then Oliver was released. The restraints holding him let go and he was able to stand. He looked back as the places that had restrained him moulded themselves back to their original form. After dusting himself off, Oliver peered into the darkness and waited for something to step out. Nothing did. He let his eyes focus, then squinted to see what was standing just yards away in the dark.

Eight blood-red eyes appeared, all different sizes, floating and blinking in the darkness. Oliver's gaze was locked on them; whatever owned them must have been easily ten to fifteen feet tall. Its legs stepped out, gigantic spider legs as thick as a lamppost. They crept out from the darkness and the body of a jet-black spider emerged and towered over Oliver, its fangs completely exposed and dripping with what looked like blood.

It was Oliver's worst fear; he was petrified of spiders and all his instincts right now were screaming at him to run, so he did. He sprinted back to his childhood bedroom, booted the door open and slammed it shut behind him. He backed up to a corner in the room and prayed that the door would hold.

With a bang one of the spider's legs burst through the door. It took a grip and ripped the door from its hinges. The massive creature crawled inside, stretching its creepy long legs around the room.

Oliver froze, frightened stiff, and watched as this hideous monster filled most of the room. Its back legs were on the wall and ceiling behind it, whilst all its other legs were on the floor and side walls. Like a helpless fly trapped in a web, Oliver was stuck with no escape. It moved in closer, and its heavy breathing gave it a spring when it crawled.

He backed himself as tight as he could into the corner and cowered with his arms in front of his face.

Looking through his arms, Oliver watched the spider's front legs go up in the air, like it was going to pounce, but all it did was open its mouth. It opened abnormally wide and inside something was moving. It looked like a large ball of wet hair soaked in blood. The hairball began to protrude from the spider's mouth and spin as it extended out on a long rigid arm. The arm reached out with the hairball at its tip, and moved towards Oliver's face, dripping blood everywhere as it did. To Oliver's horror it became clear what this hairball was. It was a human head, and once the head spun face up and the hair fell to its natural position, the person whose head this was could be made out.

'Mum?' Said Oliver, looking at the bloodied head in front of him.

Her eyes and mouth shot open, and the head tilted to the side looking back at him in shock.

'What is this?' Asked Oliver, confused.

'Oliver, my boy. Where have you been? Why did you leave me for so long?' Said his mother's head, and tears of blood ran down her face.

'Leave you? I didn't leave you, you aren't my mother. I don't know what you are, but my mother is alive.'

'You left me, alone and lost in the dark.'

'I pursued my career, which my real mother was happy for me to do.'

'I'm dead, Oliver. I killed myself because of you.'

'No! Lies... my mother would never do that,' shouted Oliver.

'It's true, and it's your fault. After you left, I knew only despair and emptiness,' said the head, and more blood poured from her eyes.

'You are not my mother; my mother is alive!' Shouted Oliver.

The head started laughing and spinning uncontrollably. The long rigid arm holding it retreated into the spider's mouth and it swallowed the head whole. The spider sprang to life; it leapt for Oliver, catching him off guard, and bit down deep into his shoulder.

Screaming, Oliver grabbed the spider's body and attempted to push it off. The spider jerked to his touch. Oliver's hands lit up and scorched the spider's underbelly. Shrieking, the spider convulsed; its legs buckled and turned in on themselves. Oliver let go and the spider backed away unsteadily. Its shaking legs could not support it properly; it fell to the floor and rolled onto its back. After one last ear-piercing shriek its legs curled up and it died on the bedroom floor, letting out one last long breath as it did.

The room started to shake violently, making the ceiling crumble and the walls split. The floor broke away, and Oliver fell through it. Everything went black and he smashed against surfaces he could not see before landing on his back on a solid floor. He covered his face to protect it from the falling debris and coughed as he inhaled thick dust. His back had taken a hard blow, so he was a little winded, but other than that there were no major injuries. He curled up, catching his breath, and after a few moments struggled back to his feet. A strong gust of wind blew around him, and the dust in it forced him to cover his eyes. Once it calmed, Oliver looked around in shock: he was inside his church.

The main entrance doors burst open and Jessica came running in. 'Oliver, you're alive,' she shouted, and ran towards him with her red rain jacket flapping behind her.

'Jessica, but how?' Said Oliver.

'Wait till I tell the others you're here, they'll never believe me. We all saw your body... it's impossible,' she said, and wrapped her arms around him.

'It's so good to see you, Jessica. I was sure I was dead. Is this real?' Said Oliver, uncertain.

'Real? Of course, it's real,' said Jessica.

'But?'

Jessica cut him off, grabbed his face and kissed him on the lips.

Oliver immediately pushed her away. 'You're not Jessica,' he said, and held her at arm's length.

'I know you want me, I see the way you look at me,' said Jessica, and tried to kiss him again.

Oliver averted his head and shook it, rejecting her.

'Don't you find me attractive?'

'Get away,' said Oliver, and looked in her eyes; they were jet black. He jumped back.

'What's wrong? Is my body not good enough for you?' She asked and took off her jacket. Underneath she wore black lace lingerie. She started caressing her breasts, pushing them together and lifting them up.

Now Oliver truly knew it wasn't Jessica; she was clearly not pregnant. Her stomach was flat and firm with no signs of pregnancy.

'Don't you want to fuck me? I'll let you fuck me all over this church,' said the imposter, and stroked her hand down her stomach and into her knickers.

341

'Stay back!' Shouted Oliver.

Ignoring him, she walked towards him, moaning in pleasure as she did.

Oliver ran away from her. There was the crack of a whip and his legs were pulled from under him. He hit the floor and rolled onto his back to see a whip wrapped around his legs. Clutching it at the other end was the thing impersonating Jessica.

'Where do you think you're going?' Asked the imposter, no longer in Jessica's voice but its own deeper and more menacing snarl.

Her skin started bubbling and parts of her body began unnaturally bulging out. Using her free hand, she reached into her mouth, took hold of her cheek and began ripping her face off like a mask. Underneath was slime and hideous discoloured flesh. The leather-like skin bodysuit was completely ripped away from the true body underneath, and the disgusting malformed archdemon stood there holding up its disguise. It flung the skin suit to the side and with both hands started reeling Oliver in. As it did, it belched and spewed a mouthful of green bile on the floor. It burned like it was acid and gave off a putrid smell which filled the entire church.

Oliver rolled onto his front and tried to grab onto anything as it dragged him across the floor.

The archdemon vomited again, and this time a much larger amount of bile was expelled from it. It melted a hole in the floor and the souls the monster had trapped reached out of it, trying to escape the cesspit they were confined to.

'No point fighting it, little worm, you're mine now,' said the archdemon, grinning with a rotten and toothless mouth.

There was nothing Oliver could do. As he neared the hole, he was filled with panic at the thought of being trapped by this monster for all eternity.

There was a huge smash; the walls on one side of the church came tumbling down as something burst through them.

'Why do you continue to pester me, Darius? You know I will just return,' said the archdemon, pausing.

'Because the look on your disgusting face every time I take you down fills me with endless joy,' said the being, and picked up a large piece of wood that had broken off one of the pews on his landing. Using it like a spear, he threw it with blistering speed straight through the demon's chest. It hit the archdemon so hard it took it off its feet and shot it to the back of the church, pinning it to the wall. The being called Darius ran and jumped onto its shoulders, gripped its head and pulled it clean off, then tossed it into the hole it had created for Oliver. Its body turned to dust, and Darius landed on the floor.

Oliver was still lying on the floor, catching his breath. Darius walked over to him and gave him a hand to his feet. 'Are you alright?' He asked.

'I am now, thank you. I'm Oliver.' Oliver shook his hand.

'Darius. Not to be rude, but I must go. Satan's hounds will be upon me shortly. They are never far behind,' said Darius, and turned to leave the building.

'Hounds?' Said Oliver, following him.

'Yes, four to be precise. Like werewolves, but bigger and fiercer. All they do is hunt. Any straying soul that's not in its designated chamber, they'll sniff out and tear to shreds. I know this because they've done it to me countless times. This is the longest I've avoided them, so they must be close.'

'But the way you took out that thing... surely you can beat them?'

'Unfortunately, no. In this place they are invincible. They will eventually catch up and rip me apart again. Then I'll wake back in the torture chamber Satan has specifically set up for me. I'll endure vast lengths of time in unbearable pain before getting my opportunity to break free and run again. A vicious, twisted cycle all built for Satan's amusement.'

'Is your escape purposely a part of this cycle? I mean, do you think Satan lets you escape so the hounds can get you?'

'Undoubtedly. Which is why I slaughter as many of his archdemons as possible whilst I'm free. They just reanimate elsewhere, but it brings me great joy taking them down. I've taken that archdemon down three times now. So instead of the hunt filling me with fear, it fills me with incentive... incentive to kill more archdemons each time before being caught. It has been my only salvation here.'

'Sounds awful. So, I guess this is my chamber. That would explain the surroundings, and the spider, because of my phobia.'

'If this is where you awoke when you first got here, then yes, this is your chamber. Every soul here has one, and each is specific to the torment of that soul.'

'I see. Well, if I've got to choose between spider or werewolf, I'll choose werewolf any day,' said Oliver, and the bite on his shoulder throbbed as he opened the church doors to leave with Darius.

Outside were not the streets of London, but a vast open landscape covered with hills, caves, lava rivers and enormous boulders. The sky was tinted red, hellspawn prowled the area, and black clouds engulfed in lightning dotted the horizon, the bolts of which stretched out for miles, scorching the land.

'This is insane,' said Oliver as he took in the alien surroundings.

'Indeed. Insanity knows no bounds here. You can't see them, but all over are hidden passageways, just like this one we've come through, all leading to other chambers. Inside each one are all kinds of different horrors, different times, different environments, different evil. Avoid entering any other chambers at all costs,' said Darius, and began walking.

Oliver looked behind at the church doors as they closed. The passageway had no door or outline that could be seen. It was just a large rock. No hint a passageway existed there at all. 'That's incredible,' he said.

'You won't be saying that when you sit down for a moment to yourself and end up falling through a church wall,' said Darius with a little laugh.

Oliver chuckled too, acknowledging that Darius had in fact just done that before rescuing him.

'So, what now?' Asked Oliver, walking behind Darius.

'We keep moving. Be under no illusion, this momentary safety will not last. Already the hellspawn around us have picked up our scent.' Darius pointed forward.

The heads of four hellspawn some distance away all turned to face in their direction.

'Shouldn't we head the other way?' Asked

Oliver, confused as to why Darius had not changed his path.

'It makes no difference which way we go. They are everywhere.' Darius continued to walk forward.

Oliver did not say another word; his current situation had really hit home. He was doomed.

It wasn't long till the hellspawn were upon them; Oliver's hands lit up, but he hid them behind his back as Darius made quick work of them. Even in a pack of four they were no match for him. He broke them one by one and threw their mangled bodies in a pile on the floor.

'How do you do that? How are you so strong?' Asked Oliver, amazed.

'I'm a soldier of heaven, an angel of God. Satan may have tricked and trapped me here, but much of my strength is still with me, even though he removed my wings and orb of strength.'

Far in the distance something caught Oliver's eye. It looked like a giant red-and-black umbilical cord, reaching from the ground to as far as the eye could see above. The cord-like structure moved like a writhing snake in the sky.

'What is that?' Asked Oliver, pointing.

'That is Satan's link to his astral projection. Because he can't walk the Earth in the flesh, he sends a projection of himself there instead. It's half his strength, but still very capable. It's what took me out. What you see there is coming out of Satan himself and reaching way up through a portal into Earth. At the other end is his astral projection.'

Oliver's gut instincts kicked in as he recalled the black shadow he had fought before arriving in hell. 'That's what killed me, too. It's up there now, killing more people. We've got to do something – we must stop him.'

'I'm sorry, but that is impossible. We wouldn't get anywhere near Satan before the whole of hell's armies were unleashed on us. A pointless effort.'

'I can't tell you how I know but something in my gut is telling me that's where we should be heading.'

Darius ignored Oliver and continued to walk in a different direction.

'Do you know of the black orb?' Asked Oliver, and Darius stopped in his tracks. 'If you do, then you should know it is up there right now, and that is why Satan is there. I died trying to stop him reaching it... others are dying as we speak.'

'It can't be,' said Darius.

'A black ball, covered in red writing with the ability to change its own attributes. Almost like it's alive. Sound familiar?' Asked Oliver.

'If this is true, then there is a war taking place right now. My brothers and sisters would not sit idly by as Satan took to escaping hell,' said Darius.

'You are right, they are not sitting idly by. Before Satan killed me hundreds of angels were shooting down like meteors from the sky.'

In the moment of silence, as Darius pondered, a fearsome howl sounded. Both shot their heads around to see four massive hellhounds sniffing at the air several hundred yards away.

'Oh no!'

'Run!' Shouted Darius.

The hounds darted for them, their prey now in sight.

'What are we going to do? We can't outrun them,' Oliver gasped while running the fastest he had ever run.

'There's only one thing we can do. Follow me,' said Darius, and headed for a large rock.

After reaching it, Darius frantically felt around it. It didn't take long for him to find a passageway: an odd edge was its only giveaway. Darius wasted no time and pushed it open.

'Didn't you say to avoid these at all costs?' Asked Oliver.

'Yes, unless the hounds are on your tail. Get in!' Said Darius, dragging Oliver inside and closing the entrance behind them.

For a split second there was darkness, but then Darius opened a door, and there was light. They stepped out onto a street and looked back to see they had come through a grocery store.

'*Épicerie,*' Oliver read from the store's overhead sign.

'So, we're in someone's memory of France,' said Darius, assessing the dozens of slow-walking, non-conscious people around them.

'You speak French?' Asked Oliver.

'*Je parle toutes les langues,*' replied Darius, and began walking down the street.

Oliver looked again at the zombie-like people around them, but as Darius didn't see them as a threat he just cautiously walked on by.

'Who are these people? Do they know we're here?' Asked Oliver.

'They don't even know they are here. They don't exist... they are just from the memory of the soul that belongs here,' said Darius.

'I see.'

'We must get out of here. There's usually more than one way in and out of these places. It's just finding them that's the issue. Let's move along this street, try all the doors and look for anything that looks odd, misshapen or out of place.'

They made their way down the street, trying every door on their way, but they were all locked. The street had an eerie, ghost-town feel to it. It felt empty, dead. Everything looked grey: the buildings, the sky, even the clothes on the people.

'I don't like it here, Darius. I'm getting a real bad feeling,' said Oliver, but Darius did not hear him.

They came to a crossroads, and Oliver went to inspect a signpost on one of the corners. 'Caen... Caen. I've heard of this place. This is a city in Normandy.'

Then they both heard it... the heart-stopping sound of oncoming World War Two bombers, hundreds of them.

The ghost-like people in the streets burst into life, screaming and shouting at the top of their lungs, and running, seemingly, for their lives. Their numbers multiplied as dozens more ran into the streets from the buildings.

Oliver's first instinct was to try one of the doors that had just opened, but for him it was locked. 'What do we do?' He asked, yanking the sealed door.

'Go back, back to the grocery store,' said Darius.

'But the hounds...' said Oliver as the first heavy bombers went over their heads and began releasing their payloads.

The pair looked up wide-eyed as the bombs fell linearly from the aircraft all over the city.

'Now!' Shouted Darius running away as explosions erupted around them.

They struggled to push through the now dense crowd on the streets. Fortunately, the flow of the stampede was going in their direction, but it was difficult to see.

'Where is it?' Shouted Darius as a massive explosion blew up behind him.

The blast sent him and many others hurtling through the air. Rubble came crashing down from above, fires broke out and more explosions battered the area, moving the very ground and buildings around them.

'I can't see it,' shouted Oliver as another explosion boomed and rang in his ears.

Dazed, Oliver froze, holding his head. Hearing nothing but the ringing in his ears, he watched as the street ahead became engulfed in fire. The explosions were happening frequently and were tearing down the street towards them. There was a hard tug on his arm; it was Darius, shouting and pointing. The grocery store was just three shops ahead. They put their heads down and charged for it side by side, batting off flying debris with their hands and arms. Each shock wave from the blasts rippled through their spiritual bodies, many times nearly taking them off their feet. Fire was all around them and the heat was scorching to their faces as it burst out from the buildings.

'We're not going to make it!' Shouted Oliver.

'Yes, we are!' Screamed Darius, using all his strength to barge past the crowd. He dragged Oliver to the store's entrance and ripped it open, just as a bomb hit the street they were on. It blew them straight through the passageway and out to the other side. They slammed onto the solid sandy ground and skidded across it before coming to a halt. Covered in soot and rubble, they looked up to see the hellhounds surrounded them.

Oliver dropped his face into the ground, feeling defeated, while Darius struggled to his feet, battered and bruised, clearly prepared to fight.

One hound stood up on its hind legs, reaching a height of around thirty feet. It snarled at Darius and with its man-like arm whacked him out the way; Oliver thought it looked more interested in him.

The huge, muscly black beast reached down and picked Oliver up off the ground. It brought him to its nostrils and sniffed him deeply. The hound snarled again, this time more viciously, and slavered at the mouth.

Oliver's hands felt warm and tingly; he recognised immediately what this meant and quickly grabbed the hound's man-like hand, which was firmly gripped around him. The hound's expression changed dramatically to one of fear. Its mouth closed, its eyes widened, and its ears dropped from Oliver's touch.

The hound staggered backwards before crumbling to the floor in what looked to be utter agony. It yelped loudly – was it asking for help from the other hounds? None intervened... *are they shocked*? Now on its back the hound desperately tossed Oliver away, then quickly got up and scurried back to the others.

The other three hounds looked ready to attack; on all fours, they raised their backs and hackles in a position to pounce with bared teeth. All three moved in for the kill, while the injured one stayed back. Fast, smoothly and in unison they darted for Oliver, who was already back on his feet and moving away.

Darius shot in from the side and smashed into two of the hounds, hurtling them off their course. The third picked up its pace; it looked eager to rip Oliver apart. Its jaw snapped open and closed as it neared him. Once Oliver was in reach, it lunged for him with its mouth wide open, ready to sink its massive teeth into him.

Oliver anticipated the attack and quickly dropped to the ground. The hound went over him, then with reactions he did not know he had, Oliver instinctively grabbed its tail. It dragged him along, but he managed to keep his grip and cling with both hands. The hound bucked like a horse, trying to shake Oliver off, but he had far too good a grip of its furry tail. The hound cried out and it took the attention of the other hounds from Darius. They turned and ran for Oliver again, disregarding Darius as any sort of threat. Side by side, they moved faster than any land animal on Earth, their enormous, muscular legs helping them to cover huge lengths per stride. Yet although fast, they were not fast enough. The hound held by Oliver crumpled up like a spider brought to the flame. Its limbs twisted and snapped as its body folded up like paper. Oliver felt its essence slipping away, and though Darius had said this fate should have been impossible, it let out one last thunderous howl before it imploded and vanished with a flash and an almighty bang.

The black clouds that had been in the distance now gathered above them and were wildly spitting out bolts of lightning, like plasma filaments in a plasma globe. They struck the ground and tore across it, leaving black trails of burnt rock and stone. The ground beneath them rumbled and seemed on the verge of ripping apart.

Terrified, the remaining three hounds turned and fled, while Darius took Oliver by the arm and ran in the other direction.

'What is happening?' Asked Oliver loudly.

'I have no idea,' Darius shouted over the deafening crackle of electricity.

The pair had to duck and weave to avoid being fried. They ran for open space, away from the abnormal storm, and managed to get some distance away from the black clouds. Lightning was still striking around them, but far less intense and less frequent.

'What now?' Asked Oliver.

'We head for Satan. What you just did to that hound was impossible – they are indestructible. Maybe you can do the impossible and stop Satan too. It's worth a try.' Darius pointed to the astral projection link in the sky, just a few miles away.

'That's more like it.' Oliver smiled, and both picked up their pace.

CHAPTER 21

Torn-apart bodies covered the stadium. Blood ran through the stands, and the black orb reacted to all of it. It had generated a visible force field around itself and the script inscribed on it was pulsing bright red.

The hellspawn had gone on a merciless rampage and killed as many as they could before the angels had gained control. The hellspawn could no longer get any further than the pitch as the angels had the sinkhole encircled and were letting nothing through their lines. However, there were some hellspawn still wreaking havoc in and around the stadium that had escaped before the angels took control.

* * *

Alexander awoke dazed and confused. Marson was at his side; he helped him to his feet and shot any hellspawn that got too close.

'Father... where's Father Hall?' Asked Alexander.

'I was going to ask you the same question. Jessica is outside, Zhang and Bear are there, that's all I know,' said Marson, pointing to the pair killing hellspawn and possessed in the stands.

Alexander looked around for Oliver but among the chaos it was difficult. Bright lights were flashing all over the stadium, like the camera flashes from a large crowd at a concert. These flashes were concentrated around the sinkhole where there were also thick clouds of black ash.

'There... I think I see him.' Alexander pointed to a body face down on the ground. They ran to the body; it was Oliver. All the colour had gone from his face, and after a quick check Alexander found no pulse.

'Is he alive?' Asked Marson.

Alexander put his face in his hands and could not reply. He closed his eyes, took a deep breath and blocked out all the surrounding noise. He needed a moment to collect his thoughts. Then a comforting hand was placed on his shoulder.

'We need to get his body out of here,' said Alexander, and stood to see an angel before him. 'My God.'

'Not God: Michael,' said Michael.

The whole battle scene unfolded before his eyes. The bright balls of light all around him became visible as angels and the true extent of the situation hit home, so much so that his legs buckled, and he fell to his knees. He could see there was an endless flood of hellspawn trying to escape the sinkhole, and the angels were just about holding them at bay.

A single tear escaped him as the sheer beauty and horror of it all overwhelmed him. Then he filled with rage. He got to his feet and looked around for his sword.

Marson had picked up Oliver's body and was calling to Alexander to follow him.

'I'm not done here. Take his body to Bishop Christopher at the church. The others know where it is, they'll take you,' said Alexander.

'But what about you?' Asked Marson.

'Don't worry about me, I'll see you all back at the church. Now go,' Alexander said sternly.

Marson nodded and walked away with Oliver's body towards Zhang and Bear, shooting any hellspawn that crossed his path as he did so.

Alexander turned back to face Michael who was, to his utter disbelief, offering him one of his swords. Without any exchange of words, Alexander accepted the sword and gave it a few test swings. Its balance and weight were crafted to perfection; no weapon had ever felt so magnificent in his hands. It gave him hope; it filled his body with motivation and an energy that made him feel he could take on the world.

'This is incredible,' said Alexander to Michael.

'Only weapons forged in heaven and infused with eternal light can destroy this presence of Satan. That's why your sword was useless. If you still wish to help, take it and stay by my side. If not, leave it and escape with your friends. You have already done more than ever expected so do not feel obliged in any way,' said Michael.

'I'll stay,' said Alexander, and Michael bowed his head.

Satan's astral projection had been caged by seven long gold spears. Seven angels had pinned the spears into the ground around it, creating a pyramid-like prison cell, trapping it inside.

'It's over, Satan. Close your portal and pull back your minions,' Michael demanded as he walked around the golden cage.

'You above all should know me better than that, Michael,' said Satan, and closed his eyes.

* * *

Michael continued to demand his retreat, but Satan was no longer listening. He had shifted his spiritual presence to the battle above with Abaddon and the fighter jets. Abaddon had taken down two of the Typhoons pursuing Luke and Vincent and was now on course to take down the third. The rogue pilots had ignored the Typhoon pilot's warning shots and instructions to land. It was now the only jet left of three, so the Typhoon pilot had been given permission to shoot down the Tornado. It posed a larger threat active than it did as falling debris, so the command had been issued. As they both soared through the sky above London, the Typhoon pilot had stopped firing warning shots from the 27mm cannon and was now lining himself up to use the advanced short-range air-to-air missile.

'Shake him!' Shouted Vincent.

'Can you not see that's what I'm trying to do?' Said Luke and flew the jet into a barrel roll. Once out of the barrel roll he went into a nosedive, heading straight down towards Wembley Stadium.

The Typhoon followed with ease, but before the pilot could lock on, Abaddon slammed into its wing and shook the jet with force. All three plummeted at tremendous speed and Luke was about to pull up when Satan took possession of his body and mind.

Luke went into a dream state; he dreamt he was in a white room. The room filled with fire, and it engulfed him. It destroyed his inner self and shattered his self-awareness, giving Satan full control of his body. Black liquid spewed out of him, but the g-force prevented most leaving his mouth, and he began to choke.

Satan, using Luke's body like a puppet, took a hold of the aircraft's joystick and steered the jet towards the stadium.

'Pull up, what are you doing?' Screamed Vincent as Satan fired three missiles at the stadium.

Two of them hit the roof but one went inside. It exploded next to the astral projection and blew apart the gold spear cage it was trapped in.

Satan's presence left Luke's mind and returned to the astral projection. He grabbed a spear that was still in the ground and pulled it out to fight with.

The Typhoon pilot fought against Abaddon's jolts and locked on to the Tornado. He fired a missile without hesitation and pulled up sharply. Abaddon lost his grip because he had not expected the sudden manoeuvre and somersaulted several times before coming to a stop in mid-air. Hovering, he watched as the missile hit the Tornado's wing and sent it straight into the arch of the stadium.

The rogue jet blew up on impact and destroyed that section of the arch. The whole structure began to break and fall into the stadium. Its cable supports, unable to hold its weight, snapped and whipped across the roof, tearing up huge chunks as they were ripped out of place by the falling arch.

'Watch out, it's coming down!' Screamed Alexander, and watched in horror as the arch hurtled towards the pitch.

It wiped out one side of the angels' defence line as they flew out of the way before it hit.

The hellspawn were now escaping into the stadium again and on the hunt for humans to kill. They spilled out in their dozens as the angels tried to find new defensive positions.

Satan wasted no time; he took advantage of the distraction and ran for the black orb.

'Michael!' An angel flying overhead called and pointed to Satan.

Satan threw the spear at Michael before he had a chance to react. It smashed into his stomach so hard that he went hurtling into the stands and ploughed through several rows of seats before stopping.

* * *

Alexander was now the only thing between Satan and the black orb. He gripped his sword with both hands and took a defensive stance, ready to defend with his life.

As he charged towards him, Satan boomed out an almighty roar that rocked the entire stadium. His face elongated with this release of immense rage, and his shape altered. His hands reshaped into claws; each limb grew larger and more muscular; his shoulders broadened, and his chest expanded to double its original size. He approached Alexander and swung an open claw at him.

Alexander reacted quickly and jumped back, slashing down on Satan's wrist, cutting off the claw. The appendage hit the turf and spattered into liquid tar.

Satan roared again and continued his advance, trying again to hit Alexander with his remaining razor-sharp claw.

Alexander jumped back once more and sliced upwards at Satan's elbow, removing the arm, then quickly thrust his sword forwards straight into Satan's chest, stopping his advance. 'I'll die before I'll let you reach this orb.'

'So be it,' said Satan, and regrew the amputated limbs.

Alexander acted fast and pulled the sword from Satan's chest, then spun around three-hundred-and-sixty degrees and chopped off his right leg.

Satan fell to the floor and once again the cut-off appendage liquefied to leave a black puddle on the pitch. Abaddon shot down from above and slammed into the ground just behind Satan. For a second Alexander was worried, but then Michael appeared next to him, spinning the golden spear Satan had used from side to side.

'Get back into your pit, Abaddon,' Michael demanded, pointing the end of the spear to the sinkhole.

Abaddon didn't speak, but instead reached behind his back and produced a long black whip. He cracked it towards them, and it startled Alexander. The whip missed them, going between the pair straight for the orb. The end of the whip penetrated the force field and wrapped around the orb, and Abaddon ripped it back before either had time to stop him.

Alexander swung his sword to cut the whip, but he was too slow. The orb was on its way. Michael flung his spear at Abaddon and ran at phenomenal speed to get the orb before it reached Satan.

Time seemed to slow down. Alexander watched the next few seconds in ultra-slow motion as his mind went into overdrive: these might be his final moments. Helpless to do anything he watched, wide-eyed, with his heart beating through his chest, as the black orb fell right towards Satan's newly formed outstretched claw.

* * *

Darius and Oliver neared their destination. Just in front of them was the daunting sight of the entrance to Satan's lair: a one-thousand-foot-high black gate with sculptures of demons, snakes and tortured souls sculpted into it. The jet-black walls either side of it ran dead straight for as far as the eye could see. The wall's surface was so smooth and shiny it looked like the still surface of a peaceful, undisturbed lake.

Oliver was tempted to go over and touch it, to see whether his touch would create ripples, but he decided against it.

'We should have faced some resistance by now... something isn't right,' said Darius.

'Maybe destroying that hound has made them think twice about attacking us,' said Oliver.

'The horde of hellspawn that guard this gate do not think, they just obey and attack. If they are not here, it must be for a reason.'

The ground surrounding them began to rumble. It felt as though something enormous moved beneath them. Holding on to each other for balance, they watched as the black gate opened inward. The gargantuan gate groaned as it moved, and its hinges sounded ready to burst. Oliver and Darius had to plug their ears with their fingers against the noise.

As an opening became clear dozens more cord-like structures, identical to the link connected to the astral projection, sprouted out of the entrance and snaked their way upwards, soaring high into the sky. All were the circumference of a train, black-and-red in colour with electrical bolts shooting through them.

'This could explain why there's nothing guarding this gate. If I'm right, all of those will be portal links leading to separate locations all over Earth. Satan must be sending everything he has there to attack, hence no resistance here. If we're going to do something we need to do it now,' said Darius.

'Let's get inside while the gate's open and see if there's anything we can do.' Oliver led the way inside.

'After you,' said Darius.

The pair walked inside cautiously and were quickly consumed by darkness. They were in a vast open area with no light. The further inside they got, the darker and colder it became.

'Any suggestions which way we should go?' Asked Oliver.

Darius looked up at the cord-like structures they could just make out in the dark. 'Follow those for now, I guess. They must end somewhere.'

Oliver nodded. After walking for quite some time, the pair were now in complete darkness with no sign of the huge gated entrance behind them. It was freezing and the temperature continued to drop; Oliver was questioning their decision to be there. 'How much further do you think we've got to go?' He asked, shivering.

'Your guess is as good as mine,' said Darius.

'Don't be angry, but I have to tell you. I lost sight of those tube things above us a while back. One second, they were there, and the next they were gone. I just didn't want to worry you,' said Oliver.

'I thought you may have. I lost sight of them too.'

They stopped to catch a breath.

'We could walk around in here forever. There's literally nothing but open space... it could be endless for all we know.' Oliver was panicking.

'You're right, this seems pointless. Surely there's something here, or something we're missing.'

They both looked around, but there were no clues as to where they should head, or what they should be doing. Then Oliver looked down at the floor and saw it was transparent. He could see straight through it to a mirrored world the other side. It looked like a castle hallway or tunnel, he thought, with brick walls either side and a ceiling. There were fire torches along the walls, yet it was still quite dark. 'Darius, look!' He said.

'I can see it too, and our legs,' said Darius.

Oliver looked at their legs, and they were sinking into the floor. He pulled his legs free and the floor became solid again under his feet. But as soon as he stopped moving, he sank again. 'Do you think we need to sink?' He said.

'There's only one way to find out. I'll go first,' said Darius, and remained still.

Oliver walked on the spot and watched as Darius sank deeper into the floor. It did not take long; the deeper he sank, the faster he went. As the floor reached his chin, Oliver prayed this was not a trap. Then the floor swallowed him.

Oliver's heart raced; he was all alone now in the vast emptiness, which unnerved him immensely. Then to his astonishment he saw Darius standing upside down in the floor waving at him and beckoning for him to come down.

'Okay, I'm coming, don't move.'

Oliver remained ultra-still and felt himself sinking into the floor. It scared him. His instincts screamed at him to escape, but he trusted Darius, so he kept his cool. Just as with Darius, when the floor reached his chin, he again prayed this would work. Then he felt like he was floating, falling up and down until he fell and landed on his feet. He opened his eyes and looked down the fire-lit tunnel he was now standing in. Behind him was a dead end, a brick wall, so the only way to go was forward. Darius was nowhere to be seen.

'Darius, Darius, where are you?'

There was no answer. Oliver saw someone far ahead of him, but they ran down a connecting tunnel to the left.

'Darius!' Screamed Oliver and ran after the figure.

He charged down the tunnel and took a left where he'd seen them go. It led to an identical-looking tunnel, and once again the person took off down another tunnel to the left ahead of him.

'Wait!' Shouted Oliver and chased after them.

He turned down the tunnel to follow them, and once again the tunnel was identical to the last. The person ahead darted off again to the tunnel to the left and Oliver stopped, confused.

'Wait,' he shouted again, but it was pointless. 'Fine!' He called, and turned, but was taken aback by the brick wall blocking the way he had come. It was a dead end again, just like where he had started.

'What the hell?' Oliver investigated the wall, pressing his palms against it and pushing.

The wall unexpectedly gave way and spun like a revolving door. Oliver stumbled inside and ended up the other side. The wall closed behind him and he now stood in what appeared to be a large dark torture chamber. There were many evil-looking devices inside he had never seen before, but each one's main function was undeniably to cause severe pain and discomfort.

He froze; he dared not make a sound - he was not alone in the room. There were tortured souls trapped and being tortured in many of the wicked contraptions surrounding him, and there were three spirits standing around one soul who was chained to the wall. The three spirits were translucent - they didn't appear to be made of solid matter. One of them was mouth to mouth with the soul chained to the wall, smothering it. After looking closer, Oliver realised it was Darius, and he appeared unconscious. The spirit covering his mouth seemed to be ejecting some type of liquid into him.

Oliver ignored the cries and moans of the tortured around him, even though they disturbed him to his core, and slowly moved towards the spirits as quietly as possible. His hands started to tingle, which filled him with confidence - he now knew he could destroy these things, like he had the hellhound. He picked up his pace and got right up behind two of the ghost-like figures, which close up resembled monks in black hoods.

Oliver placed a hand on top of each of their heads and braced himself. The two stuck to his hands like glue and began to glitch like a malfunctioning TV. They went in and out of focus, jolted in different directions and flashed on and off like a strobe light. Then, in a puff of black smoke, they disappeared. The third spirit became aware that something was happening and released Darius, then took off into the air and whizzed around the chamber like a burst balloon. Oliver's eyes were fixed on it as it did laps in circles close to the ceiling. Then it shot out of the only door in the room and escaped.

Oliver went to Darius's aid and gave him a gentle shake to bring him around. The chains holding him released.

'Oliver, is that you?'

'It's me, are you okay?'

'That abomination was in my mind – it had me believing I was trapped, burning alive. I could not tell you how long for,' said Darius, and gave Oliver a hug full of gratitude.

'We've not been separated for very long at all.'

'That thing must be able to manipulate time once it has you in a dream state. I've literally been engulfed in flames for, at a guess, about seven of your days since I fell through that wall, to put it into perspective.' Darius pointed at the wall where Oliver had also entered the chamber.

'Then I'm sorry I wasn't here sooner. Are you okay to continue? We must still find Satan.'

'Yes,' said Darius, and placed a hand on Oliver's shoulder. 'Thank you for getting me out of there, Oliver. We need to take every step further with extreme caution. There could be even worse ordeals ahead than what I just endured.'

Oliver nodded in agreement and both made their way out of the torture chamber by the same door through which the spirit had fled. The door opened out into a large cavern, a massive underground cave that was over two-hundred-feet high.

They hesitated as they stepped further into the cavern. It was filled with hellspawn, and above them were hundreds more spirits like the one that had fled. The hellspawn were countless in number and were all fighting to enter what Oliver assumed was a portal link at the other end of the cavern. The portal link snaked up into the air and left the cavern through a gigantic hole above them. The spirits were flying around like a swarm of bats and lingered around another portal link in the air.

'Look, another one of those links. It runs through this cavern and goes down that way, down that slope. It may lead to Satan.' Oliver pointed at the portal link, which went down deeper into the cave ahead of them.

'But how do we get past all of that?' Asked Darius with a tone of anguish.

Oliver could feel the power in his hands; it was intensifying, and he knew somehow, they would be okay. 'Do you trust me?' He asked, and his hands glowed.

'I do.'

'Then let's do this. I have held two hellspawn at bay before. I will not let them get to us. After three, we run for that slope,' said Oliver, and Darius joined him at his side.

'I hope you're right. This is more than two hellspawn,' said Darius.

'Stick with me and we'll make it. Three...' started Oliver.

'Two...'

'One...'

'Go!' They shouted together and ran into the cavern at full sprint.

The spirits above them burst into life like wasps protecting their nest and flew down in their dozens to attack the threat. The hellspawn on the ground spun around and growled ferociously at the two intruders.

'They're coming,' said Oliver; he could feel every presence around them. His hands vibrated and heated like he had never felt before. The glow from them grew brighter, and with the slight mist in the air it created a bright radiance around them.

'I'm thinking this was a bad idea,' said Darius, jumping over rocks and stones.

'I think you could be right,' agreed Oliver while trying to run faster.

Darius got in just behind him and held onto his shoulder as they ran towards the approaching wall of hellspawn. Both braced for impact as the hellspawn hit the light surrounding them and bounced off it. The light catapulted each one that came into contact with the light into the air. No matter how hard they tried to slash at it, they could not break through. The spirits above caught up with them and nosedived directly for them. The pair stopped running and braced again, putting their hands above their heads to guard themselves from the incoming hail of spirits.

Oliver focused on his hands and put every bit of energy he had into them. The first spirit got close but bounced off the light, and so did the second, and the third, and the rest. The illumination from his hands acted as a shield; nothing could penetrate it. The spirits all hit at once and swamped them, but there was no weakness in the light. It held out and repelled every spirit and hellspawn that collided with it.

'That's incredible!' Shouted Darius.

'We must keep moving... I don't know how long it will last. Keep going the way we were heading – we were nearly at the slope.'

They both moved as quickly as they could

over the rocky terrain and kept their footing amid the bombardment. Then they hit the slope. It was very steep and neither saw it coming. They mis-stepped and fell, tumbling over one another as they picked up speed and rolled downhill. The light that had surrounded them disappeared, but so did the hellspawn and spirits attacking them. For some reason they chose not to follow the pair down the slope. They rolled, bounced and crashed their way down until they hit flat ground with a nasty thud and both had the wind knocked out of them. After sharing a few moments of pain on the floor, groaning, they pushed themselves up and stood.

'Ouch,' complained Darius, 'are you okay?'

'I think so,' replied Oliver as he looked at their surroundings.

The portal link ran directly above them and ended just in front of them, right above a naked body that was lying on a stone altar.

Thin black streaks reached down from the portal and penetrated the skin of the body.

'Is that...?' Started Oliver.

'Satan,' confirmed Darius, and quickly checked the area for anything guarding him.

The area was clear, so both cautiously moved closer and kept their eyes fixed on the motionless body.

'Is he awake?' whispered Oliver.

'Satan does not sleep,' replied Darius as they reached the body.

Darius stood on Satan's left side while Oliver moved around to his head.

'I don't think he is consciously with us. His astral projection is on Earth, so his attention and awareness are there. I think we're safe for now,' said

Darius, and bent down to look up into the portal above Satan. Oliver, seeing Darius's attentiveness, peered up also, intrigued to see what was there.

The portal appeared to show what Satan was seeing at the other end through the eyes of the astral projection. The images coming through looked like reflections in a rippling puddle. The wavy scene moved with no sound, but it was clear enough to see what was happening. What Oliver saw made his heart skip a beat. The images showed Alexander holding a sword in Wembley Stadium, with an angel standing beside him with a spear. The black orb was flying towards Satan's outstretched claw.

Oliver realised they were seeing what was currently happening. Satan was about to have the orb in his grasp. The angel next to Alexander threw the spear and ran for the orb, but Oliver knew the angel would not make it. Without another thought, Oliver looked away from the portal and placed both his hands on Satan's temples.

Satan's eyes shot open and he let out a thundering roar. It rocked the entire cavern like an earthquake; cracks split through the ground, and rocks fell from above.

'Oliver, what are you doing? He's too strong,' shouted Darius, and took a few steps back.

The altar that Satan lay on shattered to bits under him, but the black streaks infused into his body from the portal link held him dangling in the air.

Oliver continued to keep his hands on Satan's temples, even though the connection felt like two identical poles of a magnet repelling one other.

'Do something! I can't keep this up... he's pushing my hands away,' shouted Oliver, using all his strength to keep his hands in place.

'I don't know what to do, this was your idea!' Shouted Darius.

'I can't do it, he's too strong!' Oliver clenched his teeth and closed his eyes with the strain of keeping his hands where they were. There was a bang, and Satan was gone from his grip. Panic hit, but Oliver opened his eyes to see an angel on top of Satan with his hand around his throat.

'Michael!' Shouted Darius, sounding incredulous.

Michael had one knee pressed into Satan's chest and quickly looked from Darius to Oliver. 'Both of you, back through the portal now!' He shouted as Satan grabbed his arm.

'Oliver, in the portal, quick!' Shouted Darius, darting for the portal himself.

Oliver followed his friend and jumped up into the portal with no debate. The pair flew through the portal link at immense speed. Light and colours whizzed passed them as they made their way back to Earth. There was a blinding flash and the pair were in Wembley Stadium.

Oliver did not feel right; he felt empty. He was floating; he could see Darius on the ground underneath him as he took off at speed into the air.

* * *

'You did it, I can't believe you did it... Oliver, you got us out of there,' said the angel, looking around. 'Oliver, Oliver, where are you?'

'Oliver is dead. Where is Michael?' Asked Alexander, staring at the hole in the astral projection's stomach that Michael disappeared into.

The black orb was on the ground next to the angel. *Is the battle over?*

The hundreds of hellspawn in the stadium let out a loud shriek and all began to be pulled back into the sinkhole. The crows circling the stadium above dispersed and Abaddon quickly retreated into a portal he created on the ground.

'Hit them with everything we have... they are retreating!' Shouted an angel standing on the fallen arch of the stadium.

'Where is Michael?' Asked Alexander again and pointed his sword towards the newcomer.

'He held Satan down, so we could escape. Oliver and I had to get out before it was too late,' said the angel, then stood and stretched out his newly formed wings.

'What if he needs help? You shouldn't have left him,' said Alexander.

'We were a liability. Our presence would only have put Michael at a disadvantage. All we can do now is wait.'

'We should go after him.'

'The portal this end would only have been open for a split second when Oliver pulled Satan back to his true body. It was miraculous that Michael made it through at all.'

Alexander did not respond, but he knew this angel was telling the truth. Two more angels flew down and landed next to Alexander; both looked at the newly arrived angel and seemed overjoyed.

'Darius, is that you? How can this be? We thought you were gone forever,' said one of them.

'It's me, Jade, Kleo. I wouldn't be here if it wasn't for Oliver. He got me out of there, he saved me,' said Darius as Jade and Kleo ran over to hug him.

As the three of them hugged, angels gathered around them. Most of the hellspawn had now retreated to hell, and any that had not, were being dealt with by a few angels still scouring the area.

'Where is Michael?' Asked Kleo, looking at Michael's sword in Alexander's hand.

Darius pulled away from Jade and pointed to the hole in the astral projection's lifeless body.

'In battle with Satan,' said Darius.

More angels gathered around them, all with their eyes on the astral projection.

'It's Michael, Archangel Michael, he'll come back... right?' Said Alexander.

'Satan is no match for Michael, even in hell. Though the portal link on their side will not stay open for much longer. Michael must come back through or face a more difficult alternative route out of hell,' said Darius.

There was silence for the first time since the battle had begun. Every angel now stood waiting, clearly expecting Michael's return, but with every second that passed, it felt less likely.

There was a small flash of light within the stomach of the astral projection, and then another, but this time brighter. 'Did you see that?' Asked Alexander to no one directly.

Every onlooker moved in closer for a better look, and as they did, an intense blast of bright light caused Alexander to look away. When the light died out, Michael was standing before them. The archangel looked unhurt, apart from a broken wing.

'Michael!' Shouted Alexander, and they all moved in closer.

'Your wing, it needs eternal light,' said Jade.

'It will be fine. The battle is won... let us leave this place,' said Michael, and stretched out a hand to Alexander for the sword.

Alexander handed over the sword without question. Michael struck the air with it and formed some sort of portal, right where they stood. Jade led the way and flew straight into it. Kleo followed right behind, and every other angel did the same. Michael bowed his head to Alexander and was the last to enter the portal, which disappeared as soon as he was through.

We did it, we stopped Satan. The world is safe again... for now.

There were no cheers of victory when they left, but Alexander felt a huge sense of respect and gratitude towards every one of them.

Alexander stood for a moment and looked at the aftermath. The stadium was in ruin, and parts of it aflame. He wondered if it would even be possible to repair. His phone rang in his pocket; he answered it. It was Steven. 'Steve, we did it. We won,' he said.

'I know, I saw the hellspawn retreat on what was left of the cameras. I've also been watching the news. Did you know London was not the only city hit? Major cities all over the world were. Sinkholes appeared all over the globe, hellspawn spilled out, killing everything and everyone in their path. Then for some reason they all retreated into the holes and stopped their attack. The theories and speculations going around are insane,' said Steven.

'I can imagine.' Alexander picked up the black orb with his free hand. 'The orb has gone dormant again. So strange to think that this little thing nearly brought about the end of the world.'

'What will you do with it?' Asked Steven.

'I will disappear and find somewhere safe to hide it. It will never be in the wrong hands again,' said Alexander.

'But what about us and the team?'

'No one can know where I hide the orb, not even you, I'm afraid. I'm leaving alone. The Pope and I will be the only people with knowledge of its location.'

'Will we see you again?'

'I don't think so, my friend,' replied Alexander, and there was a slight pause.

'Well, then I wish you good luck, and I'll let the others know that you're taking care of the orb.'

'Thank you, Steven, it was a pleasure meeting you.'

'And you too, Alexander. Now I must continue getting Lieutenant General Winters under military arrest. I've found overwhelming evidence that he was in on this attack and knew it would happen. He was paid to deliberately slow people's escape, an act to cause more death. He would have ordered the slaughter of the people trying to escape if he could have got away with it. There are high-ranking officers and police at the stadium now about to bring him in for questioning about the documents I sent them. They are also detaining the Natas, who caused even more carnage among the chaos. I just hope none of them slips the net.'

'Great, I hope they all get what's coming to them. Well done, Steve. And thank you for alerting the RAF to what was happening here. I don't think many would still be alive if you hadn't.'

'It was my pleasure,' replied Steven.

'Goodbye, Steven,' said Alexander, breaking the silence.

'Goodbye, Alexander.'

Alexander ran to find his sword and leave the stadium.

CHAPTER 22

James West had handed over the female member of the Natas to Mario and his men and was now standing outside the stadium. He had tried to find Alexander, but was forced to flee when hellspawn chased after him. Unable to get back inside because of the sheer number of people trying to escape, West looked around, helpless, until he spotted Lieutenant General Winters. He was outside a gate entrance surrounded by soldiers and looked to be very agitated. West quickly walked over to them and saw that Winters had a gun pointed at the soldiers around him.

'This is preposterous. I'm in command here, you do not give the orders,' screamed Winters, waving his pistol around.

'We did not give the order, Lieutenant General. It has come from above your rank and we are to place you under arrest. Put down the weapon, sir,' said one soldier as he placed his hand on his own pistol.

'Save yourself this embarrassment, Winters, and hand over the weapon. It's over,' said West.

After a short pause to piece together who this was talking to him, Winters became visibly infuriated and pointed his gun directly at West.

'You've done this, haven't you? You've framed me,' Winters said with his finger on the trigger.

'You've done this to yourself and you know you have. I will take great pleasure in watching you go down, and just so you know, I will do everything in my power to help them do it,' said West, hoping to get a reaction.

It worked. Winters looked West in the eye and went to pull the trigger. There was a bang, and Winters' facial expression changed to shock. The soldier who had asked Winters to drop his weapon had removed his pistol and shot Winters in the shoulder.

'Someone get an ambulance!' Shouted another soldier as Winters dropped his gun and fell to the floor.

West ran to his aid and placed pressure to the wound. 'Get a paramedic, quick, we must keep him alive.' He looked Winters in the eye. 'You're not getting away with it that easy. You'll pay for what you've done, and for the lives of those men you sent into that ambush!'

'If you say so,' said Winters and laughed a little, at the same time grimacing in pain.

Two paramedics got to the scene, pushed West out the way and took over from him.

'I hope you survive this, Winters – you'll be seeing me in court.' West left to find Jessica.

* * *

Cole was outside the stadium looking everywhere for Tasha, but she was nowhere to be seen. By chance, he spotted Jack Buckley in the crowd. He was wearing a baseball cap, but it would have taken more than that for Cole not to recognise him. Plus, the cap didn't quite cover the inverted cross on his forehead. After some thought, Cole decided it was best to give chase. Even though giving up looking for Tasha was the last thing he wanted to do, letting Buckley slip through the net was not an option. He ran after him with determination and vowed to make it up to Tasha. He followed unnoticed and kept a good distance, and he had every intention of keeping it that way.

Cole knew that Buckley was alone. If he could keep the element of surprise, apprehending him would not be too much of a struggle. He followed behind him and ducked his head every time Buckley looked over his shoulder. They got some distance away from the stadium. The blue lights and sirens were less frequent here, and the crowds were thinner as people branched off in their own directions.

Buckley broke away from the crowd and sneaked off down an alleyway. His movements went unnoticed to the surrounding people, but Cole had a close eye on him and followed him cautiously down the narrow passageway, using wheelie bins as cover as he did so.

Buckley ran all the way through the alleyway and turned right at the other end, out of Cole's sight. Not wanting to leave too much of a gap between them Cole sprinted to the end, leant up against the wall and peeped around the corner. Buckley was standing right there, motionless, with his back to him. 'You need to improve your tailing skills,' he said, not bothering to look at his pursuer.

Cole walked around the corner and waited for Buckley to turn around. When he did, there was a menacing look on his face.

'It's you. You just couldn't let me go, could you? You realise that's quite an ego you have?' Said Buckley, pulling out his knife.

'Enough talk. You're coming with me.' Cole stood his ground.

'If you say so,' said Buckley, and went to pounce, but halted as a sword was thrust through him from behind.

The sound of a wet thud, then a sword protruding from his stomach. Blood left his mouth and he looked at Cole, perplexed. The killer ripped the sword out, and Buckley fell to the ground. It looked to be a fatal wound.

'Alexander, what have you done?' Said Cole.

'That was for Rachel,' replied Alexander with no remorse, and began packing his sword back into its case.

'You murdered him... we could have stopped him together. There was no need to kill him,' said Cole.

'I was not willing to take that risk. I refuse to allow even the chance of him killing another person. Plus, I have the orb in my possession. If he had got the better of us, then reclaiming it would have been for nothing. You should thank me. I nearly turned the other way when I left the stadium and saw you chasing him. The orb is too important for me to be getting side-tracked. It needs to be hidden, but I decided I'd get ahead of you and cut him off. If I hadn't, it could have been you now bleeding out on this pavement.' Alexander threw the sword case back over his shoulder.

'I will have to report this, you understand?' Said Cole.

'That report will be bottom of the pile after this shit-storm and will be long forgotten by the time anyone entertains giving it a read. So be my guest,' said Alexander, and went to leave as Buckley took his last breath.

'Not if I have anything to do with it,' said Cole, and Alexander paused for a moment taking in his words. He walked away, leaving Cole to deal with Buckley's dead body on the pavement.

* * *

Jessica opened the main church door and held it open for the others. Zhang and Bear entered behind her, and Marson came in last carrying Oliver's body in his arms.

The church was full to the brim with people, all praying and crying.

'Your Lordship!' Shouted Jessica, and everyone in the room turned to look at the group.

They made their way down the centre aisle towards the altar where Bishop Smith was standing.

The bishop eyed Oliver's body and spoke. 'Everyone, may I please ask you to leave the church?' He said and gestured to his bodyguards to escort people out. 'Bring him here, lay him on the altar,' he said and cleared the altar of the crucifix and candles.

Some people were reluctant to leave and were putting up a fight with the guards. *The church is most likely giving them a sense of safety and security*, Jessica thought, so naturally they were disinclined.

'Please make your way out of the main entrance. I apologise, but the church is now closed.

Go home, be with your families. You may return tomorrow if you wish. Thank you and God bless you all.' The bishop walked to the centre aisle to escort people out.

Marson placed Oliver's body on the altar and the group waited for the church to be cleared. After the last person had left the bishop locked the entrance door, then thanked his bodyguards for their support. He made his way to the altar looking grief-stricken. 'What happened?' He asked as he approached the group and the altar.

'The Natas attacked the stadium as we expected. The black orb was also there. Father Hall tried to stop them from raising Satan. We were on our way into the stadium to help him, but when we got there, he was dead. Alexander told us to bring him here,' said Zhang.

'That was a good decision. The hospitals are extremely stretched at the moment. I will liaise with them and transport his body to the morgue as soon as possible. What of Alexander?'

'He stayed in the fight,' replied Marson.

'And the black orb?'

'It's safe, Alexander has it. Somehow Satan and the Natas were stopped. Alexander is on his way to the Pope as we speak,' said Zhang.

'The fight for the orb is over. That is great news. This victory should now put an end to the demonic possessions,' said the bishop as he stood over Oliver's body. 'My friend, you have paid the ultimate price. Your courage and sacrifice in the depths of darkness will be a lesson to us all. You have given your life trying to save this world, and for that we will be eternally grateful. I bless you, Father Hall, and may you rest in peace.' He took some holy water from the font and blessed the body.

Jessica broke down in tears and the bishop shed a tear also; the others bowed their heads in respect.

The main doors burst open. The locks broke, and splinters of wood flew from the breaks. A gale-force wind filled the church and the group had to hold on to anything they could to keep from being blown over. It felt as though a mini-tornado had formed around them and was trying to suck them up and spit them out.

'What is happening?' Screamed Jessica as her hair flapped around her face.

'I do not know!' Shouted Bishop Smith, holding on to the altar.

Marson had one hand on the altar and the other on Zhang. There was nothing for her to grab, so she clung to his arm for dear life. The wind centralised at the altar and became stronger, so much so that the group could not hold on any longer. One by one they were blown away from the altar and sent skidding across the floor, all except Marson and Zhang, who were sent over a pew and landed on top of each other. Then, out of nowhere, the wind disappeared. It vanished just as fast as it had arrived and left the group in shock and confusion.

'What the hell was that?' Shouted Bear and got up off the floor, then froze, looking stunned. 'Oh my God.'

Jessica and the others got up and looked to see what Bear was seeing.

'It can't be,' said the bishop, who looked in disbelief at what he was seeing.

'Oliver?' Said Jessica, confused; Oliver was sitting up, alive, on the altar.

'Stay back, he must be possessed,' warned Bear, and moved to protect Jessica.

Oliver slowly swivelled on the altar and pushed himself off onto his feet. He stumbled at first, but his muscles seemed to kick in and he balanced himself. Then he walked towards Jessica.

'Stay back,' warned Bear, and moved Jessica behind him.

Peering over Bear's shoulder, Jessica saw that Oliver's eyes were not jet black.

'It's okay, it's me.' Oliver stood still and raised his hands in the air, gesturing that he was no threat.

With no more discussion, Jessica went around Bear and ran to Oliver. She slammed into him and hugged him so hard that she thought she would make him die all over again.

'Jess, I can't breathe,' he said.

Jessica's hug had his arms locked at his sides. 'But how, how can you be alive?' She asked, her eyes filling up again.

'I don't know, but I must get back to the stadium.'

'You must be out of your mind, but luckily you don't have to. I spoke to Steve on our way here. The attack has stopped. Alexander has the orb and is on his way to hide it by himself,' said Jessica, and stepped back from him.

The bishop placed a hand on his shoulder and turned him around to look at his face. 'It truly is you. It's a miracle. God's presence really is within you.' He got down onto one knee and bowed his head.

'My Lord, there is no need to bow. I'm sure there's a logical explanation for this,' said Oliver.

Bishop Smith stood and looked him in the eye. 'Oh really, and what might that be?'

Oliver appeared stuck for words; he did not reply.

'That's what I thought,' said the bishop.

Zhang walked up to them with her phone in her hands. 'I've been online, looking at the news. The situation at Wembley Stadium is the main headline, and there are live updates every minute. It says here the military have entered the stadium, restricted the area and placed a quarantine. They're saying a main gas line burst following a natural disaster that occurred during the final. The death toll is unknown but is expected to reach into the hundreds. Officials have insisted that reports of monsters are solely because of hallucinations from high gas inhalation. They have also apprehended hooligans that were running riot inside and attacking fans trying to escape,' she said.

Jessica looked at Oliver. He was deep in thought; he looked like he had just solved a puzzle – as though a light switch had flicked on in his mind.

'Do people believe that's true?' Jessica asked Zhang.

'Maybe some, for now. Though the video footage online may give rise to some questions. Several news organisations across the globe have released recordings that reveal the hellspawn. Also, there're hundreds of people's personal uploads to social media that have gone viral. I can't see this gas story sticking myself.' Zhang put her phone away.

'No mention of the fighter jets?' Asked Marson.

'No, none. I guess the RAF don't want it getting out that two of their own pilots stole a jet from under their noses and got paid to cause havoc with it over London,' said Zhang, and Marson nodded in agreement.

Oliver looked like he had something he wanted to share. He hesitated a moment, but then stepped forward. 'I can't believe it worked. When I touched Satan in hell, it stopped him. My touch must have prevented him from getting the orb and stopped the attack. I saved the world.'

'What are you talking about?' Asked the bishop.

'I was in hell. Satan took my soul, and while I was there, I found his true form. When I placed my hands on his head I somehow cut the link to his astral projection, stopping him reaching the orb. Then an angel and I escaped through the portal. I didn't see what happened once the angel and I got out. One second I was there, next I woke up here,' said Oliver.

'You must tell me everything,' said Bishop Smith, and took Oliver by the arm to lead him into the vestry.

'Father, before you go. I'm leaving now to find my Dad, so I won't be here when you finish, but I'm so glad you're still with us. I don't understand how, but I'm glad. You should take it easy and rest... who knows what sort of side effects you could experience,' Jessica said.

'I will, Jessica, thank you.'

Jessica and the rest walked away to leave the church, and Oliver and the bishop continued to the vestry.

CHAPTER 23

Jessica was pushed in a wheelchair by a nurse into the waiting room, cradling her newborn baby in a blanket. Steven and Nicole stood at Oliver's side to greet and congratulate her on becoming a mother.

'Aww, Jessica, he's so cute,' said Nicole, and stroked his cheek with the back of her finger.

'How are you feeling, Jess?' Asked Steven.

'Just tired. I feel like I could sleep for days.'

'Is there anything we can get you?' Asked Oliver.

'Oh no, I'm fine, thank you. I'm content here just looking at his adorable face,' said Jessica, and held him closer.

'Still no luck finding the father?' Asked Nicole.

'None. I don't think we will ever find him, to be honest. I didn't expect I'd need to after we'd met, so I didn't stay in contact. It looks like it's just me and Ethan.' Jessica squeezed Ethan in her arms.

'You named him? Aww, I love it, Jess,' said Nicole, looking all broody.

'Ethan James West, after his granddad,' said Jessica.

'James must love it. How is he, by the way?' Asked Oliver.

'He's not great, it's been a real struggle without Mum.'

'Well, please send him our love, and remember he can come to me any time for a talk,' said Oliver.

'Thanks, Oliver, that will mean a lot to him. I'll make sure to tell him.'

'Thanks, Jess. I think it's best we leave you to it then... you should go get some rest. If you need anything, you know how to contact me.'

'I do. It was great to see you all,' said Jessica with a smile.

'Bye, Jess.' Nicole gave Jessica a kiss on the cheek.

'Bye Jess,' said Steven and did the same.

Oliver gave her a kiss last and placed his hand on hers. 'I mean it – you need anything and I'm just a call away.'

'Thanks, Father, I'll be in touch if I need anything,' replied Jessica, and the nurse pulled her away to take her back to her ward.

The three of them waved her goodbye and waited until she was gone before leaving the ward. They made their way through the hospital and out of the main entrance. It was late, and dark outside. They went to say their goodbyes when they reached the street, but were interrupted when they heard a window smash.

They looked back at the hospital in horror as they saw a hellspawn falling from the third floor, and Alexander standing in the broken window.

Zhang and Bear came at the group from nowhere and nearly made all three jump out of their skins.

'Good, you guys are safe,' said Zhang.

'What are you doing here?' Asked Oliver.

'Alexander told us to come here. Apparently when you touched Satan in hell he saw into your mind. He knows the truth about Jessica's baby, whatever that is, and is sending hellspawn to kill him,' said Zhang.

'It can't be... how does Alexander know this?' Asked Oliver.

'He didn't say anything else, I don't know,' said Zhang, and a loud roar came from within the hospital.

The whole group looked to see Abaddon on top of the building and fireballs falling from the sky.

'Jessica!' Screamed Oliver, as he ran back to the hospital entrance.

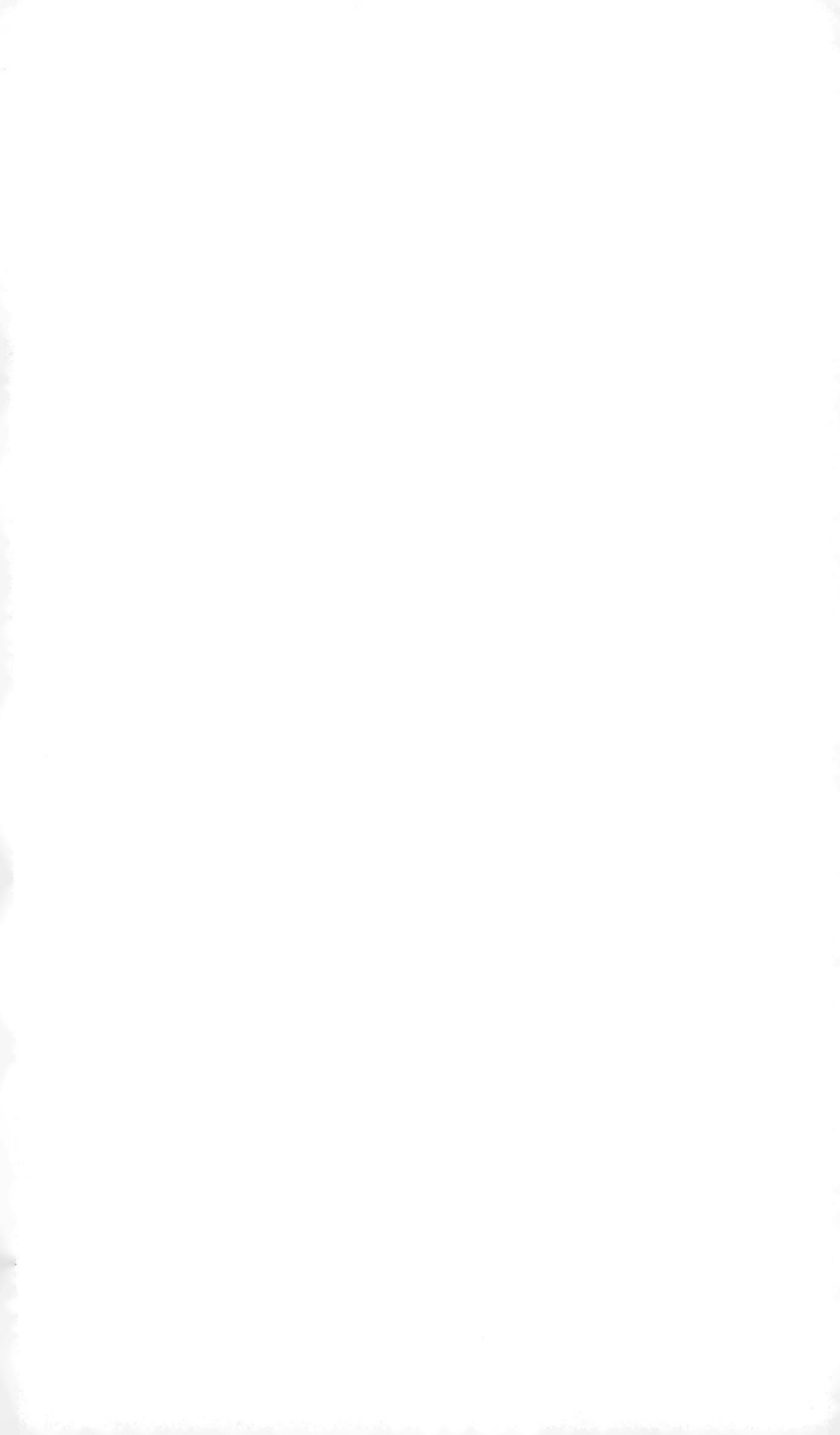

Lightning Source UK Ltd.
Milton Keynes UK
UKHW022130310321
381326UK00009B/296